SOULSWIFT

SOULSWIFT

MEGAN BANNEN

BALZER + BRAY
An Imprint of HarperCollins*Publishers*

For those who doubt,
whether you want to or not

Prologue: The Dead Forest
Ten Years Ago

The trees grew at impossible angles from the limestone escarpment, and brittle rock crunched underfoot. The sound forcefully reminded Goodson Anskar of the day he half ran, half skidded across the broken floor tiles of the monastery's chapel—the ominous crush and scattering of marble beneath his feet—before he peered down into the Vault of Mount Djall and found it empty.

That emptiness reached inside him now, two years later—two years of research and guesswork, convincing himself his hunch was right. He had arrived in Hedenskia with two thousand knights. Now only he and Brother Marton remained, trudging through the Dead Forest, taking turns carrying the precious child they had never expected to find among the heathens.

The Goodson's back ached, so he set the girl down beside a gnarled tree to stretch. In that moment, a crack rent the air like a whip. The bark split down the middle, and from within the tree came two skeletal hands pushing apart the chasm. There was an answering crack in Anskar's chest, a paternal feeling so ferocious it nearly brought him to his knees. He lunged, grasping the child by her cloak and yanking her behind him. Her body soared through the air like a bird as the monster oozed from the tree.

A telleg.

It attacked Brother Marton first, scraping a thick gash across the knight's throat before biting into his shoulder with savage teeth. Anskar drew his sword as the creature sprang at him with unnatural speed, and he sliced it in half, exposing the spine within its bloodless gray flesh. When he was certain it was dead, he rushed to Marton, only to find his friend's eyes staring blankly toward heaven.

Fighting the urge to weep, the Goodson glared down at the telleg that had killed the last of his men. On the monster's chest was a mark that resembled the Hand of the Father, the same emblem stitched across his own tunic. This was surely a sign from the One True God, a symbol of Anskar's failure and disgrace.

Silent as a fawn, the girl came to stand beside him, taking his big hand in her small one. She gazed up at him with innocent eyes, and his heart lurched. Her soft presence was like his favorite verse from *The Song of Saint Ovin*, the one that always brought him comfort:

> *When the berries of the gelya tree turn red,*
> *Then you will know that I have called you home.*

Squeezing the girl's hand, Anskar reminded himself that his name meant *spear* in Aurian. Now, more than ever, the Father required that he be sharp to protect this child, the Vessel of the One True God.

Casting aside his despair, he crouched before her, and because he did not know her name, he gave her a new one. "Poor little Gelya. Come. I shall carry you now." Then he scooped her into his strong arms and carried her through a forest full of monsters and night.

I.
The Vessel

One

As Daughter Andra plops a scoop of thick oatmeal into my bowl, I recall the last conversation I had with Zofia before she left for the Monastery of Saint Helios:

Have you met the new Daughter yet? There are three girls your age here now, and it might be nice for you to have friends other than a thirty-year-old woman and the Goodson.

Those girls look at me like I'm going to bite them.

Then be your lovely self, Gelya, and show them that you don't bite.

Well, Zofia is about to get her wish. With the other Vessels treating me like a nuisance and the rest of the Daughters avoiding me like the plague, I'm lonely enough in her absence to follow her suggestion. Girding myself, I walk past the Vessels' table and head straight for the only other teenage girls in the refectory.

Vessels are Daughters who were chosen by the Grace Tree of Saint Vinnica to sing the Father's Word for the faithful, while the other Daughters of the convent are simply women who've chosen to dedicate their lives to the One True God. These girls may not be Vessels like I am, but they are young women, and I'm a young woman, and surely that counts for something, especially in a convent full of old ladies. Not that I have anything against old ladies. It's just that I'm not one.

I try to remember the girls' names as I cross the room. Lucia? Lucretia? Something like that. And Trudi. I think. And . . . and that other girl. Most Daughters, unlike Vessels, don't enter the convent until they're at least sixteen. That means each one of these girls has a home to remember, a wider world they've seen that I haven't—at least not that I remember clearly. I was only five or six years old when the Father chose me. I watch them stiffen, then stiffen a bit more, then turn into a set of petrified wooden boards as I get closer. By the time I reach their table, I think I'd rather hide under it than pull up a chair, but there's no going back now. I almost ask, "May I sit here?" but then it occurs to me that they could say no, and that would be mortifying. Instead, I opt for "Is this seat taken?" because it clearly isn't, and lying is a sin.

"No?" Probably Trudi answers doubtfully, her blue eyes wide in her round pink face. Lucia or Lucretia and That Other Girl gape at her in panic.

My hands are shaking so badly that my teacup vibrates on its saucer, and my orange nearly rolls off the tray. "So," I chirp as I sit, my voice two octaves higher than normal and five times louder than necessary. "What do you study at the convent?"

"Um," gulps That Other Girl, her brown eyes darting between her friends. She has the fine bones of someone from southwest Rosvania or northwest Tovnia, the sort of person who makes me feel extra enormous. She stares at me like she might vomit from terror. Because I'm not just a Vessel. I'm also Hedenski, a girl from the most brutal and uncivilized place on earth, a land where people worship a tree goddess—a *tree*, for the love of the Father—and that makes me terrifying twice over. But honestly, I've lived at the convent so long that I don't remember anything about Hedenskia. It's not like I murder people, and to my knowledge, I've never carried a battle-axe. Can't they see that?

"Well," says Lucia or Lucretia, adding a third word to the girls' collective lexicon, which is promising. With her dark hair and olive complexion, I'd guess she comes from south of the Koz Mountains, and I feel a pang of sympathy for her, living so far from a home she must miss. I may not remember where I came from, but I do remember mourning its loss.

Probably Trudi finally gives me a complete sentence. "I'm studying herbalism so that I may serve the Father by treating the sick."

Her accent is thickly Degmari, and since my Degmari is pretty good, I figure that speaking to her in her native language would be a friendly thing to do. "That is interesting," I say a little too enthusiastically. "I recently translated a book on medicinal herbs from Middle Tovnian to Rosvanian. I was surprised to learn how useful goldenseal is." By now, I notice that Probably Trudi appears to be shrinking in on herself and on the verge of tears, yet my mouth runs on a few seconds longer as if it has a life of its own. "And . . . and . . . chamomile as well."

"Um, yes," she sniffs in Rosvanian, dabbing at her eyes with her napkin.

"Did I say something wrong?" I ask, feeling even more gigantic than usual. And then I realize my blunder. Many people on the continent think of the Degmari as backwater yokels, probably because of the archipelago's proximity to Hedenskia, and here I am, a Hedenski, pointing out the girl's embarrassing origins in front of her friends, who are now looking at me like I've sprouted fangs when I was trying to be kind. I wish the floor would open up beneath me, but since that's not going to happen, I escape before I can make things any worse.

"Well, nice talking with you." I lurch to my feet, and this time the orange rolls off my tray and bounces on the floor. I pick it up, clear my tray, and exit the refectory without having eaten a bite. I'll be sure to tell Zofia "I told you so" when she returns, but the humiliating pang of my failure pulverizes whatever smug triumph I might have felt.

An hour later, at Ovinsday services, I rise from my kneeler at the front of the Cathedral of Saint Vinnica, ascend the steps of the dais, and stand at the lectern. Pilgrims from all over the world fill the wooden pews in hushed wonder, waiting for me to begin the sacrament as they stare at the huge mosaic behind me. Saint Ovin stands in the center, plunging his sword into the heart of Elath, the snakelike demon at his feet. His daughter, Vinnica, stands to his right, clutching a chalice to her heart, her mouth yawning wide as the Great Demon's immortal spirit enters her body. To Ovin's left stands his second daughter, Saint Lanya, writing down *The Song of Saint Ovin* with the blue soulswift feather in her hand.

The Daughters of the convent kneel below me, their faces turned up in expectation, their shorn heads reflecting light in shades of blue and red as the sun presses through the stained-glass windows. The sacristy behind the altar once housed hundreds of Vessels in prayer. Now only twenty-three of us fill in the kneelers at the front like teeth in a beggar's gap-toothed smile, and almost all those who remain are old women. No girl has been chosen since me, ten years ago, which means the day might come when I look out over the Daughters to find myself the only Vessel left, really and truly alone in the world.

My stomach growls into the silence, as empty as I feel. I stare down at one of my least favorite passages from *The Songs*, the part where the Knights of the Order of Saint Ovin deliver the Father's punishment upon the ancient Kantari, the heathens who insisted—and insist to this day—that Elath the Great Demon is their mother goddess.

I press my fingertips to the embossed Sanctus text, and the Father's Word takes hold of me, cold and invasive. May the Father forgive me for loathing it, this sensation that something other than myself is pouring into me and using me for its own purpose—His own purpose—however divine it may be.

You're saving souls, Gelya, I remind myself, and I dutifully sing the verse as it comes to me through the sensitive skin of my fingertips.

Set the city of Nogarra alight, and I shall be the bellows of the flame.
Let the flesh burn away into ash from the bone.

Let the bone wither into dust in the unforgiving fires of the Father.
I shall melt down my enemies and make them anew
in the love of the One True God.

I tamp down the effects of my gift as I sing, lessening the way my voice makes my listeners feel the searing heat of the flames and hear the shrieking of helpless children. The Father's wrath always plants a seed of unease in my gut. It seems impossibly harsh that children should suffer simply because their parents followed the wrong faith. Aren't they human, too? Aren't they also the Father's creation? As I slog my way through the verse, unbidden words string themselves together in my mind, forming a question of the unquestionable: How can a Father who punishes His children with such cruelty be considered good?

I tamp that down, too.

Once the fires have obliterated every Elath-worshiping man, woman, and child in Nogarra, once the city crumbles to a wasteland of ash, my body sags with fatigue, and a sheen of perspiration beads uncomfortably on my upper lip and forehead. I close the holy book, clomp gracelessly down the dais steps, and drop to my kneeler beside Daughter Ina, the intimidating Vessel Zofia left in charge in her absence. Whenever Ina sings, her gift lifts her listeners' souls toward heaven, while the dark brown skin of her perfectly shorn head remains miraculously sweat-free, as if Sanctus were effortless for her. She inclines her head toward me and whispers, "That was weak."

I glance over my shoulder at the girls from breakfast. That

Other Girl whose name I don't know and probably never will shudders when her brown eyes meet mine. I face forward again and mutter, "I'd say it was adequate."

After services, I go to the scriptorium with the other Vessels and settle myself beside a window that looks out on the courtyard gardens. Beyond the latticework, daylight paints the fat pears in the orchard a honeyed gold. I allow myself one last, wistful glance before I get to work, pressing my fingers to the embossed pages of *The Songs of the Saints*. The Father's Word fills me with a cold, thick pressure that heaves upward against the back of my throat and tightens my flesh. Pushing aside my discomfort, I grasp my pen and translate the Sanctus song into Kantari.

I'm the only Vessel at the convent who specializes in Kantari, and since there are more and more Kantari converts to the faith every day, it seems like all I do anymore is translate *The Songs* for them. Or, at least, for the ones who can read.

While the Kantari do worship the Father, most of them still cling to the old belief that Elath the Great Demon is a goddess. They even call Her their "Mother." They're the reason the Order of Saint Ovin exists, the knights who guard Elath's prison against the Kantari who keep trying to set Her free. If Elath is ever released, the world will end, so the other Vessels can sneer at my translations with that I-just-sucked-on-a-lemon face all they like; my work is literally saving the world one soul at a time.

At least I think it is.

Today's translation from *The Song of Saint Lanya* explains the central tenet of Ovinism: Hundreds of years ago, Saint Ovin slew Elath the Great Demon with the sword given him by the One True God, a weapon called the Hand of the Father. As the demon's body died, Ovin trapped Her spirit inside his daughter, Vinnica, the only girl pure enough to contain such evil. He then sealed the demon inside the Vault of Mount Djall, thereby saving mankind's immortal soul from earthly suffering.

As the Sanctus text wears out my body, my gaze drifts once more to the view beyond the window. I find little joy in being trapped indoors when the world outside is green and alive. The scriptorium walls press in on me, and the stuffy air makes it difficult to breathe. I feel as though I might burst. The next thing I know, I'm on my feet, bonking my head on a low-hanging lamp as I dash for the courtyard door.

"Where do you think you're going?" Daughter Ina calls at my back, but I shut the door against her protests and take a deep breath of fresh air. I don't know how I'll get caught up on my work, but the scent of hay drying in the fields beyond the convent walls is enough reward to make me push away any misgivings. Can't a Vessel of the One True God enjoy His creation from time to time?

The pea gravel between the raised beds of the potager garden crunches pleasingly beneath my feet as I make my way to the ancient statue of Saint Vinnica. It stands in the shade of the Grace Tree, whose seedpods open in the hands of the Vessels chosen by the One True God. The tree is dying, and has been dying since long before I came to the convent. No one knows why. It's another reminder of my loneliness, of the possibility that the Vessels of the Father are dying out right alongside it. And who will sing the Father's Word then?

The statue beneath the Grace Tree is a weathered version of Vinnica, less severe than the other icons of the convent, the idea of the saint rather than the painful reality of her. I tend to come here when I'm feeling rudderless or lonely or both, which is more and more often these days, especially with Zofia gone and no one to talk to in her absence. While the other Daughters and even the laity wax rhapsodic about the way the Father fills them with love and understanding, the sad truth is that the One True God is silent when I pray to Him.

My stomach aches with a terrible word that wriggles in my guts, making itself known whether I like it or not: *doubt*. I can't unthink it, and I can't pretend that I haven't thought it before and won't think it again. My doubt is why I stand before Saint Vinnica's statue now. When I speak to her here in the garden, it feels as if someone is listening to me, so I send up a little prayer, a wish that the Father spoke *to* me rather than *through* me, some reassurance that he is the loving Father I have been taught to believe He is. I close my eyes and lift my face to the sun and listen to a swallow chirp in the Grace Tree. By the time I open my eyes once more, I feel calmer, comforted.

As I gaze at the statue, I wonder how anyone could identify it as Vinnica. She's usually associated with either snakes, which represent Elath the Great Demon, or a chalice, a symbol of her body, which she sacrificed for the world, but if there were ever snakes or a chalice carved into the stone, they've long since faded with time and age.

I crouch down to push aside the tall sorrel leaves that obscure the saint's legs and feet and find that the statue rests on a limestone block with faint Sanctus symbols carved into the stone. When I press my fingertips to the inscription, one word—one distinct feeling—jumps out at me: hand. But there's more to it than that. Wrapped within the word are other ideas, other meanings. This hand is warm to the touch. It reaches for mine, but it also holds away things that would harm me. It feels oddly personal, and makes me long for something I don't have the words or understanding to name.

It's not surprising to find Sanctus carved into a statue's base, but I've never felt a text as strong as this one. My fingertips drift across the stone, hungry for more. It's mostly gibberish until I come across a few lines that are crystal clear:

Sing, faithful, of beloved Vinnica,
Prison and prisoner,
And pity her,
The eternal Vessel,
The heart of the Father's sorrow.

I take my hand away, puzzled. Why would the Father be sorrowful when Vinnica's sacrifice allowed Ovin to imprison Elath the Great Demon? My curiosity piqued, I sneak back into the scriptorium to fetch a sheet of parchment and a piece of charcoal. Then I stop by the garden shed to scrounge up one of the wire brushes we use to scour terra-cotta pots before replanting. I work up a sweat, scraping off the moss and lichen encrusting the statue's base until I have enough cleared off to take a decent rubbing.

After all that, the results are disappointing. Sanctus is a slippery language on a good day, but I've never encountered a text this incomprehensible. I can't even find the one passage I was able to read moments ago. Growling with irritation, I fold the parchment into fourths and stuff it into my pocket. I'm about to go back inside when a series of high-pitched notes dances through the air. A bird circles above me before it comes to perch on the statue's shoulder.

Blue wings. Gold breast. A black band on each side of her face delineated by a white stripe above and below. Long wings and scissored tail tapering out of sight behind the statue. She's a soul-swift, a Vessel who has transcended her body to become a bird who carries the souls of the faithful to heaven. She cocks her head and releases a trilling more beautiful than any other sound on earth, proof of eternal life beside the Father in heaven.

This is what I will become when I die. Has the Father answered my doubt with this reminder of my duty on earth? Cowed, I grope for some sense of His presence in my heart, but a hollow ache is my only answer.

At last the soulswift takes flight, circles twice, then soars off beyond the convent walls, taking her heartbreakingly beautiful call with her.

Two

Well after dinner and twenty bells, the scriptorium is empty except for me, the lone Vessel who is staggeringly behind in her work.

I wonder what normal girls are doing in Varos da Vinnica, the town outside the convent. Knitting and gossiping with other women beside a fire? Telling stories that have nothing to do with burning cities or the end of the world? Whatever it is, I'm sure it's more fun than translating Saint Wenslas's apocalyptic visions into Kantari. It would be nice to find out what being normal feels like, if only for a day or two.

I rub my bleary eyes with ink-stained knuckles and get back to work, copying out verses that detail what will happen should the faithful fail to contain Elath the Great Demon in her earthly prison at Mount Djall.

Your forests shall become deserts.
Your seas shall become salt and sand.

Your fields shall drown in the punishing floods of the Father.
Your winters shall yawn across months, then years,
Until there is nothing left but death and death.

Most scholars believe Saint Wenslas's visions are metaphorical rather than literal, but most scholars have never set foot in the Dead Forest, the place where the souls of the sinful go when they die, where they are transformed into telleg, the monsters that haunt the earth for eternity.

Sweat glazes my shorn head and slicks my armpits. As I shift my leg to unstick the back of my thigh from my stool, I hear the rustling of parchment in my pocket. Welcoming a distraction from my troubling thoughts, I let my hand find its way to my pocket and pull out the rubbing of the strange inscription. I spread it out on the table and touch a random spot. This time the power of the Sanctus text is much stronger, grabbing hold of me, gluing me firmly to the page, filling me with one distinct word: *mother.*

Not just any mother. *My* mother.

I can't see her face, but I sense her in the room, close by. She hums a tune as I doze off in a bed of furs, the comforting scent of woodsmoke and burned sage surrounding me like a blanket. The physicality of her—the realness of her body—sends a pang of longing shooting through my chest, as fresh as the day the Goodson first brought me to the convent. I rip my hand away so fast I nearly topple over.

"Gelya?"

I let out a bleat of surprise and leap to my feet, smacking my head against the lamp for the second time today, and I find Zofia standing before me. I'm so relieved to see her that I wrap her up in a fierce hug, her steady presence calming the turbulence of my thoughts.

"I've missed you, too," she laughs as she untangles herself. The flicker of the lamp's light dances across her face, and I can't help but think—not for the first time—that someone as lovely and smart as Zofia shouldn't be hidden from the world behind stone walls. She's from Auria, like the Goodson, and with her graceful height and gray eyes, she could be his niece. When she sings *The Songs of the Saints* for the pilgrims who come to the cathedral, her gift permeates the Sanctus text with excruciating beauty, piercing her listeners' hearts with the glory of the One True God. She's everything I wish I could be.

"I think you've grown another inch since I've been gone," she tells me.

"Holy Father, I hope not. I'm going to start knocking into the ceiling beams soon."

But Zofia's eyes have already found the rubbing on my desk, and she frowns. "What are you working on?"

I touch the new sore spot on my head, suddenly nervous. "It's nothing."

Zofia crosses her arms over her chest and levels me with a no-nonsense stare. She may be my best friend, but she's also my older sister and mother and mentor, all rolled into one imposing package. "That's funny. Your 'nothing' looks remarkably like something that is completely unrelated to *The Songs of the Saints*."

I hate it when she does this. She's been Sacrist—the director of the convent—for about a year now, ever since Sacrist Larka died.

Now I never know whether she's going to be Zofia, my one and only friend, or Zofia, my boss.

"Come on. I didn't do anything wrong, and I promise I'll get my translation finished by tomorrow."

As the words tumble out of my mouth, Zofia picks up the parchment, brushes it with her fingertips, and gasps. "Gelya, what is this?"

"I don't know."

Her eyes flash. "Where did you get it?"

"I found it," I tell her, wondering just how much trouble I'm in. "It's the inscription on the base of the statue of Saint Vinnica in the garden. Did you know it was there?"

She turns her attention back to the parchment, and her voice is hushed when she answers, "No, I didn't."

"Really? So I found something— Ow!"

She grabs me by the arm and drags me into the dark library stacks, casing the room like a thief to make sure we're alone. "Have you shown this to anyone?" she whispers, flapping the parchment at me. Anxiety thickens in my stomach as she stares me down with an intensity that sharpens her eyes to pinpoints.

"No."

"For the Father's sake, keep your voice down," she hisses, looking over her shoulder as if someone might jump out from behind a bookshelf at any moment. "I need you to think. Did anyone else see this? Anyone at all?"

"I already told you, no," I whisper.

"You're sure?"

"Yes, I'm sure. Zofia, what's wrong?"

"Good. That's good." She folds my rubbing and puts it in her own pocket.

"But—"

Zofia holds up one authoritative finger, silhouetted by what little light from the scriptorium lamp shines into the library. She is no longer Zofia-My-Friend. She is Sacrist-Zofia-of-the-Convent-of-Saint-Vinnica. "Don't tell anyone what you found. No one. Not even Goodson Anskar. *Especially* not Goodson Anskar. Is that clear?"

The anxiety in my gut grows heavier. "Why?"

"Is that clear, Daughter Gelya?"

Daughter Gelya. As if she hadn't held my hand and told me Aurian bedtime stories when I was still a little girl scared of thunderstorms. My lips thin, but who am I to defy the Sacrist of Saint Vinnica? "Fine," I agree tightly, but there's a part of me that wants to snatch the parchment out of Zofia's pocket. The urge to touch it, to feel its meaning again, burns inside me.

For the first time in years, I want my mother.

Two days pass before I get the chance to return to the convent garden, but when I pull back the sorrel leaves covering the statue's base, I find that someone has chiseled the Sanctus symbols off the limestone block beneath Saint Vinnica's feet. I gape at the grooves and gouges in the rock, certain that Zofia would never go to such lengths to hide anything from me, and equally certain that she must be responsible for this.

"What in the name of the Father did I find?" I wonder aloud, but no one answers me, not even Saint Vinnica's steady presence in the garden. Before this moment, it didn't occur to me that I should be afraid of what I discovered. But now, as I stare at the erasure of a song, my instinct tells me there are things in this world I may be better off not knowing.

Three

It's been nearly a month since Zofia took the rubbing from me, but every time I try to get a private word with her, she finds an excuse to slip away. Which is why I'm shocked when she sits down beside me at dinner one night.

"Oh, did you decide to join us this evening?" I ask with a mouthful of broccoli and irony, and she gives me a weary sigh in response. After several minutes of eating in silence, I finally soften, leaning toward her to murmur, "You haven't been yourself since you came back from Saint Helios. What's wrong? Is it the . . . thing I found?"

Zofia eyes me sharply, but we're interrupted by a serving girl, who races into the refectory, bobs a curtsy, and thrusts a letter into Zofia's hand. "Knights of the Order of Saint Ovin delivered this not five minutes ago, Sacrist," says the girl as she bobs another curtsy and scurries back the way she came. The missive is sealed with the emblem of the Holy See of the Ovinist Church pressed into violet wax. I don't know if Zofia has ever received a direct message from His Holiness, but she certainly hasn't received one in the middle of dinner. She breaks the heavy seal, and as her eyes dart back and forth across the looping script, her hold tightens, wrinkling the vellum.

"What is it?" I ask, worried by her reaction. In answer, she squeezes my hand, then rises to her feet, holding herself erect before the Daughters of the convent.

"I've just received a message from His Holiness, the See. The Kantari army has crossed north of the Koz Mountains. As of this report, they have made it to Debrochen in Tovnia."

Cries of alarm fill the room, and my own heart freezes in my chest. The Kantari have never brought their war north of the Koz. Their focus has always been on defending their borders and, from time to time, trying to breach the walls of the Monastery of Saint Ovin to free Elath—their "Mother"—from the Vault of Mount Djall. The fact that an army of murderous Kantari soldiers is only a few hundred miles away makes my veins ice over. Could the Kantari make it all the way to Rosvania? To the convent, even?

Zofia holds up her hand, silencing the Daughters' alarm before she continues. "The Tovnian army is holding them at bay, but Tovnia has requested a Grand Summit here at Saint Vinnica to discuss their concerns with the other Ovinist nations. The Holy See has granted the request. The date has been set for three weeks from today. I'm placing Daughter Ina in charge of arranging accommodations for the ambassadors. I will personally oversee preparations for the summit. I'll keep you all informed as I learn more."

With that, she sits, flapping her napkin onto her lap as if she hadn't just delivered the most staggering news in decades or, possibly, centuries.

"There hasn't been a summit at Saint Vinnica in years, and there hasn't been a Grand Summit in my lifetime," Daughter Ina sputters. "How many men are we expecting?"

"Ambassadors from every Ovinist kingdom—possibly princes—and their retinues, although they'll need to be warned that space is limited within the parlertorium. I wouldn't be surprised to see at least one representative from the Empire of Yil, as well. And the Holy See is sending the Archbishop of Rosvania to facilitate. So thirty men, give or take?" Zofia looks up from her dinner. "All kingdoms but Kantar and Hedenskia will be represented."

"Of course the heathens won't be there," says Ina, spitting the word *heathens* the way you might say *roach* or *louse*.

"What exactly is a Grand Summit?" I ask Zofia. "Is it different from a regular summit?"

"Most summits deal with border disputes between kingdoms or provinces, tariffs, that kind of thing, and there are usually only a handful of men involved. A *Grand* Summit calls together representatives from all the kingdoms of our faith to make a decision regarding the best interests of the Ovinist Church as a whole. In this case, I imagine the ambassadors will want to decide as a group how to act against the Kantari threat to the north, but that's not our concern. Our only purpose at a summit is to serve the Father by translating the words of men." Zofia scans the entire table, making eye contact with each Vessel in turn as she speaks, lingering last and longest on me.

The next three weeks are a blur of scrubbing, polishing, mopping, and waxing as the ambassadors trickle in from all over the Ovinist world.

On the morning of the summit, as I walk the west wing to fill the lamps with oil, I find myself passing a narrow closet—one of my favorite hiding places when I was little. My memory stretches back to the Aurian folktales Zofia used to tell me. She's the only Vessel who ever bothered to learn a bit of Hedenski, and she would whisper the stories to me in my native language. I remember the way I would act them out in all my hidden spaces, living in an imaginary world whenever I could escape from Sacrist Larka long enough to play.

Once there was a girl.

Every story began the same way.

Once there was a girl whose mother gave her the gift of life, and she woke the dead.

Back then, I slept on a cot in Zofia's room. Many nights, I would wake screaming, my dreams haunted by the wraithlike telleg I faced in the Dead Forest.

Once there was a girl who slew the Snake of Umut.

During the day, I used to tuck myself into this closet and whisper the words to the little rag doll Zofia had sewn for me, before Sacrist Larka found it and took it.

Once there was a girl who flew like a bird, up and up, far above the earth.

I haven't thought about that rag doll in ages, but suddenly its loss hurts my heart. I was only a child. Why couldn't I have had one toy, one thing that belonged to me? I'm still lost in these gloomy thoughts when Zofia calls my name from the end of the hall. As I make my way toward her, the hard-set expression of her face warns me that I should be worried.

"What did I do?"

"Nothing." She takes the pitcher from my greasy hands and sets it on a console next to a small sculpture of Saint Vinnica, leaving a shiny wet stain beside the saint. "Come with me."

"Where are we going?"

"The parlertorium. There's been a change to the summit proceedings. Your attendance is required tonight."

All the blood drains out of my head and pools in my stomach. "Am I going to observe?"

"No. I need you on hand to translate."

"Which language?" By now, my misgivings are stomping on my chest.

"The Tovnians have captured a Kantari soldier and want him questioned."

I never dreamed I'd find myself face-to-face with a living, breathing, Elath-worshipping Kantari, and now, in a matter of hours, I will have to translate for one at a Grand Summit in front of a roomful of important men. My breakfast roils in my stomach.

Zofia stops and puts her hands on my arms. "I know this is sudden, but you'll do fine. Better than fine. Your command of Kantari is excellent, well beyond my own grasp of the language, which is why I need you there tonight. You're ready for this. Give yourself credit."

I may not think myself capable, but the fact that Zofia does warms me to the core. So despite the fact that I'm worried half to death, I find myself nodding my agreement.

"Good." She beams at me. "Now take a breath and come on."

The parlertorium sits at the heart of the convent's main building and has served as a neutral place where ambassadors, lords, bishops, and even princes have met for centuries to debate issues, resolve conflicts, and make peace. Vessels are the only women allowed to enter this room, mostly to polish the wood and to keep the Eternal Flame of Saint Ovin lit, but also, from time to time, to translate for the men. Zofia pulls up the key on a chain around her neck and slides it into the oiled lock of the gold-inlaid doors, turning the tumblers, which fall into place with a *clank*. She pushes open one of the doors and ushers me in.

There are no windows in the parlertorium. The only light comes from the Eternal Flame of Saint Ovin, whose statue stands at the front of the room. It's an oval-shaped chamber, like a giant egg, with a high ceiling that arches toward heaven. Alcoves line the long sides of the room, each containing its own statue of a saint. I wander to the one dedicated to Saint Lanya, the first Sacrist of the convent and the first soulswift. Every time I see an image of her, I imagine what it will feel like the day I die, when I transcend my mortal body to become a soulswift, too, a bird who delivers the souls of the faithful to the Father in heaven.

Zofia rouses me from my rumination. "Gelya, I'm about to entrust you with one of the greatest secrets of the convent. Do you promise to keep it to yourself?"

Her solemn tone drops a stone of foreboding into my stomach. "Of course, but—"

"No 'but.'" She lights a candle on the small altar at the front of the room, sticks it to a base with its own wax, and leads me to one of the alcoves along the south wall. The statue within depicts a saint peering mournfully into his hands, which are cupped around an object the size of a fist. I stand on my tiptoes and find that he's bearing his own heart in his hands.

"Which saint is this?" I wonder aloud.

"No one knows. Several scholars have studied it over the years and theorized who it could be, but the more important issue I want to bring to your attention is the fact that if you pull down on his head, a latch below the marble slab should release. There's a tunnel underneath. It exits into the scriptorium library."

My anxiety blooms, spreading through me like dye dropped into water. "Why are you telling me this?"

"Just in case."

"In case of what?"

Zofia softens like the wax candle she carries. "The world of men is dangerous for women. That's why, centuries ago, the Vessels built a passage leading out of this room. Because every woman should have an escape route if possible. Do you understand?"

"Yes," I say. But I don't. I don't understand at all. The

Kantari are dangerous. The telleg—the souls who roam the Dead Forest—are dangerous. But the world in general, or at least the world I inhabit at Saint Vinnica? How can I be anything other than safe within the walls of a convent?

Four

I spend the next hour helping Zofia prepare for the summit, setting up three long tables in a U shape so the ambassadors can face each other. The less impressive table where Zofia and I will sit is tucked off to the side, facing the double doors at the back.

"You are not to speak unless asked to do so," Zofia instructs me as we carry chairs to our table. "And you may only translate a man's exact words. You may not—I repeat, may not—say anything of your own volition. A Grand Summit is a sacrament, and it is considered highly offensive to the One True God if a woman, created by Elath the Great Demon in her own image, speaks during the sacred ceremony."

"Oh, my Father, I know." I'm sweaty and worn-out and nervous, and I don't need her to teach me lessons I've already learned fifty times over.

"Translating is stressful, and it's easy to lose one's composure. Bear with me." She moves to a point at the top of the U. "I will provide all non-Kantari translations this evening, and I'll do so from my seat. But when the ambassadors wish to question the Kantari directly, you will stand here, and the prisoner will stand on the other side across from you. He will be under guard and will likely be bound, so try not to worry too much about your personal safety."

"I'm more worried that I'm going to make a fool of myself."

"You won't. Just follow the protocol, and everything will be fine. And one last thing." Her lips twist wryly as she crosses back to me. "Men may have been created in the image of the Father, but they are not perfect. There are long-standing disputes between many of these countries, so be prepared to see childish behavior this evening."

I'm about to ask what she means when a Knight of the Order of Saint Ovin enters the parlertorium, his pale blue cape billowing behind him.

"Forgive me for interrupting your preparations, Sacrist, but I have come to summon Daughter Gelya to the receiving room on behalf of the Goodson."

"Goodson Anskar? He's here?" I exclaim.

"The first Grand Summit in over half a century is taking place this evening," Zofia says. "Of course he's here. He's running security."

"You didn't tell me!"

"Because I knew you'd be a nervous wreck. I doubt he'll be in the parlertorium to watch you work, but I'm sure he's going to give me an earful about your singing this morning, how I'm not pushing you to reach your full potential."

"Can I go?"

She laughs and shoos me away with a flapping of her hand. "Meet me in the scriptorium by eighteen bells," she calls as I race out the door.

When I burst into the receiving room two minutes later, the Goodson rises from his chair at one of the tables and smiles at me. Aside from the Hand of the Father emblazoned on his chest, his white wool tunic is as pure as the day it was shorn from the lamb. He wears a sky-blue cape at his shoulders—blue being the color of heaven—and the Hand of the Father in the scabbard at his side. It's an elegant if simple weapon, honed for the purpose of serving the Father in modesty and humility. He's tall like me—but unlike me, he wears it well.

"I hope I'm not calling you away from your work," he says.

The world's stupidest grin spreads across my face. "Daughter Zofia said I could come see you."

"And I must speak with her." He gestures for me to take the wooden chair opposite him. "Your singing at services this morning didn't showcase your full potential. She's not pushing you hard enough."

My stupid grin widens as we both sit. "She said you'd say that, too."

"Ah, well, the Father knows I am nothing if not predictable." His smile turns rueful, but his gray eyes dance with amusement. "Shall we play a game of Shakki? It's been a good long while."

I pour us each a cup of tea from the service as he sets up the game board. We speak of banal things—the weather, which of the Aurian translations of *The Songs* is best—but my mind latches onto the text Zofia took from me weeks ago, the one she didn't want me to mention to the Goodson. Now all I can think about is how I'm not supposed to say anything to him about it.

I've spent the past ten years trying to erase my memories of Hedenskia, but ever since I felt the word *Mother* in that inscription, I find myself doing the opposite, hunting down and clinging to anything I can dredge up from my childhood. I want to know where I came from, and the Goodson is the only person who can tell me anything about it.

"Goodson Anskar," I begin as I split my cavalry between two of the fictional countries on the board. "May I ask you something?"

"Of course." He rolls the dice and takes out half my cavalry with his army from the southwest. I didn't think he would cross an entire country for such a small threat to his borders, but then, I've never been much good at anticipating his strategies, which is why I usually lose.

"Was my name always Gelya? I mean, was that my name when you found me?" I try to sound passingly curious, but I'm quaking inside. I should be grateful that the Goodson saved me from Hedenskia, and I *am* grateful. But I had a mother at some point, a family, a place where I belonged in the world. I can't help but wonder how my life might have been different if the Goodson had never found me, and it feels like disobedience, wanting to know about those things.

"No," he says. He offers nothing more.

"Were you the one who named me?"

"I was. Did you not know?"

"I guess you'd have to be." I force a smile and move a unit of my men to back up my remaining cavalry. "Why 'Gelya'?"

He scrutinizes me but in a kind way, the same steady man he has always been, the one who fought the telleg of the Dead Forest for nights on end to save my life. When he speaks again, his tone takes on the mythic, reverent cadence he reserves for the Father alone.

"When I placed the seedpod of the Grace Tree in your hand all those years ago, it was the only time in my life I have witnessed the Father choose His Vessel. To be in the presence of the Father, to watch His hand as He chooses a Vessel for His Holy Word from heaven above . . . it took my breath away. The Father made you so that you would fill the world with His love and wisdom. His eternal goodwill, revealed to the faithful through your voice, is like the gelya berry in winter: bright and alive and lovely when all else seems to have died, a reminder of our everlasting life in heaven. So, you see, I named you after the glory of the One True God. Surely there is no greater name than that?"

I've never thought of my name in this light, and I've certainly never thought of myself as bright and alive and lovely. A hard lump of affection clogs my throat. "Thank you," I croak.

He reaches for his tea and takes a contemplative sip. "It's natural for you to wonder where you came from, a girl your age. But you must overcome that curiosity. You are a Vessel. Your life belongs to the Father. Who you were before the Father chose you, where you came from—those things don't matter now. And they were troubling to begin with."

This is the first time Goodson Anskar has spoken of my past so specifically. My pulse quickens, hopeful. "Troubling because you know what it's like there, because of your mission to convert the Hedenski heathens?"

"Because of my *failed* mission to convert the Hedenski heathens." He sets his cup down and smooths away a drop of liquid that spilled onto the table's surface. When he turns the full intensity of his gray eyes on me, I can tell I've pushed too much, too far. "You must guard yourself against the temptations of Elath the Great Demon. A Vessel is as easily filled with evil as she is with good, and a Daughter of the One True God is still a woman, made in the demon's image. You must resist this curiosity. To know of sinful things fills you with the sin itself."

"But Elath is imprisoned," I argue, both scared and empowered by this new temerity. *I just want to know,* I think.

"That doesn't erase Her subtle influence in the world. What on earth has come over you?" Reproach colors his voice. I may as well break a stone with my bare hands as stand up to Goodson Anskar. I slump in my chair, disheartened and sulking. "Nothing."

"None of us are safe from the lure of worldly pleasures," he continues when I am already defeated. "The demon's temptations permeate the very ground beneath our feet and all life that springs from it. As a Vessel, you are particularly vulnerable. That's why you live here, safe inside the convent."

I give him a weak nod as he moves his army north to meet mine. Within ten minutes, he trounces me. I stare at the board, my eyes drifting from my decimated southern armies to my nonexistent defenses on my northern border.

"Can you see your mistake?" he quizzes me.

"I should have reinforced my southern defenses?"

"Well, that is an excellent thought, but your mistake is larger than that." He leans against the wooden seat back and folds his arms. One corner of his mouth twitches upward in paternal amusement. "Daughter, who is your adversary?"

"You are, Goodson Anskar."

"I am," he agrees with false gravity. "What happens on the board is less important than what is happening here." He points to his temple. "You must know your adversary and understand his weaknesses. You must know what mistakes he will make, even before he does himself."

"But you don't make mistakes," I counter, exasperated. "Do you have any weaknesses?"

"I do. Many." He pushes the board to the side and sorts the pieces, readying them to be put away. "Here now, let's discuss more pleasant matters. I have a gift for you."

"A gift? It's not even the Feast of Saint Ovin," I protest, though I flush with anticipation. Daughters live spare lives, and gifts are extremely rare. Even my little doll was taken from me.

"I suppose I could have waited until then, but I'm as bad as a child when it comes to presents and waiting. You see? I do have weaknesses." He reaches into his pocket, produces a small, narrow box, and removes the lid, revealing a gold locket gleaming on a bed of red velvet.

"For me?" I breathe.

"For you."

I reach for the necklace but stop short. "Goodson Anskar, I couldn't—"

"Oh, I think you could." He takes the locket by the chain and hands it to me, his grin widening as I open the gold panels, revealing the triptych within. A tiny image of Saint Ovin trampling a miniature Elath beneath his feet takes up the center panel. Saint Vinnica and Saint Lanya stand on either side of him, pure and dutiful in their own panels. The artistry is stunning, but as I stare at the Holy Family, my niggling doubt rears its ugly head. Surely I don't deserve such a gift. "Thank you. It's perfect. But—"

"But Daughters are not supposed to own such fine things," he finishes for me. "Consider my gift a reminder of your purity and your purpose. You are a sacred Vessel, like Vinnica and Lanya, each serving the Father in her own way. Besides, this was made by a Kantari convert. To wear it is to keep a man's soul from becoming a telleg of the Dead Forest."

Tears spill from my eyes. If the Goodson knew of the questions I ask myself, the weight of his disappointment would crush me. It makes this reminder of my purity and purpose more valuable than he could ever know.

"Do you like it?" he asks.

I leap to my feet, knocking my chair to the ground, and race around the table to hug him.

"I'll take that as a yes," he laughs.

Five

I was hoping that my nerves would calm as I got used to the idea of translating at the summit, but if anything, the intervening hours have given me ample time to consider all the things that could go wrong tonight. Even the comforting weight of the Goodson's triptych against my heart fails to reassure me. By the time I meet Zofia in the scriptorium at eighteen bells in my best tunic, trousers, and sash, all I want to do is hide in the library stacks. She takes one look at my face and bursts out laughing. "You look like you're on your way to the gallows."

I scowl at her. "It's not funny."

"I'm sorry," she says, although she doesn't sound the least bit apologetic. But then she wraps her arms around me and whispers in my ear. "You're ready for this. I promise you."

Though I bask in Zofia's approval, my imagination keeps up a continual supply of all the ways I could mess up tonight as we walk to the parlertorium, where Goodson Anskar is stationed outside with several Knights of the Order. I expect him to greet me with words of encouragement. Instead, his tone is sharp when he asks Zofia, "What is she doing here?"

I glance at Zofia, unsure what to make of his chilly reception. "Daughter Gelya is the convent's only Kantari expert. She will translate for the prisoner tonight. I thought you knew."

The Goodson's lips tighten. "With all due respect, Sacrist, she doesn't belong here."

"What? Why?" I burst out. An unfamiliar anger bubbles inside me like boiled syrup as he pulls me off to the side, away from Zofia.

"You're far too young for this," he insists. "You shouldn't be exposed to such matters—such evil."

"He's going to be bound, isn't he? And guarded? For the Father's sake, you're the general of the Order of Saint Ovin. You carry the Hand of the Father in your scabbard. You protect Ovinists the world over from the Kantari. How could I be any safer?"

"Exactly. I'm in charge of the security of the faithful, and now I am protecting *you*."

You'd think I'd crumble under the weight of the Goodson's objections. Instead, I answer him with an inexplicable defiance, doing my best to emulate Zofia's poise as I tell him, "Forgive me, but the Father chose me for this, and I must do His bidding." Then I march through the doors, heading straight for the translators' table with my pulse slamming through my veins. Once I sit down, I grip the seat of my chair and stare at the door, waiting for Zofia as I both hope for and fear a glimpse of the Goodson, to see his reaction. But Zofia doesn't come in right away, and I can't see the Goodson from my vantage point.

My eyes shift to the ten Knights of the Order of Saint Ovin standing guard, five to each side of the entrance. Some are lean while others are stocky. Some have blond hair, while others have brown or black. Their complexions range from pale peach to raw umber, as diverse as the countries united by the Holy Ovinist Church. These brave men stand watch on the Great Wall of Saint Balzos to ensure that the telleg never leave the Dead Forest. They escort caravans of pilgrims from all over the world to visit the holy sites of our faith. Most important, they guard the Vault of Mount Djall so that Elath the Great Demon may never again walk the earth.

The knights stare ahead, their heavy longswords in scabbards strapped to their waists. I'm surprised to see that every one of them looks young. Guarding a summit at a convent in the heart of Rosvania must be an easy assignment, but their youth doesn't fill me with confidence.

"What did the Goodson say?" I ask Zofia breathlessly when she finally comes in, but she doesn't answer. She scans the room until her eyes land on two men standing across from us along the north wall, one of them a Tovnian army captain, the other a seasoned knight named Brother Miklos, a friend of the Goodson whom I've met a few times. They stand sentry in front of an alcove, presumably guarding the Kantari prisoner within. The thought of facing whoever is tucked away in the alcove's darkness makes my throat close up. That's when I notice that the Tovnian's sword sheath is empty. But of course it is. Only Knights of the Order of Saint Ovin are allowed to carry weapons into the parlertorium.

"Maybe the Goodson is right, Gelya. Maybe you shouldn't be

here," Zofia murmurs, and an icy, unnamed dread takes up residence next to my screaming anxiety. But it's too late to turn back, even if I wanted to. Nineteen bells rings. The summit is beginning.

Zofia rises to close the double doors of the parlertorium, pulling the key up from underneath her tunic to lock us all in. My stomach turns alongside the tumblers. Once she takes her seat beside me again, she touches my hand, and just in case I wasn't panicked enough, her eyes shift from mine to the statue of the unknown saint, to the escape route.

You're imagining things, I tell myself. *It's going to be all right.*

The Archbishop of Rosvania rises, the blue silk and gold embroidery of his formal vestments reflecting the flames of the chandelier above so that he seems to shine with the Father's light. He rings a small bell to call the summit to order. The room falls silent, and he leads the men in a prayer from *The Song of the First Kings,* the story of how the Father planted his seed in eight chosen Vessels, who gave birth to the eight saint-kings of the Ovinist Church.

"The sacrament of the Grand Summit has begun," he declares. "I call on Tovnia to speak his concern."

The Tovnian ambassador, a petit man in his thirties, draped in rich robes of Tovnia's orange-and-red standard, rises from his seat between his two comrades.

"That's Tovnia's crown prince, Horaccio," Zofia whispers to me.

A prince. My throat tightens, making it hard to swallow.

"On the fourth day of the month of Saint Ferda," begins the prince, "my father, King Horac, dispatched a unit of five hundred men to the Tovnian border when Ukrenti scouts sent word that Kantari troops had been spotted crossing the Koz foothills. The king's assumption was that the Kantari planned to make a move against the Monastery of Saint Ovin in a new attempt to open the Vault of Mount Djall."

"This is known," Wesmar's ambassador interjects with impatience. "We understand that Tovnia was caught off guard when their unit found themselves face-to-face with the entire Kantari army, which did not approach Mount Djall but crossed into Tovnia instead. I move to hear Tovnia's request. Let's get on with it."

"I second," calls the ambassador of Ostmar, equally disdainful.

I know that many view the Tovnian royal family with a suspicious eye since they adhere to a form of Ovinism that venerates female saints almost as much as Saint Ovin himself. The Holy See ignores the custom since Tovnia provides important trade routes between north and south, but hard-line Ovinists find the practice heretical. Even so, I didn't expect to see such petty politics here, despite Zofia's warning, and I already feel out of my depth.

"Tovnia will state his case," the archbishop directs.

Prince Horaccio clears his throat. "Tovnia requests the immediate military intervention of the Order of Saint Ovin as well as a coordinated military strike with the eight kingdoms of the Ovinist faith to repel this threat to the innocents within our borders."

I do my best to follow the rapid-fire debate that follows. Most of it is carried out in Rosvanian, but Zofia steps in from time to time to translate for the Ukrenti and Degmari ambassadors. My eyes keep darting to the alcove where the Kantari prisoner waits, tucked behind the Tovnian captain and Brother Miklos, but try as I may to catch a glimpse of him, I see only his shadow beyond the guards.

The Rosvanian ambassador, sallow in a velvet jacket of our standard's bright green, cuts through the bickering with a bombastic voice. "Why are we discussing military cooperation across borders? The Kantari pose no threat to Rosvania. This is Tovnia's problem, not ours."

"They've crossed the Koz Mountains for the first time in centuries," says the Aurian ambassador. "They're clearly heading north. Auria is deeply concerned. Why isn't Rosvania?"

"Who's to say their complaint isn't with the Tovnians alone? Rosvania has nothing to gain from committing troops."

"That's easy for the Rosvanians to say, safe as Daughters in a convent, sitting on the best land of the continent," the Wesmari ambassador cuts in. "You haven't had to deal with the Kantari threat the way your southern brothers have. We've fought those heathen monsters off our trade routes for decades, and it gets worse every year as the Kantari drought spreads. Now the devils are at your doorstep, and Wesmar would like to know what you plan to do about it."

"Enough. We're not even an hour into these proceedings, far too early to dissolve into a schoolyard tussle," calls the Yilish ambassador with his musical accent. Yil is an empire unto itself, a land of many faiths. So while there's a tentative truce between Yil and the countries of the Ovinist Church, most of the ambassadors regard him with cool disdain, and the Rosvanian ambassador doesn't even try to mask his loathing. "We don't know why the

Kantari are attacking Tovnia or why they moved north of the Koz. The answers to those questions should be illuminating to any further discussion. The Tovnians have brought a captured Kantari soldier for questioning. Well and good. Let him be questioned."

This must be news to Wesmar, because the ambassador and his two assistants whip their heads around, searching the room. "You've brought a Kantari soldier? Here?"

"He's not a Two-Swords, is he?" the Sudmari asks warily. It never occurred to me that the Tovnians might have brought a Two-Swords with them, and the possibility frays my already ragged nerves. The Two-Swords are the most elite fighters on earth, chosen by the seedpods of Elath's Tree in Kantar.

Rosvania rolls his eyes. "For the love of the Father, calm yourselves. There are hardly any Two-Swords left, and this one is only a boy."

"They don't make boys in Kantar," the Wesmari spits. "They make demons."

The archbishop beckons to the guards anyway. "Bring the prisoner forward."

Oh no, I think as Zofia touches my arm. I'm so nervous my ears start ringing, but I rise from my seat and take my place at the top of the U with my knees wobbling beneath me. The Tovnian captain and Brother Miklos pull a man out of the alcove and escort him forward.

Toward me.

Six

The Kantari is gagged, and his wrists are tied together in front of him. A length of rope pins his upper arms to his torso. His ankles are bound with just enough slack between his feet to allow mincing steps, but he only makes it a few paces before tripping.

"Can we at least untie his ankles?" the Rosvanian ambassador drawls.

"With all due respect, sir," says the Tovnian prince with no hint of respect in his tone, "this 'boy' killed twelve men in one skirmish before we captured him."

The Rosvanian smirks. "The boy is bound from the waist up, and we are guarded by the Knights of the Order. I'm hardly worried."

"Fool," the Wesmari mutters.

"Remove the ankle ties," the archbishop directs the Tovnian captain. The man's jaw clenches in objection, but he unties the rope, coils it, and slings it over his shoulder before he and Brother

Miklos march the Kantari to the opposite end of the U. I take a breath to steady myself, but it does little to ease my nervousness.

The captive's stench radiates from him like heat from an oven, a pungent combination of armpit musk, sweat, dirt, and another aroma I can't identify that is both horrible and familiar.

"Dear heavenly Father, Prince Horaccio, could you not have rinsed him off first?" jokes the Rosvanian ambassador. The archbishop eyes him with irritation but instructs the guard to remove the gag.

"Wonderful. Now he can bite us all," the Wesmari ambassador grumbles.

The Tovnian captain struggles with the gag's knot, which ratchets up my nerves with each passing second. When the cloth falls away, the Kantari lifts his head and stretches his jaw. He looks as terrible as he smells. A strand of dark, greasy hair has come loose from its binding and falls across his dirt-streaked face. His nose is large and has clearly been broken at some point in time. Even though he's young, a scraggly beard stubbles his upper lip and jaw. Two thick eyebrows hang heavily over his unsettling eyes, which are a mossy green. What remains of his black clothes leaves little to the imagination, clinging indecently to every line and curve of his long, lean body. He might as well be standing before me naked. From the top of his head to the tips of his toes, he is every bit the dangerous Kantari heathen I always imagined.

"Ask him why his people have crossed the mountains," the archbishop commands me.

I nod, focusing on the language, on the words, on my purpose.

I clear my throat and translate the question into Kantari. "Why have the Kantari crossed the Koz Mountains?"

The gag has left an angry red stripe on either side of the boy's mouth, which remains silent. I wish he would direct that intense green gaze somewhere else, but he doesn't. When it becomes clear that he has no intention of answering the first question, Prince Horaccio says, "Ask him why they're attacking Tovnia."

"Why are the Kantari attacking Tovnia?" I'm feeling steadier now, more capable, and I refuse to let a brute rattle me, even though, once again, he refuses to answer.

"The Kantari have focused their attacks on the Monastery of Mount Djall and the Vault for centuries," the archbishop presses. "Why this change in tactics? Why now?"

I translate, already certain that I'll be met with the same reticence . . . which is why I'm startled when the Kantari speaks at last. To me.

"Holy Mother, you're tall."

"What did he say?" asks the Rosvanian ambassador, but before I have a chance to translate, the boy speaks again.

"Do you shave only your head?" His tone isn't malicious, but the clear connotation is that he wants to know if I shave the rest of my body as well. A mixture of humiliation and anger makes my entire body blush.

"Translation," the archbishop prompts.

I glare at the Kantari as I translate. "He says that I am tall. He asks me why my head is shaved."

"Was that an accurate translation, Daughter?" the boy asks with a mocking grin.

The captain jostles him and barks, "Shut it. You'll speak when you're spoken to."

The Kantari looks to me. "Aren't you going to translate that?"

"What did he say?" the Rosvanian ambassador snaps.

My head is spinning with all these demands. I'm only one girl. "He asks if I'm going to translate the words of the Tovnian captain," I answer the Rosvanian.

The Wesmari ambassador snorts. "Go ahead."

But I don't. I'm too busy reassessing the boy. He would only have noticed my omission if he spoke Rosvanian. He inclines his head as I study him, and I get the feeling that he's reassessing me, too.

"Now that his tongue is loosened," says the Yilish ambassador, "ask him again why the Kantari are attacking Tovnia. What is their purpose?"

I hesitate for the span of one breath, studying the boy's face to see if he'll betray another sign of understanding Rosvanian. His face goes cool, impassive. I translate the question. This time, when the boy doesn't answer, the archbishop gives a curt nod to the Tovnian captain, who punches the boy in the lower back. An alarmed "Oh!" escapes my lips as he cries out in pain.

The Kantari sneers at me. "Do you pity me? Look at *you*, tall as a man and ugly as a buzzard. Can't you see what these monsters have done to you? Don't pity me. Pity yourself."

Each word sinks in like the teeth of a feral dog. I bite back my own infuriated response. Anger is an emotion no decent Daughter should indulge, but Holy Father, it's hard to contain.

"Daughter?" the archbishop prompts.

"He says he is not to be pitied. He says I am tall as a man and ugly as a vulture."

"Buzzard," the boy corrects me, whispering in Kantari.

"I knew it! You speak Rosvanian," I accuse him in Kantari.

"What's this?" the Rosvanian ambassador bellows.

I tear my eyes from the boy to find that every man in the room is staring at me, some shocked by my impropriety, others blazing with outrage. I bow my head in shame.

"We will not tolerate a female, who is made in the image of Elath, speaking out of turn at these proceedings, Sacrist," the archbishop seethes at Zofia, his hawkish nose red with outrage. "Make it clear to her that a woman's voice is only to be heard in translation."

"You are not to speak of your own free will, Daughter," Zofia says softly.

"Yes, Sacrist," I answer, praying that I won't start crying or do anything else that will ruin me in the eyes of men.

"See? Monsters," the boy whispers to me. When I glance up, I expect the return of that mocking grin, but his lips are unsmiling. When he speaks again, his voice is so loud it bounces off the arched ceiling. "I also have questions. Why don't you ask this Knight of the Order to my left what happened when a small band of Elathians breached the walls of the Monastery of Saint Ovin twelve years ago and opened the Vault of Mount Djall?"

The question is so shocking it borders on incomprehensible. The Kantari have been attacking the monastery for hundreds of years to try to set the Great Demon free, but they have never breached the walls, not once. When I translate, my voice sounds mechanical, distancing itself from this madness. "He says I should ask Brother Miklos what happened when a group breached the walls of the Monastery of Saint Ovin twelve years ago and opened the Vault containing Elath the Great Demon."

Behind me, I hear Zofia's intake of breath before she translates for the Ukrenti and Degmari ambassadors.

"Elath the *Mother*," the boy corrects me, but I know perfectly well what evil is contained in that vault. Every devout Ovinist knows.

The Aurian ambassador breaks the stunned silence that follows. "Nothing has happened to the Vault of Mount Djall. Has it?"

"It's a ploy," says the Rosvanian, waving his hand dismissively. "He's trying to distract us. This prisoner is worthless, Tovnia."

The boy speaks again, his alarming eyes boring into mine. "Ask this knight what Goodson Anskar and the Order of Saint Ovin did when they discovered, just as the Elathians did, that the Vault was empty."

"Translation," the archbishop demands.

I shake my head, incredulous, even as I say the words. "He says I should ask Brother Miklos what the Goodson and the Order of Saint Ovin did when . . . when they discovered that the Vault was empty."

The table bursts into sound. The Wesmari ambassador yells in alarm, while the Rosvanian ambassador continues to dismiss the Kantari's claims. The archbishop rings the bell again, thundering, "Enough!"

The Kantari shouts over all of them. "Ask him what happened to the city of Grama! Ask him what the Order did there—to women, children, the old, the sick! Ask him what the Order took from us so they could hunt down the Mother!"

"No," I answer without thinking. "The Vault has never been opened. And the Goodson would never—"

The archbishop slams the bell down on the table. "Translation!"

"Ask him where the Mother is!" cries the Kantari.

"Gelya, don't—" Zofia says, but my voice, shrill with bewilderment, cuts through the ambassadors' uproar as inevitably as an avalanche.

"He asks Brother Miklos where Elath the Great Demon is!"

It's not until the translation exits my mouth that I fully comprehend what the Kantari has said. The restless doubt that has plagued me for weeks must have gotten the better of me at last, because I am inexplicably certain of one thing: He's telling the truth.

All eyes turn to Brother Miklos, who has, until this moment, stood quietly at the prisoner's side. He answers with action rather than words, reaching inside his sleeve with a hand nearly as pale as the white wool of his tunic to pull out a dagger. Only a couple of ambassadors have time to gasp before the Goodson's old friend throws the blade across the room.

Right into Zofia's heart.

Seven

Dark blood snakes from the wound as Zofia clutches the table, gasping for air.

He killed her. I stand there, frozen, the words repeating themselves in my head over and over until they morph into a blur of meaningless gibberish. *Hekilledherhekilledherhekilledher. . . .*

And then I move, rushing to catch her under her arms before she falls out of the chair. "Fetch the convent physicians!" I shout at the ambassadors, but they all continue to gape in shock at Zofia dying in my arms.

"What the hell is this, Brother Miklos?" demands the Rosvanian ambassador with false bravado. The knight ignores him and heads straight for Zofia and me. My heart pounds with fear, but I hold tight to Zofia. When he reaches for the chain around her neck, I try to shove his hand away, crying, "No! What are you doing? Stop!"

"Brother Miklos!" the archbishop protests, ringing that

ridiculous bell as if the chime could stop the knight from pushing me aside so he can take the key. With no one to hold her up, Zofia slumps to the unforgiving marble floor, and Brother Miklos saunters to the double doors at the back of the room as dispassionately as you might carry a chamber pot to dump it.

"Do something!" I scream at the knights, who shuffle uncomfortably, glancing doubtfully at each other. One of them finally works up the courage to say, "Uh, Brother?"

Brother Miklos unlocks the doors and opens one of them. I beg the Father to send the Goodson to come rescue us. Instead, masked men enter the parlertorium, each bearing a sword, and terror turns me bloodless. Brother Miklos exits the room, and the sound of the tumblers rolling into place, locking us in once more, echoes off the vaulted ceiling.

I am going to die.

We are all going to die.

A numbness takes over my brain, as if I were seeing the world through gauze as the masked men attack the ambassadors. One of them slices into Prince Horaccio's neck as the room explodes like a henhouse when the fox gets in.

A wave of childhood memories slams into me, forcing me to relive the horrors of the Dead Forest with vivid clarity. I see the monsters floating between dark tree trunks, their black cloaks hanging from strange, skeletal bodies, their gray skin pulled taut over faceless heads, their long, unnatural hands swiping and killing, tearing apart the Goodson's companions as if they were made of rags.

A tug on the hem of my tunic makes me shriek in terror. I look down to find the Rosvanian ambassador frantically beckoning to me. "Get under here, stupid girl!"

I dive beneath the table just in time to see the Wesmari ambassador hit the floor across the room, blood spurting out of his slit throat like a fountain. The contents of my stomach surge up my throat and out my mouth, drizzling from my nostrils in burning streams. The Rosvanian ambassador grips my arm too tightly and shakes me. "Is there a way out of here?"

"The Goodson," I cough, my throat stinging with bile. "Where is the Goodson?"

But in the question lies the answer. There can only be one explanation as to why the Goodson hasn't stopped this attack. He must be dead.

And Zofia is dead.

And I am going to die.

I cover my head with shaking hands, wishing I could give in to despair, but the Rosvanian won't stop shaking me. "Dammit, girl, is there another way out of this death trap?"

My mind clings to the memory of Zofia showing me the escape route. *The world of men is dangerous for women. Do you understand?* But I hadn't understood. I hadn't understood a thing.

An inhuman gurgling comes from somewhere nearby, and there is Zofia, struggling on the floor, the knife still jutting from her body. My heart swells and breaks all at once. "Zofia!" I reach for her like a lost child for its mother, but the ambassador yanks back my hand.

"No! You'll give us away!"

I try to shake him loose, and when that doesn't work, I sink my teeth into his veiny hand until the coppery taste of his blood fills my mouth. He releases me, cursing in pain.

I don't look at the carnage around me as I crawl to Zofia—hearing it is horrible enough. I grasp her by the shoulders of her tunic and tug. At first, her limp weight holds her in place like iron to lodestone, but once I work up the momentum, I'm able to drag her under the table.

"Gelya." An unnatural pink bubble forms between her lips.

"You're going to be all right," I tell her, as if I could will it to be true.

Two men plow into the table as they grapple with one another, locked in a battle to the death. The whole table shudders and slides back a foot, nearly uncovering Zofia and me. The Rosvanian squeals like a piglet. I push him away and bend over Zofia.

"Gelya," she gurgles.

"Shh. Help is coming." Dear Father, please, let help be on the way.

"My pocket," Zofia insists, trying to move a hand that is no longer cooperating to her side. I reach into her pocket for her and pull out a folded piece of parchment.

"Hide it," Zofia wheezes, and it takes me a minute to realize she's speaking in Hedenski.

"I will," I tell her, dredging up Hedenski words I thought long gone from my mind. I'll say just about anything if it keeps her still and calm. She groans with effort as she puts her hand over mine. Already, her fingers grow cold.

"Don't let the Goodson get it." She coughs, shooting a spray of blood-dappled foam against the bottom of the table.

"Yes, of course," I agree, desperate for her to save her strength while trying to push away the thought that the Goodson is almost certainly dead.

She grips my hand with what little strength she has left. Blood trickles from the corner of her mouth. "Promise me," she rasps.

I would hand my heart in a gift-wrapped package to Elath the Great Demon if it would keep Zofia alive. "I promise," I say in Hedenski, the words light and strange in my mouth.

"Blessed be the Mother," she sighs in her native Aurian. Blood ceases to pulse from her mouth, and her gray eyes go blank, death robbing them of the brilliance that lit them in life. Disbelieving, I collapse over her and press my forehead to hers. An unbearable grief hovers nearby, waiting to crush me as soon as I comprehend my loss.

And then her words sink in like venom.

Blessed be the Mother.

The Mother.

Zofia . . . was an Elathian?

The betrayal is so thick it takes form, reaching into my chest and squeezing my heart.

The table is shoved to the side, and this time, there's no place to hide. I scream, shredding my raw throat as one of the assailants drags out the terrified Rosvanian ambassador by the legs while another skewers him. The man releases the murdered ambassador's limp legs and stalks back to the table for me. I'm frozen to the spot, waiting for the death blow with my pulse hammering in my temples. He stares down at me for a moment with cold blue eyes before turning away to help his partner dispatch the rest of the ambassadors and knights.

I'm not dead. How am I not dead?

There are so many emotions churning inside me, I can't register my relief. I crawl to Zofia's body under the table and gaze out hopelessly at the bodies strewn across the floor like garbage. I have no clue how I'm going to make it to the statue of the unknown saint without getting myself cut to ribbons, but I'm going to try for Zofia's sake, whether she was an Elathian or not. I slide her paper into my pocket, grasp the knife handle sticking up from her lifeless torso, and pull. Her body clings to the blade as it once clung to life. I yank until the blade releases its hold on her, and my knuckles smack painfully against the underside of the table. My heart beating a staccato of fear, I emerge from beneath the table like a snail oozing out of its shell, and every bit as vulnerable.

Between me and the statue, an assailant grabs the captured Kantari around his bound torso. The boy rams the back of his head into the man's face, sending a spray of blood from his opponent's nose. I turn away, scooting across the marble floor as someone screams in agony from the other side of the room. "Please, holy Father," I beg my god.

The boy's opponent kicks him from behind and sends him sprawling across the floor. He slams against the wall, bounces off the stone, and rolls into a crouch.

Right in front of me.

My mind floods with everything I've heard about the Kantari.

You shouldn't be exposed to such matters—such evil.

I should stab him before he kills me, but dear Father, I don't know how to kill anyone.

They don't make boys in Kantar. They make demons.

His focus shifts from my face to the knife. The blade shakes with the trembling of my hands. He looks me in the eye, and just in case the world had not gone mad enough, he holds out his bound wrists to me, as if he's asking me to cut the ropes.

Now he can bite us all.

My chest rises and falls with ragged breaths. I hear the masked man stagger to his feet behind me. The boy's eyes burn into mine. He reaches out, moving the ropes closer.

"Cut me free," he orders in Kantari.

I shake my head so violently my brain rattles against my skull.

"Do it. Now."

I remember the way Zofia scanned the room. She sensed something was wrong, and she was staggeringly, painfully right.

The boy shakes his bound wrists at me one last time. And for reasons I cannot begin to comprehend, my gut says to do it.

I don't think.

I don't question.

My hands quake, but I take the knife and saw at the ropes.

Eight

Once I've cut through most of the rope, the boy pulls apart his fists, snapping the last, rough fibers. He snatches the knife from my hand and lunges over the top of me, shoving the blade between the assassin's ribs. I scream as the slain assailant drops onto me and pins me to the floor, gurgling his dying breaths in my ear.

The boy cuts away the remaining ropes around his torso, fresh blood darkening his already-filthy shirt. He snatches up the slain attacker's sword, leaving me to roll out from underneath the assassin on my own. By the time I've freed myself of the dead man's weight, the boy has killed another assailant. The knife is tucked into the waist of his pants at his back, and he is now holding a sword in each hand as if he were born that way.

Oh, my Father in heaven, this boy—this *child*—is a Kantari Two-Swords?

But there is nothing childish about him now as he glides through the bloody throng of assassins and ambassadors and knights, his body moving among theirs like water easing its way between river stones. When one of the assassins lashes out at him with a longsword, he twists away and kicks off the ground, sending his body spinning, perpendicular to the floor, his blade aimed at the assailant's heart like a screw into wood. He hits his mark, then kicks off the dead man's chest as he pulls the blade out, sending an arc of blood curving through the air.

He's still airborne. How can he still be airborne?

The Kantari swings his right-hand weapon at another assailant, but the man catches the hem of his shirt and yanks him sideways to throw off his aim. The Two-Swords flips in midair and brings his left sword down hard into the crook of his enemy's neck, killing him instantly. He finally touches down with one foot long enough to regain his balance and leap into the air again, blocking maneuvers by two assassins with both swords at once.

I am not going to stay in this room long enough to find out what happens next.

The sounds of battle and death explode behind me as I sprint to the statue of the unknown saint, reaching up with both hands to pull down on its head. Nothing. I try again, letting my feet come off the floor to add my weight. Nothing.

A plume of smoke wafts past me. I turn my stinging eyes to the front of the parlertorium to see flames licking up the feet of Saint Ovin. The oil from the Eternal Flame must have spilled in the fight, and now it's been set alight. If I can't get this hatch open, I'm going to choke to death or burn alive in here.

Movement from above snatches my attention away from the fire. The boy has climbed onto the chandelier, out of reach of the other men's weapons. Our eyes meet, and his gaze pins me to the statue. Then, with a sudden lurch, the chandelier dips, pulling hard on the support beam from which it hangs. The Kantari's sweat-streaked face has just enough time to register alarm before the whole thing comes crashing down, taking half the crossbeam with it.

I turn and throw my arms around the statue's neck and heave backward with all my strength as men fight and die behind me.

Nothing.

I abandon the statue and race to the double doors, pounding them with my fists, pressing my forehead to the ancient wood as I scream for help.

An object hits the door from inside the parlertorium, silencing me. Slowly, with my heart pulsing in my ears, I turn my head to find the knife's handle jutting out from the door just inches from my nose. The wood has split around the blade, releasing the aroma of oak and lemon oil mixed with the rusty scent of blood.

"I missed on purpose. Next time, I won't. Now stop pounding the door," the Kantari commands me in his native language.

An electric current of fear zings through me. I turn and watch him step over a dead assailant to confront the two surviving ambassadors—Sudmar and Auria—as well as the only Knight of the Order left standing. The Sudmari ambassador clutches the altar statue of Saint Ovin, ready to bludgeon the Two-Swords with it.

"I saved your life," the boy points out to him in Rosvanian, but that only inspires the Sudmari to hold the statue higher so he can hit the Kantari harder. The boy huffs in disgust before he holds up his left-hand blade and declares, "I offer you the Sword of Mercy.

Throw down your weapons, and I will let you live."

The ambassadors glance at each other, but they obey, the Sudmari setting down his statue and the Aurian dropping a broken table leg, which clatters on the marble beneath his feet. The one remaining knight, however, goes on the attack, thrusting his sword straight at his opponent's stomach. The Kantari catches the young man by the wrist, holding the blade away as he knees the knight in the diaphragm. The weapon clatters to the floor, and the Two-Swords kicks it out of reach before dumping the knight on the ground.

"Let's try this again," he says sourly in Kantari before repeating, in Rosvanian, "I offer you the Sword of Mercy. Do you accept?"

The ambassadors nod, wide-eyed, while the knight gasps for air on the floor.

"Good."

The Two-Swords finally faces me. Sweaty and painted to the elbows in blood, he's even filthier than he was before. His loosened hair is glued to the sides of his face, and his perspiration ignites the air with a musky stink so thick that my empty stomach turns.

"You too," he says. "I offer you the Sword of Mercy. Do you accept?"

I nod frantically, and just to be sure he thoroughly and completely understands my will to live, I tell him, "Yes. Yes, I accept the Sword of Mercy."

"Thank you. Will you please tell these men to put out that fire if they can?"

His words run together, one garbling into the next. I've never spoken Kantari with an actual Kantari person until tonight, and

I'm finding it difficult to pick out the individual words as he speaks. I've only ever read the language or practiced speaking it with Zofia.

Zofia.

Her folded paper feels like a stone in my pocket. I will not—cannot—look at her lifeless body where it lies beneath the table. And that leaves me nowhere to look but straight ahead. At the Two-Swords.

"Hello?" he says in Rosvanian, snapping his fingers in my face. "You translate, yes?"

"Um, yes." I look over his shoulder at the three men. "He says you should try to put out the fire."

"Thank you," says the Two-Swords, and then he hurries toward the doors. On the way, he bends to pick up the rope that once bound him.

"What are you doing?" I call at his back, bewildered. Smoke stings my eyes and reaches into my lungs, making me cough.

He sets down both of his swords on the floor, then threads the rope through the iron handles. "Making sure no one can get in."

"But the fire—"

"Ten armed men just moseyed through these doors to kill us. Do you really want to find out what's waiting for us on the other side?"

"No," I reply, seeing reason where I don't want to. Any hope that the Goodson might still be alive shrivels. I push my fists against my eyes and will myself not to start bawling.

"Good. Now can you please help those men with the fire?"

A Two-Swords who just leveled a roomful of assassins is saying *please* and *thank you*. It's so ludicrous that I burst out laughing, a hysterical combination of cackling and weeping.

"Great. Wonderful. That's very helpful." The Kantari returns to me, a blade in each hand again. "Look, either make yourself useful or find a different way out of this rat trap. Those are our only options at the moment."

I'm about to entrust you with one of the greatest secrets of the convent. Do you promise to keep it to yourself?

I can't stop giggling, because it's horribly, painfully hilarious. Zofia asked me if she could "trust" *me*, when her last words in this life were "Blessed be the Mother"? If I stop laughing over the giant pile of irony the Father just heaped at my feet, I'll fall into a darkness I don't think I can escape.

"Useless," the Kantari mutters as he walks away from me. "Completely useless."

Every woman should have an escape route if possible. Do you understand? But I hadn't understood at all, not until Brother Miklos's knife went flying across the room.

I tug the knife free of the door and tuck it into my pocket beside Zofia's parchment. Then I walk to the unknown saint. He stares down at his own heart, and it seems impossible that something so achingly beautiful can do anything other than crumble to dust in the nightmare that is this parlertorium. Still giggling, I take a running leap, catching the unknown saint by the back of the head. The hinges hidden beneath the floor creak, and the nameless saint finally pitches forward several inches. Breathless and giddy, I drop to the ground, ready to run at the statue again, when I realize the boy is beside me, staring at the small gap between the floor and the tile beneath the statue.

"I take it back. You're not useless." He sets down his weapons and slips his fingers under the marble tile. "You pull. I'll push. On the count of three. One—two—three."

The movement of the secret door is stiff, but in seconds we have it opened at a right angle to the floor so that the statue stands parallel to the ground. The boy stares at it quizzically before rapping the statue's hind end with his knuckles. It's clearly hollow. "Good. That'll make it easier to pull the tile closed behind us." He scowls into the hole, and then he stalks to the other side of the room to strip two slain knights of their scabbards.

Right now I want so badly to fall apart I can taste it, but instead I opt to do something practical to keep my terror at bay. I drag a chair to a nearby pillar and reach for the oil lamp hanging from an ornate iron hook. It's one of those rare occasions when I'm grateful to be tall.

"What are you doing?" the boy calls across the room, clearly annoyed, but I don't bother to respond. If he was going to kill me, he probably would have done so by now. Maybe he feels like he owes me since I'm the miserable idiot who cut him free.

The Two-Swords and I return to the hole in the floor at the same time, me holding a lamp and he with two swords strapped to his back. I can tell by the twisting of his mouth that he thinks the lamp is a good idea. He just doesn't want to admit it.

The other men notice that we've opened an escape tunnel and crowd around us as we peer into the hole. A series of bricks juts out from the wall at regular intervals, forming a ladder into the darkness.

"Do we know when this was built? Has anyone been using it, maintaining it?" The boy speaks quickly, his consonants soft and squishy and difficult to track. It makes my head ache.

"I did not know it existed until this morning," I tell him. Even referencing the conversation with Zofia squeezes my heart with grief and anger.

"So it could be caved in, or the ventilation could be shot and we'll suffocate? Or we'll knock loose some support as we move through and the whole thing will cave in on us?" Again, his words run together. I'm mostly just registering his misgivings when the right-hand door of the parlertorium shudders as something rams against it from the outside.

"Let's go," the boy says. "You first, then me, then them."

Until this moment, I had only been thinking of escape, but it now occurs to me that I'm facing a choice: I could either go with the Kantari or stay here and, possibly, be rescued.

"Go on," the boy urges me. But how can I willingly go with him, when there's a slim chance that the Goodson is still alive?

Another thump rattles one of the doors, harder than the last.

"Go!" the boy barks.

Fear makes my choice for me, and I begin my descent into the hole.

The nerve-racking assault on the parlertorium doors continues as I climb down the bricks while holding the oil lamp. The knight sticks his head into the opening and whispers, "For the love of the Father, would you hurry up?"

"I'm going as fast as I can," I shoot back, looking up in time to see the Two-Swords haul the knight back by the hood of his cloak.

Once I'm safely on the ground, the Kantari blows out a gust of air and mutters, "Father of death," before making his way down the ladder, cursing at each rung. Once his head is level with the top, he jumps down and lands gracefully next to me, then motions for the rest to follow. You'd think he'd leave them to die, so it's a relief to know the Sword of Mercy means something to him.

The knight is the last one down, and my jaw aches from gritting my teeth by the time he heaves the hatch closed behind him. Seconds later, a clatter rings above us, followed by the sound of footsteps rushing into the room, shouts of alarm, coughing. Whoever was trying to enter the parlertorium has succeeded. I fist my hands, forgetting to breathe.

When a full minute goes by without anyone coming after us, a profound relief envelops me. I finally remember to draw air, only to discover that the boy's ripe musk has permeated the cramped space, so pungent I'd swear it's seeping into my pores. He glances past me into the darkness of the tunnel beyond, then whispers, "Tell them I want everyone in a line behind you. I'll be last. Let's go."

I translate his order, and our tragically short line begins the journey through the tunnel. The lamp swings from the chain in my hand, making the light shift and move dizzyingly in the darkness as what little relief I felt a moment ago gives way to a growing fear of whatever awaits us at the end of the corridor.

Nine

"How long is this tunnel?" the boy asks from the back, his voice strained.

"I do not know," I answer in equally clipped syllables.

"Where does it lead?"

"The scriptorium."

"The what?"

"A room for writing and study." I keep my answers short and simple. I may be stuck with this Kantari for now, but the sooner I can be free of him, the better, although I have no idea how I'm going to accomplish that.

My light is the only thing that punctures the crushing darkness as we walk for what seems like eternity. Someone's increasingly ragged breathing cuts through the silence of the passage. Concerned that one of our number is asphyxiating, I turn back to find the ambassadors and the knight staring at the boy, who leans against the wall with his head thrown back as he gasps for air and claws at the neck of his shirt. His light brown skin has turned a chalky color. The others shuffle uncomfortably, as useless as they were back in the parlertorium. I sigh and push my way past them. "Sir, are you unwell?"

I'm thanked for my concern by a fierce glare. "Move," he rasps at me. "Just keep moving."

Fine. If he doesn't want my help, he won't get it. I head back to the front of the line and march down the tunnel, coming to the end so abruptly that I smack my head against the stone wall.

"Oh, thank you, dear Father," cries the Sudmari as the Aurian ambassador shoulders in front of me, grousing, "How are we supposed to get this thing open?"

The men push in front of me, arguing over how to open the door and who gets to leave first. The Kantari hangs back and watches. In the lamplight, I can see that his complexion is still waxy. Sweat streams down his face and neck, shining in the hollow of his throat. He looks like a scared boy, not a vicious Kantari soldier.

"Get that lamp out of my face," he snaps, and I shrink away from him, my hip knocking into a brick that juts out from the wall. To my surprise, it gives way, sinking into the other bricks. The sound of a released latch reverberates through the wall at the front of the room, and a door pops outward like a loosened puzzle piece.

The Aurian shoves the other two men out of the way so he can escape first, but the Two-Swords collars him and yanks him back. He blocks the door, glaring at the men as he says, "You, Daughter, translate this: We are the only witnesses who can attest to the fact that a Knight of the Order of Saint Ovin allowed ten armed men to enter the parlertorium and murder your comrades. I'd say hiding is your best option right now. Deal?"

I do my best to translate, but I'm still having a hard time picking out every word, the reality of spoken language far messier than words written on a page. He must have been speaking formally at the summit, because he was easy to understand then. Now his speech matches his sloppy appearance. I do get his point across, though, because the knight and the Sudmari nod as if their lives depended on it. The Aurian ambassador, however, sputters protestations. The Kantari unsheathes a sword, silencing the man with the unsubtle threat of violence. "I saved your ass, so either you agree to hide and keep quiet once you're out of this tunnel, or I can leave you to die right here. Your choice."

Again, I do my best to translate, but I'm not sure what exactly *ass* means. I'll have to look it up when this nightmare comes to an end. I cling to the word, a slim hope that I have a future to anticipate.

Satisfied by the Aurian's reluctant nod, the boy steps aside. The knight, who has worked his way to the front, flings open the door, and all three men scatter through the library stacks like mice. The Two-Swords exits after them, but I'm more cautious. After all, I'm safe here in the tunnel, at least for now, and I'm not sure I'm ready to face the world beyond this door.

"It's all right. You can come out now." I can't see the boy, but his voice drifts back to me, thin and breathless. I step hesitantly over the threshold into the familiar stacks of the scriptorium library. The Kantari leans against the wall to the left of the door, inhaling air as if he had nearly drowned in the passageway. I'm afraid someone might notice my light through the small library windows, so I blow out the flame and wait until my eyes adjust before setting the lamp down carefully against the stone wall.

I study the boy as his breath evens out. I don't know what to make of him, but I do know this: He could have killed me, but he didn't, and he could have left those men to die in the parlertorium, but he didn't. So even though he's technically my enemy, I tell him, "Thank you," before I take off in search of my own hiding place.

"Where are you going?"

I stop and look back at him. "To hide."

"Huh-uh." He steps forward and grasps my upper arm. "You're with me."

My heart pounds with a desperate need to be free of him, to be free of this entire night. I fumble around in my pocket and pull out the knife that killed Zofia, ready to defend myself if I have to.

"Give me that thing before you poke your eye out." He snatches the knife from my hand, and something in me snaps. I slap him as hard as I can across his horrible face. The next thing I know, his grip on my arm is tight and painful, and he's holding the knife to my throat. My mind goes white with terror.

"You offered me the Sword of Mercy," I breathe.

"The Sword of Mercy is strapped safely to my back. The Knife of I'm Very Pissed Off Right Now is at your throat. There's a statue of Saint Vinnica at this convent. I need you to take me to it."

I give him an incredulous laugh. "There are at least thirty statues of Saint Vinnica here. It is the Convent of Saint *Vinnica*."

He presses the knife into my neck. My skin splits around the point, and a line of blood trickles down my throat. "This one's special." His voice contains as much steel as the blade at my throat.

All evidence of my defiance flees far, far away from that knife. "Please. I do not know which statue you are talking . . ." And then it hits me. ". . . about."

Because I do know. I don't understand why he's here or what he wants, but I'm certain he means the old statue in the courtyard, the one beneath the Grace Tree. And he can see that I know.

He nods and steps back, but he doesn't let go of me as he tucks the knife into the waistband of his trousers again. And then the strangest thing happens. He takes a good, slow look around him. With his free hand, he reaches out to brush the spines of the books in front of him with incongruously gentle fingertips. On any other occasion, it would be moving, the way he gazes at the books with the same slack-jawed wonder I've seen on the faces of pilgrims the first time they enter the Cathedral of Saint Vinnica, all awe and reverence.

And distraction.

I tear free of his grasp and make a run for it, speeding down the aisle, sending a pile of scrolls toppling in my wake. He curses and gives chase. This time, when he grabs me, I do the only thing I can think of to save myself. The Sanctus verse comes pouring out of my mouth, packed with the full force of my gift.

THE VESSEL

Let the flesh burn away into ash from the bone.
Let the bone wither into dust in the unforgiving fires of the Father.

I have never, not once, attempted to harm another human being with my ability, and the effect makes me nearly as ill as it makes the boy, who gasps in pain and releases me. I wobble on my feet, barely able to stand after unleashing so much force into the song, but I manage to stumble into the scriptorium to get away from him. I make it to Daughter Ina's workstation before I fall forward, catching myself on the table.

The boy takes a cautious step into the scriptorium, a sword clutched in his right hand.

"Is that the Sword of Mercy?" I ask in false defiance.

"I'm not feeling particularly merciful at the moment. This is the Sword of Wrath." He hesitates, hovering near the door. "So you're a Vessel."

"As you see," I answer coolly.

"As I *felt*."

We stare at each other, he with his sword in hand and I with my words held tight in my mouth, and nothing but Daughter Ina's neat stacks of paper between us. An impasse.

There are noises in the distance, drifting down the hallways like ghosts. Men's voices. We both look toward the scriptorium door before our eyes lock again. The Kantari puts his sword back in the scabbard and holds up his hands. "My offer of the Sword of Mercy still stands. Take me to the statue, and I'll let you go, I promise."

If Zofia were here, I'd ask for her advice. But Zofia isn't here.

Zofia will never be here again because Brother Miklos killed her. And Brother Miklos is still out there somewhere.

"I don't want you dead." The boy gestures toward the voices with a jerk of his head. "Can you say the same for them?"

He's right. I have no idea if the men who belong to those voices want me dead. Then, too, there is the less than appetizing fact that I now have Zofia's papers on my person, and the Father knows what kind of heresy they contain. I scowl at the boy, but I nod my agreement.

"Where?" he asks. My eyes dart toward the door leading to the courtyard, and he draws his own conclusions. "Let's go." He lets me walk in front of him as I step through the courtyard door. Outside, a gibbous moon blankets the garden in pale light.

"You lead," he says.

I swallow hard. My throat longs for water as I move in the shadows. At last we get to the gravel path that leads to the statue, but it isn't until we're staring up at Saint Vinnica's blunted features in the moonlight that I realize I could have lied, could have taken him to any other statue at the convent. But I didn't. I hadn't even thought to mislead him. And now he's going to do the Father knows what to the last thing I love in this world.

"Right. Well." He studies the statue, frowning, this cocksure boy who suddenly looks very uncertain of himself.

"I did what you asked. May I go?" Already, I'm easing sideways, trying to pull free, when his grip on my sleeve tightens, dimpling the fabric, and the unbearable possibility that I might never be rid of him grips my throat just as tightly.

"Wait," he hedges. "Hold on."

"You promised you would—"

The words freeze in my mouth as a bird darts out from the withering branches of the Grace Tree to perch on Saint Vinnica's shoulder.

A soulswift.

Zofia is dead, and now here is a soulswift, a Vessel transformed by the Father into this lovely bird. She looks at me with uncanny intelligence before she releases her song, piercing the night with a melody so bittersweet, I can taste the grief I've been holding at bay as it begins to leak through the dam around my heart.

"You left me," I cry, tears clogging my throat. "Oh, my Father, you left me."

Once there was a girl who flew like a bird.

"Zofia?" I whisper, begging the Father to let this be her, to keep her by my side.

Up and up, far above the earth.

I hold out my hand to her to coax her onto my outstretched finger, but to my horror, the Kantari beats me to it, taking the soulswift into his own sinewy hands.

"Stop!" The need to peel his filthy, unworthy paws off the soulswift threatens to turn me violent.

He ignores me, looking over the bird carefully before he murmurs, "Go on, then, friend, and may the Mother watch over you." With that, he opens his hands, and the startled soulswift flies off into the darkness. As she soars out of sight, the realization that Zofia is gone—really and truly gone forever—stabs me in the chest. She was my anchor as well as my guiding star, and I am lost at sea without her.

I'm still squinting into the darkness, searching for any sign of the bird, when the Two-Swords says, "Here goes nothing." He draws one of the weapons from the sheath at his back, and before I can react, he swings the sword, arcing it sideways toward the statue as if he's mowing down an enemy on the battlefield. Too late, I lunge for his arm and miss. Metal hits stone with a teeth-gritting *clang*, but the statue holds strong as the blade breaks away from the hilt and goes sailing into a garden bed several feet away.

"What are you doing?" I scream as he unleashes a stream of what I can only assume are Kantari obscenities at the broken sword.

Lights start coming on in the east wing of the convent. He's running out of time. Maybe we both are. He pulls the other sword free of its sheath, and this time I do get ahold of him by the crook of his elbow before he can strike again.

"Let me go!"

"No!"

But he's so much stronger than I am, I could never hope to stop him. He tears free of me with ease, but then he pauses, his sword held in midair. He gazes up at the statue's blank face before closing his eyes as if sending out a silent prayer to his demon goddess. With nowhere to go and no one to go to, I close my eyes, too, sending out a plea to Zofia, if there's even a part of her left to hear me: *Help me. I don't know what to do.*

Calm washes over me. I open my eyes and watch the boy's dreamy gaze shift from the statue to the Grace Tree just beyond. The blade in his hand begins to glow, a ghostly blue light like the moon shining through the trees of the Dead Forest. Logically, I know this is wrong, and yet, in my stupor, the only word that could possibly describe the sight is *beautiful*. He takes a step closer to the tree, and the sword grows brighter, then brighter again with each step, lighting up the night like an unnatural blue fire. Trancelike, he passes by the sculpture of Saint Vinnica and heads for the Grace Tree.

"Gelya!" shouts a familiar voice, yanking me out of the strange somnolence. My whole body snaps toward the sound of my name, and there, panting hard as he slumps against the jamb of the scriptorium door, stands the Goodson.

Alive.

Before I can run to him, before I can shout his name, before I can even taste joy or relief, the Kantari plunges his blade into the Grace Tree all the way to the hilt. I watch in frozen horror as he slices through the trunk like a knife through softened butter, cutting down the heart of the Ovinist faith in one terrible strike. I have just enough time to think, *There will never be another Vessel*, before the tree explodes in a burst of light so white and blinding, it shatters the night.

"Blessed be the Mother!" the boy cries rapturously when he realizes what he has done. The searing light reaches across the night and pries open my mouth as if my fingers were brushing the Sanctus words of *The Songs of the Saints*. But it isn't a song that comes out of me. It's a song that enters in as I fly into the air.

There is light.

So much light.

And then there is nothing.

Ten

In the darkness, I hear Zofia's voice.

Would you like me to tell you a story?

I nod, though I can't see her.

Once there was a girl—a very brave girl—who lived far, far away by the sea. Do you know this story?

Of course I know this story.

It's my story.

I open my eyes and find myself standing on the cliffs beside the sea. The wind whips my coppery hair into my face and, with it, the thick scent of woodsmoke and something less familiar, almost metallic. It reminds me of scrubbing scorched deer meat from the bottom of Ati's iron pot, an odor so fat and heavy I can hardly smell the salt of the sea. The ever-present sound of the waves battering the rocks below is the only familiar thing about this moment. Even the girls on either side of me seem alien now, as if I have not known them all my life.

I want to wipe my nose with my sleeve, but I don't dare.

Because of the man.

I have never feared a man before, but I fear this one. He studies each of us in turn with gray eyes the color of the sea beneath an overcast sky. I understand beyond a shadow of a doubt that this is a person whose approval is everything, so I remain very still as his eyes drift over me.

He speaks over his shoulder—a series of sharp gibberish sounds—to a group of men standing behind him, their pale clothing stark against the trees just beyond, their blue cloaks billowing like ghosts. One of them steps forward, kneels before the man, and opens a carved wooden box, revealing a soft red interior that doesn't belong to this windswept village by the sea. The man reaches inside and pulls out an object the size and shape of a small plum, only flatter. The outer husk is brown and dried and wrinkled. He holds it up and speaks words I will only come to understand much later:

"This is a seedpod from the Grace Tree of Saint Vinnica. May the Father make your mouth clean to sing His praise. May He make your tongue straight to spread His word. May He make your body pure to receive His spirit. May you be as a Vessel of the One True God."

The man gestures for us to hold out our hands, and I obey without hesitation. He walks the line, placing the pod onto the palm of each small hand. In every case, he waits for a moment and then moves on to the next child. When he gets to me, dread weighs down my insides as I stare into that unforgiving face. I want to scream for Ati to come find me, but how can I cry out for my mother when she's no longer here?

The man sets the pod on my palm, and there is a pulling at my stomach, a tugging ache in my heart. I feel like a song trapped in a cave, like the newly lit wick of a lamp, brightly burning in the darkness. The seedpod cracks and bursts, and from within the husk, oval seeds on snow-white tufts take flight, dazzling in the sooty air, flying off into the wind like snowflakes.

The song within me cannot be contained. My mouth yawns wide, and I sing like the blue swifts who live in the goddess's arms in summer. The music pours out of me in wave after ecstatic wave until the song is finished at last, leaving me sick and heaving and shaking with terror at the thing that took hold of me and would not let go.

The man kneels beside me and gently removes the empty husk from my hand. Then he bends to kiss my palm. When he looks at me again, kindness transforms his face with a softness that speaks of safety and comfort. Tears rim his eyes as he calls me what I am: a Vessel.

II.

The Song

Eleven

The suffocating stench of body odor nudges me awake. The world goes topsy-turvy as I experience the sensation of sliding, then falling, but someone catches me before I hit the ground and stands me on my feet. I open my eyes and focus on the filthy, stubbly face nose-to-nose with my own in the darkness.

The Kantari Two-Swords.

Panic jolts through my veins, and my eyes dart about, taking in my unfamiliar surroundings. High stone walls in front and behind with hardly an arm's span between them. A narrow strip of night sky peppered with stars above. The clanging of the cathedral's bell from the wrong direction. I'm not in the convent anymore. I'm standing in an alley somewhere in Varos da Vinnica, the town *outside* the convent walls, with the horrid prisoner I set loose.

The summit. Zofia. The Goodson. The Grace Tree. The light. All of it sinks into my muddled brain, like dirty water soaking into a sponge.

"How—" I begin, but the boy slaps a disgusting hand over my mouth and presses me against the wall, covering me with his body, making my skin crawl. His flesh is so hard, I feel as if I'm being crushed between two stone walls rather than a wall and a person. "Not a peep," he whispers in Kantari as footsteps approach, echoing down the cobbled streets beyond our rank alley.

I don't know if I should bite the hand over my mouth and make a run for it, or if I should hide from the men marching down the street. My paralyzing indecision makes the choice for me as the footsteps turn a corner and fade away without my having moved an inch.

The boy steps back, but he keeps a hand that tastes of dirt and rust over my mouth, while his other hand holds me under my armpit, alarmingly close to my left breast. I will scream if he doesn't stop touching me.

"Can I trust you to stay quiet?" he asks.

I nod, and he takes his hand away. I turn my head, gulping air from the direction of the street.

"Can you stand on your own?"

"Yes." I'm not entirely sure that's true, but I badly want his other hand off me. He pulls away, and while I'm unsteady, I don't topple over. My stomach feels strange, as if I had swallowed a bee, and it's now buzzing around inside me.

"Can you walk?"

I need to breathe and think for a minute. I wish that odd droning in my guts would stop.

He leans in closer. "I said, can you walk?"

I can't stand having his face in mine, and I explode, shoving him so hard he stumbles backward and smacks his head into the wall behind him. His left hand flies to the hilt of one of the swords at his back. I flatten myself against the wall, shrinking away from him, my heart slamming against my breastbone. But he doesn't draw the weapon. He slowly brings his hand back down, unarmed, then holds up both hands as if he's trying to convince me he's harmless, as if I didn't see him kill the Father knows how many men tonight.

"I told you, you're safe with me," he says.

"You said if I brought you to the statue you would set me free."

"I know."

"You lied."

"I didn't mean to," he tells me, his face stark, as if he's as unhappy to find me with him in this dirty alley as I am.

My mind digs into my memory, trying to fill in the blank between the moment the Two-Swords cut down the Grace Tree and my waking up in an alley outside the convent, fruitlessly searching for minutes of my life I seem to be missing.

"How did I get here?" I demand, my voice rising above a whisper.

"Shh!" He glances nervously toward the mouth of the alley.

"And what happened to the Goodson? Did you kill him, too?" The second the question is out of my mouth, I'm terrified of the answer.

The boy recoils, as if my words punched him in the stomach. "The Goodson? That knight in the courtyard was the Goodson?"

"Yes. Is he—"

"Death, decay, and dying—I let that monster live!"

The Goodson is still alive. Relief floods me, lighting a wick of hope in an otherwise bleak night. The boy's hands, still held up in a ludicrously ironic gesture of peace, are shaking badly, and I see my opportunity for escape. My muscles coil, readying to run, but as I bolt he grabs me and pinions me against the hard length of his body.

"Listen to me," he says in my ear, his wet breath revolting against my skin. I try to bite the muscles wrapped over my chest, but he lowers his arm and squeezes me hard under my rib cage, making it difficult to breathe.

"Listen!" he hisses. "I don't want to hurt you, and I really, really don't want you to hurt me. You're in as much trouble as I am right now. Can't you see that? When there's time, I'll explain everything. I promise. But right now? No time. None. We need to move. Our lives depend on it—mine *and* yours."

"Your promises are worth nothing," I gasp, still struggling against him.

"My promises are worth more than you think. I won't break another one to you. I swear, I'm trying to help you, and I'd rather do that the easy way than the hard way, all right?"

The little bee in my stomach buzzes so loudly I can hear it in my ears. I stop struggling against the boy and squeeze my eyes shut as if that could make it go away. When the boy releases me at last, the buzzing subsides.

The truth is, I'm not sure who is more dangerous: the Two-Swords or Brother Miklos, the man who may or may not be giving orders to the patrols. For whatever reason, it seems clear that this boy is not going to kill me. I can't say the same for Brother Miklos, and who knows where he might be right now. So while I may not relish the Kantari's company, I don't particularly want to be on my own just yet.

"Fine," I tell him tightly.

"Thank you," he says, his face slackening with relief. "Can you get to the town dyer from here?"

The question is so bizarre, I think I must have misunderstood him. "What?"

"The dyer? Do you know where his shop is?"

"I don't know. I almost never leave the convent. Why do you need the dyer?"

The cathedral's bells ring in the distance. He peeks into the street, then up at the sky, then back into the street again, and he starts muttering to himself. "We must have escaped the convent on its eastern side, which makes this either Saint Patris Street or Goodson Wike Street. So the dyer should be just three or four streets over and to the northeast, right? Along the city wall." He turns back to me. "Right?"

He doesn't wait for an answer but motions for me to follow him. We hurry down a new alley whose other end opens up onto a narrower, poorer neighborhood with houses stuffed together cheek by jowl. We repeat the process twice more, each time heading into an alley a little farther east.

"There. The shop on the corner. Is that a tree on the sign?" His lips brush my earlobe as he speaks, and I jerk away from his touch, shuddering. It's hard to tell from this distance, and I can't imagine why he needs to find a sign with a tree painted on it when he's running for his life and when it's possible I'm running for my life, too. "Perhaps?"

"Move." He steps to my side, linking arms with me as we walk brazenly down the street. "And act casual."

I wish he'd speak more slowly. My not being able to understand half the things he says is only adding to my confusion and terror. "What does 'act casual' mean?" I ask.

"It means, I don't know, to pretend this is perfectly natural."

"There is nothing natural about a Daughter of Saint Vinnica walking the streets at night with a Kantari Two-Swords."

"Good point." He ushers me into the next side street and glances out to take a closer look at the sign. "Definitely a tree."

He guides me onto the street and heads for the shop, saying "Please" under his breath. Good Father, I think he's actually praying. He breaks into a trot, dragging me behind him. The marching of the patrols approaches, and he yanks me into another alley one door down from the shop, pulling me through to the other end. Again he pins me to the wall, but at least he doesn't place his awful hand over my mouth.

I can hear the patrols pounding on doors, rousing shop owners from their beds. All I'd have to do to save myself is shout.

Unless they want to kill me, too.

"What are they saying?" the Kantari whispers. His face is close, his eyes unsettling.

"They are searching for you."

"But not for you?"

I'm about to say, "No. Only you," when I hear the word "girl" as well. The Two-Swords must recognize the word, because he curses, "Father of death," in a throaty whisper.

"Maybe they wish to rescue me," I whisper back. Why am I whispering? Shouldn't I be screaming for help?

"It is definitely not a rescue mission." He moves us into the side street leading along the back end of the shops. "Please, dear Mother and Father, let there be a door."

And there it is, a door leading out to a work yard that butts up against the city wall. He hurries to it and knocks lightly. Nothing. He knocks again, harder, but no one answers. He curses under his breath and gives it one more thump with his fist. At last, the door opens a crack, and one veiny brown eye peers at us.

"Blessed be the Mother," the boy says in Rosvanian.

Blessed be the Mother.

My memory springs to life, forcing me to kneel beside Zofia on the unforgiving parlertorium floor once more as she chokes out her last words. She's dead. Dead. And I don't know if I can bear it. But then I remember: I saw a soulswift tonight, and I cling to the hope that her soul lives on within the beautiful bird.

The boy peels back the tattered sleeve of his shirt to reveal a tattoo on his wrist of a tree similar to the one painted on the sign out front.

The eye widens, and the door opens.

The boy and I hide under a pile of undyed roving in the workroom as the dyer and his wife wait for the city guard to knock on the shop door up front. Crouched beneath a thick layer of shorn wool, I feel like I'm hiding in a storm cloud, waiting for lightning to strike me dead. The acidic scents of the dyer's trade is so strong my eyes water, so I can only imagine it masks the boy's rank stench as well. He holds tight to my sleeve as if I might run. And who knows? Maybe I should.

The pounding of a fist on the front door of the shop gallops through the stifling silence beneath the wool, and all I can think of is the moment Brother Miklos threw the knife into Zofia's heart. Any urge I had to beg the patrols for help dies instantly. Men's voices drift back to us, peppered with the clipped tones of the dyer's wife. Then the workroom door creaks open, and the patrols begin their search, their shoes hitting the floorboards like a hammer hitting a nail. I hold my breath and pray to my silent god.

"Wild-goose chase, if you ask me," says one set of footsteps.

"Holy Father, it reeks in here," says the other. "Dangerous murderer, my ass. I could be in bed with my wife right now."

"Or *I* could be in bed with your wife right now."

"Shut your hole, telleg licker."

Both men laugh.

I sense the boy coiling beside me, ready to kill if he must. As carefully as I can, I reach out my free hand and touch his arm. The men shuffle closer, their footsteps vibrating the floorboards beneath us. The boy coils tighter, so I press harder. One of the men knocks over a jar. The sound of liquid splashing on the floor cuts through the air, followed by the thick scent of ammonia.

"Ach, this place stinks like the Dead Forest."

"If I were him, I'd hide at the pub next door, not in some smelly dye vat."

"We should go look there. It's our duty."

"And if we happen to stay for a pint or two, so much the better."

The men leave, taking their laughter with them, and the boy finally lets go of my sleeve. As soon as I hear the front door close, I throw off the wool, scurry into the darkest corner of the room, and sink to the floor. The boy follows cautiously and crouches to my level, although he keeps his distance, as if he's as wary of me as I am of him.

"Why did you do that, put your hand out to stay me? What did they say?" he asks. I'm starting to get the hang of the way his words rush one into the next.

"They were not knights. They were local men, probably roused from their beds. One wanted to go home to his wife. The other only wanted a drink. They did not need to die." I turn my face away and add, "No one needed to die tonight."

The Two-Swords releases a long, slow breath. "Look, what's your name?"

Despite his rough appearance, I can see that he's trying hard to come across as kind rather than dangerous, and I decide there's nothing to lose in answering him. "Gelya."

"Gelya. Good. My name is Tavik DeSemla. Tavik rhymes with *havoc*, probably for good reason."

"Tavik," I repeat softly.

"It's nice to meet you, Gelya." He holds out his hand like I'm supposed to shake it, but then he notices that it's rusty with dried blood and filth. He ends up giving me a stupid little wave instead. When he sees that I'm not going to answer, he takes his hand back. "I'm sorry, Gelya. Truly, I am. But you're wrapped up in this now."

"I do not want to be wrapped up in this!" I protest, and that uncomfortable buzzing in my stomach feels more like a swarm than a single bee. "Can you not . . . unwrap me?"

"I mean . . ." He tilts his head and squints at me as if I were a puzzle he was trying to figure out. "You don't remember?"

"Remember what?"

His thick eyebrows scrunch together in consternation. If he was going to answer my question, the cathedral's bells cut him off as they peel again, reminding us both that the danger is far from over. Not that I know exactly what danger I'm facing right now. He glances toward the back door, but I'm not ready to let him off the hook. There's a chunk missing from my memory, a hole my mind keeps prodding the way a child pokes the vacant spot in her mouth after losing a tooth, an empty space that's not supposed to be there.

"Tavik, what happened at the statue?"

He opens his mouth, but he doesn't get a chance to answer me, because the Dyers return to the workroom, looking wrung out from stress and fear.

They're an older couple, the man uncommonly stout for a Rosvanian, the woman as fine-boned as a sparrow. I tower over her like a great oaf, but that doesn't stop me from rushing to her side the moment she enters the room. I feel much safer with her and her husband than I do with Tavik, even though they must be Elathian heathens, too, if they're welcoming a Kantari Two-Swords into their shop. I've always known that many Elathians still exist in the Ovinist world. I just always thought of them as bandits or criminals. I would never have imagined this sweet old couple.

Dyer hurries over to Tavik and asks, "What's going on? We were told to expect you, but we don't know why. What are you doing in Rosvania?"

Tavik glances nervously at me.

"He wants to know what you are doing in Rosvania," I translate.

"I know."

"What *are* you doing here?"

"Tell them . . . tell them that . . . Oh, death, can you just ask them if they have a messenger coop?"

"I want answers," I press him.

"So do I." He turns to the Dyers and tries to communicate with them in Rosvanian. "Everything is good. Do you have a . . . ?" His accent is solid, but his vocabulary isn't. He turns back to me with pleading eyes. "Please. Tell them we need help getting out of Varos da Vinnica. And a safe house on the Milk Road. And another sword. And I need to send a messenger."

His rapid-fire directions combined with his mushy consonants have me reeling, and the strange humming of my guts isn't helping matters. "You tell them since you speak Rosvanian!"

"I *understand* Rosvanian. I don't speak it very well, and we don't have time for this. Please, Gelya. I swear I'm trying to help you. I'm trying to help us both, okay?"

Dyer takes me by the arm. "Does this have something to do with freeing the Mother?"

"He asks—" I start, pulling my arm free of Dyer's grip. I'm sick to death of people thinking they have the right to touch me.

"I know what he said," Tavik cuts in. "Just tell them it's complicated, and that we need to get out of town immediately." He looks at Mistress Dyer and begs in Rosvanian, "We need to go."

She nods the nod of a deeply efficient woman, a gesture so Zofia-like it robs me of air. "I have an idea how we can get you out of town without raising suspicions."

I translate, focusing on the words rather than the events of the evening. The words are the only thing keeping me from losing my mind right now.

"Great. Thank you."

That's as far as he gets before Mistress Dyer raises one cautionary finger. "*But* we are not risking our lives or anyone else's until we know why we're helping you. What does this have to do with the Mother? Why are the Kantari in Tovnia when the Mother is in the Vault of Mount Djall?"

I translate, although he seems to catch her drift on his own. Without taking his eyes off me, he answers grimly, "Tell them that the Mother is not in the vault. And if they want Her set free, they need to help us. Now."

Twelve

As Tavik and I stand in awkward silence, watching the Dyers argue over what to do with us, my mind whirs with questions. Why didn't the Goodson want me to go to the summit? Did he know what was going to happen? Why did Brother Miklos kill Zofia? What in the name of heaven is written on the folded parchment in my pocket? And if Tavik was a prisoner of war, how could the Dyers have known he was coming?

I can't question the Goodson or Zofia now, and I think it's probably a bad idea to let anyone know that I have Zofia's notes, but Tavik is a different matter. I incline my head toward him and ask, "Who are you, and why are you here? And what happened at the statue?"

"It's complicated."

"You said that already. It does not answer my question."

He glances at me, his grubby face troubled. "Do you think you could try using a few contractions when you speak? I feel like I'm talking to an epic poem."

"I do not know Kantari contractions. Your language in its written form has none."

"Well, my language in its spoken form does. Contractions. Learn some. I'm begging you."

I shake my head in irritation. Now that I'm growing accustomed to the way he speaks, I suspect it was better when I understood him less rather than more.

He nods toward the Dyers. "They're wasting too much time. We really need to get out of Varos da Vinnica."

"'We'? I am not going anywhere with you."

Tavik pulls down on his stubbly face with dirty hands. "Holy good Mother, you really don't remember, do you?"

"Remember what?" That strange sensation in my stomach starts vibrating again, unnerving me.

He looks over my shoulder toward the Dyers. "Excuse me," he says a little too loudly, bringing their argument to a halt. He gestures first to himself and then to me, and says a Rosvanian word: "Alone?"

"I do not want to be alone with you," I protest.

"This is the price of my honesty." He looks to the Dyers once more and insists in Rosvanian, "Alone."

Mistress Dyer gives me a worried look, but she says, "Five minutes. We have work to do."

I'm tempted to bolt for the back door as the Dyers vacate the room, but there is that gaping hole in my memory that, unfortunately, only Tavik can fill. I turn on him, arms crossed tight over my chest, waiting for my answer.

He fidgets nervously with the hem of his shirt. "What do you remember after we got to the statue?" he asks.

I close my eyes and envision the last moment I can recall with any clarity. "You hit the statue with one of your swords, but the blade broke. The Goodson arrived—" Here, Tavik makes a snarling sound under his breath. I open my eyes to give him a pointed look. "The Goodson arrived, and then you drove your other sword . . . Holy Father, you drove it into the Grace Tree of Saint Vinnica."

Saying it aloud—giving words to it—makes everything solid and real when I want it to be a bad dream. He killed the Grace Tree, and that means I am the last Vessel of the One True God. Once I die, the Father will never again speak to His people. And I am completely alone in the world.

A light-headedness stretches from my brain all the way down to my knees. Everything feels loose and wobbly. I squint, seeking the lost memories trapped in my brain. "There was a bright light. I couldn't see."

"And then what?"

"The next thing I remember is that I was with you outside the convent. I don't know how I got there."

"I carried you. We escaped through a broken storm grate in the convent's outer wall. You may have a few bruises. Sorry about that. And thank you for using a contraction, by the way."

"But why did you take me? You should have left me there!" I

feel like a tuft of dandelion seeds clinging to the stem. One strong breeze, and I'll blow apart.

He opens his mouth and promptly closes it again. "Sorry," he says, rubbing his forehead. "I'm just trying to figure out where to begin."

"May I suggest you begin when you destroyed the Grace Tree of Saint Vinnica?" I say through gritted teeth.

"No. You need a quick history lesson first. Here it goes." He starts to pace like a caged tiger, as if he requires the movement of his legs to power the difficult words coming out of his mouth. "Twelve years ago, a small band of Elathians successfully broke into the Monastery of Saint Ovin on a mission to bust open the Vault of Mount Djall and free the Mother. Only the vault was empty. The Mother wasn't there. The Prima of Kantar and a few of her closest advisers knew about it, including my captain, DeRopa, but they kept it secret, worried the Kantari would lose hope if the truth got out. They've been trying all this time to figure out where the Mother is, and so has the Order of Saint Ovin. It's been top secret on both sides." He comes to a halt in front of me. "But then a spy at the Convent of Saint Vinnica figured out that the Mother was imprisoned on the grounds."

"What? That is ridiculous!" But didn't it always feel like someone was listening to me when I prayed beside Saint Vinnica's statue? Didn't someone hear me when the One True God was silent? Without realizing it, I've been seeking comfort from the Great Demon for years. Holy Father, how great a sinner am I?

"Do you want the truth or not? Because we don't have a lot of time."

I nod my head, feeling as though I have looked down at my own two feet for the first time to discover that the rock I was standing on is cracked and crumbling.

"Good. The Prima of Kantar sent the entire Kantari army to take the Convent of Saint Vinnica and free the Mother."

"Oh, my Father," I gasp, but Tavik plows ahead.

"She was worried that we wouldn't move quickly enough, or that the Order would find out what we knew and beat us to Elath's prison. That's where my mission comes in."

He starts pacing again, maybe because it's easier than telling the truth to my face.

"I was sent to Rosvania under Captain DeRopa's orders to free the Mother. I was to get myself captured at the Tovnian battlefront in the hope that the Tovnians would bring me to the inevitable summit at Saint Vinnica. The Ovinists always call a summit when we Kantari do something they don't like. And it worked. I got free—well, you cut me loose. Thank you for that—and then the sword lit up in my hand, and somehow I knew I was supposed to open up that tree, but . . ." He stops and toys with the shredded hem of his shirt again. "But the Mother didn't just reenter the world like we thought She would."

My ears start to ring in panic. "Where is She now?"

Tavik inclines his head in my direction and murmurs, "There."

I look behind me in alarm. "Where?" When I turn back, he looks like he might be sick.

"You. She's inside you."

I can comprehend each individual word, but strung together they make no sense. "I do not understand."

"All that light streamed out of the tree and . . . and . . ." He makes a vague gesture at me.

My head is spinning. I imitate the gesture and exclaim, "What does *this* mean?"

When he speaks again, his words come hurtling out of his mouth in a rush, one toppling over the other. "The light kind of hit you, like, poured into you. And you may have floated. In the air. Several feet. Please don't lose your shit."

My whole body goes numb, right down to my fingertips and toes. "No," I say in one long-drawn-out syllable as I back away from him.

"I said don't lose your shit."

"That cannot be right."

"I know what I saw."

"There is nothing inside me."

"Elath the Mother is inside you," he assures me.

My hard-won emotional control is fleeing farther and farther from my mental grasp. "I would know if a demon had taken possession of my body!"

The bees in my belly swarm and swell, and the reality of what it means slams into me. I'm no longer the Vessel of the Father's Word. I am now the Vessel of Elath the Great Demon. The buzzing. The humming. The sensation inside me.

Is Her.

I back into a shelf, knocking a ceramic pot of dye powder to the floor and sending up a cloud that wafts of walnuts. I feel like my body is about to fly apart, and I press my hands hard against my face to hold myself together.

Tavik approaches me but pulls up short. "I know this must be difficult for you."

"Difficult?" My feelings spill words out of my mouth in Rosvanian. "I watched people die tonight! One man died *on* me! And then I find out that the woman I've loved as a mentor—a sister even—was probably an Elathian spy who colluded with the enemy! I've been abducted by a heathen Kantari soldier who hates the Goodson—the Goodson who is the very best of men, I might add! And now this . . . this . . . *thing* is inside me!"

"I didn't catch all that," Tavik admits in Kantari. "And I don't deny any of it. But you're coming with me."

I shake my head, furious with myself for freeing Tavik, and furious with Tavik for getting me into this mess, and furious with Zofia for lying to me, and furious with the Goodson for failing to protect me when I needed him most, and furious—livid—with the thing that decided to take up residence inside me. Holy Father, what am I going to do?

Tavik takes a step closer. "The Goodson was there. He saw what happened to you. Do you really think he's going to just let you live out your life in peace at the convent when he knows what's inside you?"

"Shut up," I spit in Rosvanian.

"And that man who killed your friend tonight—Brother Miklos—do you know what we call him in Kantar? The Butcher of Grama. He led a massacre on an entire Kantari town, Gelya. It took everything I had not to tear his face off at that summit. And now he's out there, searching for us—searching for *you*."

He's got me there, and he knows it. He closes the distance

between us, then kneels on the ground at my feet, gazing up at me with an expression I can only describe as reverent. Because of what I am now. Because of what I carry inside me.

"Listen to me, Gelya. I know what you hold inside you. I watched Her soul enter you with my own eyes, and I have never seen anything more beautiful. The Mother is life, and life is more precious than anything else in this world. That makes you valuable beyond pearls. There are people who will want to hurt you now, people who will want to use you, but they'll have to get through me first. I promise to keep you safe. I will protect you with the last breath of my body if I have to."

His complete sincerity robs me of air. I believed the Kantari were my enemy, but now that my life has collapsed into ruin, the one person unequivocally on my side is a Kantari Two-Swords who has just made a vow so heartfelt, it almost feels like he married me. I look down on his dirty, beatific face, but in my mind all I can see is the knife in Zofia's chest, a knife that is aimed just as surely at my own heart now.

Elath's undeniable presence simmers inside me like water in a kettle right before it whistles. What will happen if I let it boil over, if I can't contain it? I wipe my tearstained face, smearing a nightmare's worth of tears and blood and dye and grime all over me. "If what you say is true, you cannot and should not protect me. You speak as if I am in danger, but I am the one who is dangerous. I should turn myself in to the Order and let them seal me in a vault just as Saint Ovin entombed Saint Vinnica to save the world from sin."

Tavik winces. "Is that really what you want?"

The word *yes* refuses to exit my mouth. Did Vinnica get to choose her fate? Did she have a voice? Did she willingly sacrifice her life for the world, or did her father make that decision for her? Maybe it would be easier if someone else chose for me, so that the fate of the world didn't rest on my shoulders alone. But how can I give up my life, all that I am, for a faith that feels like it's breaking apart beneath my feet?

"No," I admit, the word bitter in my mouth. "That is not what I want."

"Then you'll come with me? Willingly?"

I look down at Tavik, who, against all reason, has just become the person I trust most in this world. "Yes, I will come with you."

He sits back on his heels, gazes up at me in stark relief. "Thank you."

"But where are we going? How do we get this thing out of me?"

"So here's the thing. When the Mother entered you, there was this . . . shock wave, I guess? It knocked the wind out of me, and the Goodson was out cold, which is why I didn't have to fight him. I went to see if you were all right, and . . . um . . ." He rubs the back of his neck.

"Just say it," I tell him. It's not like things could get any worse, and I'm tired of being left in the dark.

"You put your hand on me. Here." He pulls back his ragged black shirt to reveal a ruddy mark over his heart in the shape of a hand, as if someone has branded him like a cow. "I guess it's more accurate to say Elath put your hand on me, and She sang to me. *Inside* me."

"What did She sing?" I ask as I stare at the place where my

hand—*my* hand—burned the skin over his heart and seared the coarse hair surrounding it. I stand corrected. Things could, in point of fact, get worse.

"They weren't words exactly, just an understanding. The gist is this: We need both the Vessel and the Sword to return Her to the world. And we have the Vessel already. That's a good thing, right?"

I can't work up the motivation to speak Kantari right now, so it's still Rosvanian coming out of my mouth when I say, "There is not one single good thing happening right now, you absolute git." This is the sort of sentiment I would normally keep to the confines of my mind, but there's nothing normal about my current situation, and Tavik seems to bring out the brutal honesty lurking in my brain.

"I'm not sure what a 'git' is, but I suspect I should just ignore that."

"And where is this Sword?" I ask, my voice as dead as I feel.

"Um." He cringes and rubs the back of his neck again.

My heart goes leaden in my chest. "You have no idea what the Sword is or where we can find it, do you?"

"Yet," he says with unparalleled optimism.

I try and fail to massage away the headache taking root at my temples. "And what happens in the unlikely event that we find this sword? What happens when and if we figure out how to remove the demon from my body?"

"Then the *Mother* can return, and Kantar's drought will end, and the balance of life and death will be restored to the world."

But that is not what I was taught to believe about what would happen if Elath were ever set free, so I force myself to say a different truth, the Ovinist truth: "Or the world will end, and the Father will close the gates of heaven forever."

"Well, personally, I think that's crap," he informs me matter-of-factly, without a hint of offense. "But I doubt I'm going to convince you otherwise at the moment, so how about this? Let's worry about one thing at a time. Right now, we need to get out of Varos da Vinnica and go into hiding. Agreed?"

"Agreed."

"Good. Let's focus on escaping with our lives. If we manage to get that far, we'll figure out next steps. Deal?" He extends his hand and makes a circle with his index finger and his thumb.

I frown at the gesture. "What are you doing?"

"It's a circle swear. You have to lock your ring with mine. Your finger and thumb should touch inside my circle."

"Your hand is dirty."

"Humor me." He wiggles his hand at me. I cast my eyes toward heaven, but against my better judgment, I link the circle of my finger and thumb with his.

"Deal?" he asks.

I shake my head, more at myself than at him. "Deal."

Our five minutes are up, and the Dyers return.

Thirteen

I have no idea how the Dyers plan to sneak us out of town, and for the moment, I don't care. Glad to let someone else do all the thinking for me, I follow Mistress Dyer upstairs to a one-room apartment where a kitchen, a table and chairs, and a bed jockey for space. Ever bustling, she goes directly to the sink, where she pumps water into a basin as I stand awkwardly by the door.

"I won't eat you. Come in," she directs me as she pumps.

I take my first tentative steps into the room and nearly jump out of my skin when I see another person moving alongside me. And then I realize it's a mirror, perched above a well-dusted chest of drawers. There are no mirrors in the convent, so I have never seen my own reflection. The girl standing before me now is horribly pale, her freckles livid against sickly skin. Her bald head gives her a rapine appearance, and the blood and dirt streaked over the long lines from her sharp nose to the grotesque length of her arms only add to the disaster in the mirror. No wonder the other Daughters—even the Vessels—kept their distance from me all these years.

Mistress Dyer stands beside me and tilts her head thoughtfully as she studies my reflection. "It's not as bad as you think."

I wonder if I stood out like this in Hedenskia when I was a little girl. Or did I fit in with the strange, wild people there? I watch a tear streak down one dirty cheek of the repulsive young woman staring back at me. "I'm hideous."

The old woman wraps an arm around my waist. "You'll feel better once we get you cleaned up."

She's mothering me, when the only person who has ever mothered me is gone. I start sobbing, a giant weeping over Mistress Dyer as she holds tight to me. She ushers me to one of the chairs, bringing over the water basin to wash this evening's nightmare from my skin with a soft cotton cloth, working her way down from the top of my head to my arms and hands, taking care of me as if I were something precious.

"Are you from Saint Degmar?" she asks.

Of course it would come to this. It always does. "No," I answer.

"Auria?"

"No."

She looks up sharply, the cloth in her hand dripping on my arm. "Oh. You're that one. The Vessel, the girl from—"

"Yes." The usual shame of my origins thickens my throat. The Hedenski kill anyone who steps on their shores without permission, and the fact that they're cut off from the rest of the world by the Dead Forest inevitably links them to the telleg. I can tell Mistress Dyer wants to ask me about it, but she doesn't push, and I'm more grateful to her for that than for anything else tonight. She gets back to work, helping me out of my sash and tunic, leaving me vulnerable and exposed in nothing but my trousers and the linen wound tightly around my breasts.

"That's lovely. What is it?" she asks, fingering the newly revealed triptych, the Goodson's gift to me, the only thing left that is truly mine. Instinct takes over, and I snatch it out of her hand, clutching it protectively in my own.

"Forgive me," she says, taken aback.

"I'm sorry. Just . . . please don't touch this."

I jolt in alarm when the door flies open, and a girl a little younger than I am dashes into the room, flushed and breathless. She clutches a thick parcel wrapped in brown paper and twine to her chest. "I got it!" she declares with a proud grin. Then her eyes bulge when she gets a good look at me, as if I were a telleg who came straight from the Dead Forest to devour her.

"It's all right, Sveta. She's one of us." Mistress Dyer pats my arm, but the truth is that I don't seem to belong anywhere or to anyone now, and that makes me feel like I'm dropping into a dark hole that just goes down and down, bottomless.

"Well, bring it over," Mistress Dyer instructs Sveta as she lifts the basin off the table to make room. Sveta sets the package down and picks at the twine's knot while the mistress takes the basin to the sink. I follow her, whispering, "I hate endangering her, a girl that young."

"Elathians are in danger from our first breath to our last," Mistress Dyer answers in her matter-of-fact way, adding, "You're not so old yourself, you know."

She shoos me back to the table, where Sveta flattens the paper and spreads a simple but finely made dress across the surface. It's a deep brown color, probably dyed with the same walnut powder I spilled all over the workroom earlier.

I gasp in dismay as Mistress Dyer tugs at the cloth binding my breasts.

"The original owner of this dress is a full-grown woman," she tells me. "You're going to have to give it everything you've got to fill out the top."

Embarrassed, I let Mistress Dyer unwrap me. Then she and Sveta put me into a corselet and pull the dress over my head. I've never worn a dress before, and it's more form-fitting than I'm used to. My clothes have always been loose and flowing, designed to hide my womanliness, not flaunt it.

"You may be tall, but you do curve beautifully in all the right places," the mistress murmurs as she smooths the fabric over my form. I'm a Vessel of the One True God. I am definitely not supposed to curve beautifully.

I walk over to the mirror to study my reflection for the second time tonight, only to find myself gaping in shock at the girl who stands before me now. I never really considered how my convent clothes washed my body out of existence, how the crimson Daughter's sash, a symbol of Elath's bloody curse on women, made me look sallow and sickly. It never mattered before. It still doesn't matter. It's only that I can't help but see how my brown eyes and pale skin and even my freckles appear healthy against a backdrop of rich, earthy color, how my breasts and hips soften my appearance.

"Blessed be the Mother," Sveta giggles, her pretty reflection appearing in the background.

"Be a good girl and help her get the veil on, Sveta," says Mistress Dyer.

"Veil?" I ask, but no one answers me. Sveta is clearly pleased to help, and she smiles as she reaches up to fit a long swath of forest-green fabric to my head with a stiff band.

With my bald head hidden beneath the veil, I look like a normal girl. The green cloth falling behind me to the middle of my back showcases a heart-shaped face and the cleft in my chin. Again, my complexion looks far healthier next to all that green.

Green.

The color brides wear.

A horrid suspicion bubbles in my stomach, and this time, it has nothing to do with the life I hold inside me. "Why am I wearing a veil?"

"Because you are to be married today, my dear." Mistress Dyer goes on tiptoe to kiss my cheek. "Congratulations."

"Wait!" I sputter as Sveta laughs and claps her hands, but the mistress pulls the other end of the veil over my face, leaving me in the dark.

My veil is down and will remain down until the end of the ceremony. I can see very little, just hazy outlines of the Dyers and Tavik and the other people milling about the workroom. I knew that there were pockets of Elathians inhabiting the kingdoms of the Ovinist Church in secret, but I had no idea there were so many in Varos da Vinnica. Now here they are, preparing for a wedding. Because I'm getting married. Today.

I explain the plan to Tavik, my voice flat, disconnected from the rest of me—the rest of me being a giant ball of throbbing unease. "The shrine of Saint Brivig is one mile north of the city. It's a common venue for weddings since Saint Brivig is the patron saint of wives. We will exit the north gate of Varos da Vinnica in a procession with music and dancing."

Tavik blows out a gusty breath. "All right."

"No! It is not all right! I refuse to marry you!"

I can hear an eye roll in his voice as he answers, "It's not real, Gelya. And for your information, I don't want to marry you either."

I appeal to the Dyers, squinting at their silhouettes beyond the green fabric over my face. "What if we have to see this ruse all the way to its conclusion?"

"It's unlikely that we'll need to go through with the ceremony, but we are prepared to take this as far as it needs to go. Your lives depend on it," says Mistress Dyer. "Now keep translating, because there are a few more things he needs to know. Tell him it's expected that a wedding party bribe the guards at the gate with an invitation. There's an Elathian family throwing together a wedding feast at their farm near the shrine even as we speak, just in case."

"Did she say something about food?" Tavik asks me eagerly, but Mistress Dyer plows ahead, addressing him directly.

"You are the son of Ukrenti immigrants. Your name is Semir Walema."

"All right," Tavik agrees. "I speak a little Ukrenti."

Mistress Dyer takes my hand. "Daughter, you are my niece, Vina. I doubt you've seen many weddings at the convent, but not much is required of you, so don't worry. Just leave the veil down until the end. If it even comes to that." She gives my hand a squeeze. "We're going to get you both safely out of Varos da Vinnica and on your way."

I'm about to leave everything I've ever known or loved, possibly forever, so I cling tight to Mistress Dyer's hand. Once I let go, I'm going to have to face my new and uncertain future with no one but Tavik at my side.

The sun is up by the time the Dyers escort us out the front door of the shop and into a waiting litter, which is hoisted onto the shoulders of several men, my "family" on the left and Tavik's on the right. Someone taps out a beat on a drum, and a pair of pipers joins in. The women have bells tied to their ankles, and they stomp along to the rhythm. Our fake families surround the litter, and we take off down the narrow street, a raucous party.

"All this trouble. All this risk. Why are they helping you?" I whisper to Tavik.

"Us," he corrects me. "They're helping you, too. The Dyers are the Milk Road contact in Varos da Vinnica. I was to report to them after my mission was complete."

"But it is incomplete."

"Thanks for pointing that out."

"What is the Milk Road?"

"Later," Tavik says, switching languages. "We should speak Rosvanian now, yes?"

"Yes," I agree, but since Tavik doesn't speak Rosvanian well, we remain silent, even though I have a million more questions to ask him. By the time we reach the north gate, my jaw hurts from the nervous clenching of my teeth. Elath's strange thrumming in my belly does nothing to help.

"Well now, I don't think I can let a dangerous lot like you through," says the guard at the gate. I'm half tempted to beg him to save me, even as my heart sinks with the fear of getting caught.

"It's all right," Dyer whispers up to us. "This is all part of the tradition."

I can hear the smile in the guard's voice as he says, "Try again on Saint Elbin's Day."

Several people in the wedding party shout, "Boo!" while most laugh.

"Hey, now," says another guard. "It's my turn to do a wedding. You did the last one."

"Oh, come off it, Tomas," says the first, but they are both shouted down by a third guard who yells, "No one leaves the city today, by command of the king of Rosvania. The Order of Saint Ovin is on a manhunt. Don't you know there's a dangerous criminal on the loose? Go back home! All of you!"

A deeply uncomfortable pause follows this declaration. Then Tavik scares me half to death when he leaps to his feet, making the litter sway.

"Gentleman! I have waited so long to bed my lady. Now you make me wait longer?" he shouts with a convincing Ukrenti accent, but I am too horrified to appreciate the effort. The wedding party roars with cheers and laughter all around us, playing along, but their enthusiasm quickly peters out. I'm not sure why until I hear the suspicious guard's voice call up to us from the foot of the litter.

"Name?"

"Semir Walema of Ukrent," Tavik answers as if he were the happiest man alive. "And you, my friend?"

"Elus of I'm-Not-Having-It. Who's the lucky bride?" the guard asks snidely.

"My niece, Vina," Dyer intercedes, coming to our rescue. "Please, sir, some of the groom's family came all the way from Ukrent for this day. We really can't postpone it. And there's a banquet waiting for us at the shrine of Saint Brivig. You are most welcome to join us."

"You know what? I'd love to join you."

Though my face is veiled, I'm certain the owner of that sarcastic voice has his shrewd gaze fixed on me.

"Wonderful," Dyer answers unconvincingly, and I sense Tavik stiffening beside me.

The man makes us wait for twenty minutes while he calls up a full contingent of city guards to escort us, enough to arrest every wedding guest if they discover anything fishy. I suppose I should be relieved when we finally make it through the gate, but the guard's humorless presence tamps down everyone's spirits. The music is quieter now, the dancing more subdued. The mile to the shrine feels more like five miles, and by the time we arrive, I want nothing more than to rip the veil from my head and make a run for it.

Just stick to the plan, Gelya, I tell myself. *One thing at a time.*

Dyer opens the litter's door on Tavik's side, murmuring, "We'll eat first. The guards always leave after the feast. We'll try to get them good and drunk. That should help."

Mistress Dyer was right. I've never been to a wedding. But I do know the basics of how one works. A feast precedes the event where everyone eats except the bride, who is expected to fast as a sign of her purity, which is just as well since I think my stomach would rebel if I tried to put anything into it right now. So I remain mute beside Tavik, who mutters, "Unbelievable," each time someone sets a plate of food in front of him. I'm sure he devours every single bite.

A baritone gets up and sings, and as the wine gets passed around, it sounds as though the partygoers are loosening up. I suppose they're all of a mind that if they're going to die or get thrown into prison today, they may as well enjoy themselves. It would be nice to join them, to feel a sliver of joy here at the end, but I just can't. I remained shrouded in my veil, surrounded by people yet completely alone.

A young man's voice pipes up close by. "Are we leaving yet, sir?"

"No, we're staying for the ceremony," answers the now-familiar voice of the horrible guard. He gives a shrill whistle, and when the music and laughter die away, he shouts, "I came here for a wedding. Let's see it."

"It will be all right," Mistress Dyer assures me, but I'm ill with dread as she escorts me under the ceremonial canopy.

Any man can perform a wedding ceremony. Today, it's Dyer,

The Songs of the Saints open in his hands as he stands in front of the statue of Saint Brivig. His wife turns me to face Tavik's blurry form to the statue's right.

I can't believe this is happening. Holy Father, please tell me this isn't happening.

Tavik takes my left hand in his right, as Dyer instructs him. His hand is steady but damp with sweat, while mine trembles in his grasp.

"The groom will repeat after me," Dyer intones.

Oh no.

"I promise to honor you with my words."

Tavik is listening so intently, his nerves practically beat me over the head. He repeats each phrase with clarity and precision and a good Ukrenti accent. "I promise to honor you with my words. I promise to respect you with my actions. I promise to protect you with my body. I promise that my heart will beat for you."

A genuine vow lingers in his words, a truth buried beneath the phony surface. He said he would protect me with the last breath of his body, if only for the Mother's sake, and he will honor and respect me as the Vessel of his goddess. His sincerity flusters me, bringing a pink tinge of confusion to my cheeks.

"My body shall be your body, and your body shall be mine," he repeats. "My soul shall be your soul, and your soul shall be mine." Each word from his mouth links his fate with mine in ways I don't know how to unravel.

"All this I vow in the name of the Father, the One True God," Dyer concludes, and while I'm certain Tavik is less than thrilled to repeat this promise, he forces the words out of his mouth.

I am faced with another choice now. I could either refuse to go any further, turn myself in, and let everyone involved be caught by the city guard, or I could save my own skin along with all these Elathians and see this sham of a wedding to the bitter end. I wish I could say that I dither, but I don't. I take the ends of the veil and pull the green cloth back, revealing my face to Tavik for the first time in hours.

The complete stranger before me is scrubbed clean, smelling faintly of lavender soap. His long hair has been cropped and surrounds his head in sleek dark curls that are beginning to show signs of unruliness, defying whatever means the Dyers used to tame them. He is clean-shaven, and his smooth cheeks make him look even younger than I thought he was. The rich ocher of his groom's attire, symbolizing the sun in the Father's heaven, flatters the warm undertone of his skin and brings out the green of his eyes.

He freezes at the sight of me. Aside from the blinking of his eyes, he's not moving at all. I don't even think he's breathing.

And I am frozen, too. Because.

Tavik.

Is.

Beautiful.

He gapes at me as if he has never seen me before, his soft lips hanging open, and even that is beautiful. How can a mouth be beautiful? And why am I even thinking this? I'm not supposed to think of men at all, beautiful or otherwise. But as Tavik continues to stare at me with those lovely eyes, a ridiculous scarlet blush paints me from head to toe.

"Your bride shows herself to you," Dyer tells him. "Look upon her and kiss her if you would take her as your wife."

A second passes. Two. Three. Tavik's eyes widen as if he has just woken up, and I realize that he didn't understand what Dyer said, that he has no clue what he's supposed to do.

And that leaves me to do it.

Holy Father, I was never meant to kiss anyone. Ever. How do you kiss a person on the mouth? Why on earth did humanity decide this was a good idea?

I lean in but hesitate, my heart pounding in my chest, my breath disappearing. Tavik's gaze shifts to my mouth, and my blush might burn me to a crisp as he closes the distance between us. He kisses me, and I go rigid, my lips dry and awkward. His lips move against mine, softening my mouth, melding into me, strange but not terrible.

Not terrible at all.

Not even remotely terrible.

The sensation pings through my entire body, sending a pleasant fizz all the way to my toes. It doesn't last long, only the span of a breath or two, although I can't truly measure time in respiration since I'm not breathing. Tavik pulls away, his unforgivably beautiful face still inches from my own, and the only words I can form in my mind are *I think I liked that*. One corner of his mouth ticks up into a perfect, lopsided smile. I'm still blinking through a kiss-induced fog when that guard who has doubted us from the first steps to the front of the wedding guests. He looks from me to Tavik and back to me again, but I can't seem to take my eyes off the groom.

"You Degmari?" he asks me.

"Yes," I gasp, finally remembering to draw breath. "On my father's side."

"Huh." He looks again at Tavik, who hasn't taken his eyes off me either. "Huh." He grins and claps Tavik on the shoulder, a big manly *thump* that finally breaks our gaze. "Congratulations," he says with a toothy grin before ordering his men back to the city gate.

For a heartbeat, I'm stupid enough to feel relief, but then reality drops on me like a ton of bricks.

I carry Elath the Great Demon within me, and I just married a Kantari Two-Swords named Tavik DeSemla.

Fourteen

For the next half hour, I sit at the banquet table with my face buried in my hands, a feeble attempt at avoiding reality as the remaining wedding guests tiptoe around me. Eventually, Tavik chucks a plate heaped with food onto the table, plops into the chair next to me, and combs his cropped curls out of his eyes with both hands, undoing what little order the Dyers managed to impose upon them. "This mess is going to be in my face and driving me bonkers for the next half year at least."

What am I supposed to say? *Even that ridiculous mop is gloriously beautiful?* Instead, I frown at his mini feast on the table. "You ate five courses at the banquet. Was that not enough for you?"

"Most Kantari don't get that much food in a week. I've had more than enough, but *you* haven't."

For a moment, I'm touched, but then I remember it's not really me he's worried about. I push the plate away. "I'm not hungry."

"In the eighteen hours since we met, I've seen you barf, but I haven't seen you eat. And nice job on that contraction, by the way. Keep it up."

"What does 'barf' mean?"

Tavik makes dramatic vomiting noises.

"I'm sorry I asked," I mutter in Rosvanian, but I drag the plate toward me. I do feel better after I force down a bit of ham and mustard greens, but I'm not inclined to admit it.

I still have a quarter of my meal left when Dyer sets down two swords in their scabbards in front of Tavik and announces, "Time to go." He shrugs out of two knapsacks and drops them on the table, making my fork rattle against my plate. "You'll head directly west until you reach the Sargo River. That's two miles out in the open, so move quickly. Once you're at the river, keep to the trees for cover, because there's a good chance the Order of Saint Ovin will have boats out on the water looking for you. Follow the Sargo north until you—"

"North?" Tavik cuts in, not needing a translation, although he's speaking in Kantari. "No. We need to head south-southwest, toward Tovnia, toward my captain. Tell him, Gelya."

"He said the Order will expect that," I translate. "That's why they're sending us north instead. But, Tavik, I cannot believe the Goodson would send a manhunt after me." If he's still in charge of the Order, I add in my mind.

"Well, he'd sure as hell send one after me."

Dyer clears his throat, impatient. "You'll follow the Sargo north to the point where it makes a hard bend west, fifteen miles or so, then head directly east from there. Dalment is about a five-mile walk from that point, again on open road, so be careful. I suggest you move at night if possible. We've sent a messenger to our contact there, the apothecary on Saint Polova Street. His name is Ambrus."

Tavik perks up. "Can you ask him if there are any more messengers?"

I pass along his request, then translate the answer back to him. "They sent the only messenger they had to Dalment, which is where we're going. Who are these messengers?"

"What, not who. And, ugh, I'd give anything to send a message right now."

He straps the swords to his back, and Dyer helps him shrug the larger of the two sacks over his scabbards. He holds out the other pack to me and says, "Come along, my beloved wife."

I glare at him and hoist the second pack onto my shoulders, surreptitiously slipping my hand into my pocket to make sure Zofia's folded parchment is there. The sooner we get to this safe house on the Milk Road—whatever that means—the sooner I can look at it, and the sooner I can look at it, the sooner I might have some answers about what happened last night and why. Dear Father, let there be something in Zofia's notes that will help me figure out what to do about the demon within me.

If it even is a demon.

Simply questioning the nature of Elath is a heresy of which I never dreamed myself capable. I can't believe the extent to which my belief has shrunk and my doubt has ballooned. But I remember the light when Tavik drove his blade into the Grace Tree. And it doesn't *feel* evil, this life I hold within me. So may the Father have mercy on me for entertaining doubt. I would not be doubtful if He were not silent.

Tavik looks to me and jerks his head west, toward the Sargo River. "Let's go, dearest."

The Sargo River unspools south as Tavik and I make our way north toward Dalment. A mosquito keeps wheezing in my ear no matter how many times I bat it away, and my feet feel like lead weights attached to the ends of my legs. I would give anything for an hour's rest, but since that won't be happening any time soon, and since it doesn't appear as if we're in imminent danger at the moment, I decide the time has come for Tavik to start answering my questions.

"Tavik?" I ask his back since he's walking in front of me.

"Yes, my beloved?"

The way he's treating this nightmare like a joke makes me want to kick in those perfect teeth of his. "You do understand that you married me today, correct?"

"Uh, no, I didn't."

"You spoke the sacred wedding vows and swore an oath to the Father. And we . . . we—"

"Which is so weird," he interrupts, saving me from having to say the word *kissed*. "Doesn't the bride get a say in the matter?"

"That is not the point!"

"It kind of is, though." He slows down so that I can catch up to him and walk by his side. "Let me ask you something. Do you want to be married to me?"

"No!"

"Do you think I want to be married to you?"

"I highly doubt it."

"You would be correct. I don't. Where I come from, you're not married unless you want to be. So there. We're not married. Problem solved. Do you think you could pick up the pace a bit?"

"Holy Father, this is my life now," I mutter in Rosvanian.

He must catch my drift, because he nods in agreement. "No kidding. You're an Ovinist Vessel, and the Mother is literally living inside you, but here I am, talking to you like it's totally normal."

"Like I am a human being?" I ask him, resenting his reminder of Elath's presence within me, not that I could ever, for a moment, forget it.

He studies me before facing forward again. "I know you're a human being, Gelya."

I don't know why, but Tavik's words make my eyes water and my throat swell. My humanity should be obvious. I have arms and legs and a torso and a head just like anyone else. And yet almost no one has ever treated me like a person, except for Zofia and the Goodson. The entire Ovinist faith thinks of me as a Vessel of the Father's Word, and the only other thing most people see in me beyond that is that I'm Hedenski, something that hardly borders on human in the eyes of many. So Tavik's simple recognition that I'm human touches a sore spot I didn't know I had until now.

This weepiness has the added side effect of making the foreign presence inside me pulse more vibrantly, which makes me want to cry all the more, so I deflect my emotions by asking another question. "What is the Milk Road?"

Tavik glances sideways again. "The Milk Road. Right.

Elathians who live in the eight countries of the Ovinist Church have to hide their faith from the Order of Saint Ovin, so there's a communication network in place, a way for us to stay connected and help each other. That's the Milk Road."

"And Kantar is part of the Milk Road?"

"Kantar is where the road begins and ends. Elathians the world over feed us and supply us, and we do the best we can to free the Mother and keep the faith alive."

"The Dyers recognized you by the mark on your wrist. What is it?"

Tavik stops, rolls back his sleeve, and holds up the image on his wrist. "It's a tattoo, the Grace Tree of Kantar, the symbol of Elath the Mother and Her gift of life."

"We call it Elath's Tree," I inform him.

"Yes, I know," he answers drily and begins walking again, his eyes scanning our surroundings in search of possible threats.

"Why do you call it the Milk Road? It is such an odd name."

"It's a metaphor. Where does milk come from? Think about it."

I think about it. And then I get it.

"Cows," I reply, humiliated. "Obviously."

Tavik bursts out laughing. "May the Mother and Her Sacred Milk bless you."

"What do you think will happen if Elath is not set free?" I ask, eager to change the subject away from the demon's breasts.

"You really are the Prima of Questions," he tells me with a comical contortion of his eyebrows. "We've been living in the Mother's Last Breath since Ovin took the Mother from us. What little life remains on earth comes from that. There used to be forests and farmland and pastures in Kantar. Now it's mostly desert and mountains, stretching into all the countries of the south. It's only a matter of time before death comes for the north, too. When the Mother's breath runs out at last, there will be only the Father's half of the world left: night and rock and desert and death. No new souls will be made, and all the souls of the dead will remain in the underworld for eternity, never to be reborn again."

"What happens in the underworld? What is it like?"

His eyes go distant, unfocused. "It's dark and underground and nothing happens. Just waiting and waiting."

I think of him as he was beneath the convent, panicked and unable to breathe. I have to believe that there is no such thing as this Elathian underworld, if only so that Tavik never has to go there.

"My turn," he says, as eager to change the subject as I was a moment ago. "An Ovinist believes that the souls of faithful people go to heaven, right? While the souls of people like me . . . what? Disappear?"

This is one of the most basic tenets of Ovinism, but having to say it aloud to an Elathian's face makes me squirm with my doubt of the Father's goodness. "The souls of heathens become the telleg of the Dead Forest."

"Seriously? You think the Dead Forest is where the mean people go when they die?"

"It is called the Dead Forest for a reason. Is that not what Elathians believe?"

"No. The telleg are just the telleg. They're just there." I'd swear

I see him shudder before he asks, "What do you think will happen if the Mother *is* set free?"

There's no criticism buried in the words. He really just wants to know what an Ovinist believes. And it would be nice if he understood what's at stake not just if he fails, but if he's wrong in the first place.

"Then Elath will shackle all souls to the physical world with her temptations, and the immortal life of the soul will remain on earth, sinner or not. It means there is no everlasting life beside the Father."

"Well, your heaven is already barred to me. And frankly, I'd rather be bound to earthly pleasures anyway."

He doesn't understand.

"It means the whole world becomes the Dead Forest, Tavik. It means everyone becomes a telleg."

He considers this before he says, "I think the Father is a lot nicer than Ovinists think He is. Just because death is weaker than life doesn't make Him a jerk."

I have no idea what the word *jerk* means, but I'm fairly certain that it would be nice to believe the Father isn't one.

We don't talk much after that, and the silence gives my brain all the space it needs to pile up even more questions. I start with Zofia. I can't understand how or why she hid so much from me. I thought I knew her well, and now I wonder if I knew her at all. Was she an Elathian before she came to Saint Vinnica, or did she come to doubt the Father slowly, over time?

Like me?

It's an oddly comforting thought.

As I mull this over, my mind fixates on one question in particular: Why did Brother Miklos kill her? Tavik said there was an Elathian spy at the convent, someone who figured out where Elath was truly hidden. It had to have been Zofia. Was Miklos trying to silence her before she could tell anyone else that Elath was imprisoned at the convent? Was he punishing her for betraying the Holy Ovinist Church? And what did the Goodson have to do with any of it?

It's the Goodson's actions that make the least sense of all. I can't imagine a world in which I would not trust him with my life, and yet here I am, living in it. My suspicions grow like a thicket all around me, barbed and poisonous. Why did he try to stop me from going to the summit? How could he have allowed Brother Miklos to let armed men enter that room last night? Why wasn't he there to protect us? None of it adds up, and that's all the more reason to avoid the Order until I know more.

"You look terrible," Tavik observes, rousing me from my thoughts.

"Oh, thank you very much."

"Was that sarcasm? Thank the Mother. You do have a sense of humor. I was starting to worry."

Tavik makes my head throb. I stop and put my hands over my eyes, pushing against the pain.

"Hey, sorry," he says. "You don't look terrible. I meant you look like you *feel* terrible. There's a difference."

"Mm-hmm," I mumble, leaving my hands where they are.

He pulls them away gently so that I have to look at him. Every time I get an eyeful of that handsome face, I can feel my skin turn red and blotchy. How on earth do normal girls navigate a world full of boys?

"You know what?" he says. "We've made it a good distance, and we should probably save the remainder for the cover of night anyway. Why don't you get some rest?"

The instant the word *rest* exits his mouth, my eyelids grow heavy and every muscle in my body goes slack. He moves behind me and coaxes me out of the knapsack.

"Here." He holds out the blanket from my pack before shrugging out of his own knapsack. As I spread my blanket on the ground in the clearing where we've stopped, he takes the blanket from his supplies and holds it out to me as well. My exhausted brain can't figure out what he's doing, and I frown at the wool, confused.

"Take it. One to lie down on, one to go over you."

"Don't you need to rest, too?"

"I'll keep watch."

"Aren't you tired?"

"I'll be all right. I'm used to it." He rises and presses the blanket into my hands so that I have no choice but to take it. Gelya of Twenty-Four Hours Ago would not have dreamed of falling asleep in front of a stranger. Gelya of Right Now could not possibly care less. I curl onto my side on the soft wool, facing away from Tavik as I pull his blanket up to my shoulders. The earth beneath me is hard and lumpy, but sleep closes in anyway.

"Gelya?" he whispers.

"Hmm?" I answer sleepily.

"Can you feel Her? Does She talk to you?"

Her.

Elath.

I wish I could forget, but the knowledge that something lives inside me never fully goes away. I feel like a simmering pot on a stove, and I know without being told that I could lift the lid if I wanted to sniff what was inside.

"I sense that She's there," I tell him. "But no, She doesn't speak to me."

He nods and looks away. As I drift off to sleep, I hear him whisper, "I'm sorry, Gelya. You have no idea how sorry I am."

The last thought that randomly pops into my mind as sleep finally catches up to me is, *Tavik is right. Why don't brides get a say in the matter?*

I wish I had.

I tap lightly on the door with freckled knuckles.

"Come in."

One of the hinges squeaks familiarly as I push open the door, and there, sitting at the old polished desk in the Sacrist's office, sits Zofia, sifting through a stack of papers. I hover at the door, drinking her in with disbelieving eyes.

She looks up from her work. "Well, don't just stand there."

In a daze, I cross the small room and take a seat at the wooden chair opposite her. "Zofia?"

"What's wrong?" she asks, and I can see that my confusion amuses her.

"I thought you were dead."

She plays along, holding out her arms to get a good look at herself. "Am I?"

I glance around the office. Everything is as familiar to me as my own body, even the scent of lemon oil used to polish the oak desk to a mellow sheen. "I thought so."

Zofia rises from her seat, and suddenly, she seems much taller than I remember. She crouches down in front of me and takes me by the arms, a warm smile on her face. "Do you know what we haven't played in a long time? Hide-and-seek. What do you say to a game? Would you like that?"

I nod.

She rises and sprints out the door, calling, "Come and find me!"

I follow her down the long convent hallway, both of us giggling like mad, but when I round the corner after her, I find myself chasing her along a forest path. The ground beneath my feet rises and falls irregularly, making it hard to navigate, and I fall farther and farther behind.

"Come on, Gelya!"

I run so fast I can hardly breathe. A lock of red hair comes loose from my braids and tickles my face as I burst into a wide clearing. An enormous tree stands in the center, its branches stretching toward heaven, grasping at the clouds in the sky. The roots reach out like the tentacles of an octopus, straddling a brook that seems to come from the tree itself.

A stag stands in the clearing, regarding me with curiosity. His antlers remind me of branches, as if he were an extension of the great tree. A woman stands beside him at the circle's center. She is fuzzy, indistinct, faceless. She holds a dagger in her hand.

And she slits the stag's throat with it.

The poor creature lets out a horrid, gurgling cry before he can make no more sound at all. Dark blood pours from the slash in his flesh, gushing in waves with the pumping of his dying heart.

The woman has no eyes, and yet she looks at me. And when she speaks, it's Zofia's voice that comes out of her mouthless face.

"Hurry."

Fifteen

I wake to find myself sore and cramped on the hard earth as the river whispers behind me in this living world where Zofia cannot go. She was so real in my dream, and waking to the realization that she's gone is like losing her all over again.

The urge to start bawling is cut short when I realize that Tavik isn't here. A spark of panic snaps me, but then I see him standing a little farther on between the trees. He's naked from the waist up, with the scabbard straps crossing his torso just under the mark my hand made over his heart.

"Blessed be the Mother," he says under his breath. Then he draws the swords from their scabbards, pushing the blades skyward in two parallel lines, arcing them slowly downward to his sides before following their path back in the opposite direction.

Each movement is slow, precise, one moving smoothly into the next. It's absolutely mesmerizing, and I tiptoe closer for a better look as the sun sets behind him, peeking between the narrow trees, outlining him in amber light. He bows low, his swords extended outward before he transitions into an asymmetrical position, the blades shifting in opposite directions as he raises his knee toward his ribs.

He is lean and rangy, his bones outpacing his flesh so that his frame seems a little too large, hinting at the man he'll grow into. His muscles shift and tighten beneath a layer of scarred, taut skin. One series of scars in particular stands out, forming a shiny silver crescent on his arm.

As he continues through the movements, the strain begins to show. His blades are not as steady, and his muscles tremble. He sweeps the blades in a long, low swipe parallel to the earth before arching his back and crossing the swords behind his head. How is he not falling over? This is incredible, beautiful in a way that goes beyond the surface, transcendent.

He straightens, shifting his torso upright as he casts his arms behind him, up and over until his hands reach the same level as his shoulders. He bends in his elbows and spins the pommels of the swords over the back of each hand. But then he loses control of both weapons, and they drop like a pair of bricks onto the soft earth.

"Father of death!" He leans down to pick the swords off the ground and mutters, "Hello, Gelya," without looking in my direction.

I watched him that entire time, and he knew it, and now I'm burning with embarrassment. "I apologize. I did not mean to—"

"Snoop?"

I taste the new word in my mouth. "*Snoop*? That is an odd word."

"*That's,*" he corrects me. "Contractions, remember?" He takes off the scabbards and sets each one gently on the ground as if they are as delicate and precious as babies before he picks up his tunic, which, to my surprise, is neatly folded. *Thank the Father, he's putting on his shirt,* I think, but he pauses, squinting at me with amused suspicion, and it's clear he knows I'm staring at his chest. Well, what am I supposed to do? I haven't been in close contact with many men before, especially half-naked ones, and it's extremely distracting.

"Does that hurt?" I ask, nodding at my handprint over his heart, feeling remorse when I wasn't really the one who did that to him.

He looks at the brand and frowns. "No. You'd think it would, but it doesn't."

That's a relief at least.

"What were you doing?" I ask him. "Were you dancing?"

He raises his thick eyebrows. "You thought I was dancing?" The tunic hangs from his hands. I wish he'd put it on. How hard is that?

"If you were not dancing, what were you doing?"

"Praying."

"Really?" I take a step closer. "It looked like dancing to me. You pray with swords in hand?"

"Yes, all men do, although most pray with only one."

"But you are not yet a—" I stop myself just a little too late. In his mind, Tavik fills in the blank, as evidenced by the sour look on his face. He puts his tunic on at last and picks up his swords. I follow him to our packs and attempt to undo the offense. "How do women pray in Kantar?"

"Without swords," he answers curtly.

"Do you pray to Elath? Or to the Father? How does it work?"

"Both. We pray to both. All things in balance." He folds the blanket he lent me with sharp efficiency, irritated with me for implying that he's not a man. But in my defense, he isn't. I'd bet he's only seventeen or eighteen. How bizarre that Kantar sent someone so young on such an important mission.

"Would you like to know how Ovinists pray?" I offer.

"Not really." He stuffs the blanket into his pack and straps on his scabbards, leaving me to fold and pack my own blanket. He holds up his knapsack and asks, "Can you help me get this on?"

"Why do men pray with swords and women without?" I ask as I pick up his knapsack. It's decidedly heavier than my own, plus he has to carry it over the swords at his back. I'm half tempted to offer to take it, but he shrugs into it before I can say anything.

He turns back around to face me. "You and the questions. You're like an expectant pigeon waiting for a crumb."

"Is that a colloquialism?"

"No, it's Tavik's Brilliant Simile."

He's teasing me, but it's a strangely nice kind of teasing. I think I'm forgiven.

"Men are made in the image of the Father," he explains. "Women are made in the image of the Mother. So men are deliverers of death, while women are givers of life. In this way, all things are in balance. The world has been out of balance since the Mother was taken from us. The world is full of death and destruction now, and so men, who are associated with the Father's death, pray with swords. And because the world is empty of the Mother's life, a woman's hands are empty. Until now."

He nods his head in my direction, at the being I contain within me. He's all reverence again, the way he was in the Dyers' workroom when he told me what I was. I squirm under the weight of his stare and the impossible expectations behind it.

"I don't want this," I tell him.

He throws up his hands. "You carry the Mother inside you. A *goddess*. And yet you stand there, sulking and whinging and crying like it's the worst thing that could possibly happen to you when it's an honor."

"Says the boy whose body is entirely his own." I grab my blanket off the ground and fold it with a rigorous efficiency to rival Tavik's, taking my anger out on the wool. The next thing I know, I'm crying again, and I couldn't even tell you why. I am sick to death of weeping at the drop of a hat. It's so frustrating, and yet completely out of my control.

"I'm sorry." Tavik takes a tentative step toward me. He holds out a hand, but he doesn't touch me. "Hey, now. It's all right. It'll be all right."

And now I'm laughing and crying at the same time. "I'm fairly certain it will *not* be all right."

This time, he does touch me. He takes me by the shoulder and gives me an encouraging squeeze, and his hand feels warm and kind when I feel so cold and empty. It helps. "Then I'll be positive for both of us. One thing at a time, right? We're already halfway to that safe house in Dalment. Plus, you just used a contraction, so I think there's reasonable cause for optimism."

I wipe my blotchy, tearstained cheeks. "How can you find humor in any of this?"

"I'm always funny. It's one of my most charming qualities."

"Yes, that's just what I was thinking."

"See there? Another contraction. If that's not cause for hope, I don't know what is."

Before I can respond, I'm on the ground, the wind knocked out of me. The contents of my knapsack press into my back as Tavik's body lies atop mine, pushing me into the damp earth.

"What—"

"Knights on the river," he hisses, slapping a hand over my mouth just as he did on the streets of Varos da Vinnica even though I don't for one second need help staying quiet. We lie there and wait. It feels like eternity before the boat approaches, and when it does, I freeze, sandwiched between my knapsack and Tavik's weight, and listen with my entire body as the splashing of oars in the water passes just beyond the shrubs that barely hide us. I'm too scared to draw breath, as if these men on the river could hear my lungs contract and expand from twenty feet away. Tavik's heart thuds so hard it's audible.

We wait until the liquid sounds of the boat pass us.

And wait.

Finally, Tavik takes his hand from my face and rolls off me. He lies on his back between me and the Sargo, his right arm pressed against my left.

"Did they see us?" I whisper.

"I don't think so."

"I still cannot believe that I am hiding from the Order of Saint Ovin."

We lie there, neither of us moving.

"What?" I ask. "No vulgar insults about the Order or my religion?"

"When am I ever vulgar?" He rises and gives me a hand up. "Come on. The sooner we get to Dalment, the better. I want to reach that safe house before dawn."

"Tavik?"

"Yeah?"

"If I never again have your hand over my mouth, it will be too soon."

He raises his eyebrows then breaks into a sheepish grin. "Fair enough."

Sixteen

It's well before dawn when we hit the bend in the Sargo, the point at which we're supposed to head east toward Dalment.

"Do you see the road?" Tavik asks me softly.

"Hello?" comes a voice out of the darkness. Tavik steps before me and draws his swords as my heart leaps into my throat. For a second, I assume the Order has caught up to us, but on further thought, it seems unlikely that a knight on a manhunt would say *hello*.

"Blessed be the Mother," says the voice, which belongs to the black outline of a man against the dark landscape. The silhouette of his hands goes up in surrender. "My name is Ambrus. I'm your contact."

Tavik nods and puts the blades back in their sheaths as Ambrus approaches. He's a short, bald man, neither fat nor thin, wearing round metal-rimmed glasses that reflect the moonlight. He looks like someone's grandfather, the kind of man who gives a piece of candy to every child who enters his shop.

"Oh my," he titters. "That's the closest I've been to a sword in my life. Come along, now. I've bribed the guards at the west gate to let us in. One of them is Elathian. Good lad, that one. Here, I've brought a pilgrim's cloak for each of you. I thought they would be a good disguise since Ovinists depart from the Cathedral of Saint Markos for trips to Saint Vinnica and points beyond, although you'll have to forgive me, my dear, this one is going to be a bit small on you."

For the first two miles of our trek to Dalment, Ambrus keeps up a steady stream of chatter, as sweet and normal and comforting as birdsong, if slightly exhausting, but he quiets down once he gets winded. As promised, the guards at the gate let us through without incident, and one of them even hugs Ambrus—the Elathian, I assume. There's a hackney waiting for us as well, so we don't have to walk all the way to Ambrus's apothecary after traveling over twenty miles on foot.

"Come in, come in." The little apothecary left a lamp burning in his absence, and he takes it in hand to light our way up a flight of stairs, talking the whole time. I struggle to keep up the translation, but the gist is that no one seems to be looking for us here in Dalment, so there's definitely cause for relief.

As we reach the top of a second set of stairs, he opens a door and gestures us through. We find ourselves in an attic bedroom, where a serving girl probably slept at some point in time. Now it's me and Tavik and a small table with two wooden chairs and one narrow, rickety bed.

We set our packs on the floor, and Tavik puts the two swords on the table, after which he rolls his shoulders and stretches his neck. I'm trying to decide if I should collapse onto the bed before Tavik gets it or read Zofia's notes at once, when Tavik asks, "Can you tell him I need to send a message if possible?"

"Of course," answers the apothecary once I've translated. I keep hearing all this talk of messages and messengers, so I follow Ambrus and Tavik down one flight of steps, where our host opens a door off the landing. When I peek in, I can see this is clearly his bedroom, and I hover at the door, hesitant to enter a man's private space. I take a few reluctant steps into the room and watch Ambrus pull out a quill, a pot of ink, and a long, narrow scrap of paper, setting them neatly on his desk.

"Thank you," Tavik says in Rosvanian as he dips the nib into the ink and scratches out an extremely tiny message with his left hand. Once he's done, he blots the paper, rolls it up, and stuffs it into the equally tiny canister that the apothecary hands him.

"What did you write? And where is this messenger?"

Ambrus goes to the window and throws up the sash. "Here."

I cross to the window to get a better look. There's a small wicker coop built onto the exterior wall. The sun has begun to rise in the east, but it's still very dark. I can barely make out the flutter of wings within the open cage.

"A bird?" I ask. In answer, Tavik reaches beyond the window frame and takes the creature from its perch. Blue wings. Gold breast. A black band on each side of her face delineated by a white stripe above and below. Long wings and scissored tail. He might as well be clutching Zofia in his muscled grip. Or me.

"It's . . . it's a soulswift," I stammer.

"These birds carry messages between Elathians. Hence, 'messenger,'" Tavik explains as Ambrus helps him tie the canister to one of the bird's delicate legs.

"How can you . . . ? These are . . . They carry . . ." For the second time in as many days, I want to pry his fingers off a soulswift, this innocent creature who was once a Vessel just like me. And then I want to wrap my own fingers around Tavik's ropy neck and squeeze the breath out of him.

Tavik gives me an utterly unmerited long-suffering look. "I know Ovinists believe these birds carry the souls of the dead, and I can see you're really pissed off right now, but I'm tired, and it's hard to be sympathetic to a religion that has tried to stomp out my own for literal centuries. They're just birds, all right? Really handy birds."

"Let her go," I insist, my breath hitching in outrage.

Tavik obliges, holding the soulswift up to the window to release her. The bird flaps her wings and takes off on the wind, heading south and west in the direction of Tovnia. As the three of us watch her disappear into the distance, Tavik murmurs the same desperate word Zofia's voice spoke to me in my dream a few hours ago: "Hurry." The bird darts through clouds dyed deep purple by the coming sunrise. I watch her until she disappears from sight, carrying Tavik's message and a piece of my heart with her.

"How does she know where to go?" I ask.

"They just know. That one is heading for my captain now." Tavik shrugs as if none of this were shocking. With each second he's in my life, I find myself with more questions and fewer answers, and I had so few answers to begin with, as it turns out.

"Wait!" I call as he stalks past me, heading for the door.

Ambrus and I glance at each other and follow him as he clomps up the stairs. In seconds, I'm at his shoulder, hounding him. "What message did you send your captain? And how could you use a soulswift to send it?"

I can hardly believe I'm uttering these words, and yet I just watched a soulswift willingly take Tavik's message. Why would a soulswift help Elathians? It makes no sense. Unless what I was taught to believe is the thing that makes no sense. The alien humming within me throbs, reminding me of Her unwelcome presence.

"Is everything all right?" Ambrus asks from behind me, breathless on the stairs.

"No." I hustle to catch up to Tavik, who pushes open the attic door. "Do not ignore me!" I fire at his back.

He stops beside the bed and faces me, his eyes bloodshot. "You can yell at me later. I promise."

He drops onto the tick without bothering to take off his road-dirty boots and nestles into the blankets as if lying in a bed were the greatest thing that's ever happened to him. Maybe it is. He probably sleeps in a pig's trough back home.

"Tavik!"

But he's already out cold. Ambrus and I stand over him, staring at his slack face before the apothecary turns to me and asks, "I don't suppose you play Shakki, do you?"

I itch to read the parchment in my pocket, but what can I do when Ambrus comes back a few minutes later with two tankards of ale, a Shakki board, and a tray of bread, cheese, and salami?

"Thank you for helping us," I tell him as we set up the game pieces.

"Certainly, although I must admit it would be nice to know exactly why I am helping you." He says this in a conversational tone, but the content leaves me at a loss for words. I decide to take a page from Tavik's book and answer, "It's complicated."

"I gather that." He smiles at me and makes his first move. "So the Mother is no longer in the Vault of Mount Djall?"

Tavik admitted as much to the Dyers. There's no point hiding it from Ambrus. "Correct."

"But She is still imprisoned?"

"Yes."

"Where?"

I flounder before I repeat, "It's complicated. We're working on it."

"May the Mother help us all," Ambrus says with a sad nod as he provisions his army in the mountains when he should be shoring up his defenses along his coastline. I get a strong roll of the dice, confident that I might win for a change.

"She can't help anyone if She's imprisoned, can She?" I point out with a hint of bitterness in my voice as my army charges through the paltry defenses he set up along his northern border.

"Is She truly absent from the world?" Ambrus challenges me, raising his thin eyebrows over the tops of his glasses. "There is still life. You and I are here. Our hearts are beating in our chests."

I reply with a noncommittal sound as Elath's presence makes my stomach churn.

Ambrus frowns at the board. "Frankly, I think the Ovinists have it right to a certain extent."

Now it's my turn to raise my eyebrows. "Really? How so?"

"They believe a demon's temptations permeate the world, but I believe it is the Mother's life. Here. Let's say this light is the Mother." He slides the Shakki board to the side and sets the candle down closer to the table's center. Then he retrieves a basket from the corner and places it over the flame. "The basket contains the candle, but it cannot contain the light. The room is darker now, but the fire still shines between the splints. So the Mother may be imprisoned, but Her life finds a way out, even if the way seems quite dim to us. Now, I'd better take away the basket before I set the whole house on fire."

He grins and places the basket on the floor beside his chair, and I mull over his theory as he contemplates his next move. If I believed Elath was the goddess of life and not a demon, Ambrus's basket analogy would make sense. Rosvania is the most powerful country of the Ovinist Church, its lands rich and productive. Could that be a result of Elath's presence in the heart of the country? Merely asking myself this question feels as dangerous as playing with fire, yet how can asking a question be a sin?

Ambrus interrupts my spiraling thoughts as I eviscerate his northern army. "What's that chain you wear around your neck? It looks fine, not the sort of thing a Daughter usually wears, is it?"

I doubt Ambrus could connect me to the Goodson, yet tension seeps into my spine. "It was a gift."

"May I see it?"

What can I say to that without drawing Ambrus's suspicion? I pull up the triptych and hold it out to him, unopened. He studies the floral engraving on the outside. "Lovely. Such craftsmanship. Will you open it? If the interior is anything like the exterior, I'm sure it must be exquisite."

I can't stand to look at Saint Vinnica right now, a reminder that my fate is tied to hers, that my only choice may be to sacrifice myself as she sacrificed her own life. I snatch back the triptych and stuff it down the neck of my dress, wishing I could hide from Ambrus's shrewd gaze. "It's very personal to me."

"I see." He shores up that inexplicable naval force, and I get the sense that I'm not winning this game as handily as I thought. "Are you our spy at the convent, then?"

I give him a nervous smile, but I don't correct him.

"You're not a Vessel, though," he says as if it's a statement when, really, it's a question.

"No." It's my first bald-faced lie to him, and I'm ashamed to admit the deceit trips off my tongue with ease.

"There aren't many Vessels left, are there? Just as there aren't many Two-Swords." He rolls the dice. "Is it true? Did the boy kill the Grace Tree of Saint Vinnica?"

The memory is fresh and painful, but there is no point in hiding it. "Yes."

"Why?"

"I don't know." Another lie, just as easy as the first.

Ambrus nods sadly as he contemplates my last move. "It was already dying, and now it's gone. And the Grace Tree of Kantar is dying as well. The drought stretches beyond the borders of Kantar, and the long cold winters reach down on us from the north. It's all happening so fast now."

"What is?"

"The end."

"The end of what?"

He looks up at me, his eyes somber, his face grave. "The end of life."

Until two days ago, the end of the world has always been distant and theoretical. Now it's immediate and imminent. Because *I* am the end. If what I was taught to believe is right, and I release the demon inside me, the earth will become a wasteland and eternal life beside the Father in heaven will disappear forever. But on the off chance that my faith is wrong, I could end the world simply by holding this spirit inside me.

These thoughts are so dark that I'm almost grateful to Ambrus for pushing his navy upriver, a move I didn't see coming. Suddenly it is very clear to me that this man is a far better player than I gave him credit for.

"We must do all we can to stop it," he says as he obliterates my army and wins the game. "I'm sure you wouldn't stand in the way of that, would you?"

I don't give him an answer, but he doesn't seem to require one. He rises and says, "I'm afraid I can't stay for a second round. The shop opens in an hour, and I have much to do. I'll bring up a tea tray later."

With that, he leaves me to sit alone at the rickety table, my head spinning with questions and worries. I wait a couple of minutes to make sure he's not going to pop back in before I finally take Zofia's notes from my pocket.

Seventeen

I unfold the page to find not one but two pieces of parchment in my hands. The first is a rubbing of an unfamiliar Sanctus text, but the second I recognize with a slithering dismay. It's the rubbing I took in the courtyard. Could Zofia have died for this, for something I did simply because I was curious? But what could I have discovered in the convent garden that led to a war, and to Tavik's mission, and to my becoming the Vessel of a thing that is either a demon or a goddess?

"Is that a bedtime story?"

I look up with a start. Tavik sprawls across the mattress, his eyes opened to slits, his hair mussed. His physical presence, the very maleness of him, takes up an astonishing amount of room. A blush oozes over my skin, which is exasperating. How can I be distracted by—what do I even call this? attraction? allure?—when I'm facing the literal end of the world?

"Have you had many bedtime stories in your life?" I ask

cuttingly, annoyed with myself and taking it out on him.

He stretches like a cat. "I've had loads of bedtime stories, as a matter of fact. Have you?"

The question stings. Zofia's stories are one more thing I have to grieve.

"So what are those?" Tavik asks when I don't rise to his bait.

"I don't know. Zofia gave them to me before . . ." My voice trails off as grief sinks in.

"Zofia? The other Daughter at the summit?"

I nod.

"I'm sorry for your loss. May your friend be reborn in the Mother's breath."

It's the most heretical thing anyone has ever said to me, but he's being kind, and I could use a little kindness right now. "Thank you."

"Was she the one who wrote to my Prima?"

"I think so."

He sits up, alert and attentive. "And you think those papers might be important?"

"Maybe."

"Well, let's read them."

I clamp my lips, unsure what exactly I should share with him.

He leans toward me. "Oh, spit it out, Gelya. We're partners here."

"Yes, but I am your unwilling partner."

"You want to get the Mother out of you. I want to get the Mother out of you. We both want the same thing."

"That's not true. I don't know what I want."

He's all theatrical arms and hands as he speaks—overwhelming when I have lived such a quiet life before now. "Well, I want the Mother's soul to return to Her immortal body so She can walk the earth again and breathe life back into the deserts of Kantar. I want the souls of the underworld to be reborn again. I want to save the world. If that's not good enough for you, what is?"

I open my mouth, but nothing comes out. Because I have no answer.

What would the Goodson think if he could see me now, full of questions and doubt? But then I also have to question what exactly I think of the Goodson. I hate this uncertainty, this growing suspicion that the world is not what I thought it was, that I've never truly known or understood anyone in my life.

"I just want the truth," I tell Tavik at last.

"I'm telling you the—" He stops himself and drops his gaze. "I haven't lied to you."

"That is very reassuring, but I am more than capable of finding my own answers." I give up on keeping secrets from Tavik—what's the point?—and spread the first page on the table, pulling it at the corners so my fingers don't touch the text until I'm ready. "It's written in Sanctus, so I will have to sing it."

"Can't you just read it?" Tavik's face betrays his misgivings. I'm sure he recalls with perfect clarity how he felt the fires of Nogarra when I sang to him at the convent.

"Sanctus must be sung, and only a Vessel has the ability to do so," I explain. "The language is not learned. We simply know how to sing it. There are subtleties that shift and change depending on the reader and the listener, so understanding a song's true meaning is a bit like catching a fish in a river with your bare hands."

"I would love to see you catch a fish with your bare hands. Can that be arranged?"

I bat away the joke as I look over the unfamiliar rubbing. "I haven't sung since Elath entered me. I'm not certain how to fill myself with the Father's Word when this thing already resides inside me."

"Let's not call the Mother a 'thing,'" Tavik suggests. I glance up to find him sitting cross-legged, his elbows on his knees, as comfortable as you please, when I am anything but.

"I'll just sing a bit at random," I tell him. "Will you stop me if it gets too loud?"

"You got it. But, just to be clear, there's nothing in there about fires and sinners and burning cities, right?" His tone is light, but I see the fear in his eyes. I should probably be grateful that he fears me, but instead, it makes me feel lonely.

"I don't think so."

"Good. I'm listening."

I'm worried about what is going to come out once I touch the text, but honestly, there's only one way to find out. I imagine myself pressing down on the lid that covers that burning cauldron inside me before I brush my fingertips to the Sanctus symbols. The words enter, pouring inside me, filling me up, but they refuse to come back out. It's a different sensation than I'm used to, hot when it's usually frigid. The pressure builds. The buzzing soars up from my core to my ears, deafening.

"Gelya? Are you all right?" Tavik's voice sounds muffled, but I can't answer. I lift the lid the barest crack to let out the steam, and the text vibrates through my body like a long, low note on a violin, richer and more resonant than ever before. My voice becomes a living spirit that pours from my lips into Tavik's being, from my breath into his lungs, from my flesh into his body. My song dances along his skin, trembles in the muscle beneath the surface, grips the bones within.

Water of my thirst, blood of my body.

I sink deeper into the song, gliding into the words. For the first time in my life, it's a pleasure. I *want* to read it. I *want to* sing.

"Gelya," comes Tavik's strangled voice, and I force myself to rip my hand from the page. Outside the song, I shake with fatigue and grip the table to stay upright. And yet I want to dive back in to take pleasure in this gift that has never felt good before.

And then I remember poor Tavik. I look up to find him staring back at me with glassy eyes, his pupils large and black. He's breathing so hard his chest rises and falls. You'd think I'd be used to the fact that my gift has this visceral effect on people, but Tavik's expression is one I've never seen before, and the intensity of his gaze makes my skin inexplicably hot. His eyes go wide, and he grabs a pillow from the bed to plop into his lap, which seems strange. "Whew" is all he says.

"Sorry. That was stronger than usual. Are you all right?"

"Yeah," he gasps.

I frown down at the Sanctus symbols. "I think it's a love story. Can that be right?"

"Definitely a love story," he concurs, his voice deep and throaty. What on earth did the song do to him?

"Sometimes the listener experiences the song more clearly than the singer. What did you hear? How did it feel to you?"

He folds his hands over the pillow and considers his answer

carefully, a quizzical expression playing across his face. "Familiar, actually. That's weird. Could you translate it into Kantari?"

"I think so." I brush the Sanctus text as lightly as I can, doing my best to hold back the power inside me as I attempt to re-create the verse in Tavik's language.

> *Come to me, my beloved,*
> *My wellspring, liquid and lovely,*
> *Water of my thirst, blood of my body,*
> *What the Mother joins in life*
> *Cannot be separated in death.*

I feel like a cup, and the text is wine. I'm growing drunk on it. Again, I tear my hand away, as troubled as I am pleased by the power of the verse. "I think that's as far as I ought to go."

Tavik crosses the room, tucks a piece of leftover sausage from the tray into his mouth and chews ruminatively. "I'd swear that's from *The Ludoïd*. I thought you said this was some kind of religious heresy or something."

"I don't know what it is. But you do?"

"Yeah. It sounds like the wedding of Ludo and Vinnica from *The Ludoïd*."

He pulls up a chair and begins to shovel what's left of the food into his mouth. I gape at him until the words he uttered fully sink in. "The *what*?"

He speaks with a mouth full of cheese. "The wedding of Ludo and Vinnica from—"

"I heard what you said!"

He swallows. "Then why did you ask?"

"Vinnica as in *Saint* Vinnica?"

"We don't have saints."

"But we are referring to the same person?"

"Well, yeah. What happened to those contractions?"

"So you believe Saint Vinnica, the purest of all Vessels, was married to . . ."

"Ludo."

"First of all, that is ridiculous," I inform him, on the verge of apoplexy. "Second of all, who is Ludo?"

Now it's Tavik's turn to be apoplectic. "You've never heard of Ludo? Or *The Ludoïd*? Aren't you supposed to be some kind of Kantari expert?"

"I translate *The Songs of the Saints* into Kantari. I don't read heathen texts."

"Oh, for the love of the Mother, *The Ludoïd* is one of the greatest works of Kantari literature."

"So you know what this is?" I ask, holding up the rubbing.

Tavik gapes at the parchment, and then he leaps to his feet to snatch it from my hand, knocking over his chair in the process and making a horrible racket.

"Tavik!" I protest, but he ignores me and spreads Zofia's rubbing out on his side of the table, his hands splayed across the page. He releases a shuddering breath as if on the verge of tears.

"What's wrong?" I ask uncertainly.

"Where did your friend get this?" he chokes without looking up, echoing Zofia's words the night she returned to the convent: *Where did you get it?*

"The Monastery of Saint Helios, I think. She was sent there to do translation work." I stare at him as he remains bent over the page.

"This stone was in my mother's library in Grama. I asked her to read it to me once, but she said only a Vessel of Saint Vinnica could read it."

"You've seen the original?"

"I just told you. My mother was the librarian of Grama."

That man who killed your friend tonight—Brother Miklos—do you know what we call him in Kantar? The Butcher of Grama. Tavik's mother is dead because Brother Miklos led the attack that killed her. I keep hoping things will get clearer and easier. Instead, they keep getting muddier and more complicated. When Tavik finally looks up, his eyes are wet and bloodshot, making my own well up in sympathy.

"May the Father lift her spirit up," I whisper. He offered me a Kantari platitude for my loss. I can at least offer him this.

He steps away from the table, turns his back to me, and holds his hair out of his face with both hands. "So for some reason, an ancient epic Kantari poem led your friend to figure out where the Mother was hidden. How?"

"I can't answer that unless I know what *The Ludoïd* is about," I tell his back.

He lets his hands fall and turns to me wearing a sad, crooked grin. His curls fan up and out like a halo around his handsome face. "Then it looks like I'm the one telling the bedtime stories today."

Eighteen

"'Call down the Mother's voice, the song of the lark, to sing the tale of Ludo, Breaker and Broken,'" Tavik intones.

Impressed, I ask, "Have you memorized the entire poem?"

"No, I've been a little busy—fighting Ovinists, surviving, feeding a hungry nation, that sort of thing. But it's a great first line, isn't it?"

I purse my lips in annoyance, which makes him grin, which annoys me even more. "Please, continue."

"Here's the gist: Once there was an orphan named Ludo, and because he had no mother, Elath took him as Her own son. This was in the days before men killed men. But then the Northmen decided that a man could take a life more easily than a woman could give it. They came to believe that one was better than the other, that life taking was more powerful than life giving. Clear so far?"

"I suppose so?"

"Good. Ovin was the best hunter in Kantar. He—"

"*What?*"

"I'm two seconds in, and you're interrupting me? Really?"

"This is very shocking. I was taught that Ovin was from the area around southwest Rosvania. How could Saint Ovin have been a Kantari? I had no idea this is what Elathians believe."

"Well, it's high time you learned, so less talking and more listening. Ovin was a great hunter, so when the Northmen crossed the Koz Mountains to conquer the south, it fell to Ovin to teach men how to use the gift of the Father—death—to hunt their fellow men like animals.

"The Mother saw this and took pity on the Kantari. She sent Her son, Ludo, to help them. 'You were born with the Sword of Wrath, as all men are,' she told him, 'but you must also carry the Sword of Mercy so that you will always remember to balance death with life.' That's why we carry two swords—the Father's Wrath and the Mother's Mercy—so that death alone will never rule the world. Tuck that away, because it's really important later on.

"So Ovin and Ludo fight all these epic battles together and fend off the Northmen, and eventually, Ludo ends up falling in love with Ovin's daughter, Vinnica. Actually, Ovin has two daughters. The other one is Lanya, but she's not really important here."

"Saint Lanya, the first Sacrist of the Convent of Saint Vinnica and the first soulswift, isn't important?" I protest, but Tavik waves away my comment and continues.

"The Kantari nearly have the Northmen pushed back to the Koz when Ovin gets drawn into the faith of the enemy. He comes to believe that he's better and more powerful than the Prima because, as a man, he can take her life more easily than she can take his. He ends up converting and leading the armies of the north. Under his command they shred the southern armies. As you can imagine, his betrayal really tears Ludo up."

"And the Prima. And Vinnica. And Lanya, the sister who is apparently not important in this story?"

"Yeah, them, too. Eventually, there's a giant battle in the forest surrounding Mount Djall between the northern forces led by Ovin, and the southern Two-Swords led by Ludo, but this one is different, because Vinnica has come to beg Ovin to stop. And not only does Ovin ignore her pleas, he actually tries to slay his own daughter with his sword."

"Is his sword the Hand of the Father?"

"This is a Kantari story. We don't care about Ovin's stupid sword." At this point, Tavik's flair for all things dramatic inspires him to act out *The Ludoïd*'s finale with an imaginary sword in each hand.

"Ludo gets there in the nick of time and blocks Ovin's blow, but he's so enraged by Ovin's betrayal that he casts aside the Sword of Mercy to fight Ovin with the Sword of Wrath alone. Huge mistake, Gelya. Huge! Can you feel the tragic ending breathing down our necks?"

"Um, yes?" I answer, a bit overwhelmed by his theatrics, but I want to hear the end.

"An incredible fight ensues, skill against skill, two warriors, equally matched, one sword to one sword. But then Ludo, lunging at Ovin, accidentally runs his sword through Vinnica, who has stepped between the two men she loves most in the world. Ludo's own true love goes down! Oh, the tragedy!" Tavik falls to his knees in mock despair. "Then Ovin plunges the same sword into Ludo's broken heart, and the hero falls. When the Kantari bring his body back to Nogarra, the Grace Tree of Kantar, whose seedpods choose Two-Swords, grows from his grave."

His story complete, Tavik drops into the chair opposite me.

"So it's a cautionary tale about not putting one's own feelings before faith and country," I surmise.

Tavik raises a thick eyebrow, perplexed. "Not at all. The point is that you should never throw away the Sword of Mercy. No one should kill out of hate. Hate is an imbalance of two souls, and death thrives in imbalance. If the greatest Two Swords in history is susceptible to such weakness, we must all guard against it."

I huff in disbelief.

"What?"

"How many men have you killed?"

His mouth forms a thin line before he answers, "I don't know."

"So many that you cannot count them? And you tell me that you killed none of them out of hate?"

His jaw tightens and his eyes go steely. "I kill out of necessity. I don't relish it."

"I imagine your victims do not relish it either."

"I'm not the monster you think I am." He leans closer to me, his elbows resting on either side of the rubbing. "Every life has worth, even the life of my enemy. And I'll tell you something else we Elathians believe, Miss High and Mighty: love is the only thing worth dying for, because in love there is balance between souls, and in that balance life flourishes."

"So, by that logic, it is better to die for the love of one person than to sacrifice what you most love for the benefit of many?"

"Yeah, that sounds right."

"Really?" I'm certain he must be kidding again, but he looks at me quizzically, as if I've suddenly sprouted a mustache. "You think entire nations should fall for the sake of the love between one man and one woman?"

"Or a man and a man, or a woman and a woman, or a parent and a child, or whatever. We're talking about a soul and a soul here. A life and a life." He leans in, resting his forearms on the table. "Love trumps hate. Every time. Even in the face of world destruction, love is the better choice. Vinnica tried to stop Ovin and Ludo out of love, so even though she was killed by Ludo's hate, she lives on as the true hero of the story, the example to which all humanity should aspire. The Father gave men the gift of death, but we Two-Swords fight with the understanding that each life has value and power, because life is the gift of the Mother."

I'm supposed to be the Kantari expert of Saint Vinnica, but these are concepts I've never learned. I was taught that the Kantari are mindless killers, yet here is a Two-Swords telling me how much he values life. My ignorance is beginning to feel like a gaping sinkhole beneath my feet. I had hoped I would find answers in Zofia's notes, but now I'm stuck with more questions. Stumped, I ask Tavik, "Do you mind if I sing the end?"

"All right. But can you go light on the magic? I'm afraid you're going to make me bawl when the Mother cradles Her dead son in the Grace Tree, and a Kantari never wastes his water."

"Meaning you are not supposed to cry?"

"Yep."

"Because a display of emotion is considered unmanly?"

"No, because there's so little potable water left in Kantar, it's considered an insult to the Mother to waste the water of the body. That's why you never, ever spit at someone."

"I would not spit at someone anyway."

"Except me, possibly?"

I raise an eyebrow at him, and he laughs. *It must be nice to laugh so easily,* I think as I place my fingertips toward the end of the passage and sing softly:

> *From within Ludo's shattered heart came the seed,*
> *Planted in his Mother's creation*
> *And watered with his blood.*

I sweat from the effort of holding back the grief buried deep within the words, trying to protect Tavik from the gut-wrenching emotion of the verse.

> *But Ovin could not see the life*
> *That Ludo's heart would become.*
> *His beautiful boy dead, his daughter broken,*
> *Ovin—*

My voice trails off, and I pull my fingers from the parchment.

"What in the name of the Mother was that?" asks Tavik. "Is there more?"

"I think so."

"Well, keep going."

"I can't. The text ends there."

We stare at each other across the table, Tavik's face a mirror of my own confusion. Then I hear the memory of Zofia's voice in my mind: *Don't tell anyone what you found. No one.* I snatch up the other rubbing—*my* rubbing—and compare it to Zofia's. My pulse ratchets up in excitement, and I turn to Tavik. "If we can assume Zofia was your spy at the convent, when did she write to your Prima?"

"I got my assignment a month ago, so shortly before that, I guess? Why?"

"I took this rubbing of the base of the statue of Saint Vinnica nearly two months ago. Zofia seemed to think it was important. And right after that, she must have sent a message to the Prima of Kantar saying that Elath was imprisoned at the convent."

Tavik's eyes meet mine, and I know we're both thinking the same thing. He hustles to my side of the table and watches as I push the first rubbing back to make room for the second, careful to keep my fingers away from the Sanctus symbols. The pieces aren't touching yet, but it's clear they fit together perfectly. I don't know how it's possible, but the statue of Saint Vinnica sat on the end of the story Tavik just told me, separated for centuries from the piece that resided at the library in Grama until Brother Miklos's invasion.

"Are you ready?" I ask Tavik.

"No," he answers, both joking and starkly honest at the same time.

I give him an apologetic grimace, then slowly, carefully, I slide the bottom half up to meet the top.

Nineteen

The second the two pieces connect, my body goes rigid, every muscle locked tight. My hands, planted on either side of the completed text, latch hard to the parchment. I couldn't move if I tried. The ringing of my body thrums in my ears and swells into a deafening clamor.

"Gelya?" Tavik calls to me, but he sounds so far away I can hardly hear him. He tries to take my hands off the text, but his grip tightens around my wrists as he's drawn into the force of the words, too. I'm fully conscious, but the Sanctus takes over my body like a cramp that squeezes every muscle at once, relentless and entirely out of my control. The pale figures against the charcoal's sooty darkness burn my eyes.

I picture the window over my desk in the stuffy scriptorium. In my mind, I open that window, and Elath's life force slips in, soaring through me, joyous, like a bird taking flight. I sing the song from beginning to end with music so bright and searing that my throat feels like it will burst from the beauty and pain of it.

> *Call down the Mother's voice,*
> *The song of the soulswift,*
> *To sing the tale of Ludo,*
> *Breaker and Broken.*

The story is just as Tavik told it. The war is brutal, the love consuming. Tragedy approaches like a stampede nearing a cliff. A great tree towers over the forest. Beneath its canopy, the final battle between Ludo and Ovin plays out.

Vinnica is there, too, but Ovin doesn't try to kill her. Instead, he aims a blow at the tree's massive trunk. His daughter flings herself against the tree, protecting it with her body, as Ludo parries. Livid, Ludo casts aside the Sword of Mercy, and the two men fight, sword against sword and rage against rage, until, at last, Ludo disarms Ovin and draws back his blade to finish the fight. His eyes, like his hand, hold nothing but wrath.

There is a bump in the narrative, a wobbling of the tale as my singing steps over the place where the two pieces meet.

Ovin dives as Ludo lunges. The Sword of Wrath misses its target and sinks into Vinnica's stomach, and because she stands before the tree, Ludo buries his blade into bark and sap and wood as well.

The Mother.

The tree is Her body, and the sword pierces Her soul.

The blow rings deep inside me, a pain so exquisite I can't even cry out. There is no sound for this. The whole world trembles violently as the Sword of Wrath cleaves life in two and separates the body from the soul. As Ludo withdraws his blade, he drags out his Mother's spirit with it, pulling Her soul through his beloved's body as if threading a needle.

Ovin watches with helpless eyes as his daughter becomes the Vessel of the spirit he hates. He turns on Ludo, wrenches the sword from the younger man's grief-slackened grip, and runs him through with it.

The Hand of the Father.

The tree withers and dies as Ludo's blood drenches Her roots. A wave of death washes over the forest in a hot wind, blackening the trees in one giant exhalation.

When Ovin's men arrive, they tear his still-living daughter from his arms. Afraid of what she is, they send her down a well and cover it tight, but in the night, Ovin takes his precious girl from the well and covers it once more so that no one will know what he has done.

Poor little Vinnica. Come. I shall carry you now.

North and north they travel, all the way to the prison where his daughter Lanya lives with the other women who refuse to kneel before the Father. Vinnica holds her father's and her sister's hands to breathe her last breath, yet Elath's soul remains trapped within her, alive in death.

From the Vessel's heart grows a tree, a twin to the one that will grow from Ludo's grave, for what the Mother joins in life cannot be separated in death.

The day Ovin dies, the tree flowers, and the flower bears fruit. When nothing is left but the dried husk, Lanya dares to pluck it, and it opens in her hand.

> *She felt like a song trapped in a cave,*
> *Like the newly lit wick of a lamp,*
> *Brightly burning in the darkness.*

Elath's soul remains imprisoned, but Lanya holds the seed of Her body in her hand. The sorrow and the beauty are too much. She becomes a bird of the Father's grief. Blue wings. Gold breast. A black band on each side of her face delineated by a white stripe above and below. Long wings and scissored tail. She takes flight, singing a song so lovely that it hurts to hear it, as she carries away the seed to plant Elath's body anew.

> *And the Father said,*
> *The sons of Ovin have aligned themselves with death,*
> *So they will live and live until the Sword cuts them down.*
> *Only the Vessel and the Sword may set Her free,*
> *beginning and end,*
> *body and soul.*
> *Until then, the Father bars the gates of heaven to you.*

The text releases its hold on me, and my gift releases its hold on Tavik. I fall face first onto the table as Tavik stumbles to the floor. I try to sit up, but my head weighs a ton.

"Gelya?" Tavik's hand is on my back, warm and trembling. Then he pulls me upright by the shoulders. My head lolls to the side, and I watch his eyes widen when he sees my face. "Father of death."

He darts away. I hear a ripping sound, and he returns a moment later with a strip of red cloth, which he presses beneath my nose.

"What's happening?" I whisper.

"Your nose is bleeding. Are you all right?"

The truth I thought I wanted comes crashing over me. Saint Ovin, the founder of the Holy Ovinist Church, was not the one who slew Elath. It was Ludo, the first Two-Swords and the hero of Kantar, who did it, and the Sword of Wrath became the Hand of the Father, passed down from Goodson to Goodson for centuries. It was Saint Ovin who took Elath out of Her prison at Mount Djall, Ovin who brought Vinnica to the convent.

Then again, who's to say the text Tavik and I put together is any more the truth than *The Songs of the Saints* is? It was right about Elath's whereabouts, but that doesn't mean it's right about everything, does it? If I accept that one thing I was taught to believe is wrong, do I have to question everything? Or does the whole system collapse like a house of cards the moment you remove even one bastion?

"I'm farther from the truth than I have ever been," I tell myself more than Tavik. His eyebrows pull together, a tragic line across his forehead. He's having to grapple with hard truths, too, like the fact that his hero, Ludo, is the one who slew Elath, while Saint Ovin, the man his faith reviles, is the one who saved Elath from the Vault of Mount Djall. It's a bitter irony that Ovin's rescuing Vinnica manages to turn not one but *two* faiths on their heads at once.

Finally, Tavik says, "The Mother is true. Our goal is true. Nothing's changed, not really."

I glare at him, frustrated by the obstinacy of his faith when my own faith is cracked and breaking. "Everything has changed."

He holds my gaze, but I can see in his eyes that my words strike deep, hitting a dissonant chord.

"Elath's body is a tree," I harangue him. "How many trees are there in the world, Tavik? And if we happen to find the right tree, what exactly are we supposed to do with the Vessel and the Sword? What are we supposed to do with *me*?"

He pulls the cloth away from my nose to examine his work, and I realize that he's using a piece of my Daughter's sash to stanch the bleeding. He speaks, his words calm when mine are fiery. "One thing at a time, remember? We have the Vessel. We need the Sword. And now we know what that Sword is and who has it." He stops dabbing my face and meets my gaze again, his face made soft and lovely with a new sadness. "Let's get the Sword. Then we'll worry about finding the Mother's body, all right?"

"So in addition to becoming the Vessel of the demon that the Goodson loathes, I must steal the Hand of the Father from him?"

"Elath is not a demon. Please tell me you understand that now."

"The only thing I understand is that I understand nothing. I never have, and maybe I never will." I stare down at the text that has just shaken my belief—my life—to the core, and Tavik's as well, the bottom corner stained with my blood. Somehow, Brother

Miklos must have found out what Zofia discovered, and he killed her for it. If he figures out we have it, he'll have another reason to hunt us down.

I wish I knew where the Goodson stands in all this. In my mind, I see him kissing my hand the day I was chosen. I see him slaying the telleg to keep me safe. The triptych, his gift to me, rests against my breastbone, a reminder of his steady and unwavering presence in my life when the only other person I loved and trusted was lying to me all along. Even if the faith the Goodson gave me turns to dust, at least he believed he was telling me the truth, and the only reason I'm alive today is because he saved my life in the Dead Forest. I can't imagine he would want to harm me, no matter what I know or what I've become. So I resolve to find him, not to take the Hand of the Father from him but to beg him to save me, just as Ovin saved Vinnica. He may be the only person in the world who can.

"You're right," I tell Tavik at last. "One thing at a time. We need to find the Goodson."

"Thank you," he breathes as he blots away the remaining blood under my nose with a gentleness that makes my heart hurt.

Twenty

There's a tap at the door, and Tavik barely has time to stuff the parchment pieces down his shirt before Ambrus pokes his head in. "Thought you might want some tea and toast." The apothecary crosses the room to set a tray down on the table. "Also, er, I'm not sure what it is you're doing up here, but could you do it more quietly? I can hear you two floors below, and the shop is open, you know."

"I am sorry," Tavik tells Ambrus in Rosvanian without the need for a translation, and it occurs to me that I'm not the only one who sounds like an epic poem when speaking a second language.

"Contractions," I murmur. "Two can play that game."

Tavik wrinkles his nose in annoyance. "Can you ask him if he has any news of the war or the Order or where the Goodson might be?"

"I don't know where the Goodson is, but I might be able to find out," Ambrus answers after I've translated. "As for the rest, you'll have to wait until I close up. Hopefully, the messenger will have come back by then." With that, he returns to his shop downstairs.

Ambrus's last words remind me of yet another pressing question I need Tavik to answer. "Who exactly is this man you sent a message to, and what did you tell him?"

"Rusik DeRopa is captain of my Two-Swords division and one of the team who opened the Vault of Mount Djall twelve years ago. When the Prima proposed this mission, he suggested me."

"Why would DeRopa send you? Why not send someone older and more experienced? You are so young."

"DeRopa sent me because, in case you haven't noticed, I'm really good at what I do," he informs me in a voice soured by offense.

I nearly retort, "Killing people, you mean?" but I bite back the words. It won't do either of us any good to start sniping at each other. "I am sorry," I tell him. "I am grateful for your help."

He gives me a nod, and a truce settles between us.

"What did the message say, the one you sent to DeRopa?"

Tavik picks up a Shakki piece and rolls it between his palms. "Everything."

I give him an incredulous laugh. "How could you fit everything on that tiny slip of paper?"

"We use shorthand. I told him that the Mother wasn't free and that you were the Vessel and that we're in Dalment. Please advise."

I blanch so quickly I feel light-headed. "Oh my Father, you really told him everything."

"It's all right. I trust DeRopa with my life."

"But I do not trust him with mine. The Goodson is like a

father to me, and yet I doubt very much that you would trust him just because I asked you to. Even if this DeRopa is the most trustworthy man alive, what if Brother Miklos intercepts that message?"

"I get that you're concerned, but we don't have a lot of options right now, and we need all the help we can get. If anyone can help us, it's Captain DeRopa."

"Define 'help.'"

"Help is help."

"Help is killing people, as far as you are concerned." When Tavik opens his mouth to speak, I hold up one long finger. "If you tell me to use contractions right now, I swear I shall sing the apocalyptic hymns of Saint Wenslas at you."

Bone weary, I rest my palms on the table and let the wood take my weight.

"Are you all right?" Tavik asks, genuinely concerned when only minutes earlier I think he wanted to shake me until my teeth rattled.

"I need to sleep." I look up and meet his worried eyes. "But I would like to pray first."

"Of course."

"In private."

He gestures around the room. "Where am I going to go?"

"Fine, then. Watch me pray." I'm half tempted to sing *The Song of Saint Wenslas* out of spite. I take myself off to the corner of the room farthest from him, kneel, and press my forehead to the dusty floorboards.

Holy Father, I think, *if ever you wanted to answer my prayers, now would be the time.* Keeping my voice low so no one can hear me downstairs, I sing "The Vessel's Prayer" from *The Song of Saint Lanya.*

> *Father, most high and most exalted,*
> *I am your humble Vessel.*
> *You have made my mouth clean to sing Your praise.*
> *You have made my tongue straight to spread Your word.*
> *You have made my body pure to receive Your spirit.*
> *You have given me life to reflect the light of Heaven for all to see.*
> *You have given me death that I may live eternally*
> *In the light of the Father.*

I fill my prayer with the notes of my longing to be heard, to be understood, to be valued in the eyes of the One True God. But there is no answer, no sense that the Father is listening. There never is.

My prayer done, I climb into the lone bed and bury myself beneath the blankets.

I stand next to Zofia in the convent courtyard, gazing at the statue of Saint Vinnica. "You lied to me," I fume. "Then you left me."

"Most people just say hello," she says, managing to sound both joking and a little hurt at the same time.

"You started a war, Zofia. Men are dying because of what you did."

"Ovin started this war long ago, Daughter, and I have to believe on some level you understand that."

I cross my arms. I can tell she's looking at me, but I don't return the favor.

"I used to think it was a blessing that you had forgotten who you were, where you came from," she says. "The world is an easier place to bear when you don't have to question it."

I've been grasping at thin memories of my past for months now, even though I know it's wrong, and now here is Zofia—or, at least, the memory of her—telling me my life is easier without them. I finally turn on her. "You think I wanted to forget?"

"Yes, I do. But by the time you decided to remember, it was too late."

I turn away once more to glare at Vinnica, prison and prisoner.

"You have to remember who you are and where you came from," Zofia tells me. "For everyone. And everything."

"I know who I am!" I shout, but no one is there. Her absence is tangible, a marked emptiness, a hole in a lovely cloth that no one can mend.

Twenty-One

I wake hours later to Ambrus's rapping at the attic door. "The messenger is back," he says as I drag myself awake, and Tavik is on his feet and out the door before I can untangle myself from the bedding.

"You asked for news? I have conflicting reports," says the apothecary as I catch up with them on the stairs. "Official channels say the Tovnians are holding the Kantari at bay, but my Milk Road contacts indicate that the Kantari are cutting their way north at an astonishing pace. I suspect reality lies somewhere between the two. As for the Goodson, he was last spotted crossing the Sargo on the Kings Road, so all I can tell you is that he may be heading west. His retinue is extremely small, and it seems odd to me that he's traveling away from the Tovnian front rather than toward it. What I *can* tell you beyond a shadow of a doubt is that Brother Miklos is actively searching for you two, although I do not know his exact whereabouts. Additionally, the kings of Rosvania, Auria, and Ukrent have warrants out for your arrest at the behest of the Holy Ovinist See."

"Oh," I say, the most inadequate syllable ever to exit my mouth. I translate for Tavik.

"It gets worse. King Horac of Tovnia has a price on Tavik's head. The Tovnians say he assassinated Prince Horaccio. As a matter of fact, they say he single-handedly killed nearly thirty men. Is that true?"

"Nice," Tavik says in Kantari with no little bitterness when I translate Ambrus's avalanche of bad news. "Can you explain reality to this man?"

I'm not champing at the bit to defend Tavik, but the reports aren't true, so I set Ambrus straight. By now, we've reached the window, where Tavik takes the soulswift from her coop with a careful hand. He can be as gentle as he likes; it's still upsetting.

"What does the message say?" Ambrus asks. "And what did you send to begin with?"

"He requested his next orders from his captain," I explain, keeping only to the vaguest details. The less Ambrus knows, the better as far as I'm concerned.

Tavik removes the note from the canister and places the soulswift back in its coop. A frown pulls down his mouth. "He says the Kantari army has made it to Varos da Lotharo. I'm supposed to stay put. He's sending help."

I don't really want to translate for Ambrus, but I see nothing for it. "DeRopa is sending men?" I add warily in Kantari.

Tavik is already scribbling a new note as he answers, "I'm

telling him not to come." Then he switches to Rosvanian for the apothecary's sake. "Ambrus, a map?"

Ambrus scurries over to a small bookshelf and pulls out an atlas, which he sets on the desk, opening it to a map of the north.

"Where is Varos da Lotharo?" Tavik asks, still speaking in Rosvanian as we bow over the book. Ambrus points a neat fingernail at a town in east central Tovnia. It's much closer to Rosvania than I thought.

"I'd say your Milk Road contacts are closer to the truth than the Rosvanian reports," I comment to Ambrus, troubled. I can't believe the Kantari army has made it this close to the Rosvanian border.

"So the Kantari are here," says Tavik, placing his finger next to Ambrus's. "We're here." With the index finger of his opposite hand, he points to Dalment. "And the Goodson is . . . ?"

The Kings Road is the main highway running east and west through the north, and I point to the spot where it crosses the Sargo on Saint Nadel's Bridge. "Probably around here."

"Where would he be going?" Tavik muses in Kantari.

Ambrus frowns at my finger. "You're not traveling *toward* the Goodson, are you? Shouldn't you be running in the opposite direction?"

"Why are we telling him any of this?" I murmur to Tavik in Kantari.

"Because we need the help of the Milk Road to track down the Sword. Tell him we need to follow the Goodson."

My necklace feels like lead around my neck. "To be perfectly clear: I will not help you if you plan to kill or hurt Goodson Anskar. You don't need to kill a man to disarm him."

"Of course I'd rather steal the Sword than fight him for it, but I'm not making any promises I can't keep. Do you have any idea how hard it would be to take a sword from me? Same goes for the Goodson." Tavik switches back to Rosvanian to ask Ambrus, "Can you help us find the Goodson?"

"Possibly. If you're heading west, I can mark a few places where you can stop between here and Juprachen, and I'll do my best to keep you off the Kings Road. The farther you get from Dalment, the fewer contacts I have, so if you track the Goodson beyond Juprachen, you'll have to rely on others for help." Ambrus tears the map from the atlas and adds, "It would be wise for you to leave any valuables in my care. Is there anything you'd like to store under the protection of the Milk Road? That necklace, perhaps, my dear?"

I get the sensation that Ambrus and I are playing another game of Shakki, and that I am about to lose badly. I pull up on the chain around my neck. The Goodson's gift to me dangles from my hand, reflecting the light of Ambrus's candle. "It's just a necklace."

"So you tell me."

Perplexed, Tavik looks from the triptych to Ambrus, then puts a hand over mine, pushing it back down. "We will keep it. Thank you."

"I see." Ambrus smiles thinly. "Give me an hour. I should have your map ready for you by then."

We leave Ambrus's room, but Tavik stops me on the stairwell. "What was that about?"

I glance at Ambrus's closed door over his shoulder. "I'm not sure. He wanted to look at my triptych while you were sleeping, but I wouldn't let him. I didn't let Mistress Dyer look at it either back in Varos da Vinnica."

"Why not?"

"I don't know. It's personal. They must think I'm trying to hide something."

"Like the Vessel that holds Elath the Mother, for instance?"

My hand flies to my mouth. "Does he think . . . ?"

Tavik looks behind him at Ambrus's door, before nodding up the stairs. We don't start talking again until we're back in the attic with the door shut. "I'm trying to decide if this is a good thing or a bad thing," he says, pacing the floor. "Might be a good thing. Maybe? It's definitely A Thing now."

"I could go prove him wrong."

"No, I'd rather he and his northern buddies believe some worthless trinket holds the Mother rather than—"

I step in front of him, forcing him to stop. "It is not worthless."

"All I'm saying is let them believe what they want to believe, as long as it keeps you safe."

"Because of what I am." I walk over to the bed and plop down on the mattress. It feels like the weight of the world is pushing me farther into the tick. Tavik comes to sit beside me, so close his hip presses against mine, but I don't scoot away from him.

"Can I see it?" he asks.

I hesitate. My necklace is the only thing that truly belongs to me, and showing it to Tavik feels like an act of friendship. We're not supposed to be friends.

"I know it's important to you, but it's just a necklace, right?

You're not actually hiding the Mother in that thing."

I relent, taking the chain from around my neck and handing it to him. He turns it over on the palm of his callused hand, studying it. "This looks Kantari."

"It is. A Kantari convert made it."

"That explains why it's so beautiful. May I open it?"

I wouldn't let Mistress Dyer or Ambrus look inside, but it's different with Tavik. I don't have much to hide from him at this point. I nod, and he pulls back the gold panels with careful fingers.

"What am I looking at? Saint Ovin, obviously, but who are the other two?"

I lean in to point at the two girls, close enough to notice that Tavik still smells faintly of lavender. "Saint Vinnica and Saint Lanya."

"His daughters. Of course. What's their story? In Gelya-land, I mean?"

"Now I am the one telling bedtime stories?"

He looks up, his face just inches from mine, and I can feel my own face go red and blotchy. I don't let my gaze falter, much as I might want to. I don't want him to know he makes me . . . uncomfortable? Shy?

"Vinnica was the most innocent girl in the world, a young woman without sin," I explain, covering my embarrassment. "That made her the only person pure enough to contain the Great Demon and trap the evil spirit within her body. When Ovin slew Elath with the Hand of the Father, Vinnica was there to receive the demon's immortal soul."

"Wait a minute. So when Ovin sealed Elath in the Vault of Mount Djall, he actually imprisoned his own daughter at the same time?"

"Yes."

"Was she dead?"

"No."

"He buried his own daughter alive?"

"Her sacrifice saved millions of souls. She was glad to do it." But even as I say the words, I have to question them. If I were happy to make the same sacrifice, I would already be locked away now. The truth is that I'm terrified by the prospect, which is why I'm sitting side by side with a Kantari Two-Swords in an Elathian's attic.

"I highly doubt that," says Tavik. He stares down at the little Saint Vinnica in his hand. "Wow. She died cold and alone in the vault with a thing she thought was evil incarnate inside her."

"Actually, while the Great Demon lives, Vinnica cannot die."

"Are you kidding me? Holy good Mother! Did Ovin at least bury her with a good book?"

He looks up when I don't answer right away. The words that spill off my tongue are so heretical that I can't help but feel a stab of guilt for saying them. "She wasn't buried in the vault. We know that now."

His face grows more pitying, not less, but I don't think it's Vinnica he pities at this moment, and my eyes well up.

"And what's Lanya's story?" he asks softly.

"Lanya, the sister who is not important?" I joke, holding the sadness at bay.

He gives me a crooked grin. "Yeah, her."

"She grieved for her sister, so the Father planted the Grace Tree in Saint Vinnica's honor. Lanya would visit the tree and be comforted. One day, the tree grew a single flower—"

Tavik's eyes go distant. "Five white petals turning pink toward the heart."

"Yes. And from that flower came a seedpod. When Lanya held it in her hand, it burst, and she felt . . ." My words trail off, trying to recapture the moment when the Father chose me.

"Like a song trapped in a cave . . . ," Tavik fills in.

". . . like the newly lit wick of a lamp." I look at Tavik, making the connection, finding this strange similarity between us that I had never before considered. "Did it feel the same when you were chosen?"

"Yeah." For once, I can look him in the eye without feeling self-conscious. There are so few people in the world who understand what it's like to be chosen by a god, whether you want to be or not.

"When the seedpod burst in her hand, she found that she could speak all the languages of the world, even Sanctus, the Father's Word. The One True God told her to sing the story for the faithful, and it became the first of *The Songs of the Saints*."

"*The Song of Saint Vinnica*?" Tavik guesses.

"No, *The Song of Saint Ovin*. There is no *Song of Saint Vinnica*. We learn of her sacrifice through her father's song."

Tavik frowns at my open triptych in his hand. "That's so depressing."

He's right. It is depressing. How could I have failed to see that before now? *Because you didn't have to see it until two days ago,* I remind myself. *Of course you see it now. You* are *Vinnica.*

Tavik wears his pity, as clear as glass. Pity for Vinnica. Pity for me. It's all the same. As I tell him the rest of the story, the words feel empty, because the story we put together today negates so much of what I was taught as absolute truth.

"Anyway, Saint Ovin founded the Convent of Saint Vinnica in his daughter's honor, with the Grace Tree at its heart, and Lanya became the first Sacrist. When she died, she was so dedicated to the Father that she transcended her mortal body and became the first soulswift."

"And soulswifts carry the souls of the faithful to some wonderful afterlife in the sky?"

"To heaven, yes."

"How did souls go to heaven before Saint Lanya?"

"They didn't. Back then, when a body died, the soul remained on earth in the Dead Forest. Only by containing Elath's worldly influence are we able to live eternally beside the One True God in heaven. If Elath is set free again, it will be the end of the soul's everlasting life in paradise. That's why the Order wants to find us."

"They want to find *you.* They want to *stop* me."

I take my necklace from his hand, close the triptych, and put it back around my neck. "They want to save the world, just like you do."

Twenty-Two

We've only been back in the attic for twenty minutes when Ambrus comes rushing in, the map from the atlas clutched in his neat hands.

"What is it?" I ask, a fresh fear taking root in the pit of my stomach.

"Brother Miklos and his men were last spotted in Oltagov." Ambrus is already flattening the map of the north on the table as Tavik asks, "Oltagov? Where is Oltagov?"

"Here," Ambrus and I answer in unison, each of us with a finger on the same point only three miles from Dalment.

"Father of death."

"Time to fly, my birdies," says Ambrus.

We're ready to go within minutes. It's a simple matter of leaving the way we came, only this time there's no hackney. Cloaked in our pilgrims' robes, Tavik and I walk a quarter mile down Saint Polova Street and take a right at Market Row, heading straight for the west gate, where, hopefully, Ambrus's guard friend will wave us through without batting an eye. You'd think we would stick out like a pair of sore thumbs, but Dalment is one of the larger cities in the province, and we blend in far easier than we might have in a smaller town. I pass plenty of foreign faces in this crowd, many of them wearing pilgrims' robes like us, so no one gives us a second glance. My newfound anonymity is short-lived, however, because once we're in line to exit the city gate, we see four Knights of the Order a few yards ahead, slapping Ambrus's guard.

One of them is Brother Miklos.

"Oh, death," Tavik curses. He takes me by the arm and drags me in the opposite direction. Just before my head turns with the rest of me, Ambrus's "good lad" spots me, and he points at us.

"You!" Brother Miklos's deep voice rings out behind us. The word feels like an arrow shot into my back. Tavik and I come to a halt.

"Follow my lead, and do exactly as I say," Tavik murmurs quietly before he plasters a grin on his face, turns, and calls out, "Brothers!"

He still has me by the arm, only now he escorts me *toward* the knights. Holy Father.

"Young man." Brother Miklos acknowledges him while I pull my hood down as low as it will go. "You look remarkably like the killer we're looking for. A Kantari. Have you seen him?"

Tavik laughs and steps into his Ukrenti accent. "Oh, you northerners. You think all southerners look the same."

Miklos doesn't return Tavik's smile. "And I suppose that's your 'wife'?"

I'm tempted to rip my arm out of Tavik's grasp and make a run for it. I don't know if he senses my panic, but his hand tightens around my arm as he draws me in close for a fake cuddle. "My little tick," he calls me in Ukrenti, and if I weren't about to vomit from fright I'd be impressed that he knows an Ukrenti endearment.

"My sweet wine," I offer back in Degmari, with an unconvincing smile that no one can see with my head buried in my hood.

They can help you, Gelya, a small but mighty voice shouts in my head even as a larger and mightier voice screams, *That's the man who killed Zofia, you idiot.*

I glance up and see Brother Miklos nod at one of his men, the gesture that probably sent an army to destroy Tavik's town. The knight yanks back my hood, revealing my shorn head. It doesn't hurt, but there's a violence to it, a sense of violation just as hurtful as a slap to the face, leaving me as scared and powerless as I was in the Dead Forest all those years ago.

"Your 'little tick' is a Daughter of Saint Vinnica," Brother Miklos's lackey sneers at Tavik.

Tavik's smiling veneer transforms into a glare deadlier than the blades he carries beneath his robe. In a voice that could freeze blood, he tells the knight, "Oh, that was a bad idea."

With unnatural speed he whirls out of his robe, whipping the fabric across the knight's face. The man reels backward, flinching in pain, a hand coming up to cover his scratched eye as he blindly stabs his sword point in Tavik's direction. In one motion, Tavik pushes me behind him and dodges the attack, wrapping the man's arm in the cloak. He twists and pulls, and the man collapses to his knees, screaming in agony as a bone breaks with a nauseating *crack*.

Tavik's eyes flash at me. "Run!"

I sprint through the streets of Dalment, weaving through crowds and plowing into anyone who gets in my way. Tavik is hard on my heels, panting behind me.

Until he isn't.

I slow down to look for him as panicked Dalmenti rush past me, and I find him several feet behind me, fighting Brother Miklos and the other two knights at once. When one of the men swings at his legs, he leaps into the air, higher than any normal boy could. When another slashes at his airborne torso, he bends in midair, flipping all the way around until he lands on his feet, facing them again, swords out and ready. He blocks two blows from two different men while kicking the third hard in the stomach, knocking the knight into a wall.

He fights the way he prays, with his whole body, a beautiful and deadly dance, but the combined skill of three knights is too much. He inches closer to me with each defensive maneuver.

My instincts bellow at me to run as far from Brother Miklos as I can, but while I've only known Tavik for two days, I can't leave him to get cut to ribbons. My eyes land on a weathered brick lying in the littered street. Without a second thought, I pick it up and hurl it as hard as I can at Brother Miklos. When it hits him in the ribs, he cries out and staggers sideways in pain.

Tavik uses the advantage to fall back, but instead of telling me to run again, he slams his right-hand sword into its scabbard and reaches for me. The next minute is a terrifying fog of sight and sound and feeling as Tavik physically moves me wherever he needs me to be while fending off two knights with the Sword of Mercy alone. He rolls me over his back, casts me sideways, catches me before I plummet down a city well, but he's wearing down fast.

One of the knights takes hold of my cloak and pulls me to him. Tavik lashes out, cutting through the fabric. The next thing I know, Tavik has me pinned against him, my full length plastered to his front as he sweats against my cheek and breathes hard in my ear.

The Sword of Mercy is at my throat.

Brother Miklos regains his footing just in time to call a halt, and the men freeze. A long pause thunders between us, with Tavik gasping in exhaustion and me gasping in terror.

"You wouldn't," Brother Miklos pants.

"Would I not?" Tavik seethes in Rosvanian. "What will happen if I open the Mother's prison here, now?"

"Tavik?" I whimper. For once, my body responds rationally, quaking in fear, while my mind refuses to accept reality. All I can think is *He was supposed to be my friend.*

"Shut up!" He grips me so hard I can't draw breath. The blade at my throat presses in, cutting into the skin of my neck.

I trusted him.

First Zofia, now Tavik.

Why did I trust him?

Even now, as he holds a blade to my throat, there's a part of me that trusts him, the part of me that clings to the moment he vowed to protect my life with the last breath of his body.

Without warning, Tavik charges at the men, pulling me behind him as he slashes his way past the knights. We're heading straight into the wall of a house. I scream, my body bracing for impact, when Tavik leaps, taking me with him all the way to the roof above us. I have no time to adjust to the new perspective because he's still running, dragging me behind his madness.

"Tavik!"

"Jump!" he shouts, and I do. My stomach drops as I rise, and now we're on the next roof over, even higher than the last.

We're still running, Tavik as sure-footed as a cat and me stumbling, sending roof tiles raining down to the street sickeningly far below. Our breakneck pace is leading us straight to the edge of the building with nothing but the top of the city wall and the earth below us. I scream so loudly, I feel as though I've set fire to the inside of my throat.

"Jump!"

His arm wraps around my waist, and we're flying.

Then falling.

Down to the top of the wall.

Another jump. Tavik's arm is hard around my middle, and we drop, down and down. The ground rises, and Tavik's whole body wraps me up as we hit the ground, the two of us one body rolling and rolling until we finally come to a dizzying stop.

I'm spread-eagle in the grass, the air knocked clean out of my lungs. Tavik's face is in mine, sharp, focused, a pinpoint of energy. "Are you hurt?"

"I . . . I . . ."

"Any broken bones?"

I cough, fighting for air.

"Good. Let's go."

He pulls me to my feet by the scruff of my cloak and takes off running again, straight for the queue of people waiting to pass through the city gate. Every man, woman, and child in that line gawks at us as if the circus has just arrived.

Tavik grabs one man's horse by the bridle. "I need this."

"Um." But that's all the man has time to utter before Tavik forcibly removes him from the saddle and leaps up to take his place.

"Hey!" the man protests as Tavik reaches down and pulls me up in front of him.

"Thank you!" Tavik calls back in Rosvanian, and we gallop off to the west, leaving Dalment behind us and nothing but the slimmest hope ahead.

Twenty-Three

We make it to a stable beside a run-down farmhouse before we stop and dismount. I'm not used to riding horses, and I've lost all feeling from the waist down. I fall over when my feet hit the ground. Tavik helps me up, but not before he slaps the horse's rump, sending it running off to the south.

"Come on. We need to hide."

Thankfully, the stable is empty except for a tabby cat and a cow. My body is so thoroughly out of commission that Tavik has to shove me up the ladder to the hayloft by my bottom, but I'm too shaken by our narrow escape from Brother Miklos to care much about the indignity of it. Once I'm safely stowed away in the loft's darkest corner, we spend the next hour in silence, Tavik crouched and waiting by the ladder, the Sword of Mercy clutched in his left hand.

Silence is a fresh torture, giving my mind the required space to reconsider and question and doubt as the uncanny presence within me hums, unwilling to be ignored. I can't tell right from wrong anymore. Is staying with Tavik the right thing to do? Should I have turned myself in to the Order in Dalment when I had the chance? Yet how could I give myself over to the man who murdered Zofia?

An idea strikes me, a plausible answer for Goodson Anskar's actions—or *in*action—the night of the summit. What if there was a coup? What if Brother Miklos wrested command of the Order away from the Goodson? Tavik said Miklos massacred an entire Kantari town, and I witnessed his murder of Zofia with my own eyes. He let assassins slaughter a roomful of men. I can't believe the Goodson would hurt me, but I can well believe Brother Miklos would. The more I consider this possibility, the more it rings true. For all I know, Goodson Anskar's position is as precarious as mine. What if he can't help me?

The sound of the barn door creaking open below cuts through my thoughts and turns my body into a vise tightening with fear as the farmer comes in with his workhorse shortly before dusk. He spends an eternity rubbing the beast down and brushing it out, but I think it's safe to assume that my screeching anxiety makes time stretch unnaturally. Once the farmer finally leaves, I let the back of my head hit the wall behind me.

"We're going to be caught, sooner or later," I tell Tavik bitterly as he scuffles toward me through the hay. He looks worn in the dim light seeping in between the barn's wooden slats.

"No, we're not."

"Yes, we are." And is that such a bad thing? To be caught? To have my choices taken from me? An answer bubbles up from deep inside me, and I don't know if it comes from myself or from the spirit my body houses. In either case, it's loud and clear: *Yes, that is a bad thing.*

Tavik puts the Sword of Mercy back in its scabbard and squats in front of me. "I vowed to keep you safe. Don't you trust me?"

The cut on my neck stings, reminding me of what he did to me today, and I give him a hard look. "You held a blade to my throat. Again."

"I was bluffing."

"Then you essentially told Brother Miklos that I'm the Vessel of Elath."

"Uh, hello? He's the Goodson's right-hand man. He already knew. Why do you think the Order is after us?"

"You don't know that," I argue, my theory taking root and growing steadily in my mind.

"Pretty sure I do."

I sigh as he sits down next to me. I don't have the energy to debate this with him right now. Eventually, he breaks the silence.

"You saved my life today."

I shrug. "Maybe."

"You did. A knight like Brother Miklos only lives that long because he's a fantastic fighter. If you hadn't taken him out of commission when you did, I'd be a dead man." He holds up the ring of his index finger and thumb in front of me.

"This again?" I ask wearily.

"The last time was a bargain. This is an oath. We are going to make the Official Circle Swear of Friendship." He traces a line around his circle with the index finger of his opposite hand. "You see this? A ring is infinite, no beginning and no end. That's what I'm offering you."

"Eternity?"

"Eternal friendship."

I breathe out a humorless laugh. "You are ridiculous."

"I'm very serious here." Irony tinges his voice, letting me know this is all hyperbolic, meant to amuse me. And yet there's an odd sanctity in the moment, the sense that if I lock my ring with his, I'm attaching a part of myself to him that I can't take back.

He shakes his circle at me, insistent. "Friends?"

I remember how he knelt before me in reverence as he vowed to keep me safe.

"Gelya," he says softly.

Not a Daughter. Not a Vessel. Me.

Maybe he can see the girl who lives inside this body after all.

I lock my ring inside Tavik's, my fingers pale against his. "Friends," I agree, and as I stare at our intertwined rings, my resolve to leave Tavik when we find the Goodson suddenly feels more like a suggestion than a firm course of action.

Tavik takes both my hands in his and rubs them briskly.

"Um?" I ask in alarm. I'm not used to being touched, and I'm definitely not used to being touched by a boy, friend or not. My stomach flutters in a way that is completely unrelated to the immortal life inside me.

"Your hands are freezing, pal."

"I'm all right," I assure him, taking my hands back, even though they're cold as ice.

I know I might have to leave Tavik eventually. I know I might have to go my own way and let him go his somewhere down the road. But I also know this: given the opportunity, I would throw that brick at Brother Miklos again and again and again.

Tavik promised to protect me. As it turns out, I'd do the same for him.

III.

The Sword

Twenty-Four

According to Ambrus's map, we're heading to a safe house in the Pavane Forest, sixteen miles northwest of Dalment. We're definitely not going to make it that far before daybreak, but hopefully we can get under the cover of trees.

"How much do you trust Ambrus?" I ask Tavik as we trek across a pasture and try not to trip over the sheep.

"More than you do, I think. Look, even if Ambrus is not the sweet old man we thought he was, the Milk Road is our best bet to find the Goodson and get our hands on the Sword. And with a price on our heads—or my head, at least—we don't have much of a choice now, do we?"

I can't disagree with that.

A drop of water plinks on my head, followed by another that trickles down my cheek. I turn my face to the night sky and scowl as the raindrops grow fat and plentiful, drenching my skin, making my clothes wet and heavy. Considering everything that's happened over the past few days, the sudden storm takes on an ominously prophetic tone, as if the thunder is Saint Wenslas shaking his apocalyptic verses at us, shouting, "I told you so!"

Tavik moves through the muddy fields with sure-footed grace. I, however, slip and slide and trip over every rock in our path and a few sheep as well, mostly because I'm exhausted. Normally, when I use my gift, it takes me an hour or so to recover, but singing *The Ludoïd* took so much out of me that my body is still sluggish and clumsy. Then again, can I really say I relied on my own abilities? To be honest, I'm not certain what happened in Ambrus's attic. All I know is that singing *The Ludoïd* felt good and right when the Father's Word has only ever felt cold and heavy before. Whatever the case, I'm worn out, and by the time the sky begins to lighten, my right big toe is nothing but a giant bruise, and my legs hate me.

The Pavane Forest evolves from a dark distant blur to an army of oaks, beeches, and—my namesake—gelya trees. Once we're safe under the canopy and moderately drier as a result, Tavik inexplicably grows more fretful rather than less. "What if we're wasting all this time moving west, only to find that the Goodson has veered off in a different direction? Or what if the Milk Road loses track of him altogether?"

"The world will not end if we don't find the Goodson tomorrow," I tell him wearily.

He looks at me sharply, then drops his gaze. "Help me build a shelter, will you?"

We prop fallen branches against a tree trunk to fashion a rough lean-to and stuff wet leaves into the cracks. The second it's complete, I crawl inside to sleep, to dream of Zofia and of a slaughtered stag beneath a great tree whose roots give birth to a stream.

I don't know if Tavik slept beside me, because by the time I wake up, he's already up and praying. The movements are exactly the same as before, only now the rain makes his skin wet and slick. Once again, his shirt is off, and once again, I can't tear my eyes away. As he comes out of the logic-defying backbend and sweeps his blades low to the earth, he gives me a full view of his many scars. I have the giddy urge to run my fingertips over his skin, to read him like the embossed text of *The Songs* sitting on my desk in the scriptorium. Could I sing the song of his body, or would I feel only lean muscle, rough skin, the heat of him?

The fact that I'm asking myself this question unnerves me. Many of *The Songs* warn the faithful of the earthly temptation of another's flesh outside of wedlock. I just never in a million years thought such a warning would apply to me. Well, I'm fairly certain that it applies to me now, and a sense of shame settles in my stomach right alongside the unwelcome spirit who has taken up residence inside me.

I always thought beauty belonged to the realm of women, but Tavik challenges that assumption, just as he has challenged my entire world from the second I met him. Even the crooked line of his nose is a work of art. If he had been a snaggletoothed ogre, would I have followed him as far as I have? And what does that say about me that I did and am? If Elath really is the Great Demon, what better instrument than Tavik could She have devised to tempt me away from the path of the One True God? He is walking, talking temptation.

He loses control of his swords and drops one in the exact same place he dropped both weapons the last time I watched.

"Father of death!" he spits. "And hello, Gelya."

Caught again. How annoying. I take my cue to crawl out of our makeshift shelter as he puts his shirt back on, thank the Father. "I hope you don't mind my watching."

He shrugs. "What do I have to be ashamed of?"

Would that my own faith were as steadfast. I wouldn't be in this mess if it was.

"I don't always mess up that last bit," he adds. "It's just that these northern swords are much longer and heavier than Kantari blades. I feel like they're trying to rip me in half when I bend back for the Acceptance of Death, so by the time I transition into the Triumph over the Dark Night, I'm kind of done for."

Those are unusually poetic words pouring out of Tavik's mouth, and I'm never one to turn down the opportunity to learn something new. "What is the Acceptance of Death?" I ask him. "Or the Triumph over the Dark Night?"

"Each gesture of the prayer has a name. Those are two of the gestures."

"Are you required to pray with your shirt off?"

"Why?" He cocks an eyebrow at me. "Like what you see?"

"That is not what I meant! I am simply curious." Except I do like what I see, and I'm sure that I'm wearing the telltale blush as a result.

He comes a little closer than I find comfortable and explains, "You're showing the Mother and Father that you have no breasts, that you are death giving, not life giving."

The word *breasts* hovers in the air between us, and my skin grows hotter. Tavik throws his head back and crows with laughter.

"What?" I ask, irritated.

"You're blushing so hard you've turned purple. You know breasts exist for feeding babies, right? Like, even camels have them. Holy Mother, your face! This is hilarious!"

I could single-handedly light up a small city with the humiliated burning of my skin, which makes me want to poke holes into what Tavik believes the way he keeps prodding my own faith. "What if a woman does not want to give life? Or cannot? What if a man would rather raise children than fight or kill or hunt? Is there no room for people who don't fit into either of your narrow boxes?"

"I didn't say that. I'm just speaking in generalities here."

"Generalities are small-minded and annoying," I inform him.

He holds a hand to his heart in mock offense. "Are you saying that I'm annoying? Because I'm pretty sure you find me charming."

"Are you sure of that? Are you really?"

He laughs again, careless and full-throated, dissolving my embarrassment as easily as he might blow steam off a cup of tea. A Vessel is supposed to remain pure to be worthy of the Father's Word, but the way Tavik inhabits his own skin makes me wonder what it's like to live in a world that doesn't threaten your immortal soul.

Walking. Talking. Temptation.

Father above, I hope we find the Goodson soon.

A damp ten-mile hike leads us to the first safe house on Ambrus's map, a cottage belonging to a middle-aged forester, his wife, and their seven children. Two of them—a boy and a girl who are no longer babies but not old enough to understand personal boundaries—beg to touch the top of my head. Their sticky hands are child plump and none too gentle, but I let them, and I find myself laughing as they giggle over my stubble.

I don't know why, but I always imagined the secret Elathians as adults. It never occurred to me that they would have children whom they would raise to worship Elath as their Mother. If the Father is good, how can He believe these innocents deserve to become the telleg that haunt the Dead Forest for eternity?

I look at Tavik, speaking his broken Rosvanian with Forester beside a roaring blaze in the fireplace, believing himself a man when he is anything but, so confident and comfortable in the world and his place in it. Does that make him right? Or does that make him an arrogant fool? In either case, I envy his immovable faith.

"Hey, Gelya, can you come here for a minute? I think I understand what he's saying, but I want to be sure."

I'd rather stay where I am. All the girls of the family have congregated around the kitchen stove, and I don't feel at ease crossing the room toward Tavik and Forester. I had to borrow one of Mistress Forester's dresses to wear while my own clothes dry out in the rafters, and because I'm so much bigger than she is, it clings too tightly to my body.

"Gelya, I need you," Tavik insists in his overly dramatic way.

I sigh, cross my arms over my chest, and come to his rescue. "Yes?"

"How would you like to be a man for a little while?"

I eye him suspiciously. "I don't think I heard you correctly. What?"

It's Forester who replies. "The wife and I thought about it, and it doesn't make sense for you to be traveling like pilgrims when you're heading away from the holy sites, not toward them."

"And I can't carry my weapons if we're disguised as pilgrims," Tavik adds in Kantari.

"Also, sorry, miss, but that head of yours ain't normal for a girl."

"I missed that. What's he saying?" Tavik asks.

"He says that I'm hard to hide because of my shorn head."

"But you could disguise yourself a man," says Tavik, speaking eagerly in Kantari. "That's what he's getting at. Men wear their hair short up here."

"But most men don't carry swords," I point out.

"Knights do."

I switch back to Rosvanian to ask the next question, although I can't believe I'm uttering the words: "We're going to disguise ourselves as Knights of the Order of Saint Ovin?"

Tavik grins. "It's a great idea, right? We're the prey, but we're going to disguise ourselves as the predator. Now we don't have to worry about hiding your head, and I'll have easy access to my sword *and* yours."

Forester studies me and shakes his head. "You might pass for a boy, but you'll still stand out. Guess we'll say you're Degmari. Not enough of them around for anyone to know you don't pass for one."

"What is he saying?" Tavik asks me.

"Nothing," I answer. I don't know what the Kantari think about the Hedenski, and I'd rather not find out.

"The Goodson?" Tavik asks Forester in Rosvanian. "You know where he is?"

"Still on the Kings Road, heading west."

"And Brother Miklos?" I add.

"Last seen scouring the towns south and southwest of Dalment, so he seems to have lost your scent, at least for now."

"Well, that's good news," says Tavik when I translate the answer for him. "How do you say 'messenger' in Rosvanian?"

"I think you mean 'soulswift,'" I tell him flatly.

"Whatever. I need to send an update to Captain DeRopa."

It takes Mistress Forester and her girls a few days to sew our new uniforms. Despite what Forester said about Brother Miklos losing our trail, I still feel antsy, especially since the Goodson is getting farther and farther away from us while we wait. Tavik's incessant pacing leads me to believe he feels much the same way.

It's bizarre to see him dressed like the Goodson once we're finally back on the road, although he wears the Order's uniform as if the Father had painted it on his body with His own divine hand. For my part, I can't believe how comfortable men's clothing is, how much easier it is to move through the world in a well-cut set of trousers rather than a skirt or the voluminous pants of my Daughter's habit. Considering the fact that Tavik and I have fourteen miles to cover before we arrive at the next stop on Ambrus's map—a town on the upper Sargo called Lithgate—I'm grateful for my new attire.

Tavik frowns at the sky, which continues to weep on us. "Fourteen miles of this, Brother Elgar," he grouses. At least he's calling me by my alias rather than *my beloved bride*.

"Complaining will do us little good, Brother Remur."

"Sorry, Brother Elgar, but I have more complaining to do." He stops, hands on his hips, his thick eyebrows drawn together. "If that text we put together is the truth—and it *feels* like the truth—why were we both taught a . . . a . . ."

"Lie?" I suggest, the word cutting on my tongue.

"Something that was not quite the truth," Tavik amends. "Why keep Elath's prison a secret? How does that benefit anyone?"

"Maybe the early Ovinists thought that keeping the true location of Elath's soul a secret was the best way to guard it against the Elathians."

"But why keep up the ruse that the Vault of Mount Djall was Her prison? How many men have died on both sides, trying to either open it or protect it?"

"I don't know. I don't think we'll ever know why."

"Maybe," he says, unconvinced. He hands me an apple from

his pack and changes the subject. "Your hair is starting to grow back."

"I know."

"Why do you shave it off? I don't mean to sound like an ass. I'm just curious."

"To have hair is to have vanity."

"Nothing wrong with a little vanity." He rubs the shadowy beard growing on his chin, a feature that makes him look even handsomer than before. I don't say anything. I just tug down on the tunic, which keeps puffing up over my sword belt as I walk.

Tavik looks at me askance, as if I'm an exotic specimen on display. I suspect I know what's coming, and I suddenly yearn to hide behind a tree to avoid it. "Your hair," he says. "It's orange . . . ish."

"As you see." I pull the blue hood over my head. Why does it always come to this? Why does where I come from matter so much?

"Do a lot of people have hair that color around here?" he asks.

"It's called *red*, and no."

"Do a lot of people have hair like that where you come from?"

"I don't remember. I was very young when I came to Saint Vinnica." *Holy Father, I wish he'd take the hint and let this go,* I think as I hold the half-eaten apple out so that the juices won't drip on my white wool.

He studies me with those ridiculously pretty eyes. "You're Degmari, right?"

"No."

"Didn't you tell that guard at the wedding you were Degmari?"

"I lied."

"You lied? I didn't know you had it in you." He gives me an approving smile, but any hope I might have cherished that our conversation has come to an end deflates when he asks, "So where exactly are you from?"

"North." I take another bite of my apple, wishing I could swallow my shame and bitterness with it.

"North," he repeats slowly. "Auria, you mean?"

"No."

His confusion clouds his face. "Northern Rosvania?"

"No." I walk a little faster, but he catches up.

"Wait. North? Like *north* north? Like *Hedenskia* north?"

"Does it matter?"

Tavik's eyes widen, and he nearly chokes on his next words. "Yeah, it matters!"

"Why? You are foreign-born, too," I point out defensively.

"There's a bajillion Kantari. How many living, breathing Hedenski live outside Hedenskia? They hardly have any contact with the outside world, and they shut down their only two ports years ago. Even stepping foot on Hedenski soil is punishable by death."

"A Vessel has no nationality. We belong to the Father alone." I'm now hiking so fast, I'm nearly trotting, as if I could somehow outrun this conversation.

"How did you become an Ovinist Vessel, though? I thought the Hedenski worshipped trees or something."

"Can we not talk about this?" I beg. I finally make a friend, and my stupid Hedenski past has to go and ruin it.

"But . . ."

"But what?" I stop and turn on him. The expression on his face is not the ghoulish pleasure most people take in the discovery of my origin. He looks genuinely upset to find out I'm from Hedenskia, fearful even. I think I'd prefer the ghoulishness.

"How did you get to Rosvania in the first place?" he asks me.

"The Goodson brought me."

His eyes bulge. "The Goodson? The Goodson went to Hedenskia? When was that?"

"He led a missionary trip to Hedenskia ten years ago. When he placed a seedpod of the Grace Tree in my hand, the Father chose me, so he brought me to the convent."

"By boat?"

This is my least favorite part. "No."

I watch his eyes as his mind fills in the rest. If I didn't come to Rosvania by boat, there's only one way to go: through the Dead Forest, through the telleg, through the pale, faceless monsters that haunt the trees and devour anyone who comes near, the souls cursed to live on the earth for eternity. No matter how hard I push against the memories, someone is always forcing me to dredge up those days crossing through the Dead Forest, the way the telleg floated silently between the trees, the way they ripped every knight but the Goodson to shreds without care or emotion.

Tavik regards me with a face full of awe and horror. "Mother and Father. Did you see . . . ?" His voice trails off. He can't even bring himself to say the word.

I don't answer. I move. Tavik puts a hand on my arm to halt me, but I tear myself free, not just because I don't want to be touched, but because the humming inside me swells, deafening in my ears, and I'm not sure I can keep a lid on it. I take a deep breath in and out through my nose to quell the thing inside me before I speak.

"Yes, I have seen the telleg. Yes, they are terrifying. Yes, I nearly died. And no, I do not want to speak of it." My words are sharp and cold to freeze the burning inside me. I throw what's left of the apple as hard as I can and listen for the satisfying *thud* as it lands before I keep walking, leaving Tavik to follow in my frosty wake.

Twenty-Five

We left the Pavane eight miles back, but a pall has settled over us—or over me, at least—since Tavik figured out where I'm from. We continue in somber silence until Tavik stops—just stops—right in the middle of the barley field.

"Is something wrong?" I ask him. It makes me jittery standing out in the open like this, especially when it's not just raining but thundering as well, but he stays where he is. He folds back one of his sleeves and lets the rain wash over his bare skin, slicking the strange silver scars on his arm.

"Unbelievable," he says.

"What is unbelievable?"

"All this water. All this rain. All this *life*." He gestures at the expanse of grain surrounding us.

At the convent, on the rare occasion when someone spoke of the Kantari drought, it was distant and irrelevant, something that didn't affect us. Tavik's spare frame brings the reality of a drought into sharp focus. I'm half tempted to touch his arm to comfort him, but it seems to me that a well-fed girl doesn't have that right, so I keep my hands to myself.

After a moment, he sighs and nods toward the outline of a town in the distance. "I think that must be Lithgate."

"Should we wait for sunset before we go in?"

He shakes his head. "We're wearing these uniforms for a reason, so let's test them out and see how they do."

Twenty minutes later, we're walking down the main thoroughfare of Lithgate, Brother Remur with a confident swagger and me—Brother Elgar—mincing along with my heart in my throat, waiting for someone to point at us and scream, "It's them! Call the patrols!" Instead, our entry into Lithgate goes unnoticed. The few people we encounter pay us no attention. It's as if the uniform of the Order makes both of us invisible and anonymous, two things I've never been in the whole course of my life. How incredible to move through the world without anyone knowing or caring. It's a luxury I never knew I wanted until this moment.

I read each shop sign along the way until I find the one that says *Brewers*. The ornate lettering is formed from the branches of a painted tree like the one tattooed on Tavik's wrist. I'm about to knock, but a handsome man in his thirties opens the door before my knuckles hit wood.

"You made it! Excellent! We've been on pins and needles," he says as he stands aside to let us enter and drip all over the well-swept floor of his shop.

"Are they here?" a male voice calls from the back, and a moment later, another man comes into the shop. "Thank the Mother. We were on pins and needles."

The first man grins. "I already said that. I'm Danov, and this is Rek. We're very glad to see you, obviously. Here, let me take those cloaks. Can we get either of you a pint of ale? It's the one thing that's never in short supply here."

I'm surprised when Tavik answers, "No, thank you," at the same time I do.

"Don't give me that look," he chastises me. "The Kantari aren't big drinkers, you know."

Danov is tall and blond while Rek is stout with a southerner's darker complexion, but I get a sense that there's a family connection here, cousins maybe. They escort us upstairs to their living quarters on the second floor. Tavik and I take turns changing into the Brewers' spare clothes in the single bedroom so we can hang our knights' uniforms in the rafters to dry. Once we're both warming ourselves by the fire in the main room, I ask for an update on the Goodson's whereabouts, and Danov fills us in.

"He's still on the Kings Road, but I'd guess he's got a good fifty miles on the two of you. Why exactly are you following him?"

"It's complicated," I tell him. This has apparently become our stock response for any question we can't answer.

"I gather that. Forester's message was less than enlightening. So the young man there was sent to Rosvania to free the Mother, who is, apparently, no longer in the Vault of Mount Djall, but it sounds as if he was unsuccessful?"

Rek leans in. "What he's trying to ask is, where is the Mother?"

My eyes shift between the two men as I try to figure out how much to say. "We're not sure. The Goodson may have information that could help us. That's why we need to find him."

Danov shudders. "Better you than me. I wouldn't want to run into any Knight of the Order, much less the man himself."

This complete mischaracterization of Goodson Anskar makes me bristle, but I decide to use this opening to put my theory to the test. "Do you happen to know if there's been a coup in the Order? Is the Goodson still in charge?"

Both men raise their eyebrows, and Rek glances at Danov before he answers. "We've heard nothing of it, but information on the inner workings of the Order is extremely hard to come by. I assume you have reason to believe such a thing?"

"I do, yes."

He nods thoughtfully. "We can put feelers out on the Milk Road, if that helps."

"What did you ask him?" Tavik butts in.

"I asked if there had been a leadership change in the Order."

"Why? Because you think your precious Goodson had nothing to do with what happened at the summit?"

"I trust the Goodson as much as you trust *your* precious captain," I snipe at him.

Tavik purses his lips at me before asking the Brewers in Rosvanian, "And where is Brother Miklos?"

"He must have caught your scent. Ambrus sent word that he and his men are now heading west," Danov answers.

"Father of death," Tavik moans when I translate.

"Sorry to be the bearer of bad tidings."

"Oh! I nearly forgot," Rek exclaims. "A message arrived about an hour ago. I can't begin to make out what it says, so I assume it's for you?" He reaches into his pocket, pulls out the tiny missive, and holds it out to Tavik. When Tavik's done reading it, he steps to the fireplace and tosses it into the flames.

"Is it from your captain?" I ask his back.

He nods, but he remains at the grate. "You can tell them it was from our Kantari contact, that we've been reporting our progress—or lack thereof—to him, and that he commands us to stay the course and keep him posted."

"And?" I press, because I get the sense that he's leaving something out.

He rubs his face. "You know what? I'll take that ale after all."

After dinner and Tavik's third pint of ale, the Brewers offer to give us a tour of their operations. All my knowledge of the world has come from books, so I'm excited to learn about something that I can see with my own eyes and touch with my own hands. But when I translate the offer for Tavik, he raises his drink and says, "Super," his green eyes glassy, and I have the sinking suspicion that this is not going to go well.

The brewery on the main floor comprises the largest portion of the building. There are two enormous casks, one for weak ale and one for strong. Tavik sways in the corner and scowls at them.

"Which did you give him? Weak or strong?" I ask Danov quietly.

He grimaces apologetically. "Weak, I swear."

I decide to leave Tavik to his own devices as I listen to Rek explain how he and Danov crush the malt and combine it with barley and oats before pouring boiling water into the tun, adding the grain mixture, then pouring on more water at carefully timed intervals.

"This really is fascinating, you know," I call to Tavik, who has stuck his face in a strainer.

"I'm sure it is."

"Do you not have ale in Kantar?"

He pulls his face out of the strainer to glare at me. "No. When we manage to get our hands on food, we *eat* it. We don't make it into some fancy drink."

"Perhaps you have had enough of that fancy drink, then," I suggest, my patience gone.

"Perhaps you can shove it."

"Should we hide his swords?" Rek whispers to Danov.

I march over to Tavik and pull him to the side. "Why are you so angry?" I demand in a low, warning tone.

"Just look at this," he cries, not bothering to lower his voice. "Mother and Father, this room could have fed my family for a year. Do you know what it's like, seeing all this rain and all this food here in the north when the summer rains have all but stopped in Kantar? Our land has dried up. The goats are skin and bones. There's no food. None. The Two-Swords spend more time attacking trade caravans than anything else, just to feed our people. But here you have so much that you *drink* this stuff."

"Everything all right?" Danov asks nervously from the other side of the brewery.

"I'm so sorry," I tell him before turning on Tavik. "I understand you're angry, but you're being unpardonably rude right now." I grab him by the arm with the dim hope of ushering him upstairs and convincing him to go to bed early, but he yanks himself free, barely staying on his feet as he glowers at me.

"Good Mother, you're probably the one who's been translating *The Songs of the Saints* for all those Kantari converts, right? What you Ovinists don't get is that the Kantari don't care about your faith. They just want you to fill their bellies. But no one starves in Rosvania, do they? No one goes without. And do you know why?"

I answer him with thin-lipped silence. I know he's going to answer his own question anyway.

"Because hundreds of years ago, Ovin imprisoned the Mother and shut Her up in that convent, trapping Her life force here in this perfect, miserable country. Meanwhile, my people, the ones who stayed faithful to Elath, have slowly starved. We've watched our lands dry up over the centuries. Even the *Ovinist* countries south of the Koz Mountains suffer, their fisheries dwindling to nothing, their orchards and olive groves shriveling up, while the Mother's life has remained trapped here. All so the northern Ovinists can pray to the Father alone."

I have Ambrus's basket analogy on my mind when I counter, "If Elath's presence has brought life to Rosvania, what has caused the drought in Kantar? Doesn't it follow that the deserts began to stretch over your country once Ludo was buried near Nogarra? It seems to me your great hero is the one who brought your people death, not the Ovinists."

Now it's Tavik's turn to answer with sour reticence, so I keep going.

"And as for the rain, there is such a thing as too much, you know. If it doesn't stop soon, it will drown the fields, and the people of the north will starve just as surely as the people of the south, and these nice Elathians who are helping us right now will be out of business."

Tavik blows air between his ale-loosened lips, making them flap wetly. He pushes past me to head back upstairs, but not before throwing one last jab over his shoulder. "What would you know, when you've been imprisoned yourself all these years?"

I never knew how much anger a girl could contain until I met this boy. The presence inside me simmers in my veins, and I wish I could let myself tap into it. It would serve Tavik right if I unleashed such power on him. Instead, I stomp up the stairs after him. "I am not a prisoner," I snipe at him, but he's already helping himself to another pint. He gulps down half the glass, belches, and says, "You know, food tastes pretty good when you drink it."

I take the pint from his limp fingers, and he looks at his empty hand in confusion. After I set the glass down out of his reach, I hold his slack face between my palms and make him look me in the eye. "Would you please stop?"

He droops and grows heavy in my hands, as if I'm supposed to hold him upright. "Sorry," he tells me. Father above, he sounds like he's about to start crying.

"It's all right."

"It's not all right." The next thing I know, Tavik is hugging me. But he's also not terribly steady on his feet, and he nearly knocks us both over.

"Really. It's fine," I assure him. He has his body plastered to mine, and I can feel myself go pink with mortification.

"You're so nice, Gelya. And you're so smart."

"You can let go now," I tell him as I give him a half-hearted pat on the back, but he's still got me in a bear hug when the Brewers make their way into their own parlor.

"How is he?" Rek asks.

"A little drunk," I answer over Tavik's shoulder, my arms pinned awkwardly to my sides.

Tavik finally sets me free so he can face the Brewers, point a thumb at me, and ask them, "Isn't she adorable?"

"What did he say?" Danov asks.

"Nothing," I answer, because there's no earthly way I'm translating that.

They help me get Tavik to a small sofa. "I love all of you. I want you to know that," he slurs as his bottom hits the couch cushions.

"Apparently, he loves you," I translate for the Brewers. If we have to put up with Tavik in this condition, it seems only fair that we should get to laugh at him, too.

"How nice!" says Danov, smiling wide.

"Have I ever told you about Captain DeRopa?"

"A few times. Here, drink this." I try to get Tavik to take the cup of tea Danov has just handed me, but his hands don't appear to be working properly.

"He's so nice," Tavik tells me. "And he's really smart."

"I bet you love him, too."

Tavik nods solemnly. "He's like a father to me. I wish he were here. He'd know what to do. Although, Father of death, he's going to be so mad at me if I ever see him again."

Rek produces a blanket from a trunk and drapes it over the inebriated Kantari on his sofa. I take Tavik by the shoulders and urge him to lie down. "Go to sleep," I tell him, and he does, but not before giving me a sloppy grin and saying, "Why are you so adorable?"

He doesn't see the irrationally pleased and equally stupid smile that answers his.

Twenty-Six

"Do I even want to know what I did last night?" Tavik asks shortly after we leave the Brewers and Lithgate behind.

"No," I tell him, staring straight ahead as my cheeks burn with embarrassment for both of us.

He grimaces and rubs his temples, but he doesn't press me for details. I'd rather forget myself, but my mind keeps latching onto that one word: *adorable*. I'm fairly certain I know what it means, and I'm also fairly certain it's a word used to describe puppies and kittens, not a tall, gawky Hedenski girl with freckles and red stubble on her head.

Our uniforms never fully dried out in the Brewers' rafters, and now the interminable rain has us soaked through again, which may be why I fail to notice the telltale wetness in my drawers until the uncomfortable bloating of my abdomen alerts me to my problem.

"Oh no," I moan.

"What?"

"Nothing. I'll be right back," I answer, inwardly wailing at the fact that not only am I going to spend yet another day walking in the rain, I'm going to have to do it while going through the demon's curse.

"Oh. Got your monthly bleeding?" Tavik says the word *bleeding* so loudly that every village and town and farm within a fifty-mile radius probably hears him.

"Tavik!"

"Well, I mean . . ." His forehead crinkles. "Go take care of it?"

"How can you be so . . . ?"

"I'm trying to figure out what word you want here. Cavalier? Nonchalant?"

"Ugh!"

"What is the big deal?"

"First of all, I would rather not discuss something so private with you, and secondly, I don't know what you mean by 'take care of it.' At the convent, we went to the House of the Unclean."

"*Unclean?* Seriously?" Tavik shakes his head and rubs at the ale-induced headache behind his bloodshot eyes. "Your bleeding is natural and normal, all right? Just tear off a piece of fabric from your old clothes and stick it in your drawers. It'll be fine."

My instinct is to argue with him, but a trickle down my thigh reminds me of the reason why this mortifying conversation started in the first place. I grumble in defeat and head into a patch of trees to our right.

"Don't stray too far," he calls after me.

"Where would I go?" I mutter. I make sure that Tavik and I are separated by so many trees and shrubs that he can't possibly see me as I tear a swath of cloth free of my old Daughter's sash and use it to fashion a humiliating diaper for myself.

I've grown grudgingly fond of Tavik, but he's a poor substitute for Zofia. She haunts my dreams when I really need her here in the living world. There are things only another woman can understand, and it's at times like these when I miss her steady presence most of all, especially when the only other person I can rely on is so very male and so very not her. He may be at my side, but the truth is that I feel more alone in the world than ever.

"Sing, faithful, of beloved Vinnica, prison and prisoner, and pity her," I sing under my breath, letting the Father fill me with the cool invasiveness of His Word while the other presence churns beneath the lid I keep over Her. I fist my hands, refusing to accept myself as either prison or prisoner. I may hold Elath within me, but that doesn't mean I have to be Her pawn. I still have free will. I still have control over my choices and actions.

I walk farther away from Tavik, farther than is necessary. Farther than is wise.

"Gelya?" His voice grows faint behind me, but I don't turn back. I walk until I come to a place where the trees thin and I stand on the edge of a cliff overlooking the Kings Road far below. Even if the Goodson were on that road now, he'd never find me here. He'd never think to look up. But I tear another strip from my Daughter's sash and tie it to the branch of a gelya tree anyway, a cry for help to the man who named a little girl after the gelya berry, which is bright and alive and lovely when all else seems to have died.

As the weeks go by, our stops on Ambrus's map grow few and far between. We stay with a miller in a small town a few miles north of the Sargo's headwaters, with the steward of a great estate, with a farmer whose flood-soaked wheat fields bring us within spitting distance of the Kings Road. Each time it's the same news: the Goodson is moving west. He is always too far away, while Brother Miklos is too near. The constant worry that the Butcher of Grama could very well catch up to us pulls at my nerves until I feel threadbare.

Whenever and wherever I can, I tie a strip of my Daughter's sash to a gelya tree. I know the Goodson will never see these flags, but it's comforting all the same, giving me a sense of control in a world in which I have none.

The messages between Tavik and DeRopa fly back and forth. Literally. Since I don't know the coded shorthand they use, I have to rely on Tavik to tell me what they say. There's very little variation. DeRopa always asks for our location, and Tavik always sends "an update." Considering his clear adoration for his captain, Tavik is remarkably out of spirits every time he receives a message, and it takes him ages to compose his brief responses. I can't shake the sense that when it comes to this correspondence, there are things he's not telling me.

As our safe houses become sparse, we have to find other places to shelter overnight: an abandoned farmhouse, a dilapidated mill, a termite-ridden shed. In between, we walk and walk as it rains and rains, the air smelling of rot and the earth beneath us squishing sickeningly with decay. We have to circumnavigate fields so flooded they look like ponds, and each day of unrelenting rain makes our journey feel increasingly prophetic.

"Tell me again how the entire world is supposed to become a desert when Elath's Last Breath runs out," I joke half-heartedly one morning, but it falls flat.

"All this rain is making Kantar look like your heaven right now." Tavik jokes back before tilting his head thoughtfully toward the sky. "Did you mean what you said back in Lithgate? That Elath's presence has made Rosvania rich, while Ludo's body in Kantar caused the drought?"

"I thought you didn't remember anything from that night."

"I remember the less embarrassing bits, but you didn't answer my question."

"It's only a theory," I tell him, but it feels more like truth than guesswork.

"So when we opened the Mother's prison . . ." He holds his hands out, letting the rain plink on his palms. "This?"

"This," I agree reluctantly, the heaviness of the idea leaning on my stooped shoulders. No matter how often we stop or how much rest I get, I can't seem to recover my strength. Each day saps energy from my body, a cumulative exhaustion that weighs down each step I take. One afternoon, I catch Tavik looking at me, worried. His expression reminds me of the statue of the unknown saint in the convent's parlertorium, mournful, as if I were someone to mourn.

"What's wrong?"

He wipes his face clean of emotion. "Nothing. I'm going to pray."

I've seen Tavik pray so many times over the past few weeks, I could go through the motions myself, so I only half watch him now as he worships not just the Father but the soul inside me whom I was taught to think of as a demon. But with each passing day, She feels less and less like something I could call demonic, and Tavik's prayer does not look evil. There's a sanctity to his movements, a clear indication that his own spirit transcends his physical body while I, a chosen Vessel of the One True God, feel nothing but the Father's coldness when I pray.

It isn't fair.

I find my own place to pray beneath the relative shelter of an oak tree. I kneel and press my forehead to the damp ground and sing the familiar verse from *The Song of Saint Lanya*.

Daughter Ina used to wax on and on about the Father's love, the warmth He brought to her heart, but as I pray the Vessel's Prayer, the Father fills me with His purpose alone, cool and distant. There is no sense of value or worth in who I am, only in what I can do for Him.

Elath's humming grows more insistent inside me. I push against it, begging it—Her—to go away. She pushes back, terrifying, yes, but also dangerously beautiful. I remember how easy it was to sing *The Ludoïd* when I tapped into that power, how strong I felt, how right it was. I don't lift the lid, and yet a hint of that power escapes, billowing through me like steam, intoxicatingly warm.

You have given me life to reflect the light of Heaven for all to see.

I am filled with the symphony of life and death, melody and harmony, mingling into one complete whole. I'm supposed to be a Vessel of the Father, but when the prayer draws to a close, the only spirit who remains inside me now is Elath, not the One True God. Who may not be true. And who may not be the only one.

Considering the circumstances, it makes sense to challenge what I was taught, but in my heart, it feels weak to let my faith die so easily. I sit back on my heels, wishing with all my heart that I could turn back time and spend the rest of my days at the Convent of Saint Vinnica, blissfully ignorant of the world. I want to live in a universe where Zofia is still alive, where neither one of us has turned her back on the god who chose us. In my dream, she told me that the world is an easier place to bear when you don't have to question it, but now, thanks to her, I have no choice but to question it.

I don't want to doubt! I shout at her in my mind since I can't argue with her in person. *I don't want any of this!*

Tavik's voice cuts into my thoughts. "So, do you press your forehead against the earth when you pray because the Father is the source of life, in your view, and all life comes from the earth?"

Startled, I get to my feet. Tavik stays where he is, lounging against a tree with a blanket draped over his shoulders. He doesn't care if I watch his prayer, but it feels so invasive to know he has watched mine.

"Because . . ." My long hands try to articulate what my words cannot. They're like a pair of birds fluttering before me. "Because as a Vessel, I submit myself to the Father so that He will favor me and fill me with His Word." Only I didn't exactly submit myself to the Father's will alone this time, did I? But Tavik doesn't need to know that.

"And by submitting yourself to the Father, you earn your spot in heaven?"

"No. A Vessel's place is not in heaven."

He cocks his head, confused. "But if you don't go to heaven, what happens when you die?"

"I'll become a soulswift."

He leans toward me, disbelieving. "I don't think I heard you right. What?"

"That's what a soulswift is: a Vessel who has transcended her mortal body to become a bird who carries the souls of the faithful to the Father in heaven. That is how a Vessel attains eternal life after death. Did you not know?"

"That would explain why you don't enjoy watching me man-handle messengers. I wish I'd known."

"Now you do."

"So you've seen this happen, this transformation of a woman into a bird?"

"No. No one has seen it. No mortal can watch the transformation, because to see it happen is to see the Father. A Vessel's body is placed in the Crypt of Saint Vinnica, and after the miracle, she is able to fly free through one of the tunnels that lead to the outside."

"Then how do you know it's true?"

"How do you know the Father is true? Or, in your case, the Mother? Faith." It's hard to have this conversation when my own faith feels like it's burning up right alongside the fiery presence inside me.

"So this bowing you do is all about submission to the Father's will. It's not about the fact that the Father's ribs are the bones of the earth?"

Now it's my turn to tilt my head in confusion. "The Father resides in heaven above. He has no ribs. He has no body."

Tavik gives an incredulous laugh, pushing his growing mop of dark curls out of his face with both hands, but they spring right back into place. "This is the craziest conversation I've had in my life."

"Bodies are earthly vessels," I tell him, repeating the lesson by rote without feeling anything resembling conviction. "They are inherently sinful. The Father is without sin, so He does not have a body."

"If your god doesn't have a body, how do you know he's a he?"

"Well . . ." My eyes shift back and forth. I feel like I'm standing over a trapdoor that's about to open under my feet. "He just is."

"So he has a penis? An aphysical penis? Is that a thing?"

My face burns with embarrassment, and I'm not even the one who said the word. "Would you please stop saying that?"

He looks at me like I'm the one who's being ridiculous. "What?"

"That . . . word."

"Penis?" he guesses completely without shame.

"Tavik," I warn him.

"You Ovinists are so weird!" he laughs. "You do know that half the population has a penis, right?"

"Stop!"

"Penis!" he sings operatically. "Penis, penis, penis!"

I level him with an icy glare, but he only cackles in reply.

"I'm sorry," he tells me as he wipes away a tear of hilarity from the corner of his eye. "It's just so much fun to poke holes in Ovinist absurdities."

"I was not put on this earth to entertain you."

"Whew, you've got that right," he says, and not only do I stop scowling at him, he even manages to coax a grudging smile out of me. Honestly, it's hard to stay mad at Tavik, and not just because he's nice to look at.

Although he is very nice to look at.

Twenty-Seven

There's a soulswift waiting for Tavik at the last stop on Ambrus's map, a farm called Illesmaat—the family name, Illes, plus the Old Rosvanian word for *freehold*, maat. Whatever the message says pulls down on the corners of Tavik's mouth.

"Are you going to read it to me?" I press him.

"It's just the usual," he mutters, but *the usual* appears to be something that makes Tavik increasingly uneasy each time he hears from his captain. He's so distracted by the contents of De-Ropa's tiny missive that he fails to notice the very pretty girl who lives at Illesmaat with her mother and father and two older brothers.

Mera is petite and has thick honey-colored hair, and is the picture of femininity when contrasted with my towering, knight-garbed form. Ten years in a convent didn't equip me to interact with a normal girl like her, and my mouth feels as if it's been glued shut. I keep thinking of the new Daughters back at Saint Vinnica, what a disaster I made of that, and they weren't even normal like this girl. What am I supposed to say to her? How am I supposed to act? Making matters worse is the fact that she hasn't taken her eyes off Tavik since we arrived. It's irritating, even if I was guilty of the same thing when I first met him. He's just a boy, for the love of the Father.

Tavik crumples the message in his fist, spreads out Ambrus's map on a long dining table, and asks Illes, "Where is Gulachen?" in Rosvanian.

"Here." Illes points to a place in southest Rosvania.

"The Kantari army has made it all the way to Gulachen?" I ask in alarm.

Tavik nods.

"Your people have been battling their way northeast for weeks, but no one can figure out where they're going or why. Where *are* they going?" Illes asks.

Tavik and I look at each other over the table, and an unspoken question bubbles up between us, one I can't believe we haven't asked ourselves until now: If Tavik sent word to DeRopa that he has the Vessel containing Elath's soul and that we're on the move, why are the Kantari still trying to reach the Convent of Saint Vinnica?

"Is the Goodson still on the Kings Road?" Tavik asks Illes, redirecting the conversation, but I'm determined to discuss the movements of the Kantari army with him the next chance I get, especially since something in DeRopa's message clearly has him rattled.

In the meantime, Illes is shaking his head in answer to Tavik's second question. "The Milk Road lost the Goodson at Juprachen.

The only thing I can tell you is that he's no longer heading west, at least, not on the Kings Road, and he doesn't appear to have taken any of the major trade routes running out of the city either."

I snap to attention. "Is he still in Juprachen?"

"Possibly, but if he is, he doesn't seem to be staying at any of the religious houses, so I think it unlikely."

Tavik nudges my elbow, and I fill him in as my finger brushes over the map until it lands on Juprachen. "Where would he go from here?"

"You know him better than I do. You tell me," Tavik says in Kantari.

Not wanting to be rude, I stick with Rosvanian for the sake of our hosts. "What if he's not moving *toward* something, but *away* from something. Could it be that Brother Miklos is after him too?"

Tavik makes his opinion known via a heavy sigh rather than words.

"We heard you thought there might have been a coup," says Illes. "If there's dissent within the Order, then the Mother is truly blessing us."

"Where is Brother Miklos now?" Tavik asks.

"The last report says he hanged five Elathians in Varos da Manveld," Illes answers, his words sharp with resentment.

Tavik frowns at the point on the map labeled *Varos da Manveld*, only twenty-five miles to our east, but my eyes scan ahead, searching all roads leading out of Juprachen. If I look long enough and hard enough, I know I can figure out where the Goodson has gone, and why. I'm so preoccupied with my search that I don't pay much attention as Tavik scribbles a hurried reply to his captain and sends it off with the same soulswift who delivered DeRopa's message. He stands at the back door, watching the bird fly south, and he keeps his back to me when he says, "I think we should rest here a few days."

Considering the fact that Brother Miklos is hard on our heels, it's probably foolhardy to let down my guard, but when Mistress Illes offers to pour me a bath the next morning, I'm tempted to hug her. I peel the knight's uniform from my body like a snake shedding skin, and I'm deliriously grateful to be a girl again. That, at least, puts me on equal footing with Mera.

I watch her with wary eyes as she fetches water from the well and helps her mother heat it, a good and obedient daughter with her "Yes, Mama" and "Thank you, Mama" and "How can I help, Mama?" If she finds me strange, at least she doesn't show it.

As I ease myself into the blessedly warm water of the tub, I can hear Tavik outside playing some kind of game that involves kicking a ball around with the two older boys, shouting and laughing and not feeling a need to save the world for a change.

"Don't you worry. I'll make sure you have as much privacy as you need," says Mistress Illes, handing me a soft cloth so I can rub weeks' worth of road grime off my skin.

"Would you like the verbena soap or the rose soap?" Mera asks, blinking her big brown eyes at me. It's so rare that anyone offers me a choice in anything that I'm stymied. Is one better than the other? Is there a right answer?

"I like the verbena better," she says, giving me the bar that looks yellow rather than pink. Then she leans in with a conspiratorial grin and whispers, "The rose soap will make you smell like my grandma."

She holds my gaze, her eyes twinkling with amusement, and I have to stifle a giggle. Then, just as quickly, I have to stifle the urge to bawl. Because being with Mera is like being with Zofia. It's like being normal.

Three male voices outside shout at once, followed by a cacophony of clucking chickens. Mistress Illes rushes to the window and shouts, "What on earth? Petor, get that ball out of the chicken run! You're scaring them half to death." She growls in irritation and tells Mera to look after me as she dashes out the kitchen door to save her hens from the boys' game.

As soon as her mother is gone, Mera props her elbows up on the side of the tub. "Holy Father, I thought she'd never leave. Now we can finally talk."

"Oh. Okay." I am naked in a bathtub in a stranger's kitchen, and though I appreciate the fact that Mera treats me as if I'm not terrifying, I am suddenly feeling very trapped and very, very vulnerable.

"Are you really a Daughter of Saint Vinnica?"

"Yes," I say, then amend, "I *was*."

"A Vessel?"

She's looking at me with an eagerness that makes me lie just to protect my own sense of privacy, what little is afforded me in my current situation. "No."

"What is it like? I mean, wow. A Daughter."

I scrub at my skin a little faster, trying to get through my bath and escape Mera's questions as quickly as possible. "We just pray and study. You know."

"No, I definitely do not know." She looks over her shoulder before leaning in a bit closer. "Is it true, what they say about Daughters?"

"I don't know. What do they say?" I cross my arms over my small breasts.

"That the women . . . you know."

"Heal the sick?"

"No."

"Grow medicinal herbs?"

"Fall in love with each other," she whispers. "Kiss."

"No!" I nearly shout. But then I remember Daughter Miv and Daughter Lunella, and how I once walked in on them in the garden shed, the way they stepped apart from one another like opposing magnets. I was so young, I didn't understand what I saw, but now I have to wonder. "At least, I never kissed a girl. Or a boy. There's not a lot of kissing at a convent."

"Well, *I've* kissed a girl before," Mera declares, moving back to hop up onto the kitchen table, her legs swinging back and forth.

"You have?"

"Mm-hmm." The satisfied grin on her face informs me that she either enjoyed it or enjoyed the daringness of it.

"Oh." My first reaction is shock, but then again, what do I care who kisses whom? I'm hardly in a place to judge anyone.

"Please tell me you've at least kissed that boy you're with," says Mera.

"What? No!" But then I remember that I have, in fact, kissed

Tavik on our fake wedding day. And then I think of all the times I've watched him pray, the times I've had that giddy urge to touch his skin. The bathwater has gone cool, but all of a sudden the kitchen feels stiflingly hot.

"So you're not together?"

"Of course we're together." I wish Mera's mother would return. She's easier to handle with her mother around.

"Honey, when I say *together*, I mean *together* together."

"He's my friend."

Mera goes over to the window to watch the boys. "He's a mighty fine friend," she says before looking back at me. "Come on. Be honest. Are you seriously trying to tell me you haven't been even a little bit tempted?"

"Tempted to what? Kiss him?"

"At the minimum."

"No!"

Elath's presence inside me stutters, and I get the oddest sensation that She's laughing at me. Now all I can think about is the way Tavik linked his fingers with mine when we made our ring swear or whatever he called it. I feel like I'm reminding myself as much as Mera when I say, "I'm a Daughter."

"You're something. Let me just say, if it were me on the road with that guy, we'd definitely be sharing the same tent."

She's staring out the window at Tavik once again. I stand up so fast I nearly slip and fall. "I'm ready to get out now."

She takes an unembarrassed eyeful of my naked body as water streams off my skin. "Wow, you have freckles everywhere."

I breathe my irritation in deeply through my nose. "Yes, I

know. May I have that towel now, please?"

"It wasn't an insult," she says, reaching up to drape the towel over my shoulders. "You're really pretty, you know."

I draw the towel closer around me, feeling strangely small. "Am I?"

Mera nods and gives me an encouraging smile I probably don't deserve considering how distrustful I've been of her.

I've spent so much time worrying about my appearance, but it never had anything to do with beauty. What use is beauty to women who will live their lives behind the high stone walls of the convent? But out here in the larger world, it matters more than I care to admit, especially when I think of how I must look compared to Mera.

"I wish I were tall like you. You're so elegant," she tells me wistfully, and I don't think she's lying. I grin at her, feeling at once sheepish and pleased.

"I'm a giant," I joke awkwardly.

"No, you're a girl."

She helps me step out of the tub and exchanges the towel for Mistress Illes's robe, which is too small for me, but at least it's clean and smells good. We stand side by side at the window in companionable silence and watch Tavik kick a ball around with Mera's brothers. He plays fair, passing the ball with his foot as if he were a regular boy, not a Two-Swords who can bend the laws of reality. He catches us watching at the window, and one of those big bright smiles spreads across his face.

Mera sighs beside me. "You are so lucky."

I have something that is either a goddess or a demon inside

me, two different religious factions believe they have the right to dictate my actions, I'm exhausted every day and all the time, and whatever I choose to do with my body will determine the fate of the world. *Lucky* is not how I would describe myself.

But then Tavik waves, not at pretty Mera, who is a normal girl, but at me, and a little knife of longing jabs me in the heart, an emotion that I could not possibly define as friendship.

Don't, I tell myself. *Just don't.*

Tavik is still smiling and waving when the ball hits him on the side of the head and bounces off. He cringes, and it's clear that his ego smarts more than his cranium. Mera bursts out laughing, and her brothers laugh, and even Tavik laughs, but no one laughs as hard as I do. Mera has to hold me up, because I'm staggering under the hilarity of it.

"Holy Father," I cackle. "That was an absolute gift!"

Twenty-Eight

I share a room with Mera, the pair of us staying up later than we ought to, laughing over the local gossip that pours from my new friend's mouth with comical flair. As I drift off to sleep, I remember staring at my translation work in the scriptorium, wondering what normal girls were doing. I know I'm anything but normal, yet staying at Illesmaat makes me feel like . . . a girl. Just a girl. Which is really nice.

After another blissful night of sleeping in a warm, dry bed, I wake to find that Mistress Illes has taken it upon herself to wash our uniforms while the rain gives the world a reprieve. Illesmaat is truly a place of miracles.

Tavik borrows a set of clothes from one of Mera's brothers, and since I'm too tall to wear anything belonging to the mistress or Mera, I have to borrow a tunic and trousers from the younger of the Illes boys. I've grown so slim since leaving Saint Vinnica that the trousers keep sliding down my hips as I stand at the kitchen window and watch my knight's uniform dangle from the clothes-line beside Tavik's, damp and limp in the moldy air.

While my body feels well rested today, Elath's spirit roils more insistently than ever, leaving me with a strange sense of foreboding. It's almost as if She's giving me trouble simply because I'm contented for a change. I wish we could stay at Illesmaat, where it's not currently raining and where I feel like a normal person and where, if left to my own devices, I might form a lasting friendship with a girl my own age. But we can't stay, so I sit at the table to study Ambrus's map, trying to figure out where the Goodson might have gone. Juprachen is one of the biggest cities in Rosvania, and there are so many roads branching into more roads leading out of it that I can't begin to guess where he is.

I sit back in my chair, close my eyes, and picture his familiar face smiling at me from across a Shakki board, and I let myself sink into a memory of him.

"And what have you been studying since my last visit, Daughter Gelya?" he asks me as he shifts his cavalry westward, a move I didn't anticipate.

"I've been assigned Kantari as my focus language," I answer absently, trying to figure out my next futile move.

"Kantari? You?" His shocked tone jolts me out of the game. I look up to find disappointment plastered across his rugged face.

"Daughter Miv was the only Kantari expert left at the convent. When she died last spring, Sacrist Larka assigned it to me," I explain, feeling ashamed even though I had no say in the matter.

"Of course. The Sacrist knows best." His expression softens, but I can see that this news saddens him all the same. He's the only person other than Zofia who doesn't see a Hedenski when he looks at me. I hope he won't think the less of me because of my language focus.

"I wasn't thrilled about it either," I admit to him. "And yet it's interesting, too. I've been learning the strangest things about what the Kantari believe. Did you know that there's a tree in Kantar that chooses the Two-Swords just as our own Grace Tree chooses Vessels?"

"I do know about Elath's Tree. As a matter of fact, when I was a young man, I held one of those seedpods in my hand." He raises an eyebrow and takes a sip of tea, knowing full well he has lit the wick of my insatiable curiosity.

I lean forward, a grin splitting my face. "Really?"

"I'm ashamed to admit this now, but I was young and stupid, and some of my friends and I . . . er . . . had enjoyed a little too much wine that night." He sets his cup down. His eyes go distant, and a smile pulls up on one corner of his thin lips. "We were stationed at the Monastery of Saint Helios for a fortnight, waiting for pilgrims to gather for a journey to Mount Djall, and we had a great deal of time on our hands. We broke into the library and got into all manner of mischief. We found a box labeled 'Seedpods from Elath's Tree of Kantar.' One of the fellows dared us to hold a pod in our palms to see if it would open and make Two-Swords out of us."

"Did the seedpod open?" I ask with all my twelve-year-old eagerness.

He toys with one of his generals, rolling the piece between his hands. "We passed it from man to man—boy to boy really, we were *hardly men then—and nothing happened until . . ."*

His voice trails off. I don't think I can stand the anticipation. "What?" *I demand.*

"My friend placed the seedpod in my hand, and it opened."

His manner is nonchalant, and yet his admission takes my breath away. "It chose you?"

"It opened," he corrects me, but the memory of my own seedpod rises like a specter. I can still feel the way the gift tugged at my insides, the way the song burst inside me.

"Did you feel anything?" I ask, hushed, reverent.

The Goodson gives me an indulgent smile. "No. Of course not. Do I look like a Two-Swords to you?"

I laugh at the absurdity of it. "No."

"No," he agrees as his smile widens.

As I think on that memory, my mind paints Goodson Anskar's smile in a new light. His grin didn't reach his gray eyes. Could he have lied to me? Did he experience what Tavik and I experienced when we were chosen? And what does it mean if he did? As my mind whirs with questions, my gaze randomly lands on one spot on Ambrus's map: Varos da Helios.

We were stationed at the Monastery of Saint Helios.

I bolt upright in my chair and draw Ambrus's map close. The tip of my finger traces a line backward, beginning at Varos da Helios, the university town just south of the monastery, following one road, then another, then a third until it stops at Juprachen.

Zofia was doing translation work at the Monastery of Saint

Helios when she began to piece together the true location of Elath's prison. The monastery must be where the stone from the library of Grama was taken. That's where Zofia made her rubbing of the first half of *The Ludoïd*.

It all starts clicking into place. The Order attacked Tavik's town for the library, for the information it contained, for anything that might lead them to Elath's whereabouts. They took the library's collection to the Monastery of Saint Helios, and they brought in Sacrist Larka, then Zofia, to translate anything the monks couldn't read for themselves.

The Goodson isn't running from Brother Miklos. He's going to Saint Helios. He's looking for knowledge, for information. Of course he is! Wouldn't I do the same?

I snatch up the map and barrel out the kitchen door to search for Tavik, my pulse slamming through my veins. I hear low voices nearby. Talking. Laughter. A boy and a girl. Tavik and Mera.

I race toward the familiar sounds, but I pull up short when I find Tavik leaning against the stable wall out of sight of the house and Mera standing just inches in front of him. She leans in close, smiling her pretty smile.

And he smiles back at her.

And she presses her lovely body against his lovely body.

And his hand lands on her waist to pull her closer.

And her lips touch his lips.

And his lips respond.

And I'm pretty sure he eases his tongue into her mouth. My logical brain asks, *Why would people want to put their tongues in someone else's mouth?* My illogical heart whispers only, *Why?*

The map flutters in my hand, forgotten. I stand there, watching them, feeling stupid when, really, Tavik is the one who should feel stupid, not me. We're facing the end of the world, and here he is, indulging in this ridiculous display of superficial pleasure. And I'm so angry with Tavik for making me feel stupid, even if I'm not sure why I feel this way or why in the name of the Father I'd want his stupid tongue in my mouth anyway.

You're really pretty, you know, Mera told me, and maybe that's true, but this is also true: I'm not as pretty as she is, and for the first time in my life, it matters.

"Oy!" shouts a deep male voice behind me, yanking me out of my self-pity. Tavik and Mera separate in a hurry, and I spin to find Mera's brothers standing a few feet behind me.

"Gentlemen," Tavik says, slowly backing away. "Let me explain."

"You can explain it to my fists, you little shit," says the older and bigger of the boys.

"Petor! Stop it!" Mera shouts, but unsurprisingly no one pays attention to her. The boys shoulder past me, advancing on Tavik.

"I don't want to hurt you," Tavik tells them, still stepping backward, his hands held up in surrender.

"I think you're confused about who's going to be hurting who in three . . . two . . . one."

I don't stay to watch. I race back to the clothesline, yank down our wet garments, and trip into the house, where I struggle into the damp knight's uniform before slinging my necklace over my head and grabbing both our packs. I slide the map into my knapsack, cursing Tavik's name—the only time in my life I have ever uttered such words—as I pick up his swords as well. With a bag over each shoulder and the scabbards in my hands, I stand out front and wait for Tavik as my wet uniform clings to my skin, clammy and itchy and horribly uncomfortable. I gaze longingly at the house with its warm fire and its dry bed and its promise of a girl who might have been my friend.

A few minutes later, Tavik comes sprinting back, alone. He has the gall to present himself like an actor onstage, shouting, "Behold, the daring knight, Brother Remur, returns without so much as a scratch on him!"

"Oh, very well done, Brother Remur." I make the words *Brother Remur* sound like *you idiot* as I shove the swords and pack into his hands.

"You are the smartest, most wonderful friend ever, Brother Elgar," he gushes, but I'm in no mood.

We run until it seems clear that no one is chasing us. For now, at least. When we finally slow down enough for me to catch my breath, I want to give him the earful that's been building up inside me for at least a mile, but I'm so livid, the only word that comes out of my mouth is a long, seething "You."

"I didn't do anything wrong."

"Except break that poor girl's heart. Do I even want to know what you did to her brothers?"

"I didn't do anything to them. And as for that *poor girl*?" He rolls his eyes, dramatic as ever. "Please."

Indignation on Mera's behalf makes my nostrils flare. "How can you just kiss someone and not care?"

"You're making a big deal out of nothing."

"Ugh. Poor Mera."

"Mera . . . ?" He puts a finger to his chin, thoughtful. "Who's Mera again?"

A fury that is all mine and not Elath's boils in my veins. "You arrogant, selfish, repugnant—"

"I'm kidding!" Tavik reaches out his hands, imploring. "Come on. Messing around is fun, all right? Fun for Mera. Fun for me. Fun. Ever heard of it?"

"Messing around?"

"Fun. You should try it sometime. Besides, do you have any idea how long it's been since I kissed a girl?"

Is he actively trying to fan the flames of my anger? I glare daggers at him and spit, "Yes, I do, as a matter of fact."

I can see the moment when he realizes I'm talking about our wedding. He crinkles his artfully crooked nose in disagreement. "That doesn't count."

"Oh, thank you very much!"

"Can we keep moving, please?" He walks ahead of me, but I catch up in a heartbeat, eager to keep berating him.

"Yes, we must keep moving, since *you* lost us a warm, dry place to sleep tonight. That was the last stop on Ambrus's map, Tavik, and we didn't get a chance to ask the Illeses for the next place to stay, thanks to you."

His pace slows. He bites the inside of his cheek. "Sorry. Father of death, I was waiting for a message from Captain DeRopa, too. I just wasn't thinking."

"Correct. You weren't thinking. Fortunately, *I* was." I hold out the map to him, jab my finger at the point labeled *Varos da Helios*, and leave it in his bewildered clutch before moving on.

"Oh. Oh!" he says in my wake, but while my feet may take me away from Illesmaat, my brain stays behind, not letting me erase the sight of Tavik's lips on Mera's, his tongue in her mouth, his hand at her delicate waist.

"Idiot," I fume under my breath in Rosvanian.

Twenty-Nine

The rain starts up again, so a night spent sleeping—or trying and failing to sleep—under the cold, damp shelter of branches and leaves when I could have been in a dry bed sharpens my anger. Raindrops pelt my hood as we slog through mud toward Juprachen the following day, souring my mood even more.

"Do you have any idea how much I want to strangle you right now?" I snarl at Tavik, breaking the thick silence between us.

"Yeah. Got it," he snaps, as if he has the right to be angry. My shoulders hunch in resentment, and I take the first opportunity I can to excuse myself to the cover of trees so I can tie another flag to a gelya branch. The gelya has lost its leaves, but its berries cling to its twigs, drab little globes in a muddy brown landscape. You don't really appreciate their beauty until winter arrives.

When I return to Tavik on the road, I find him rubbing his temples. "Look, I get that you're mad, and I'm not saying that you don't have a right to be, but can we please figure out how we're going to get from here to the Monastery of Saint Helios? And what we're going to do once we get there?"

I fold my arms. "Fine."

"Good. Thank you." He moves toward me, but I step away, keeping an arm's length between us. He heaves a sigh before continuing. "There's a messenger coop at Illesmaat. We'll go back, and I'll apologize to Mera or whoever, and then we can send a new message to Captain DeRopa. The Kantari army can't get through enemy lines, but a small unit of men might be able to sneak past and meet us at Saint Helios."

"You want to attack a peaceful monastery?"

"Why not? The Order attacked Grama, and the Goodson's sword belonged to Ludo in the first place. I'm calling it fair game."

"So the plan is to kill the monks of Saint Helios so you can get the Hand of the Father?"

"Look, I'd love to get in and out with no one being the wiser, but we need to be realistic. It's going to be hard to get into any building that belongs to an Ovinist religious order without some level of risk."

"I won't do it."

He throws his head back and growls, "Gelya!"

"Besides, I have a better idea," I add, annoyed that he's annoyed when I am clearly the one who should be annoyed.

He looks unconvinced, but he says, "I'm listening."

"I'm a Vessel. I can simply walk through the front door."

"No way. I'm not going to let you waltz into a monastery where

I can't protect you." His tone is infuriatingly condescending.

"I don't need your protection for this. Or your permission."

"Okay, so you can walk through the front door. Whoop-de-do. How do you think you're going to get the Goodson's sword once you're inside? He's the guy who saw you levitate after Elath the Mother entered your body, remember?"

"He's also the man who rescued me from Hedenskia, saved my life in the Dead Forest, and has been, for all intents and purposes, my father for the past ten years. He's not going to just lock me up and throw away the key."

Tavik bursts into a fit of harsh laughter. "Locking you up and throwing away the key is exactly what the Goodson has in mind. Holy good Mother, how can you not see that?"

"So I'm supposed to put my faith in your Captain DeRopa, then?" I counter. "If he's so wonderful, why is the Kantari army still moving toward the Convent of Saint Vinnica?"

"What does that have to do with anything?"

"Your captain knows where we are. You've been in communication with him the whole time. So why are the Kantari marching on a convent full of helpless Daughters if they know Elath isn't there?"

His eyes falter. "I don't know."

"What do you mean, you don't know?"

"I mean I don't know, all right? My mission was to get to the convent and free the Mother. I'm not the one commanding military units. I'm not privy to every scrap of information out there. I'm just obeying orders." His voice falters on the words *obeying orders*, and he kicks a rotted walnut into a tree trunk.

"Well, *I* don't have to obey orders," I point out, but Tavik talks right over me.

"And you can stop shitting all over DeRopa, because that man—that *hero*—is the one who broke open the Vault of Mount Djall. He's dedicated his entire life to serving the Mother. I'm pretty sure you're a lot better off in his hands right now than in the hands of an Ovinist zealot like the Goodson."

The more wound up he gets, the more my own anger subsides. "Listen—" I begin, putting out a hand to stop him, but he's like a boulder rolling down a hill, and I couldn't halt his avalanche of raw feelings if I tried.

"If you want to compare father figures, let me just point out that Rusik DeRopa rescued me when I was six years old. He pulled me out of the well where I was hiding when the Order burned Grama to the ground and killed my entire family. DeRopa found me a good home with his cousin, and when the Grace Tree of Kantar chose me two years later, he personally oversaw my training. So don't you dare try to tell me I can't trust him, because in a country full of starving, homeless children, he didn't have to take care of a kid with no family, but he did. I owe him my life. I owe him *everything*."

By the time Tavik gets through this tirade, he is ragged with emotion, his voice rough, and I realize, to my shame, that up till this moment, I have known next to nothing about his past, his hurts, his grief. Now, all of a sudden, I'm drowning in it.

For a moment, we stare at each other, me feeling uncomfortably exposed and Tavik feeling the Father knows what, when his eyes shift from my face to a point below my breastbone, and his face transforms into a mask of alarm. "Oh, death."

"What?" I ask faintly, my stomach dropping.

"Death, decay, and dying. Gelya, look."

He reaches for the chain around my neck and pulls it up. The pendant dangling before my eyes is the correct size and shape and weight, but it's not my triptych, not the gift the Goodson gave me. It's only some cheap locket, a trinket. A nothing. Tavik wraps his fist around it and squeezes hard, as if he could crush the metal in his grasp. It makes the chain dig into the back of my neck.

"You're hurting me. Let go."

He relinquishes it and paces up and down the road. "That apothecary back in Dalment is behind this. You mark my words. He got it into his head that your necklace was the Vessel of Elath, and this is what's come of it. What, did he think the northern Elathians could free Her when we couldn't?"

"Probably."

"Thank the Mother we didn't tell anyone what the Vessel really is."

"*Who*, you mean. *Who* the Vessel is," I remind him. My body feels like a teakettle just before it releases its shrill, piercing whistle, but Tavik carries on as if I haven't said anything.

"I bet it was the Illeses who took it. That Mera. Mother and Father, the Milk Road is supposed to be on our side. Well, these northern Elathians will figure out soon enough they've been duped. Serves them right."

"It was mine," I say, tears of rage brimming on the rims of my eyes, thickening my words.

"At least they didn't take anything valuable."

"It was valuable to me!" I explode, and I finally lose control of the lid I've kept so carefully in place over Elath. It opens a sliver, a hair, and Elath's power surges through me, setting my eyes alight.

Tavik stumbles away from me in terror and lands buttocks-first in a muck-filled wagon rut, his face bloodless. "Father of d—"

"Do you know how few gifts I've received in my life? Do you have any idea how few things in this world truly belong to me?"

"I'm . . . I'm sorry," Tavik stammers.

Blood trickles from my nose, hot and salty. My eyes burn so brightly, they light Tavik's beautiful face.

"These clothes are not mine! This life is not mine! Even my body is not my own!"

My rage slips farther out of my grasp. Holy Father, it feels right.

"I didn't choose to be a Vessel of the One True God, and I didn't choose to become Elath's Vessel either! Every path in my life has been chosen for me, and I had no say in any of it!"

I glare at Tavik, my breath heaving, my anger a conflagration. He's shaking badly, but he gets to his feet and takes two timid steps toward me.

"Gelya." He speaks my name as if he's talking to a cornered dog.

"You *say* 'Gelya.' You *see* 'Vessel,'" I spit. "You're no better than the Ovinists. I'm nothing but a box to any of you. I'm just the thing that contains the only life you actually do care about."

"That's not true." He holds out a trembling hand and forms a circle with his finger and thumb.

That's all it takes. The lid slams down, and I crumple inside and out. Tavik moves another tentative step closer and holds out his arms. "Come here."

I stand there, swaying with misery and exhaustion, limp and blubbering. "Come where?"

"Gimme a hug."

"What? No."

"Bring it in." He makes a beckoning motion with both hands.

I swipe at the tears streaming down my cheeks and the blood dripping out of my nose. "You are so—"

"Right now, pal."

I'm too worn out to resist when Tavik pulls me to him the way the sea carries driftwood out with the tide. His arms are warm around me, his beard softer than I would have expected against my cheek.

"I'm sorry. I shouldn't have said those things about Captain DeRopa," I cry on his shoulder. It's so much easier to apologize when I'm not looking at him.

"And I'm sorry about messing things up at Illesmaat. Let's face it, we're both complete telleg lickers." He says *telleg lickers* in Rosvanian, coaxing a sad, pathetic laugh out of me.

"I'm glad to know you're picking up the most elegant vocabulary from my language."

He releases his hold on me but keeps his hands on my arms as he gives me his very best Tavik Face, the one full of sympathy and understanding, the one that inspires a million problems in my chest.

"Are we good?" he asks.

I sniff one last time, wipe the rest of the blood from my nose with my sleeve, and nod.

Then that brat reaches into the unruly red thicket on top of my head and tousles it without mercy. "Quit being so serious, will you?"

"Tavik!" I struggle out of his reach and smooth my short hair back into place, a hopeless endeavor from the outset.

"Divine Mother, I've been wanting to do that for weeks." He slings an arm over my shoulders and starts walking back the way we came, dragging me with him. "Come along, my beloved wife. Let's go get my ass kicked, send a message, and get your stupid necklace back."

"It's not stupid. *You* are stupid."

"*You're* stupid."

I shake my head. "You are going to be the end of me."

"Probably," he agrees with his charming, rueful grin, and that ridiculous hurt in my heart with Tavik's name on it throbs and aches.

Thirty

The trek back is brutal, five times harder than our escape from Mera's brothers was. All I did was dip a toe into Elath's power, and now I can hardly stand on my own two feet, even after a night of semirest under the same shabby shelter we built the night before. The closer we get to Illesmaat, the more my feet drag.

We've nearly arrived at our destination when Tavik asks me for the millionth time, "You all right?"

"Fine," I mumble. Even my lips are numb with fatigue.

"You don't look fine."

I give a humorless laugh. "Thanks."

"Hold up." He puts a hand on my arm to stop me. When we're with other people, he hides his thoughts better than the world's greatest Shakki player, but when it's just me, he wears his worry, head to toe. His concern makes it hard to tamp down the sudden urge to cry.

He points back in the direction we came from with his thumb.

"Can we talk about what happened yesterday? Your eyeballs . . ." He makes a gesture with both hands, like fireworks exploding out of his eye sockets. "And now, a day later, you can still barely stand up."

I rub at the bleak headache blossoming in my sinuses. "I know."

"Was that you, or was that Her?"

"Both? Maybe? I don't know." I let my hands fall away from my face, and for the first time, I try to tell Tavik what it's like, how it feels. "Her presence is always there. This buzzing. Simmering. It never goes away, not even when I sleep. I think of it as a pot over a fire, and if I don't keep the lid clamped down tight, the whole thing will boil over. When I read *The Ludoïd* in Ambrus's attic, I pulled the cover back, and I used this power—*Her* power—to sing the song, and it made using my gift so much easier. But just now the lid popped off, and I couldn't control it."

Tavik lowers his thick eyebrows and presses his lips into a thin line. The silence between us stretches until I say, somewhat jokingly, "You're the Elath-worshipping heathen here. Any words of wisdom? Any advice?"

His voice is low and deadly serious when he answers, "Keep the lid on. Do whatever you have to do to keep that lid on. Do you hear me?"

I was expecting reassurance, maybe even a bit of answering humor. Instead, he looks at me as if I'm as dangerous as a Hedenski shield maiden wielding a battle-axe.

"It isn't as if I did it on purpose! That's what I'm trying to tell you. I thought I could contain it—Her—but I lost control yesterday, and it only gets harder with each passing day. Sometimes I feel as if my skin might burst if we don't get Her out of me soon, as if my whole body will crack open, and it scares me. I'm so scared."

He gazes at me with the sorrowful expression of the Unknown Saint. I press my hands to my cheeks and try not to cry until he steps close to me, snapping out of his mournful stupor. "Hey, I made you a promise, remember? And I keep my promises." He makes the sign of the circle swear again and says, "Don't leave me hanging this time, dearest wife."

A sound that is both a groan and a laugh escapes my mouth, but I link my ring with his and feel a hundred times better.

"We're going to get Elath out of you, all right?"

"All right."

He releases the swear, and we resume walking. As the outline of the Illeses' house becomes visible in the distance, I start to panic at the prospect of facing Mera again. Will she be mad at me for running away? Will she think I'm stupid? Or jealous? What will I say to her? I'm lost in thought, paying no attention to my surroundings, when Tavik suddenly pulls on my arm so hard he nearly rips it from the socket. The next thing I know, he's got me shoved up against a tree trunk, the rough bark abrading my back. He looks over my shoulder, his eyes bright and sharp.

"What is it?" I whisper.

He breathes through his nose, in and out, as he stares at Illesmaat. Then he presses his forehead to mine and curses, "Oh, death. Death, decay, and dying."

"Tavik?"

"How far is it to Saint Helios from here?" He speaks so quietly I can barely make out the words. His forehead is still pressed to mine, his sweat dampening my skin.

"A hundred miles at least."

"By road or as the crow flies?"

"By road. It's probably closer to seventy miles directly. What happened?"

"Brother Miklos happened."

I can't bear the not knowing, so I turn my head to look. The Illeses' front door hangs crookedly open from one hinge, and the words *Elathian Traitors* have been scrawled across the front of the house in red paint. Posted on the wide trunk of an oak tree in front is a sign with rough-drawn sketches of Tavik and me. My eyes catch the words *By Order of the Holy See of the Ovinist Church* in bold letters over our faces. I slap a hand over my mouth to push back the fear rising up my throat.

Tavik hooks his arm around my waist and pulls me deeper into the trees. "Listen to me very carefully. You are going to stay right here while I sneak back in to send a message to DeRopa."

I grab his sleeve so hard the wool wrinkles in my hand. "No!"

"We need help. *I* need help." Tavik looks much more like the frightened boy under the Convent of Saint Vinnica than the confident friend I've come to know, and I remember his drunken words about DeRopa at the Brewers' house: *I wish he were here. He'd know what to do.*

It's exactly how I feel about Goodson Anskar.

All this time, we've been heading toward the Goodson, Tavik for his sword but me for his guidance. And now Tavik is reaching out to the man who is like a father to him for the same purpose. He's right. He needs help. I need help. *We* need help. And I don't know that I care whether that help comes from the Goodson or Captain DeRopa so long as a competent, experienced person who genuinely cares about us takes charge.

"Stay here," Tavik says, but before he can leave me, I pull the sword from the scabbard at my side.

"Take it. It won't do me any good, and you might need it."

He hesitates, but he nods and takes it from my hand, brushing my fingers with his in a way that doesn't feel accidental before he leaves me hidden in the grove, alone.

As the minutes pass, I can't keep still. I think of Mera, hoping she's alive and fearing she isn't. How could Brother Miklos take her life from her? How could her life be worth so little? It's a difficult possibility to swallow, but easier than worrying about Tavik, who is definitely still alive and might not be in the very near future if he gets caught. The longer he's gone, the more my imagination takes over, envisioning all the horrible things that could be happening to him as I wait here, useless. When I can't stand it anymore, I head toward the house, following in his footsteps.

"What are you doing? Get back!" Tavik's voice nearly makes me jump out of my skin.

"Don't do that!" I gasp.

"Then don't go sticking your nose out where Brother Miklos can cut it off! Father of death!"

"Were the Illeses there? Mera?"

Tavik licks his lips and opens his mouth, but nothing comes out. He simply shakes his head.

I ask the question I wish I could keep bottled up inside me. "Do you think they're still alive?"

He shuffles his feet. "Maybe. But . . . there was blood. A lot of it."

My eyes well up. My lips fatten with the urge to cry. I sniff, trying to keep a grip on myself. "Did you send your message?"

"The coop was bashed in and there was no bird in sight." He holds out his hand, and my necklace dangles from his fingers. "I found it on the kitchen floor." I take it from his hand and put it on, but the weight around my neck feels heavier than I remember, less comforting.

Tavik rubs his chin. "Seventy miles as the crow flies, huh? That makes us a pair of crows. Can you make it, Brother Elgar?"

"I think I preferred 'my darling wife.'" I'm trying to lighten the mood, but when he looks at me as if I were as fragile as a china plate, I tell him, "I won't break."

I hope that's true, because it doesn't feel true.

He draws my arm over his shoulders. "Come on, my darling wife. We need to move."

Thirty-One

"Unbelievable. Does it ever *not* rain in Rosvania?" Tavik complains four storm-soaked days later as we trudge between the grapevines of Rosvania's western wine country. Any fruit that survived the rains has long since been harvested, and the remaining vines are black with rot. Even their wooden supports are decaying and toppling over. The rosebushes at the end of each row, planted there for the purpose of alerting the vintners to any diseases in their precious vines, perished long before our arrival, and I can't help but remember a line from *The Song of Saint Wenslas*: *Your fields shall drown in the punishing floods of the Father.*

The south is drying up, while the north is drowning.

Until there is nothing left but death and death.

Ambrus was right. It's all happening so quickly now. The end. And the fact that I still don't know what to do about the soul inside me—the cause of this disaster—weighs me down a thousand times more than my muddy boots.

"What if I'm the cause of this?" I ask Tavik, giving voice again to that theory that has been gnawing at my insides since Lithgate. "What if Elath's presence inside me is flooding the earth? What if the world is coming to an end right now, right this minute, before our eyes?"

Tavik gazes off over the ruin stretching out in all directions. "That's why we're going to get the Hand of the Father," he answers grimly, and we keep walking. And walking.

I've never been drunk, but I think this must be how it feels, the complete inability to put one foot in front of the other in a way that will guarantee I'll stay upright. Mud squelches beneath my feet, making it hard to move in a straight line. The air stinks of mold, and the rain taps incessantly against my body.

When we stop for the day, Tavik prays, and I move away to give him privacy he doesn't need. I'd pray, too, but why bother? The Father never answers, while the immortal life inside me is ever-present. She pushes upward and outward, straining against the membrane I keep stretched taut over Her. If I am as lost to the One True God as I seem to be, there's no point in keeping my most daring question buttoned up inside me: What if the spirit I carry is, in fact, a goddess?

Goddess.

I can taste the word on my tongue as the presence within me vibrates, like the satisfied purring of a cat. Ever since Elath entered me, I have assumed that somewhere down the road, Vinnica's fate would be my own, as inevitable as the sun setting in the west. But what if the opposite is true? What if the world could have a hopeful future instead? What if *I* could have a hopeful future in it? Even whispering the words in my mind feels like freedom.

I kneel as if to pray, pressing my forehead to the rot at the grapevines' roots, but it isn't the Vessel's Prayer I sing. It's a Sanctus verse of my own creation.

I pray the song of myself.

> *Sing, faithful, of Gelya,*
> *Prison and prisoner no more.*

The life inside me stirs, and an unnerving sensation overtakes me. I hear the flapping of a Daughter's sash in the wind, and a familiar scent—ink and tea, melding together—cuts through the mist.

Zofia.

I don't look up, but I'm certain she stands before me, real and alive. I've seen her in my dreams, but her physical presence in the living world is something else entirely. Understanding sinks in slowly, like water soaking into the soil of a potted herb, the realization that the Zofia of my dreams is not Zofia at all. This being I hold inside me—the one who spoke to me in the convent courtyard—is wearing the face of the only mother I've ever known. This is how She chooses to speak to me.

Look up, She says in Zofia's voice.

It's one thing to pray, to be heard. It's another thing to bow before an immortal being and hear an answer. Terror emanates from my skin like heat.

What have you ever had to fear from me? Look up, Daughter.

Trembling on my hands and knees, I do as I'm told. I look up.

No spirit dressed in Zofia's body stands before me. But there, stiff and unmoving on the ground just inches from my nose, lies a bird. Death has dulled her blue feathers and her gold-colored breast, but the black and white markings on her head are unmistakable. A soulswift.

A dead soulswift.

Tavik comes up behind me, and when he sees what I see, he crouches beside me. "Poor little thing."

"They're immortal," I tell myself as much as him, my voice reedy.

"Not this one," he says softly as he removes the canister from the creature's leg.

"Is there a message?"

His face is drawn and worried. "No."

No.

I asked the forbidden question, and someone, somewhere, handed me my eviscerated faith on a platter. I start to cry. Tavik puts a comforting hand on my back, unlocking an even deeper grief I didn't know I had inside me. I throw my head back and wail at the sky.

"Shh!" He puts his arm around me, but my mouth refuses to contain the sound of my sorrow. It just goes on and on, and selfish sinner that I am, I know I'm not weeping for this bird. I'm weeping for myself, because I *am* the bird and the bird is me.

As I touch my long fingers to the soulswift's feathers, I fling back the blanket that shrouds Elath, and I drink deeply from Her power. The border between us blurs. Our souls overlap, and in that juncture, there is more power than I ever dreamed I could hold inside me. I didn't know my eyes were closed until I open them, and the world is full of light. Tavik cries out, but I could not stop this now if I tried.

Elath's strength sears my flesh, rising from my toes and careening from my mind, all of it streaming through my fingertips into the bird's lifeless body. My mouth yawns wide in agonizing rapture as the light pours out of me, running down my chin, streaming across my shoulders, shimmering down the skin of my arms and hands. Beneath my fingertips, the soulswift twitches. Her death-dulled feathers brighten, a lively blue against the backdrop of a dying world. I pick her up tenderly, cupping her between the palms of my hands, and I hold her high, blowing on her, riffling the feathers until her chest expands with breath. The bird takes flight, circling upward, higher and higher, singing her ecstatic song.

The light leaves me, and I collapse into the mud, numb and joyous and frightened by what I have done.

"Gelya!"

Tavik sounds far away as he hoists my limp body out of the sludge to hold me like a baby. My head lolls, so he props me up against his strong shoulder and cups my cheek. His face—his beautiful face—is painted with panic.

"Come on! Don't do this!"

I try to say his name, but I can't move my tongue. All I can do is watch and listen as Tavik falls apart.

"I've done everything You asked! Why are You doing this to her?" he shouts, not at me, I realize, but at Elath. At his Mother.

I see the fingertips of my handprint on his chest peeking out from beneath his tunic as he leans over me. It's not one solid mark, but a series of tiny symbols all coming together in the shape of my hand—Sanctus, right there over his heart. My body comes back to me, and I place the tips of my fingers against Tavik's song.

A skinny boy pushes a stool just below an enormous book with the words Atlas of the World *embossed in gold down its spine as the nib of his mother's quill scratches its familiar music behind him. The book is half as tall as he is, and he nearly topples over as he wrestles it free from the shelf. But when he lies stomach-down on the floor and opens to the first page and sees the vibrant colors of the book's illuminations, he knows it was worth the effort.*

He's just old enough to sound out the name of each country: Sudmar, Wesmar, Ostmar, Ukrent. There are deserts and mountains, goats and olive orchards, each illumination lovelier than the last. His eyes drink in the blue-gray-green color of the seas hugging the coastline, an unimaginable horizon of water.

The pictures grow stranger as the pages move north, an alien landscape of forests and grain fields stretching through Tovnia and Rosvania to the hills of Auria and the Great Wall of Saint Balzos. He knows what the wall is for, and it makes him shiver, though the library is hot and stuffy.

He turns the page.

The Dead Forest. Its trees grow close together, punctuated by ominous black spaces between the trunks. He's certain that if he stares into the darkness long enough, he will see the monsters that lurk there—the telleg—hungry and waiting.

He turns the page.

And there they are, thin and ragged, their cloaks billowing around them like phantoms. One of them has its hood thrown back, revealing a skull-like head with a mouth full of jagged teeth. The boy scoots away in terror, and his mother races to him when she hears him sobbing.

"What's wrong?" she asks, stroking his dark curls with a gentle hand.

He points to the open book without looking at it and sniffles. She sighs and takes her son by the chin. "Listen to me, my little soul. There are no telleg in Kantar. And even if Grama were full of monsters, you'd be safe. Do you know why?"

He shakes his head.

"Because your mother will protect you. Always."

He nods, but he knows that a book has told him the truth in a way no adult ever could.

She holds him by the arms and gives him an affectionate jiggle. "Would you like me to read you a story?"

Mollified, he grins back at her and leads her through the stacks to the place where ropes cordon off a great stone slab carved all over with lines and swirls. "That," he declares.

She undoes the rope and brushes the symbols with her fingertips. "I can tell you the story, but I'm afraid that only a Vessel from the Convent of Saint Vinnica could truly read this."

"That's all right," he assures her.

She looks on him with warm eyes, the same green as his, and she begins, "'Call down the Mother's voice, the song of the lark, to sing the tale of Ludo, Breaker and Broken.'" She tells him the story of the greatest Two-Swords of all time, and for once, he regrets that he prefers the library to his brothers' sword games. But his regret is short-lived, because his mother cocks an eyebrow at him and says, "Didn't I ask you to fetch water an hour ago?"

Grumbling, he trudges home and slings the yoke over his narrow shoulders, the pails squeaking from rusty handles. As he passes the Temple of the Mother and Father on his way to the well, he peers into the courtyard, where boys can always be found playing Ludo on the pitch. When he doesn't see Raran or Barri, he tiptoes past the iron gate, but a moment later, he hears Raran's voice behind him. "What's this? Too good to play Ludo with us, little brother?"

He turns, his shoulders slumping as he answers, "I was sent to fetch water."

Snorting, Barri yanks the yoke from the boy's shoulders and hands it to Raran, who casts aside the buckets, plants his foot at the yoke's center, and pulls on one end until the wood breaks in half. Then he tosses the pieces at the boy's feet. "There. Now you have two swords. Play me."

With shaking hands, the boy picks up the two halves, but before he can speak or move or think, Raran raps him on the hand, cracking a birdlike bone beneath the skin. The child cries out and drops the sword as Raran strikes him behind the knees, forcing him to the ground. The gathering crowd of boys roars with laughter, but Raran is not amused. He pokes his little brother in the penis with the tip of his weapon. "You were born with a sword. Use it. Get up."

The boy obeys, fighting the urge to cry. He blocks his brother's hit this time, but the blow strikes his knuckles, and he drops the sword again.

"Pick it up."

A single tear leaks from the corner of his right eye. Raran throws down his own weapons, grabs him under the arms, and hoists him off the ground, nose-to-nose with him. "Don't you dare waste your water."

The little boy spits in his brother's face, and the square goes deadly silent.

Raran's cheeks turn purple with fury. "If you're so eager to waste your water, let me help you."

"No!" the boy shouts, fighting to free himself as Raran carries him toward the dark mouth of the well.

Barri's smirk evaporates. "Raran, stop."

"He can't keep hiding in that library, Barri. This is for his own good."

"Please, no! I'm sorry!" The boy wraps his thin legs around Raran's torso, but Barri, nodding sadly, pries him loose.

"Catch!" says Raran as he hurls the child at the dangling pail. The boy flails his arms but grasps the bucket, sending a sharp pain shooting through his injured hand. He hangs over the opening as Barri operates the crank, lowering him into the shaft. By the time the rope halts, he's sobbing shamelessly. "I'm sorry! Please!" His voice ricochets off the brickwork before Raran's last words echo down to him: "You need to learn how to use your sword, Tavik."

"Raran! Barri!" But there's no answer, so he pulls himself up onto the pail with his good hand, making the bucket swing back and forth *like a pendulum, his stomach lurching with the motion. The dark water below is awake and waiting—a living thing. He squeezes his eyes shut and hugs the rough fibers of the rope to his cheek, and still no one comes for him, not even his mother.*

Horrible noises crash down on him from above, clashes and cries and booms, blending one into the other like a terrifying chorus. Tendrils of smoke billow into the well's shaft, burning his lungs, making him wheeze and gasp for air until he's so weak he can't hold on any longer. The bucket tips, pouring him out, and he falls.

He falls.

His body sinks into the murk like a stone, and he is in complete and utter darkness. He hangs suspended in the water like a baby in his mother's womb. Then the darkness thins, and a light rises up to meet him, as gray and insubstantial as a ghost. He can no longer see the walls of the well. Instead, he finds himself drifting inside a ring of trees far wider than the well's circumference. Beyond the ring is an entire forest, more trees than he could imagine.

And he is not alone.

The telleg drift toward him from between the tree trunks, caped wraiths with hoods thrown back, revealing faces grown over with pale gray skin, so pallid they glow in the gloom.

He screams, the last breath in his lungs bubbling out of his mouth in silent terror, as a telleg reaches for him, moving unnaturally fast. He darts away only to back into another, and he watches in petrified horror as a mouth cuts itself across the monster's face and bites into his arm. Pain like nothing he has ever felt sears his entire being.

His mother comes for him then. Her eyes are his eyes. Her dark hair fans out around her in the water. He reaches for her, longing to be held, but when she stretches her arms out to him, it isn't warmth that touches his hand. It's cold, sharp steel.

His mother has handed him a sword.

Tavik wrenches my hand off his heart, yanking his song from my body, leaving me limp and powerless again, as if he had ripped my bones out, too. I can't move, and to be honest, I'm not entirely sure I want to reclaim this body of mine with all its hurts and griefs.

Tavik dabs at my bloody nose with this damp sleeve, coaxing me back to myself. "Come on. Come back. You can come back now." He sounds calm, but his sweat and waxy complexion and terror show me the scared boy I saw in the tunnel beneath the convent when we escaped the parlertorium.

"Gelya," he calls to me.

The pain of living in the world begins to seep in, a coldness that freezes me to the bone.

"Can you hear me?"

My voice is small when I answer at last. "Yes. I could hear you all along."

"Thank the Mother. Can you move?"

"A little. I just need to rest for a minute." Even saying that much is exhausting.

"Whatever that was, don't do it again. Do you hear me?" Tavik focuses his attention on cleaning my face, avoiding my eyes.

"I won't," I tell him, but there's a part of me still drifting beside his childhood self in the water of the well, scared and alone in a world full of monsters, just as part of me never left the Dead Forest.

"You've seen them," I say.

He shakes his head. "I was just a kid. I imagined the whole thing."

I put my icy hand over his warm one, and I have the strength to sit up after all. I take his left arm in my hands, and he lets me. I pull back his sleeve, and he lets me. I trace the silver scars on his skin.

He lets me.

"This is not your imagination."

He shuts his eyes tight.

"Don't you understand?" I press. "I've seen them. And you have seen them. And we're still alive. And neither of us is alone anymore."

He opens his eyes, his striking irises made lovely with threatening tears. I'm not sure how long we stay like this with my fingers pressed against his scar, brown eyes looking into green with very little for either of us to hide behind. But then he pulls away, slipping out of my hands. "You're going to make me waste my water all over the place," he gripes as he lodges his fingers in my hair and dishevels it like mad again.

"This is my new least favorite habit of yours," I protest, annoyed that he destroyed the moment.

He gives me a lopsided grin. "That's too bad, because it's my new favorite thing to do."

"You are a nightmare."

"Tavik: rhymes with *havoc*," he reminds me. "I need to get you out of this rain so you can rest. Think you can make it to some shelter?"

I nod, hoping that I have the strength to do what must be done. He hauls me to my feet, and we walk in the pouring rain, albeit slowly. Each step takes us a little closer to the Monastery of Saint Helios, where the Father knows what is going to happen, but at least I'm not alone in this.

We cross paths with an abandoned shed, which seems like a miracle beyond asking. Tavik breaks a rusted lock to let us inside. "I wish I could light a fire for you tonight, but we can't risk it," he says as he clears some old rakes out of the way, "You're sleeping with me. No arguments. We need to get you warm."

I don't have it in me to protest, and frankly, I don't care. There's nothing amorous or romantic about the ad hoc bed I share with Tavik. It does me little good anyway. No matter how tightly he holds me, I can't get warm, and neither of us can dry out.

I could dip into the burning heat at my center. I know if I touched Her, She would fill my veins with fire. Temptation unfurls like a spring fern, but Tavik's words burn brighter in my mind. *Whatever that was, don't do it again.* So I lie awake, bitterly cold as I nestle against his lean heat. I think of his mother, the woman in the library who promised to keep him safe from the monsters.

Always.

How strange to know her face when my own mother's face remains a mystery to me. I even know her name: Semla.

Thirty-Two

I spend the next day grappling with the fact that I raised a soul-swift from the dead. Or Elath raised a soulswift from the dead. Or we both did. The line between us is becoming disturbingly blurry. I'd be more panicked about this if I weren't a walking, talking coma right now. Besides, I can tell Tavik is worried enough for both of us.

After another night of inadequate shelter, he insists that we take the risk of knocking on the door of a farmhouse and begging a roof for the night, even though we're within a few miles of the monastery. I want to tell him it's too risky, but I also want to melt into a useless puddle in front of a fire. Thank the Father, we're not approaching the monastery from the south, so we can avoid the town at the very least.

A young woman answers the door, and her eyes bulge when she sees two Knights of the Order dripping on her doorstep.

"Forgive us, miss, but could you ask your father if we might stay here for the night?" I ask in my deepest voice. "We're headed for the Monastery of Saint Helios, but I don't think we'll make it before dusk."

"You'll have to ask my husband," she answers doubtfully. "Um, come in."

"Thank you," Tavik says, stepping past her, and I follow him inside.

The house consists of two rooms, one that serves as a kitchen, dining room, and parlor, and another that I assume is the bedroom. Statues and icons of the saints sit on every dusty shelf, and there is a yellowed painting of Saint Ovin cleaving the Great Demon in two framed on the mantel, a brutal and bloody depiction that makes Elath's presence inside me squirm uncomfortably.

"Tea?" the woman asks us.

"Yes, please," I answer. As she busies herself over the stove, I whisper to Tavik, "You see? Ovinists can be charitable."

He eyes the tiny saints. "I'm pretty sure she wouldn't be as charitable if she knew who we really were."

"Here." She thrusts a mug of weak tea at each of us. As she turns back to the stove, I notice the swell of her stomach. She's pregnant, though I'd swear she was about my age.

Tavik and I hang our dripping cloaks from the rafters, then steam ourselves dry in front of the fire, a simple pleasure you only learn to appreciate when it's been taken from you. As our boots and socks bake on the heart stones, I begin to feel better, stronger.

"What's your name?" I ask the young woman, more and more

convinced that she can't be more than eighteen.

Her frightened eyes dart between Tavik and me. "Pruda."

I speak gently, trying to set her at ease. "Pruda, my name is Brother Elgar, and this is Brother Remur. We are truly grateful for your hospitality."

She gives me what I think is meant to be a smile before turning back to the stove, where something gamey boils in a stockpot.

Tavik is using the privy when Pruda's husband returns. He's much older than she is, a man in his late thirties or early forties with a wiry frame and piercing blue eyes.

"What's all this?" he asks his wife, tracking mud across the floor as he crosses the room to her, glaring at me all the while.

"They're Knights of the Order," Pruda tells the side of his face in a rush. "They asked for shelter from the rain. The other is in the privy."

Something about him sucks all the air out of the room. I'm frightened of those blue eyes.

You're supposed to be a man, Gelya, I remind myself. *For the Father's sake, act like one.*

I feign ease, even though the husband's hard look makes me quail inside. "I'm Brother Elgar. Your wife was kind enough to let us in to dry out. We're on our way to Saint Helios but would be glad of a roof over our heads for the night."

His icy eyes catch sight of our pale blue cloaks hanging from the beams above. "Of course," he says, suddenly servile. "Pruda! Make these men a feast fit for the Holy See. Go get a chicken."

"That won't be necessary," I assure him as Pruda looks down at her feet and says, "That will take hours to prepare and . . . and . . . we only have three hens left."

He steps intimidatingly close to her. "You know I never ask for anything twice."

She shrinks back from him, pressing herself against the shabby cupboard. "Yes, Husband." She turns hurriedly and goes on tippy-toe to fetch two onions and a potato from a meager store on top of the cabinet, her bulbous stomach hanging over the work surface. For a breath, she pauses and looks to the statue of Saint Brivig, the patron saint of wives. I know she's sending up a heretical prayer to a saint, the way I used to pray to Saint Vinnica when I didn't know where else to turn. I'm looking at only one piece of the puzzle, but I can already see the whole picture, the way this man ruins her life every day and all the time simply because he was born in the image of the Father. The spirit inside me roils, swirling together with my own anger.

Tavik comes back and shakes the rain out of his hair before he notices the husband.

"Come in, come in," the man says as if his home were a mansion and he were welcoming an old friend. He's treating complete strangers with the esteem he should be showing his wife, the mother of his child.

I step between him and Tavik, and it's all I can do to keep Elath's rage from setting my eyes alight.

"Gel-el-elgar?" Tavik calls uncertainly behind me.

I ignore him as I draw myself up to my full height. I want this man to see just how much taller I am than he is. "I don't care for the way you treat your wife, sir," I tell him in a voice edged with frost. "She is not your property. She is not your chattel. She is not yours at all. And you will treat her with dignity and respect as the Father commands you. Do you understand?"

I've rendered him speechless. He nods as he gazes up at me with eyes full of fear simply because he believes me to be a Knight of the Order.

"If I ever return to this place and find that you have hurt that girl in either body or spirit, I will unleash something far worse than words on you." I lean in so that he has to look me in the eye. "As the Father commands *me*."

We eat rabbit broth and hard bread in silence. I make sure Pruda saves her hen. After the husband, whose name I haven't bothered to learn, goes to bed, I pull Pruda aside. "If he ever hurts you, in any way, you should seek help from the Monastery of Saint Helios, all right?"

She smiles weakly but says nothing in response. She knows the truth as well as I do. The monks of Saint Helios would only send her back, instructing her to obey her husband as the One True God wills it, because a man is made in the image of the Father, and it is her duty to submit to him.

I want to help Pruda clean up the kitchen, but a man would never do such a thing, so I'm left to watch her work as I sit with Tavik by the fire. What little warmth and energy filled me after I first arrived drains out of me all over again.

"Was it me, or did you kick ass this evening?" Tavik asks as we lie down by the fireplace after Pruda goes to bed.

"I'm not entirely sure what that means."

He laughs. "Probably for the best. Good night, Brother Elgar, Kicker of Ass."

"Good night, Brother Remur."

As the fire's flames turn to embers, I consider what little good I've done today. Pruda is as much a prisoner as I am, and a prison, too, when I consider the baby inside her, especially if that baby is a girl. It reminds me of my wedding, the way I had no say in what happened. At least it was fake.

I roll over and look at Tavik, his face slack in sleep, angelic by the light of the fire.

Fake. Definitely fake.

Probably.

After a while, as sleep continues to elude me, my mind drifts to Mera, the girl she was, the woman she'll never be, the friend she might have been. *You're so lucky,* she told me, and maybe she was right. At least I'm still among the living, and at least I still have a few choices left.

Which is more than I can say for Pruda.

In the dream, Zofia-who-is-not-Zofia sits on a stool beside me, frowning at my work, Her arms crossed, Her lips puckered in disapproval. "You're taking too long with this."

I stare at my desk. Usually, I keep it fairly tidy, but today there are stacks and stacks of books and papers and scrolls. The sight of so much work overwhelms me. I don't know where to begin. "I can't remember the assignment," I admit sheepishly.

Behind me, the sound of drumbeats drifts into the scriptorium. I turn in my chair and gaze into the darkness beyond the door in confusion.

"That," She says in a tone of exasperation. "How can you forget?"

The rhythm grows louder as I step into the hallway and follow the sound through an ever-thickening forest. I dance, feeling the drumbeats in my chest like the beating of my heart. The path carries me to the clearing, the stream, and the huge tree towering above me, so expansive that it would take twenty men linking hands to encircle the trunk. The drumming swells, and the stag waits at the clearing's center.

No.

Not a stag.

Tavik.

On his head, he wears a crown of antlers.

The drums stop, and I am no longer dancing.

The woman is there again, as indistinct as before, but I know who she is now.

"Ati!" I try to call out to her—the Hedenski word for mother— *but no sound comes from my mouth. I am powerless to move or speak as my mother drags the blade of her dagger across Tavik's throat, letting his blood onto the roots of the tree. The stream of his life pours into the river, and my heart splits with its own cut.*

My mother's voice is Zofia's voice, ringing sharply into the night. "The son gives his death so that the Mother may live!"

Thirty-Three

The first thing I see when I wake is Tavik's back, curled away from me in the predawn light. I listen to him inhale and exhale like the ebb and flow of the sea, reassuring myself that his death in my dream wasn't real.

But the tree was real—*is* real.

Everything falls into place like a well-played game of Shakki.

Elath's body is a tree, just as it was in the text Tavik and I put together. I have seen it with my own eyes, danced before it in my forgotten childhood.

I know what it is and where to find it, but there's only one way to get to the great tree that is Elath's body in Hedenskia: through the Dead Forest. Tavik swore he'd protect me, but how can I ask him to face the telleg again? How can *I* face them again? Goodson Anskar was the one who got me through that nightmare ten years ago, and he may be the only one who can help me now, no matter what Tavik promised.

My mind is certain of this. My heart is not.

Careful not to wake him, I rummage through my sack for the last strip of my Daughter's sash and sneak out the front door. If only I could slink away from the dreadful truth as easily.

There's a gelya tree in the yard, visible from the road that leads to the Monastery of Saint Helios, and I tie the red strip to a low branch. I'm not sure why. I know he's not looking for me, and I know he'll never see it. It's just that there's something comforting in the gesture, like hugging my old rag doll to my chest. The fabric flaps in a gust of wind that smells of decay and the early approach of winter. I kneel on the carpet of wet leaves, clutching the Goodson's triptych in my hand. I don't press my forehead to the earth. I no longer know to whom I'm praying, but I do know that I'm not subjugating myself to any god's will, the Father's or the Mother's.

"Let me be wrong," I pray. I beg. "I don't want to go back. Don't make me go back."

It takes nothing to recall how a telleg's mouth rips itself across its chalky, faceless head. I can still hear the screams of the murdered tear past me, even when I'm awake.

How can you forget? Zofia's voice asks me.

But that wasn't Zofia, was it, the life humming inside me, speaking to me in the guise of the only mother I have ever known?

Mother.

Elath.

Goddess.

Demon.

I rise to my unsteady feet, close my eyes, and breathe deeply through my nose as I begin the sequence I have seen Tavik perform more times than I can count, slow, methodical, deliberate.

Beautiful.

It's harder than it looks to move so slowly, to turn and stretch so precisely, although that may be my own exhaustion at play. I open my eyes a hair to keep my balance, but my focus is on the movement. *I'm praying,* I tell myself. *This is a prayer.* And it is. It feels the way a prayer should—reverent, clear—only now I'm praying with my whole body, not just my words.

I reach my arms outward and back, my elbows pointing skyward. Then I bring my hands down to my sides, remembering the way Tavik turns the swords over his hands, or tries to. I've never appreciated how difficult that maneuver is until this moment, how hard the entire prayer must be for him, holding the weight of both swords steady through each painstaking sequence. I feel the tugging sensation I felt so long ago, mild in comparison to the moment the seedpod burst in my hand, but related, similar. An answer from within.

I start from the beginning, my eyes glazing over, my breath like a bellows. In my mind, each movement has a name: Zofia, Mera, Pruda, Vinnica, Lanya.

"Gelya?"

I stumble to a halt. Tavik stands before me, sleep rumpled and confused. Like me, he left his cloak and sword belt inside, and his tunic is wrinkled around his waist.

"I—I'm sorry," I stammer, mortified by what I've done and

even more mortified to be caught doing it. "I'm so sorry."

"Was that my prayer?"

I can't look him in the face. "Are you angry?"

"No."

"I was just . . ." I begin, but that's as far as I get. I smooth down my hair, unsure what to say to him. There are suddenly so many things unsaid between us.

He comes to stand by my side.

"What are you doing?" I ask him, his proximity like a fire blazing next to me.

"I've never tried it without swords. Can we start from the beginning?"

I hesitate, but Tavik doesn't wait for an answer. He gives me a nod and says, "All things in balance." Then he moves his arms directly skyward in two parallel lines, arcing them slowly downward to his sides.

"This is the Greeting of the Morning Sun," he tells me, and by the time he's retracing the movement back the way he came, I'm with him.

"The Farewell to the Morning Star," he says.

He names each movement.

The Celebration of Birth.

The Gift of the Mother's Love.

The Creation of Life.

"The opening sequence begins as my own life did, with the Mother," he explains without pause, moving directly into the next pose.

The Molding of Woman from Whom All Life Comes.

The Flooding of the Delta.

The Gathering of Grain to Feed the Hungry.

Together, we bow low into the Supplicant Child and reach outward. "The swords extend from the soul at the center of your being," says Tavik.

The Offering of Man to the Father's Service. Here, the arms move in different directions. "I lead with what would be the Sword of Wrath if we were carrying blades, the weapon of the weaker hand, because death is weaker than life."

The Sweeping Away of What Came Before.

We arch our backs, and our arms cross behind us in a gesture Tavik calls the Acceptance of Death, followed by the Triumph Over the Dark Night, the part where he struggles, the moment when he spins the pommels of his weapons over the back of each hand. But without the swords, there is no possibility of failure.

The final gesture closes with our fists brought together before our hearts.

"The Promise of Right Action," Tavik murmurs.

We stay like that for a moment as an awkwardness creeps in, at least on my part.

"How did I do?" I ask him with a nervous laugh.

"The execution wasn't perfect, but the sanctity of it was." He faces me, and something in that look makes my skin light up. He rubs the side of his leg, his eyes shifting away from me. "It isn't strictly a Kantari prayer, you know. I mean, it is, but . . ."

"But?"

"It's my prayer, specific to me."

He bites the inside of his cheek, and I think I may have done something really and truly offensive. "Oh. I didn't realize. I'm sorry."

He scrapes the toe of his boot through the rotting leaves. "There are lots of poses and sequences for prayers. When you become an adult, you string together the ones you find most meaningful."

"Is it bad to pray someone else's prayer?"

He smooths out the trough he made in the leaves with his foot. "No."

"Have you ever prayed someone else's prayer?"

"No. It's kind of complicated."

I want to make certain that I haven't offended him, so I ask, "Does a woman ever pray a man's prayer? Or a man a woman's prayer?"

His gaze shifts away again. "Not often."

And then his eyes find the flag I tied onto a branch of the gelya tree, and my cheeks burn with regret as I watch the understanding of what it means sink in.

"What is that?" he asks icily.

"It's . . . It's . . ." How can I tell him about the tree in Hedenskia, about the Mother's body, about the path I must take to get there? I told him I wanted the truth, but now that I have it, I can't seem to say it aloud, to give voice to all the fear rushing into me.

"How long?" he spits.

"Please don't yell at me."

"Well, yelling is what people do when they're really mad! Go figure!"

"Let me explain."

"Explain what? That you're leaving a trail for the Goodson so he can come save his precious Daughter? That *is* what you're doing, isn't it?"

There are so many things I need to tell him, but my hurt and fear come bursting out of my mouth instead. "I am a Vessel and a Daughter of the Convent of Saint Vinnica, and the Goodson means the world to me. What did you expect?"

"I expected you to know good and well who you carry inside you. I expected you to do the right thing by Her. But you would willingly put Her into the hands of the monster who is going to lock you away if he ever gets his hands on you."

"That's not true."

"He's already kidnapped you once, so why in the name of the Mother do you trust him now? And what was he doing in Hedenskia in the first place, I'd like to know? He showed up ten years ago, and then the Hedenski coincidentally shut down their only two harbors and cut off what little contact they had with the outside world? Have you ever thought about that? Because I'd lay even money you haven't. What kind of man takes a child through the Dead Forest, through the telleg? Ask yourself that."

"It wasn't like that. You don't know him."

Veins pop along Tavik's neck as he leans his livid face into mine. "I know he sent Brother Miklos to level my town. I lost my family—my brothers, my *mother*. And then he shows up in Hedenskia and did the Mother knows what to your own people. At least you have the luxury of forgetting. And he did all that to hunt down a goddess he thinks is a demon, the same 'demon' who's inside you, I might add. So let me just remind you that if he ever gets his hands on you, he's going to lock you up and throw away the key. The one thing he is absolutely *not* going to do is help you."

Tavik might as well run me through with the Sword of Wrath, and he's not even finished yet.

"And here's something else you might want to think about, my beloved wife. If you've left a trail for one Knight of the Order, who's to say another knight hasn't followed it? You wanted to bring the Goodson to us, but what if you've led Brother Miklos right to our doorstep? Good job! Well done! Brilliant!"

Holy Father, I never considered that possibility. What if Brother Miklos has been following my flags? What if Mera and her family died because of what I did? My chest heaves with remorse. I turn on my heel and head straight for the road that will take me to the Monastery of Saint Helios and to the Goodson and as far away from Tavik as I can get.

"Fine! Go!" he calls to my retreating backside. "Go find your savior! But don't come crying to me when he leaves you to die in a dungeon, and then the whole world shrivels up because the Mother will be dead and gone, too!"

I pick up the pace. I can't get away fast enough. By the time I hear him hawk and spit behind me, wasting his water out of pure spite, I am no longer walking.

I'm running.

Thirty-Four

I run so fast that the world around me becomes a blur and my lungs scream for air. The burning of my muscles feels better than the ache in my heart, so I pump my legs harder, pushing my body until I can go no farther. I stop in the middle of a harvested barley field, so close to the monastery I can see the chapel's spire in the distance, but as I try to catch my breath, I look behind me, not ahead.

There's no sign of Tavik.

I've been tethered to him so long that I have no idea what to do with my newfound freedom. Only it doesn't feel like freedom at all. It feels like the unmooring of a rudderless boat, like setting out on a journey under a starless sky.

I turn in a circle and take in the rolling land in all directions. The world is vast, and I'm so small within it.

I wish I could run all the way home to Saint Vinnica, but even as I think the words, the dream dissolves. Once you rip the flower from the soil, you can't replant it and expect it to grow and thrive.

You can only hope it lives, and what kind of life is that? What life is left to return to at Saint Vinnica when Zofia is dead and when I hold a being inside me that the Goodson hates?

He's going to lock you up and throw away the key.

Why did Tavik have to say it?

The impulse to throw something as hard and as far as I can makes my fingers curl, and with no stones in sight, I bend over, yank what remains of the ruined, rain-spoiled barley stalks from the earth, and hurl them into the air, flinging them every which way.

"I don't want this!" I shout to the sky, raising hooked fingers toward heaven as if I could claw my salvation directly from the Father.

"I don't blame you. You've been dealt a lousy hand," comes a stranger's voice in Kantari.

An electric charge of alarm bolts through me. I spin to find three men to my right. One of them, a man in his late twenties with a black patch over one eye, holds up his hands, signaling his goodwill. "Sorry. I didn't mean to startle you. I'm Rusik DeRopa. And may I say that it's a pleasure and an honor to meet you at last, Daughter Gelya."

He holds out a hand to me. I'm still trying to figure out if shaking it is a good idea or a terrible idea when Tavik crests the hill, out of breath. He's got a sword buckled to each side of his waist and he's carrying both our packs, but when he sees DeRopa, he skids to a halt.

"Oh, hey, nice of you to join us, soldier," DeRopa calls to him in a voice dripping with irony.

"Captain," Tavik utters, clearly stunned to see him. "When did you get here?"

"About three seconds before you." DeRopa gives him an impatient wave. "Why don't you join us?"

"Yes, sir."

Tavik walks the rest of the way, his face drawn. When he comes to stand beside me, DeRopa smacks him upside the head. "Father of death, DeSemla, if you disobey orders again, I'll strangle the life out of you. And watch your back, you idiot. I could have drawn and quartered you five times over while you were shouting at a defenseless female."

Tavik stares at his captain, then throws his arms around the man's waist and hugs him for dear life.

"Missed you, too, kid," DeRopa tells him gruffly, pounding him on the back with a thick fist.

"Sorry, sir."

"I'm not the one you should be apologizing to."

Tavik releases DeRopa to scowl at me.

"I don't want your apology," I mutter, my feelings still bruised.

"Good. Because I have no intention of giving you one."

DeRopa rolls his eyes and looks at the other two men before addressing Tavik. "You can go back to your unit, DeSemla. De-Tana will accompany you. DeLuthina and I will take it from here."

I snap to attention. It? Does he mean me?

"Tavik?" I ask uncertainly, my anger with him vanishing in an instant. He looks at me with matching alarm, then turns to DeRopa. "No, sir, I think I should see this through to the—"

"The end?" I finish for him. I feel like the little boy he was, falling into the dark waters of the well.

"No, that's not what I meant," he tells me breathlessly before pleading his case to his captain. "Sir, there's a trust between us. I can't leave her with men she considers strangers."

"A trust? You were just screaming at her," DeRopa points out with a sardonic grin.

"But I've come so far. Why would you take me off this assignment now?"

"Are you kidding? How many times did you fail to report your location? How many times did I tell you to stay put? How many times did you feel free to disregard direct orders?"

Tavik winces.

"Orders? What orders?" I demand.

DeRopa crosses his arms over his chest. "The orders he didn't follow for weeks on end. That's why you're off the assignment, DeSemla."

Tavik stands ramrod straight. "Sir, I—"

The captain's temper sparks at last, and he points a savage finger at Tavik. "You don't question orders. You follow them. Period. Is that clear?"

Tavik shrinks. His eyes falter. He's backing down when I most need him to stand up for me. "Yes, sir," he whispers.

"No!" I beg him.

DeRopa softens and speaks to Tavik as if I'm not standing right here. "I know this is hard, but Daughter Gelya is in good hands now, all right?"

Tavik goes very still, his eyes distant and unfocused. "Yes, sir," he answers as if his words are an afterthought.

"What are you doing?" I ask him, my voice tight with panic.

DeRopa acts as if I've said nothing and claps Tavik on the shoulder. "You've done well, DeSemla. I'm proud of you. But your watch is over."

Tavik regards his captain, then glances at the other two men, and I am forcefully reminded of that moment in the parlertorium when Zofia looked about her and knew something was wrong. "Can I say goodbye?" he asks DeRopa.

"Of course."

I shake my head, my eyes wide and frantic. "Don't leave me."

"It's time."

"No!"

He takes me by the arms with his warm, strong hands. "I'll miss you."

"Don't do this," I plead.

His face contorts, and a hard, sad laugh escapes his mouth. "Remember how you wanted to walk right through the front door of the Monastery of Saint Helios, Brother Elgar?" He pulls me into his arms and hugs me tight, whispering in my ear, "Do it. Run. Now."

"What?" I gasp as he pulls away.

He's still looking at me, his deadly serious face hidden from his captain as he mouths, *Run*. Then he turns back to the Kantari and draws both his swords.

Shock roots my feet to the earth, and my mind reels with confusion as the knights behind DeRopa draw their weapons, too. The captain keeps his sheathed and puts out a hand, staying the others. "What's this, DeSemla?"

"How did you know her name?" The only part of Tavik's body that moves is his mouth. The rest of him is still and coiled, ready to pounce if he has to. I can't believe what I'm seeing.

DeRopa snorts. "Because you told me."

"No, I didn't. How did you get here so fast? Aren't you supposed to be in Gulachen?"

"You sent for me, remember?" DeRopa answers with an incredulous laugh.

"Why are the Kantari still moving toward the Convent of Saint Vinnica when you know Elath is no longer there?"

"Let me explain—"

"And how in the name of the Mother did Brother Miklos find us again after the trail went cold? Because I sent you a message from the Pavane Forest letting you know we were following the Goodson."

Holy Father, Tavik is right. If the Elathians had a spy at the Convent of Saint Vinnica, why couldn't the Ovinists have one among the Kantari Two-Swords? My flags didn't put Brother Miklos on our trail. DeRopa did.

"You're jumping to some pretty ridiculous conclusions," DeRopa says calmly.

"Am I? How did Brother Miklos know he'd find us at Illesmaat? Because I finally obeyed your order and told you where we were."

"See, this is exactly what I'm talking about, DeSemla. You think you're so smart. You think you're the only one who knows anything. That's why I'm sending you back before you make things worse than they already are."

"Except you're not sending me back, are you? You've already ordered DeLuthina to take me out the first chance he gets, because I got a lot closer to freeing the Mother than you ever thought I could, and now I know too much."

DeTana and DeLuthina move into defensive stances, and my heart jumps. DeRopa's voice is as cold and cutting as a knife when he says, "Soldier, put down your weapons."

"You didn't send me because you thought I could free the Mother. You sent me because you thought I couldn't. Father of death, how could you do this to me?" Tavik finally breaks, his face crumpling with hurt and anger.

"Oh, for the Father's sake, Tavik, save your water," DeRopa barks. "You're eighteen years old, and you're thinking with your sword instead of your head."

"No. I'm a Two-Swords, chosen by the Mother, and you trained me well enough to call your bluff. Gelya, run."

Every feeling revolts. "I'm not leaving you."

"Now!" he bellows, never taking his eyes off his captain, the father who betrayed him.

This time, DeRopa does pull his swords free of their scabbards and gives Tavik a face full of sorrow and regret. "Don't make me do this, DeSemla."

"Now, Gelya!"

I open my mouth, ready to pull back the lid I keep tight over Elath, but I close it again just in time. How can I hurt DeRopa and his men without also hurting Tavik?

"Run!"

The only person in the world who can help either one of us is at the Monastery of Saint Helios, so I do what Tavik says. I bolt for the monastery with the sounds of steel clashing against steel at my back.

My body runs, but everything I am on the inside stays behind with Tavik.

Thirty-Five

I burst straight through the front doors of the Monastery of Saint Helios, just as I told Tavik I could. Not a soul stirs in the cavernous hall or on the stairs leading up to the dormers.

"Goodson Anskar!" My voice ricochets off the ceiling. "Is anyone here? Goodson!"

In less than a minute, two monks arrive from two different directions, both of them telling me to "Calm down, Brother."

But there is no calming me. I grab one by the sleeve of his brown tunic. "I need to talk to the Goodson! Now!"

More and more monks pour into the hall, their voices and bodies swarming about me. Each second they dally is another second Tavik may not live. "Goodson!" I shout, searching the faces all around me. None of them belong to him, the one person I need.

I hold up my hands, trying to sound calm so that they'll take me seriously. "Listen to me." But the monks are all speaking at once, a dissonant, overwhelming chorus.

"Good Father, it's a girl!"

"—knight's clothing?"

"—sacrilege—"

"You don't understand. Please," I beg them. But they refuse to take me seriously.

"Miss, you must—"

"—hysterical female—"

The room is spinning. There are too many bodies and voices pressing in all around me. The buzzing of the spirit within me fills my ears. My head feels like it will burst. One of the monks grabs me by the arm.

"Don't touch me."

The buzzing ratchets higher. Another man takes hold of my other arm, a Knight of the Order this time.

"Let me go."

"What is the meaning of this?" the knight spits.

And the lid blows. Fury sets my veins on fire, and the words that come out of my mouth are not spoken in Rosvanian but sung in Sanctus. "Let me go!"

The two men with their hands on me shriek and stumble back. The monk's sleeve is on fire, and his comrades bat out the flames as I look on, panting, blood streaming down my chin.

"Holy Father. Gelya?"

The familiar voice parts the sea of men, revealing the Goodson. He stands in the hallway directly ahead of me, his white tunic pristine, his gray eyes heavy. I've followed his trail for hundreds of miles, tied flags to gelya trees to show him where I've been, prayed to the silent Father that I might find him, and here he is at last.

The knowledge that he will lift the burden from my shoulders is nearly unbearable, and relief fills me to the brim.

I turn inward to face the spirit that insists on wearing Zofia's face and speaking in her voice. *I'm sorry,* I tell Her as I slam the lid back down.

I want to run to the Goodson and bury myself in his strong arms. Instead, I drop painfully to one knee on the unforgiving floor, barely able to keep myself from toppling over completely.

Goodson Anskar races to me and scoops me up. It's not as easy as it once was—I'm so much taller than his poor little Gelya in the Dead Forest—but he staggers to his feet, holding me in his arms, his voice breaking as he murmurs, "You're safe now. You're all right."

Tavik. The name curls through my blood like steam escaping a kettle.

"Goodson Anskar," I begin, the words as limp and useless as my body.

"Shh."

"You have to help Tavik."

"Everything will be fine."

I grip the front of his tunic with my weak hands, grasping at the blue Hand of the Father emblazoned on his chest. "There's a boy fighting three Kantari on the road. Send men."

"Gelya—"

I tighten my grip, my fingernails scraping against the skin beneath. "Send as many as you can."

"I . . ." His eyes shift over my head to a knight standing behind me. He gives the man a nod and shifts his focus back to me. "I'll see to it."

I press my hand over his heart and breathe, "Thank you!" before I try to squirm out of his arms.

The Goodson holds me tighter. "What are you doing?"

"I need to go with them."

"Who?"

"Your knights."

"You'll do no such thing," he says as he carries me toward the stairwell.

For a moment, I forget who I am and who the Goodson is. All I can think of is Tavik. "You can't stop me," I say, as if the words come from the mouth of the Father Himself.

The Goodson stops and gapes down at me, the powerless girl in his arms. "Gelya," he says, his tone chastising. It's like that moment before the summit when I defied him, the thing I swore I would never do again.

"I have to go," I whimper. "Can't you see that?"

"What I can see is that you're distraught, and you need to lie down at once."

"But he—"

"But he is in more capable hands than yours now, and I'm not letting you go anywhere near a fight. My job is to protect the faithful, not send them into a bloodbath." He looks past me again and asks a monk, "Can you have something brought up that will calm her?"

"Of course, Goodson."

"I don't want to calm down," I plead. My legs sway with each step as Goodson Anskar carries me upstairs.

"And what good will you do this boy in your current condition?

Will you be helping him or hurting him?"

I answer his question by bursting into tears and pressing my face to his shoulder. I let him carry me to a dorm room, put me in a bed, and hold a mug of something "that will calm her" to my lips. As I fade into the darkness of sleep, I hear him murmur, "Poor little Gelya."

I wake in a strange bed with a headache and a throbbing sore throat. I'm somehow both cold and sweating beneath a heavy quilt. The room is dark, but gray light outlines the thick curtains at the window. I push the blanket off me, only to shiver in the cold air that greets my skin. I've got nothing on but a thin shift. I pull the quilt back over me, my movements heavy and sluggish. Everything is fuzzy.

The door opens, and the Goodson's square face peeks in, at which point I begin to sob with pure, unfiltered relief.

"Don't cry, Daughter. I'm just glad you're awake."

He steps into the room, drags a plain wooden chair from a nearby table next to the bed, and sits beside me. His kind heart is in his eyes as he takes my hand in his warm grasp, and the tenderness of the gesture makes me weep harder.

"Only the Father can know what you've suffered," he says, his voice as warm as his hand. "But you're safe now. You mustn't cry anymore."

I sit up, reining in my tears. "But are you all right? I've been so worried. Have you regained control of the Order? What happened to Brother Miklos?"

"Calm down. You'll make yourself ill. I'm perfectly well, as you see, and I have the Order firmly in hand. I'm far more concerned with your well-being at the moment, not mine."

The wrinkles pulling down the corners of his eyes have grown deeper since the last time I saw him, probably because of me. He gives me a handkerchief so I can wipe my face. I need to get this over with, the moment I've been dreading for weeks.

"You know what I carry inside me?" I ask him, although it's not really a question, and I already know the answer.

He regards me with a gut-wrenching mixture of directness, pity, and sorrow. "Yes."

"Can you get Her out of me?"

He takes my right hand in both of his and kisses my palm the way he did on the day the Father chose me. "I can help you."

His words are my deliverance, and for one blessed moment, I let myself dissolve into it. And then I remember my true reason for coming to the monastery. I bolt upright and push back the bedding. "Holy Father! Tavik!"

"Gelya—"

"How long have I been out? Father of death!" I say the last part in Kantari, as if the words will make Tavik materialize before me.

"You need to rest." The Goodson takes me by the shoulders and tries to urge me back down, but I bat his gentle hands away.

"I can't rest until I know he's all right!"

He grips my shoulders again, and this time his hands are not gentle. "Then I'll save you the trouble. I'm so sorry. He's . . . gone. My men found the boy's body."

The boy's body.

Tavik's body.

My mind refuses to catch up.

"What are you saying? Tavik's dead?" The word *dead* burns like a brand, searing my heart, my lungs, my throat.

Goodson Anskar squeezes my shoulders, his touch tender once more. "Clearly, he meant something to you, and for that, I honor your grief."

I slip from his grasp and fall back against the pillow as if a heavy weight is pushing me down. Tears wait behind my eyes, but I can't let them loose. If I do, it means he's really gone, and I don't accept that. I can't. I won't.

The Goodson lays his heavy hand on my head and looks down on me with the full force of his paternal love. "May the Father bless you, Daughter. You've done extremely well. You rest now."

He kisses the top of my head and leaves me alone in the spare, shadowy room.

Tavik is dead.

Zofia. Mera and her family. And now Tavik. I have no words for this, the loss that pierces me to the core, so painful I curl my body around it, helpless as it throbs through me.

Then I hear the unmistakable sound of the door being locked from the outside, an eerie echo of the moment Brother Miklos took the key from around Zofia's neck in the parlertorium.

If he ever gets his hands on you, he's going to lock you up and throw away the key.

But Tavik sent me here. In the end, he knew the Goodson was our only chance. My only chance.

I shove the quilt away and swing my legs out of bed to get to my feet. The room lurches. I grab the bedpost and hang on until the world stops spinning. I take one cautious step, then another and another, and by the time I reach the door, I'm steady enough to walk without falling on my face. I hope rather than believe I'm wrong when I try the handle, but the door is locked, and I'm a prisoner.

I refuse to accept this. Tavik's father may have turned on him, but I'm certain my own has not. He knows what I am, and he's not taking any risks. He's keeping me safe.

Or is he keeping the faithful safe from me?

I pull back the curtains of the single window to let in more light and find that I'm too high up to jump.

I look around the room and locate my knight's uniform bunched up into a ball in the corner, cast aside, as if someone crumpled up a part of me and threw it away like garbage.

Brother Elgar, Kicker of Ass.

I clutch the sword belt with its now-empty scabbard, breathing hard through my nose. I will not cry. I will not grieve. I will not fall apart right now, for Tavik's sake if not my own. *Let's worry about one thing at a time,* the memory of his voice reminds me.

I take off the clean shift and step into my filthy knight's uniform, trying to formulate a plan.

The sound of a key sliding into the lock makes my heart stutter. The tumblers turn, and the door opens, revealing the last person I expected to see at the Monastery of Saint Helios.

Thirty-Six

"Daughter Ina?" I breathe.

"It's *Sacrist* Ina now," she corrects me with thin-lipped disapproval. "Come on. We don't have much time."

She disappears into the hallway, but I'm so stunned I remain frozen to the spot. A moment later, she pokes her head around the jamb. "Don't stand there. I need to get you out of here before someone notices I took the key. Let's go."

I have no idea what to make of this, but it's a better option than staying locked in my room, so I follow Ina down the unlit hallway.

"What are you doing here?" I whisper.

"I've been sworn to secrecy, but I assume you already know that the Vault of Mount Djall is empty?" she whispers back. I don't trust her enough to give her a response one way or the other. She waves her hand impatiently and carries on. "I assume you also know that twelve years ago, Knights of the Order raided the

Kantari library at Grama and brought its collection to the Monastery of Saint Helios. They hoped to uncover information that would lead to the Great Demon's whereabouts. Zofia found evidence that Elath was imprisoned at the Convent of Saint Vinnica. Since she died at the summit, the Goodson brought me here to piece together her research, but it looks like you got your hands on it first."

She comes to a halt at the top of the servants' stairwell, where she reaches into her pocket, pulls out the rubbings, and hands them to me. "I found them when the Goodson had me change your clothes. You were out cold."

Dread grips me like talons as I stuff the papers into my own pocket. "Did you put them together?"

She nods. Oh, my Father, this is very bad.

"Did you sing it for the Goodson?"

"Of course I did. I thought I was doing the right thing," she snaps as my soul crumples under the weight of guilt. I can still feel Zofia's fingers growing cold over mine as she begged me not to let the Goodson get the text.

Ina starts the descent down the stairs, and I have no choice but to follow. "You know every listener brings his own faith to a song," she whispers as she takes each step with grim efficiency. "The Goodson only heard what he wanted to hear, that Ovin brought the Great Demon to a better prison than the one he took Her out of. He never wavered, even with such proof pouring into his ears. He still doesn't believe that Elath is the M—"

She stops on the stairs and levels me with a brown-eyed glare, as if the collapse of her entire worldview is my fault. "I think you are something more than the Vessel of the Father's Word now, Daughter. Is that right?"

I don't answer, but I guess I don't have to, because Ina shakes her head and mutters, "You always were trouble." Then, to my amazement, this curt woman, who never had a kind word for me a day in her life, takes two steps up to match my height and wraps her sturdy arms around me. Equally amazing is the fact that I hug her back fiercely, seeking and giving comfort in the last place either of us ever thought to find it. She understands my loss as I understand hers, and there are so few people in the world who know what it means to have one's belief crumble to ash.

She pulls away, wiping her face. "Well, I, for one, do not intend to find out what the Goodson has in store for you."

"The one thing he is absolutely *not* going to do is help me," I quote Tavik under my breath, choking on the urge to start weeping and never stop. The pang of grief is so sharp, I'd swear Elath has taken hold of my lungs and is strangling me from the inside. Tavik was right about the Goodson. He was right about everything.

At least you have the luxury of forgetting, he told me.

As Ina and I wind our way down the stairs, I cast my memory back and back, landing not on the beginning but on the end, the moment when I stood on a windswept cliff outside my village, when Goodson Anskar placed the seedpod in my hand and it burst open. Smoke filled the air.

Because my village was burning.

Because the Goodson and his knights had set fire to it.

And the tangy scent of iron in my nose was the smell of blood, because the Goodson and his men had killed as many Hedenski as they could, just as they killed Tavik's family—his entire town—all to hunt down the Mother. The only difference is that Tavik remembered, whereas I let myself forget.

I think of the young knights Goodson Anskar assigned to protect us at the summit, lambs sent to the slaughter, just as Tavik was.

How could I have ever believed the Goodson would help me get to the Mother's body?

Ina presses her finger to her lips when we arrive on the main floor. As we tiptoe past the central corridor, I hear men's voices drifting toward us from a room at the end of the hallway.

". . . never should have killed the spy." The words are barely audible through the crack between the door and the jamb.

"The Goodson's orders that night were to silence anyone who found out the Great Demon wasn't in the Vault of Mount Djall. That included her, and if you ask me, she deserved worse than she got," argues a second voice.

My stomach drops to my knees.

Holy Father, the Goodson ordered the massacre on the night of the summit. He might as well have thrown that knife into Zofia's heart with his own hand. The truth is obvious, but that doesn't lessen the shock or the hurt that follows right behind it.

"Then why is the girl still breathing? We wouldn't be in this situation if she were dead."

This time, it's Goodson Anskar who answers, his voice as familiar to me as my own. "Because the girl was innocent. Sacrist

Zofia most certainly was not. There's no point arguing over it. What's done is done, and at least now we've pieced together what Zofia knew."

Each word from that mouth is a bludgeon, hitting me hard and forcing me to remember one terrible and inescapable fact.

I still need the Hand of the Father.

My stomach drops lower. How am I supposed to take the Sword from the Goodson when, for the first time since I was a little girl standing on the cliffs of Hedenskia, I'm scared of him?

"What are you doing?" Ina hisses at me as I move toward his voice rather than away from it. I take her hand in mine, wishing I could explain and knowing I can't. "I'm sorry," I tell her before slinking down the hall with her mincing footsteps close behind.

"Daughter Zofia knew too much. A smart woman is a dangerous woman. Just look at the damage she's done."

I approach the door, trying to peer through the crack without being seen from the outside, but it's hard to make out details.

"We can't change that now. We can only play the hand we've been dealt, and if you ask me, of all the players in this game, we are holding the best cards right now." Whoever this man is, he speaks excellent Rosvanian, but with a slight accent.

"There's only one card worth having, and it's finally in our possession, thank the Father," says the Goodson.

"The question is, how do we play it?"

I inch forward, ignoring Ina's frantic gesturing until I can get a good look into the room. Goodson Anskar stands at a table, peering down at Ambrus's map with two other men. One of them is DeRopa, the man who betrayed Tavik.

The other is Brother Miklos.

The blood drains from my face. I throw myself back against the wall of the corridor with my heart thundering in my chest.

"Let's review the bidding," the Goodson suggests, ever calm and rational when I am a seething ball of emotion on the other side of the wall. "Thanks to Sacrist Ina, we now know that the Great Demon's spirit was separated from Her body. She cannot return unless body and soul are reunited. One must have the Vessel and the Sword to accomplish this, and thankfully, we have both. The only piece of the puzzle we're missing is the location of the body."

"It doesn't matter where the body is," Brother Miklos interjects. "All we have to do is bury the Vessel in the Vault of Mount Djall. We already have the security in place at the Monastery of Saint Ovin, and the world can go on as it did before with no one being the wiser."

"Except your security failed twelve years ago," says DeRopa.

"And whose fault was that?"

"Enough, Brother," the Goodson cuts in. "Rusik has been a faithful servant of the Father since his conversion. We wouldn't know about the traitor's message to the Prima if it weren't for him, and we might never have found the Vessel either. We owe him our thanks, not our scorn."

Ina tugs on my sleeve, but my feet refuse to move as the Goodson continues.

"And it *does* matter where the body is, Miklos, because as long as it exists, the threat remains that Elath's body and soul may be reunited. We know that the body can die, even if the soul cannot, and that means we must find it and destroy it once and for all."

"How? There must be a million trees in the world."

The Goodson heaves the deep sigh of a man who carries a great burden. "I don't think we were wrong about Hedenskia. They believe trees are the souls of the dead, and their goddess is symbolized by a tree. It makes sense."

"You were the only one who came back, Anskar," says the knight. "I doubt the Holy Ovinist Church will fund another 'missionary trip' after that disaster."

"All I know is that the Hedenski were willing to give their lives to protect something in that forest. We'll find a way to get back. In the meantime, there's a more pressing matter to attend to: we need to secure Elath's immortal spirit immediately and permanently. Since we have the Vessel in our possession, I propose that we move her to the Great Wall of Saint Balzos."

The Vessel.

A card to be played.

Me.

"Saint Balzos? Shouldn't we take her to the Vault of Mount Djall where she belongs?" Brother Miklos argues.

"Balzos is closer, and we've wasted enough time already. We will build a new vault in the north. We will guard it with our very souls, and we will see to it that Elath the Great Demon never again escapes Her earthly prison."

Fury brews inside me. The Goodson didn't save me. He stole me. I clung to him for protection in the Dead Forest, and I clung to his truth and his beliefs as well. Now he's going to lock me away, just as he believes Ovin buried Vinnica to keep Elath out of the world.

"I'll see to it myself. What the Father asks of me, I must do." I hear in the Goodson's voice the same anguish welling up inside me. Because what he believes he must do is bury me alive. I am Vinnica, but he is no Ovin.

Ina grasps me by the arm, but I wrench myself free. I'm not going anywhere without the Goodson's sword. I owe it to Tavik to finish what we began.

I can hear a shudder in DeRopa's voice when he says, "I feel like we're sitting under a powder keg with the Vessel in a room just over our heads."

"It's only temporary, and the Vessel is easily managed," the Goodson assures him.

He can't bring himself to call me by name. I'm only the Vessel now. And because I am the Vessel, it doesn't matter what I believe or think or want. I'm nothing but a shell, a hollow space that contains a spirit that is not my own.

"She burned two men in the entry hall before you arrived, Anskar," Brother Miklos points out. "I doubt they'd say she was easily managed."

He's right. The Vessel will not be managed.

I pull back the softening membrane between me and the immortal life I carry. Elath's burning light fills my eyes and builds at the back of my throat like a dragon's mouth just before it breathes fire. When I look back at Ina, terror overtakes her face.

"Cover your ears," I tell her, a million female voices blending into one. She cowers before me, pressing her hands to the sides of her head as she turns to scurry away from what I'm about to do. I wish I could help her, but all I can do is hope, for her sake, that she finds a way to escape this place, to free herself of the cloistered existence that was thrust upon her, just as it was thrust upon me.

I step forward and push the door open slowly, deliberately. I want to be seen as I approach a table full of men who think my life is theirs to discuss, to plan, to end.

Brother Miklos is the first to see me. He cries out and bumps into a stool, knocking it over.

"Daughter Gelya," the Goodson says, poised as ever on the outside, but I can smell his fear, a terror that is nothing to the rage building inside me. I am Mount Djall. I am the fiery pit. My eruption is inevitable.

I tap directly into the source at my center, drinking deeply. The Mother's light pours out of me as I sing, and I swim in its exquisite glory.

Set the city of Nogarra alight, and I shall be the bellows of the flame.
Let the flesh burn away into ash from the bone.
Let the bone wither into dust in the unforgiving fires of the Father.
I shall melt down my enemies and make them anew
In the love of the One True God.

By the time I finish the verse, the men are writhing on the floor, my voice filling them with agony even after the song is over. I don't feel weak or used up. I am the goddess, immortal and immutable and unstoppable. My gift, merged with Elath's power, crackles in my veins like lightning. If it is a sin to use it, then may the Father condemn me to the Dead Forest. I refuse to live my life by His rules anymore, and I will not die for Him.

I step over DeRopa to glare into the Goodson's face with my eyes on fire.

"Daughter," he rasps at me, pleading.

I rip the triptych from around my neck and fling it onto his chest. My sacred blood snakes from my nose and pools on my upper lip, sprinkling red droplets all over Goodson Anskar's white tunic as I speak the last words I ever intend to say to the man who was my father: "I am not your daughter."

I take the Hand of the Father from the sheath at his waist and put it in my own empty scabbard with the satisfying ring of metal against metal. Then I leave the men on the floor to wallow in my wake as I exit the room and leave the Monastery of Saint Helios the same way I came: by the front door.

Thirty-Seven

I stand in the yard, facing east. The sky churns with storm clouds, the spitting rain made icy by winter winds that approach too soon. I see the world now with the Mother's eyes as well as my own. Death surrounds me in the shriveling of ivy on the monastery walls, in the drowning of crops in the fields, in the last gasping breaths of the cypress trees, in the beetles curling up to die in the bark. And yet there is so much life here, too, exquisite in its tenacity. Creation clings to the living world, taking my breath away and filling me with hope. I'm still alive, and as long as my heart beats, as long as I can draw breath, I can think and act and be.

"Gelya?"

The sound of my name from that mouth is more beautiful than any song, more stunning than the call of the soulswift. I turn toward it, toward him, even though the world had me convinced that he was dead.

He steps out of the long shadow on the north side of the stable. In the gray light, he is blurry and insubstantial, a ghost. But with every step he takes toward me, he comes into focus, each detail revealing itself, inch by exquisite inch. He wears the evidence of a skirmish—an eye swollen shut, a cut seeping blood into the fabric of his sleeve—but he is just as alive as everything and everyone else clinging to life against all probability.

"Tavik?" I whisper as he comes to stand before me, his living body lit by the Mother's flames still burning in my eyes.

He made me a promise, and he keeps his promises.

"I was just on my way to . . . um . . . rescue you?" He looks past me into the open front door, his confusion plastered all over his battered, beautiful face. Someone within moans in pain, but I'm disconnected from that world now. The only world that matters is the one in front of me.

He was dead, and now he isn't, and my heart can't seem to come to terms with either. The only thing I can think to say is "I rescued myself."

His forehead wrinkles in bewilderment. "I see that."

I know he fears the way the Mother's life burns bright inside me, my eyes ablaze with Her fire, but I tackle him anyway, wrapping my arms around his waist and squeezing for all I'm worth.

"Okay," he says, his voice strained and high-pitched. He holds a sword in each hand and stiffens awkwardly in my arms. I don't care. I hug him harder.

"Bruised ribs! Bruised ribs!" he grunts, and I release him. Fiery tears streak down my cheek as he puts his swords back in their sheaths. I must look like a volcanic eruption oozing lava, because as he stares at me with his nonswollen eye, it's clear he doesn't like what he sees.

"Can you stop . . . with the . . . I just want Gelya back, all right?"

Not the Vessel. Not a card to be played. *Me.* So despite the fact that I'm probably going to drop like a brick the second I let go of Elath's power, I pull the cover back over Her burning life. And then I do, in fact, drop like a brick, but Tavik is there, catching me under my arms so I don't fall over. He glances at the open doorway once more.

"The stone from my mother's library is in there."

"I know." I pause, drawing as much strength as I can from my own store of energy to say what must be said. "We can't stay. I don't know how much time we have. I'm sorry."

He grimaces the way he always does when he knows I'm right but he badly wants me to be wrong. Then he looks at my face, and whatever he wanted for himself evaporates. "Oh, death, what did you do?"

"Long story," I mumble, still drooping from his hands.

"Can you walk?"

"Yes," I answer, but then I have to reconsider that answer. "Maybe."

He pulls my arm over his shoulder and half carries me into the shadows on the stable's north side. Blood continues to seep from my nose. He looks anywhere but at my face as he hoists me onto one of the waiting horses. I grip the pommel of the saddle, trying not to fall off as he climbs on behind me with his usual grace. I guess we're only taking one horse rather than two since I can't be trusted to stay upright. It's a relief to have his arm around my waist, partly because I really might fall off otherwise, and partly because it's a reminder that he's real and solid and alive.

"Where are DeRopa's men, DeTana and DeLuthina?" I ask.

"Dead." In that single syllable, I hear the weight in his soul, the burden of killing his own countrymen. But neither one of us has the luxury of wallowing in all that has happened in the past day, so I say, "One thing at a time. We're heading north."

"Okay. Why?" He's already got our horse moving off the road and into the rolling hills northward.

My body is so wrung out that I feel like I have no bones left, and my head falls back against his shoulder. "Because I have the Sword, and I know where the Mother's body is."

IV.

The Forest

Thirty-Eight

We opt for speed rather than distance, but after ten miles, the stallion is too tired to go on, so we abandon the horse and trek north on foot. Tavik slogs ahead of me in the pelting sleet, holding my hand to drag me up a hill. And I do mean *drag*. I don't regret using the Mother's power at the monastery, but my body is paying for it after the fact.

"What if this tree you remember isn't the Mother's body?" Tavik asks, helping me over a puddle. "What if it's just a tree?"

"It *is* the Mother's body. It's why the Goodson went to Hedenskia all those years ago. He guessed they were protecting something up there, and he was right. The only difference is that the Goodson went there to destroy Her. But you and I can put Elath back together again."

"I thought you didn't want to put the Mother back together."

"Maybe what I want has changed." How bizarre that we've reversed positions. His devotion to freeing the Mother has lessened, while I'm more committed than ever to getting Her out of my body.

"You've got to be kidding me." He lets go of my hand, leaving me to stagger behind him on my own. "If the Hedenski catch us on their soil, they'll kill us. I can fight a lot of men at once, but not an entire country."

"But *I'm* Hedenski."

"Well, I'm not."

"Why are you fighting this?" I pant at him, struggling to keep up.

"You know why," he fires back at me over his shoulder as the unsaid word drifts through the stormy air between us: *telleg*.

"Would you stop for a minute?"

"We don't have time to stop!" He ironically stops to shout at me. He's been angry with me before, but there's a different flavor to his venom now. Up until a few hours ago, he was very sure of the world and his place in it. Losing DeRopa must be like losing a piece of his soul, and now I'm the one bearing the brunt of all the hurt welling up inside him. He's not the only one feeling the sting of betrayal, but he is right on one point: we don't have time. So I close the gap between us, reaching out to take his hand again in my own meager grasp.

"If we're not going to Hedenskia, it doesn't matter whether we stop or keep going."

We stand on the side of a gently sloping hill, me teetering on my feet and both of us breathing heavily from the effort of hiking and arguing. Tavik shoves a stray curl out of his face but says nothing. In this moment, it's so easy to see past the near invincibility of his exterior, right to the delicate fragility of his heart. Staring into his vulnerability makes my own chest ache.

"'Only the Vessel and the Sword may set Her free,' and we have both. I don't want to go to the Dead Forest or Hedenskia, and I can't tell you how much I don't want to put you in harm's way, but we have no choice. Now that the Goodson has lost the Vessel—and the Sword for that matter—he has to destroy the body. The only way to end this is to get there first."

Icy rain falls on Tavik's shoulders as surely as the truth, but he's going to need something greater than truth to cross through the Dead Forest. I put my hands palms up in front of me and tell him, "Hold out your hands like this."

He frowns but mirrors the gesture. I pull the blade from my scabbard and place it across his palms. Then I put my hands under each of his so that we're holding the weight of the weapon together.

"This is the Hand of the Father, Ludo's sword, given to him by his Mother. This is the sword Goodson Anskar carried through the Dead Forest ten years ago, the sword that slew every telleg in our path. You promised to protect the Vessel, Tavik DeSemla, and you never break your promises."

He blows out a shuddering breath as he takes the full weight of the sword into his own hands.

"We're in this together," I tell him. "You and me."

Church bells ring to the south, rousing the local patrols from their dinner tables and pub stools. Our time is running out. Tavik gives me the saddest excuse for a smile I've ever seen. "To the bitter end," he agrees. It's been a while since he's made me blush, but he holds my gaze long enough to make my ears turn pink.

"I'm a Two-Swords, not a Three-Swords. You'd better take one of these," he jokes weakly, turning his back to me so I can free up space for his new weapon. As I pull one of the swords from its scabbard, I spot a bird over Tavik's shoulder, flying past us in a blur of blue feathers.

"Do you see that?" I whisper when it stops to perch on a cypress branch.

He nods and takes several tentative steps toward the soulswift.

"Does it have a message?" I ask him.

"I don't see a canister."

The bird studies Tavik with one eye, turns her head to blink at me with the other, then darts off, flying to a shrub ten feet away. Tavik and I glance at each other in unspoken agreement before we follow her. When we get close, she flits away again, this time landing on a signpost pointing the way back toward Saint Helios.

"Why are we doing this?" Tavik pants as we follow her from the sign to a copse of pines at the bottom of the hill, where she disappears into the thick branches. I'm too out of breath to answer. All I know is that my instincts are screaming at me to follow the soulswift.

When we burst into the trees, we barely stop in time before crashing into a couple of rough-looking men and three barrels we did not expect to find in the clearing. The astringent scent of alcohol cutting through the air alerts me to the fact that we've barged in on a pair of bootleggers and their illegal distillery. The men gape at us, both of them wiry and a little dirty.

"Saints and sinners, it's them," cries the leaner of the two.

Tavik's swords are out a second later, the Hand of the Father bright and dangerous in his left hand.

"Whoa!" both men shout repeatedly. One of them rolls up a pant leg while the other pulls down on the neck of his shirt. For one alarming moment, I think they're disrobing, but then I realize that each of them is showing us his tattoos. Trees, just like the one on Tavik's wrist.

"Blessed be the Mother!" the sturdier man says, his eyes wide as he stares at Tavik's swords. "Every Elathian between here and Juprachen's on the lookout for you."

"I missed that last part?" Tavik says in Kantari without taking his eyes off the scraggly men.

"I think we're getting back on the Milk Road," I tell him as I grapple with the fact that a soulswift seems to have led us here deliberately.

Tavik puts his blades back into their scabbards and shakes his head. "Holy Mother, divine intervention is kind of terrifying."

The people hiding us from the Order are a family of smugglers named Bennik, which makes Tavik and me smuggled goods. We sit beneath a storeroom's hatch, Tavik huddled on a sack of grain with the Hand of the Father in his white-knuckled grip, and me sitting slightly higher on a barrel of whiskey. We're surrounded by enough black-market wool to clothe every Daughter in the Convent of Saint Vinnica, but we can't see any of it at the moment, because we're hiding with all these illicit goods in a cramped space beneath our rescuers' house, and we don't have a lamp. I only know these things are present because I caught a glimpse of them when we were shooed down the ladder.

I don't bother to ask Tavik if he's all right. I know how much he hates dark, tight spaces. There's a part of him that will always be a frightened child stuck in a well. I reach for his hand, petting my way down his arm until I'm able to twine my fingers with his. His uneven breathing is the only sound in the room except for the occasional footsteps and voices from above.

Tavik makes a startled sound and jerks away, scaring me out of my skin.

"What is it?" I whisper.

"I think a rat just crawled over my foot."

He is definitely not all right. I reach for his hand again, and he grips mine painfully. Time stretches on. And on. Tavik's breath stretches and thins with it, moist with unspoken panic.

At last, the moment we've been dreading arrives, the cacophony of footsteps, sharp voices, and furniture groaning across the floorboards.

Someone has come looking for us.

My breath grows as thin as Tavik's, and my hand, clutched tightly in his, goes numb.

I sense him moving beside me, silent as a cat. He touches his way up my arm and shoulder, all the way to my face, cupping my cheek in the palm of his hand. "Don't be afraid," he whispers. "They won't find us here, and if they do, they'll have to get through me. I won't let them hurt you. I won't let them touch you. I won't let them take you away."

It feels like a prayer, the way he says it, comforting himself as much as me. He wraps his arm around my shoulders and pulls me in close. I breathe in his scent, which has gone a bit ripe, and even that is a comfort. I curl into him, my head tucked into the crook of his neck, my face pressed against his chest.

"You're safe," he whispers as we cling to each other in the darkness, each of us counteracting the other's fear like weights on a scale. I listen to the furious beating of his heart and feel his lungs expand and contract through the storm of men above us and through the ominous silence that follows.

At last, the hatch opens, sending a square of light into the darkness.

"All clear," a woman calls down to us. "Damn telleg lickers made a mess, but they didn't have a clue how to find you, them being men."

"Mom," one of the bootleggers complains behind her, but she only cackles in response, the sort of sound I imagined old crones making in the stories Zofia used to tell me.

I pull myself free of Tavik's arm and get a good look at him. Sweat shines on his skin, and his waxy complexion makes his bruised eye lividly purple.

"Get. Me. Out of here," he says in a thick, harsh rumble.

The house is a large, one-room block that contains the entire Bennik family—a widow, her two grown sons, their wives, six children, five sheep, and a cow—but compared to the cramped darkness underneath our feet, it feels like a castle. Technically, property is supposed to pass from father to son in Rosvania, but it quickly becomes clear that Widow Bennik rules the roost here.

Tavik and I sit with the adults at a large, rough-hewn table while the children run riot around us. The elegant tea service on the table's rustic surface contrasts mightily with the rest of our surroundings.

"Is this Yilish tea?" Tavik asks in Rosvanian after a decadent sip.

"From Ulu Province," the widow answers with a semitoothless grin. "We serve only the best at Bennik Palace."

Tavik takes an indelicate slurp and rolls his one good eye in ecstasy. "Tell her I might actually kiss her," he says to me in Kantari. When I refuse, he rolls his good eye again and raises his teacup to the old woman. "Blessed be the Mother."

She snorts. "Honey, I don't believe in gods. I believe in people. So be someone I want to believe in, and maybe I'll help you."

"If you're not an Elathian, why are you a part of the Milk Road?" I ask her.

"Well, my boys got religion from their old man, and for my part, I make good money smuggling for the Elathians, mostly wool and grain, but I do smuggle people on occasion, helping them get somewhere safe." She leans back in her chair, pulls a pipe from her pocket, and starts puffing away. I had no idea women like this existed in the world. "The Prima of Kantar pays particularly well," she adds, "which is why I agreed to smuggle the two of you out of Rosvania."

"What? Where?" I exclaim.

"What'd she say?" Tavik asks, picking up on my alarm, but Widow Bennik keeps talking.

"We're going to transport you in a shipment of wool to Port-ham in Auria, where you'll board a packet sailing to Yil. My Yilish connections will then smuggle you into Kantar through the usual black-market channels."

"I'm afraid we can't do that," I tell her, while Tavik nudges my elbow, struggling to follow the widow's twang.

She eyes the pair of us as if we had just sprouted horns. "Why not?"

Tavik nudges me again, but I swat his hand away. "We have a plan already, and we could use your help with it."

"Oh boy, this should be good," Widow Bennik says, releasing twin streams of smoke from her nostrils. "Let's hear it."

"Hello? Remember me?" Tavik growls, and I finally bring him up to speed. He glances around the room at the two men, their wives, the children, the sheep, and the cow before he turns his handsome face to Widow Bennik again and asks, "Do you have a messenger?"

Thirty-Nine

There's nothing to do but wait until the Prima of Kantar answers Tavik's message. How appropriate to be waiting on a soulswift, at once the harbinger of death and the symbol of eternal life. I wonder which of those things the Prima's answer will bring us: life or death.

I sleep for nearly two days solid, but no amount of rest fully replenishes my depleted strength. Each time I dip into the Mother's power to take one step forward, I wind up taking two steps back in the long run. The constant buzzing of Elath's presence inside me also refuses to subside. If anything, She's getting louder, more insistent, a brimming life I can't ignore.

Waiting is pure torment to Tavik. He's not good at sitting still, and having time to think rather than to act makes him broody. I've spent the past several weeks slowly easing my way into the annihilation of my worldview, while Tavik is having to deal with DeRopa's betrayal in one sudden burst. He bites off my head any time I try to talk to him about it, so instead I've taken to reading books, of which, as it turns out, Widow Bennik has many.

Rain drenches the thatched roof overhead and funnels down into several pots on the floor, making a repetitive rhythm—drip-DRIP-pause-drip, drip-DRIP-pause-drip—as I sit at the table with a book of Ostmari poetry and read by the light of a candle. I was never allowed to read secular texts at the convent, and I feel as if my mind is devouring a decadent dessert. Each poem extolls the beauty of a different landscape—mountains, the sea, a desert—a lyrical catalog of a world I've hardly seen and would not have known at all if it weren't for Tavik.

Widow Bennik sits across from me smoking thoughtfully on her pipe. She doesn't seem like the sort to keep works of literature on hand, but I'm coming to accept the fact that people are surprisingly unpredictable. "That one's easy on the eyes," she comments to me, jabbing her pipe toward Tavik, who's trying to practice sword drills indoors without jabbing a small child with one of his blades.

"Mom!" Hroth chastises her. He's the older of her two sons and the one more easily embarrassed by his mother's frankness.

"What's she saying?" Tavik asks. "Is she talking about me? She's talking about me, isn't she?"

I pinch the bridge of my nose. "I'm trying to read."

He gives up on drills and plunks the swords on the table with a dramatic sigh. One of the pommels covers a page of my book, so I also heave a sigh and scoot it out of the way.

Drip-DRIP-pause-drip, drip-DRIP-pause-drip.

I look up when another sound joins the rhythm of the rain.

Tavik has taken a wooden spoon and a ladle from the daughter-in-law cooking dinner and is now on his knees, drumming the sides of one of the pots to the drip-DRIP-pause-drip rhythm, wiggling his hips back and forth in an alarmingly obscene fashion.

"Would you stop, please?" I protest. I expect the women to back me up, but they and their children are laughing at Tavik's antics while Hroth and his brother grunt in irritation.

Tavik continues to clank the spoon and ladle against the pot as he sings in Kantari, "I'm so bored I'm going to die."

"You are not going to die."

"Not of boredom, but since the world is a horrible place, I've decided to have fun tonight."

"I'm familiar with your idea of fun," I mutter, turning my attention back to the poetry.

He changes up the rhythm so that it dances around the steady beat of the rain, one complementing the other—the leaks constant and predictable, his own beat syncopated and driving and persistent. I gurgle my annoyance under my breath. Tavik either doesn't hear me or takes this as encouragement, because he begins to sing, belting out a love song in soulful Kantari. One of the sheep bleats in alarm.

"Thank the Father we're miles from where anyone can hear you," I comment when he finishes the verse, but this only has the effect of encouraging him rather than deterring him. Now the widow and her daughters-in-law and grandchildren are clapping along, egging him on. I share an annoyed pursing of lips with the men.

Tavik lifts the kitchen utensils into the air and begins to dance on his knees, ticking the spoon and the ladle to the rhythm of his rocking shoulders and gyrating hips. He closes his eyes and sings another verse, loudly and badly, an overwrought metaphor comparing a woman to an inventory of precious stones.

"The lyrics are dreadful," I inform Hroth, and he snorts appreciatively. But Tavik keeps singing, his eyes shut tight. I wonder if he is escaping the world around him at this moment, imagining himself back in Kantar, dancing with his friends in some mosaic-lined hall. And there are girls there, too, I'm certain. I can easily imagine Tavik, crooning in the center of them, surrounded by an amorphous group of sensuous femininity. When he opens his eyes, how disappointed he must be to find my irritated face staring back at him. The thought that he might not like the sight of my face at all plucks an out-of-tune string in my chest.

"Contain yourself," he says, hitting the pot lightly with the wooden spoon. "I know you may never have seen such a manly display of singing and dancing before in your sheltered life. It's all right if you need to swoon from the intensity of my talent and beauty."

It needles me, the way he inhabits his own skin, how he navigates the physical world without any thought of others' judgment, especially when my own body feels weak and used up.

"You are so . . . ," I huff.

"Gifted?" he offers. "Dazzling? Glorious?" He raises first one eyebrow and then the other. I'm irked with myself for grinning back at him, but how can anyone fail to mirror that smile? Before I can look away, he tosses the spoon and the ladle heedlessly behind him and begins to scoot across the floor toward me, moving as sinuously as a snake on his knees, his torso swaying in the air like a cobra poised to attack. Only he's no snake. He's more like a snake charmer, and as long as he holds my gaze, I'm the cobra. Our eyes are locked, and I can't bring myself to look away. He dances closer and closer to me, sliding seductively forward on his knees, his eyes burning into mine as he sings.

> *What is better?*
> *The capture or the chase?*
> *You are the huntress*
> *And I the prey.*

I want to tell him that the hunting metaphor of his stupid song is trite, but my mouth twists and won't cooperate. He's almost reached me, when Widow Bennik claps and hoots and draws his attention away from me. Tavik answers her gummy smile with a mischievous grin. He leaps to his feet, dances to the old woman, and holds out his hand. I guess the meaning is clear enough, because she says, "Don't mind if I do."

He doesn't know any Rosvanian dances, so he lets her chatter at him, showing him first this step, then this turn, until he's mastered a country dance with her, both of them giddy and giggling.

I hunch my shoulders, trying to read despite the frivolity thundering all around me, the whole household joining in the revelry. I hardly notice when the old woman plops herself down in the chair across from me again, winded.

Suddenly, Tavik's bouncing on the balls of his feet beside my chair. "Come on, Gelya, dance with me."

I ignore him.

"You know you want to," he insists.

"I don't know how to—" But I remember the girl I was in Hedenskia, twirling by the sea, my red hair fiery in the wind.

I remember.

"Aha! You *do* know how to dance!" Tavik cries, and before I know what's hit me, he scoops me out of my chair by my waist and sets me down on my feet right in front of him, a display of physical strength that he plays off as effortless.

"Like this," he directs me, showing me a quick series of movements, mostly broad gestures with the arms and hands while springing on the soles of his feet to the rhythm of the rain. "Now you try."

I start to move, but I flounder, feeling like an idiot.

"With me," he says, humming the song from the beginning and mirroring the movement in front of me so I can follow.

To dance is to love the body, so a Daughter is not supposed to dance. But I am no one's daughter anymore, and an ebullient joy that is not Elath bubbles inside me as I sink into the rhythm, the music giving me a boost of energy I desperately need right now.

"Again!" Tavik cries, and I repeat the movement until I get it right. He adds to it, teaching me each step until I've mastered an entire string, and I'm starting to move more confidently, more smoothly.

"Now turn like this," Tavik says in the beats between the verses, demonstrating for me. I follow along with each new direction until I have all the steps memorized for two verses and the refrain.

"Again!" Tavik laughs, and we run through it once more.

"Again!"

This time, when I start the sequence, Tavik unexpectedly steps behind me, so close I can feel the heat of his body along my back, and he whispers in my ear, "All things in balance."

I gasp in surprise when his hands land on my waist, and when I turn this time, it's because he's spinning me out and then back into himself. My hand arching over my head meets his arching over his own head in the opposite direction. Every step along the way, his movements counterbalance mine, making it easier to work my way through the dance. I realize he's taught me the female half, and now he's stepping in to complete it with the male movements.

I start giggling uncontrollably. "Fun!" I whoop as the dance brings him sliding in front of me. "I should try it sometime!"

"Yes, you should!"

We break apart and come back together. He grasps my hand and spins me out and then back into him. We're about to risk life and limb to get past the Great Wall of Saint Balzos and cross through the Dead Forest, and I have never been happier in my life than I am at this moment, dancing with Tavik in a smugglers' house.

Each time we turn in to each other, there's an instant, not even the length of a breath, when we face each other. Out and in, out and in. At first, he makes a ridiculous face at me each time it happens, and I burst out laughing. But eventually his clownish antics dissolve into a grin, and my smile back to him is so warm I feel like I'm glowing.

The next time I spin into Tavik, his eyes lock with mine, and my heart flutters like a bird's wings in my chest, and heat rises in my cheeks, and neither one of us is smiling now.

The next time I spin into him, his hand pulls me in closer than before, my hip pressed to his, and I watch, hypnotized, as his gaze moves from my eyes to my lips.

Time slows to a halt, a window half open. In this unending sliver of a second, I remember the way he froze when I pulled back the veil on our fake wedding day. What did he see when he looked on my face? Something hideous?

Something lovely?

The sliver stretches and thins. In my mind, I lean into my groom, who is not really mine at all, and he closes the distance between us to touch his lips to my lips. It's nothing like the way he kissed Mera. It's only the smallest shift of one mouth softening against another.

The window of time slams shut, and when Tavik spins me out, my exhaustion catches up to me. My grip isn't tight enough to hold on, and I turn with too much momentum, sending myself stumbling across the room. I bump hard into the table, knocking the book of verse to the floor with a percussion as loud as thunder.

I didn't realize until this moment that the entire Bennik family had stopped their own revelry to watch Tavik and I dance. "It's getting hot in here," Hroth's wife teases us, and I feel my already-flushed face go mortifyingly scarlet.

"Are you all right?" Tavik asks me breathlessly. I can't look at his face. I'm not sure how I'm ever going to look at that face again.

"Fine," I tell the floor.

I get through dinner without meeting his eyes and excuse myself to an early bedtime. The problem with this escape plan is that since the house is one room, I have to tuck myself into a dark corner while everyone else except the children is still awake. My body is limp with fatigue, but sleep refuses to come. With my eyes shut tight, my mind has the blackened canvas it needs to paint its own picture of Tavik's face each time I turned in to him. The rain still drips into the pots, and as far as my restless mind is concerned, Tavik is still dancing.

Back at the convent, I always believed that my Hedenski past posed the greatest threat to my soul, but now I understand the true reason why Vessels are cloistered. No matter how tightly I close my eyes, I can't escape the warmth of Tavik's hands on my waist, his body dancing so close to mine that parts of him brush up against parts of me, jolting me with shock waves everywhere we touch, anchoring me to the pleasures of the physical world.

Tavik.

Liquid and lovely.

He is dancing across the floor to me, sliding on his knees, coming for me.

For me.

His eyes simmer from behind the thick fringe of his eyelashes as he inches closer, and I don't know what I'll do if and when he reaches me at last.

It doesn't feel like a sin to find out.

I stand on a precipice overlooking a river, wearing my bridal dress, the veil pulled back, my face uncovered. Trees expand across the horizon as far as the eye can see on the other side, but while I'm certain Zofia-who-is-Elath waits somewhere close by, I don't see her.

"Hey!" someone calls out. I turn to find Tavik standing beside me, shirt off, scabbards strapped to his back, ready to pray. "I need some answers here!"

No one responds to him.

"I deserve some answers!" he shouts heatedly.

Silence. There's only the rushing of the wind rustling in the trees, the buzzing of insect wings, the chirps of birds and frogs.

"Where are you?" he yells. He demands.

"I'm right next to you."

He turns and seems surprised to find me at his side.

"What are you doing here?" I ask him.

"What do you mean, what am I doing here? What are you doing here? It's my dream."

I look in confusion across the river, but I see no one. "Are you sure?"

He looks across the river, too, and clicks his tongue. "I'm not sure about anything anymore. Not that I'd ever admit that to you."

"You just did, though."

"Yeah, but you're not real."

"None of this is real," I muse.

"Just a dream," he agrees.

Just a dream, a world where nothing matters and nothing comes with a cost. Suddenly unburdened, my body is light as air. I step in front of Tavik to stand between him and the river, and I let myself stare at him, as openly and obviously as I please, because none of it matters here.

"What are you doing?" he asks with a breathy laugh. I'm making

the dream version of Tavik nervous, and it's intoxicating.

"Just a dream," I remind him or me or both of us as I hold out the finger of my right hand and press it to the bridge of his spectacular nose, slowly sliding down the perfect, crooked line of it.

"Gelya?" He sounds uncertain, but he doesn't stop me.

My fingertip slides down to his lips to trace their soft lines, remembering how they felt pressed against my own for the barest of seconds. My gaze follows my finger, but from the corner of my eye, I see Tavik's body go very still, the way my own does when I happen to find myself unexpectedly close to a rabbit in the convent garden and I don't want to frighten it away.

It makes me braver.

With the fingers of both hands, I touch the place where his unruly hair meets the smooth skin of his forehead and let my fingers drift downward, following the lines of his face: his eyebrows, his cheekbones, his jaw.

I meet his eyes, asking for permission to keep going. He gapes at me, his eyes the color of moss on the oaks beyond the river. He nods.

I take his left hand in mine and stretch out his arm, brushing the silver bite marks a telleg made when he was six years old and trapped in a well. My eyes meet his again, and he is soft as lamb's wool in my grasp. Beginning with the tattoo of the Grace Tree of Kantar on his wrist, I stroke my way up his arm, feeling the texture of him, the skin, the scars, the tendons and muscles beneath the surface, all the way to his shoulder. He watches me, mesmerized, unmoving as a statue. His body, in all its hard and soft solidity, sings its own song beneath my hands. I run my fingers across his collarbones, careful to avoid my handprint over his heart. Then I feel my way downward, *moving my touch over the unfamiliar roughness of his chest, the ridges of his ribs, the corrugation of his stomach.*

He makes a noise, a quick release of air from his lungs, and when I look into his face this time, his pupils are huge and black and bottomless. Something about it makes me giddy, and I reach behind him to draw both his swords from their scabbards. They're heavy, but I'm strong enough to hold them up before Tavik's glazy stare.

"I thought you said it would be difficult to disarm you," I tell him, triumphant.

He closes his eyes. His forehead creases as if he were in pain. "Oh, Tavik," he says. "This is very bad, and very, very wrong." But when he opens his eyes, he is no longer still. He is heat and life and movement. His hands reach for my waist, hot through the fabric of my wedding dress.

And then he's gone—just gone—and even his swords have disappeared from my hands.

I wake to Widow Bennik singing, "Rise and shine. The messenger is back."

She stands by the table, holding a soulswift in her knobby-knuckled hand. I will never get used to the sight of that.

"What does it say?" Tavik asks, flinging off his blanket.

The dance. The dream. Tavik. Thank the Father above the Prima's message has arrived, something—anything—to get me back on track and thinking about the more important issues at hand. Feeling a little more solid than I did yesterday, I rise from my pallet and join them at the table.

Hroth decants the paper from the canister around the bird's leg, gives it to his mother, then takes the soulswift from her hand. As Widow Bennik reads the message, her face creases in astonishment.

"What?" Tavik and Hroth ask at the same time but in two different languages.

She holds up the tiny slip of paper. "I'd think your Prima had accidentally added an extra zero to that sum of money if what she requested wasn't the most ridiculous thing I've ever heard in my life. She damn well better pay me this much if she expects me to pull it off."

"What did she say?" I ask.

"She asked me to smuggle you over the Great Wall of Saint Balzos. You two got a death wish or something?"

"May I read it, please?" Tavik asks in Rosvanian.

"Go ahead. There's a part there that must be for you, because I sure as death can't read it."

Tavik slides the paper out from between her fingers, holds it in the palm of his hand, and scans the symbols no one but he can read. The way he cups the note reminds me once again of the statue of the unknown saint in the convent's parlertorium, holding his own heart in his hands.

"What did you write to the Prima?" I ask, still feeling shy of him, my embarrassing dream floating between us.

He keeps his eyes on the message when he answers, simply, "The truth."

"Hey, Hroth," Widow Bennik calls to her eldest, slicing through the moment with her gruff voice. "We still got that Yilish gunpowder?"

Yil's gunpowder is the reason why the Holy Ovinist Church keeps a careful truce with the empire. It's highly illegal in Ovinist countries and very dangerous, and the fact that we're taking any amount of it to the Great Wall of Saint Balzos fills me with grave concern.

Hroth eyes his mother warily. "Yeah, we were going to make a king's ransom off it, weren't we?"

"Just did, thanks to the Prima of Kantar. Pack it up, sweetheart."

Forty

The shipment of Aurian wool that was supposed to smuggle Tavik and me to Yil is now a shipment of Yilish silk smuggling us to Varos da Balzos by way of the Fev River. We've swapped our knights' uniforms for simple men's clothing, so we are no longer Brother Remur and Brother Elgar, Knights of the Order, but Remur and Elgar, a pair of smugglers on Captain Hroth's crew.

The farther north we travel, the colder it gets. We're bundled in fur-lined leather jackets and caps, but the chill bites me to the bone anyway, one more way my body's continued frailty drags on me.

While I may be dressed as a man, the disguise does me little good. I don't know how I've changed since leaving the convent, but I don't seem to be fooling anyone these days. The one and only woman on the crew, other than myself, tried to give me her extra shiv a few days ago, and when I declined, she said, "Suit yourself, just so long as you know the world ain't kind to girls."

Now all I can think about is Zofia's warning that the world of men is dangerous for women, a point she proved just a few hours after she said it.

The crew hides us inside two ingeniously devised bolts of fabric at various checkpoints along the Fev, which is an absolute nightmare for poor Tavik, who might actually prefer death to being stuck in a tight space. The constant fear of getting caught never goes away, but it's a less pernicious presence than the constant buzzing and churning and roiling of Elath's relentless spirit inside me, growing louder with each passing day.

I'd confide this to Tavik, but we don't talk much. I'm stupidly shy with him, although I don't know why. It's not like he can pry open my brain and find the embarrassing dream I had or know how my heart fluttered just because he danced with me. I'm not Mera. I'm just me, and now, all of a sudden, I don't know how to be me around him anymore.

He seems as eager to avoid me as I am to avoid him, spending most of his time staring at the Fev with a distant, glassy look in his eyes. I suspect it makes him uneasy to travel by river. He doesn't know how to swim, after all, and he's certainly had his fair share of bad experiences with water, which is why I'm surprised when he sits beside me on the deck one evening and lets his legs dangle off the side as mine do, hovering above the frigid river below.

We both gaze straight ahead, neither of us saying anything. His proximity is like sitting beside a fire, viscerally present, but something I don't dare touch. And if I'm being honest with myself, I do want to touch him. I remember how his arms felt around me in the smugglers' cellar, and how I ran my fingers along his skin in my dream. But now that he is very real and sitting next to me, he may as well be on the other side of the boat.

"Fifty-four," he says out of nowhere. I glance at him, but he gives me only his profile.

"Fifty-four?"

He nods.

"Fifty-four . . . what?"

"You asked me once how many men I've killed. The answer is fifty-four. There may be more, men I left wounded who died later, but as far as I know for certain, fifty-four, including the assassins in the parlertorium and DeTana and DeLuthina." His tone is disinterested, but there's a stiff squareness to his shoulders that tells me the burden is heavy, bordering on unbearable. Heartsick, I watch him as he stares at nothing.

"Why are you telling me this?"

"I don't know. I just feel like you should know that about me."

"Is knowing this supposed to lessen my good opinion of you?"

"Does it?" He goes very still as he waits for my answer.

Fifty-four men. I feel bad when I step on a cockroach, and Tavik has killed fifty-four men. It's hard to wrap my brain around such a sum, such a toll. But what options did he have? The seedpod opened in his hand, too. He didn't choose this life. It was thrust upon him, just as mine was thrust upon me. At least he feels the consequences of his actions. Could he say the same for Captain DeRopa? Could I say the same for Goodson Anskar?

Sing, faithful, of Tavik, prison and prisoner, I sing in my mind before I answer, "No, it doesn't lessen my good opinion of you."

"Well, it should." He turns his face slightly. He still won't look at me, but I can see the stark sadness in his eyes.

"I've spent most of my life adoring the man who attacked my village and kidnapped me," I point out. "I'd say admiring you is a step in the right direction."

His lips twist into a weak smile. "You are a terrible judge of character."

"I can't argue with that." After a moment's pause, I add, "When DeRopa caught up to us, why did you tell me to run to the monastery?"

"It was a less immediate threat than the one we were facing. I knew DeRopa must have been working with Brother Miklos, but I guess I hoped you were right about the Goodson after all. I'm sorry you weren't." Here, he finally looks at me, and I feel like I'm being jabbed in the heart with the shiv I refused to accept.

I decide to match Tavik's honesty, giving voice to a painful fact that continues to bore its way through my heart. "Goodson Anskar was going to lock me up and throw away the key, just as you said he would."

"He'll pay for that," Tavik promises me, his voice gravelly with barely contained fury. "I'll make him pay for everything he's done."

My hands grasp the air between us as if I could pluck my logic out of the wind and hand it to him. "I don't want the Goodson to pay. I don't hate him. I know I'm supposed to, but I don't."

"Then I'll hate him enough for both of us."

"That's not what I would wish for you either. You're not so different from each other, you and the Goodson."

Tavik's mouth hangs open in outrage. "I am *nothing* like the Goodson."

"You are *exactly* like the Goodson, both of you so faithful, so certain of your truth. You see the world as if it were split into halves: good and evil, life giving and life taking, man and woman, and on and on. But the world isn't black and white. There are shades of gray, ideas you can't cram into your well-ordered universe, people who stand outside your definitions but who are just as valuable as you or I or the Goodson. Just because *he* is wrong doesn't make *you* right."

"Oh, for the love of the Mother, how can you not believe what I believe at this point? After everything you've seen? After everything that's happened to you? Are you seriously going to cling to the religion of the man who kidnapped you? Took you from your home? Killed your people? And after all that, after everything you know now, with the full knowledge that a goddess—a *goddess*, Gelya—is living inside you, you want to pretend *I'm* the zealous nutjob?"

"That's not what I said. I'm only saying that he's a good man who happens to believe the wrong thing. What if *you* are also a good man who's a little bit wrong?"

"I'm not wrong."

"You were wrong about DeRopa."

Tavik recoils as if I had hit him, and I instantly regret saying the words. But since the specter of Captain DeRopa now looms over the conversation, I plow ahead. With the two of us barely speaking to each other, who knows when I'll have another opportunity?

"Back at Saint Helios, DeRopa said you didn't follow his orders. What did he mean by that?"

Tavik stares at his hands pressed between his knees. "He ordered me to remain in place and report our location. Twice."

"But you didn't?"

He shakes his head.

"Why not?"

"Because I made you a promise, and . . . It's complicated."

Everything about Tavik and me is complicated. We sit side by side, miles apart, and listen to the sounds of the river that carries us to a terrifyingly uncertain future in the Dead Forest and beyond. After a few minutes, Tavik nudges my shoulder, sending an unexpected shock wave through my body.

"So you think I'm a good man, huh?"

It's a peace offering, one I know I'm expected to accept with a joke. "A good *arrogant* man," I amend.

"You say that like it's a bad thing."

I lean back on my hands. "For weeks, we've been focusing on one thing at a time: Escape Varos da Vinnica, then figure out what to do. Get the Sword, then find the Mother's body. But now we have the Vessel and the Sword, and we know where the body is. Is it strange that this is the first time I've wondered what exactly is going to happen if we get to the tree?"

"When," Tavik corrects me. "Not if."

"Fine. What happens when we get there?"

"The Mother's spirit flies out of you the same way She entered in. She inhabits Her own body and saves the world."

"That's the best-case scenario. What's the worst-case scenario?"

A muscle ticks in his jaw. "There isn't one."

"I think there are many," I insist. "We need the Vessel and the Sword, but for what exactly?"

"The Sword is to get the Vessel through the Dead Forest. It's for killing telleg. That's why the Goodson was able to protect you ten years ago. He had the Sword."

It's a good theory, and there's a ring of truth to it, yet I feel like there's more hope than reality behind it. I stare at Tavik's hands tucked between his knees, wishing I could slip my own between them but too uncertain of his reaction to try.

"The Goodson told me you were dead. He said his men found your body," I admit, my roundabout way of telling Tavik I'm glad he's alive.

He nods thoughtfully. "Good move, cutting ties like that. He probably saw how very attached you are to me."

"He probably did," I agree, tired of masking my truth with humor but not sure how to talk to Tavik about the hardest things without it. My eyes meet his as an unanswered question plops itself between us. Neither of us seems to know how to get it out of the way.

His expression turns somber and makes my breath go shallow. "There's something I need to tell you," he says, but he doesn't get any further than that. He goes on staring at me with a gravity that thins my breathing so much, my lungs begin to cry out for air.

The first white flakes of winter begin to fall, quickly turning into a torrent of fat snowflakes. Tavik looks up, his troubled expression slowly softening into the reverence I saw on his face in the library of Saint Vinnica.

"Snow?" he asks.

"Snow," I agree, seeing it from his perspective, the newness of it, the beauty falling all around us.

He holds out his arms as if he could embrace the sky and smiles, his teeth bright in the darkness.

Forty-One

The Great Wall of Saint Balzos comprises over half the northern border of Auria before the line between civilization and the Dead Forest plunges into the Rannig Mountains, a natural barrier the telleg can't cross.

There are no gates in the wall. The point is to keep things out, not let them through, so the only opening that connects Auria on the south to the Dead Forest on the north is the Five Gate Bridge, which allows the Fev River to flow from the land of the dead to the land of the living. That's where we're going, the same place where the Goodson and I crossed into the safety of Auria ten years ago, although I have no recollection of it.

This is our last time to go over the plan before Tavik and I separate from the crew, so I pay close attention. Hroth has re-created the Five Gate Bridge out of odds and ends from around the barge: a collapsible telescope, a teacup, a tankard, some blocks of wood. It would be comical if our lives didn't depend on it.

He points to the tankard. "The easternmost garrison of the Great Wall is built into the side of Mount Saint Osgart. The knights stationed here man the watchtowers on both sides of the river"—here, Hroth points to the teacup and the telescope—"as well as three sentry points along the bridge, which is about a hundred yards across. An assignment at the wall is considered light duty. The knights can see the telleg from time to time, but only at night, and the things never get too close to the wall."

"Has a telleg . . . ?" At a loss for the Rosvanian words he wants, Tavik picks up a saltshaker and animates it from the north side of the model wall to the south, making a growling sound. The fact that no one laughs is a strong indication of just how dangerous the telleg are.

"No," answers Hroth. "And the knights sure as death won't expect anyone would want to cross from south to north."

"Can we go here?" Tavik asks, sticking his finger through one of the gates made by a gap in the blocks.

Hroth shakes his head. "The Fev is running too high, but this part of the wall is the lowest point, so it's the place where it will be easiest to climb down to the other side without breaking your stupid necks. Not that it's going to be easy." He sets a crumpled piece of paper on the table next to the tankard. "We'll set off the first explosion in front of the garrison. That should empty the building and bring the men from the western watchtower over the bridge to see what's happening on the eastern shore. At that point, you two fools will go up the west tower and set off the second bomb on the bridge. You'll have thirty seconds or so to get clear once you've lit the fuse, so don't mess around."

Hroth directs this last part at Tavik. I can tell Tavik gets the gist, but I translate anyway, because I want to make sure he thoroughly understands the danger.

"Once the bridge is damaged, we hook the rope ladder onto the wall and climb down on the north side," I complete the plan.

"Where no telleg licker in their right mind would follow you," Hroth adds unhelpfully.

Tavik and I wait with our backs pressed against the wall of the western watchtower for at least an hour before the explosion erupts on the opposite bank. The ground beneath my feet rocks with a violence I was not anticipating, and the three sentries posted on the bridge race toward the east side of the Fev to investigate. Seconds later, five knights rush out of the western tower and pelt across the bridge after them.

"Let's go," Tavik says, leading the way through the ground-level door and up a winding staircase before the ringing in my ears subsides. Thank heaven my body has had a chance to rest and regain at least a little strength, because I'm already winded halfway up. I'm not sure how I would have made it a couple of weeks ago, especially since I'm carrying a knapsack full of supplies to help get us through the Dead Forest. We make it to the top in three minutes and find it empty, just as we hoped.

"So far, so good," I say between wheezing breaths.

"Let's not pat ourselves on the back yet." Tavik dumps his pack on the ground and hands me the rope ladder coiled around his shoulder.

I hold out my ring to him before he leaves me to set the second bomb. When he links his ring with mine, I tell him, "Don't you dare lose any body parts, beloved husband."

"I won't, darling wife. That's a promise." He grins, then sneaks across the bridge, keeping his head down so he won't be noticed from the ground.

It's time to get to my own task. I look over the edge to find that the slope on this side is much steeper than on the south. We've got about twenty-five feet to scale down, twice the height of the wall around Dalment, and I thought that was dizzyingly high at the time. I pull two lengths of rope from my pack and tie one to each knapsack, lowering first one and then the other onto the ground on the north side of the wall. The ropes aren't long enough in either case, so each pack falls a fair distance before hitting the earth.

In the meantime, Tavik stops a third of the way across the Five Gate Bridge, right over one of the arches, where he wastes no time lighting the fuse. The second he has it lit, he turns and sprints back the way he came.

I'm frozen to the spot. My heart stops beating as I watch him run back to me with a lit bomb at his back.

"What are you doing? Take cover!" he shouts, but I've gone wooden, and I can't move until I know he's safe.

Tavik tackles me, his body flattening mine against the floor, one fitting into the other like opposing magnets snapping together. He's panting so hard I can feel his chest expand and contract as his breath steams my face, and my mind goes blank.

"Hi," he says, looking equally blank.

"Hello."

The bomb goes off, making the tower lurch and my stomach

right along with it. Tavik rolls off me so I can grab the ladder, and we both secure the grappling hooks to the north-facing wall. It doesn't reach all the way to the bottom, so we both can look forward to an eight-foot drop from the end of the last rung to the ground, although I'm sure that distance is nothing to Tavik. He curses on my behalf rather than his, I assume, but he says, "Nothing for it. You first."

He helps me over the wall and holds on to me as I get a solid footing on the first few rungs, which is why neither of us notices the man creeping up behind him until he's right over Tavik's shoulder: Brother Miklos.

I don't have time to scream, but Tavik must see something in my face or sense Brother Miklos's presence behind him because he releases me and draws the Sword of Mercy—the Hand of the Father—in time to block the knight's blow.

"Go!" he shouts to me as he draws the Sword of Wrath, too, but there's no way I'm leaving him. I pull myself back onto the wall.

"Father of death! Go!"

Tavik lunges at Brother Miklos with one blade, and even as the knight blocks the first blow, Tavik is already following it with the second. But Brother Miklos has fought Two-Swords before, and he spins free, making Tavik correct course with a full turn into the momentum. His feet leave the ground, and his body goes impossibly horizontal in midair. Miklos is too slow to respond, and Tavik drives both blades into his stomach. The Butcher of Grama slams back against the tower's wall and sinks to the ground, his blood pooling beneath him.

I catch sight of two more men in the distance on the other side of the bridge, and even from a hundred yards off, I recognize them: the Goodson and DeRopa.

"Go, go, go!" Tavik shouts at me, waving his arm at the ladder, and this time I swing onto the ropes without his help, scurrying like a spider down the side of the tower as fast as my long arms and legs will carry me so that Tavik can get on the ladder that much sooner.

"Come on!" I shout up to him when I'm halfway there.

"Not till you're all the way down."

I go as fast as I can, but I know it's taking too long. When I hit the last rung, I let go and roll across the ground the way Tavik did all those weeks ago when we jumped off the wall surrounding Dalment. The impact jars me, but I'm unhurt, and I'm far more worried about Tavik than myself at this point.

I look up to watch Tavik's descent when movement from the left catches my eye. DeRopa has nearly reached the chasm on the east side of the bridge, with Goodson Anskar lagging several feet behind. The Goodson slows as he approaches the edge, but DeRopa sprints in a burst of speed and, to my horror, launches himself across the impossible distance, stumbling as he lands on the western half—*our* side—of the bridge, but landing it all the same.

"Tavik!"

He looks up, and there's his captain, his father, the man who betrayed him looking down at him over the wall. But it's not the sharp end of a sword DeRopa offers him. It's his hand, reaching out, offering to pull Tavik back up. Tavik freezes on the ladder and stares at that hand for one long, heart-wrenching moment before he shakes his head and climbs down another rung.

"Father of death, DeSemla, can't you see I'm trying to help you?" DeRopa says, his voice rough with emotion as he stretches his hand out even farther.

Tavik answers by climbing down another rung.

DeRopa pulls a knife from a scabbard on his arm and holds it to one of the ropes.

"No!" I leap for the end of the ladder, but it's too high. It makes me want to claw off my own skin to be powerless when Tavik needs my help the most.

"It doesn't have to end like this, kid."

Tavik looks down, first at me, then to the ground. I know he's judging the distance, and I know it's too far for him, Two-Swords or not. He looks back up at DeRopa. "Then don't let it end like this."

"I made my choice when I was your age, and I know you'd make the same choice if you'd just stop and think."

"You chose death," Tavik spits, and he makes a break for it, climbing down as fast as he can.

DeRopa saws at the rope.

"Please," I beg the Father and Mother and all the saints, but the rope snaps well before Tavik can jump down safely. The remaining rope swings wide as it takes his full weight. His feet hit the tower wall, running along the brickwork, gaining momentum. He pushes off and swings himself back onto the top of the tower just as DeRopa cuts the second rope, and the ladder falls at my feet, as useless as I am.

The Two-Swords face each other on the wall, blades out, and my heart screams in my chest.

"Impressive," DeRopa says, his mouth the only thing about him that moves.

"You underestimated me." Tavik coils tighter. "Again."

"I'm going to sheathe my swords. I just want you to listen to me. Can you give me that?"

Whether Tavik moves or speaks I can't tell from my vantage point twenty-five feet below. DeRopa slowly sheathes his swords anyway and holds up his hands, just as Tavik did with me in the Dyers' workroom, a sign of good faith. The danger isn't over, but I breathe in relief.

The captain chooses his words slowly, carefully. "I was like you once: ignorant of the world, full of sanctimony, blindly serving a religion that died hundreds of years ago. And for what? How many Kantari lives have been wasted because our country won't give up the ghost?"

"You've never looked into the Mother's eyes. You've never seen Her light."

"Don't fall for that! She only shows you what you want to believe. Imagine what good you could do in the world if you would only see reason. You've got so much talent, Tavik, so much potential. Don't waste yourself on this."

"You didn't think I had talent or potential when you sent me on a suicide mission."

"That's not true. It was the hardest thing I've ever done in my life. Good Father, do you have any idea how proud I am of you?"

Tavik lets loose a bitter laugh. "I'm sure that will be a great comfort to me when you try to send me to the underworld. Now bring out your blades, because I'm not going to kill you unless your swords are in your hands, you backstabbing traitor."

Part of me wants to kiss him for those words, but the other part of me wants to kill him myself for choosing to fight this man, who could more easily take his life than any Knight of the Order ever could.

DeRopa reaches behind his back to draw his swords. "So be it," he says darkly.

They fight at a pace that's hard to track, their movements so swift they become blurs, two smudges of men, fighting to the death. I have to keep shifting position, tripping over tree roots and fallen branches in a desperate attempt to follow along, all the while praying to any god who will listen to keep Tavik safe.

The fight slows as it drags on, making it easier to track. Tavik launches himself off the wall to hack downward with the Sword of Wrath, while DeRopa leaps, blocking the blow with such force that Tavik goes careening through the air and flies clear of the wall. He sheaches a sword, catches the iron hook of a crossbow support, and swings himself back around, kicking DeRopa full in the chest and sending him slamming into the tower wall. By the time DeRopa recovers, Tavik has both swords in his hands once more.

Watching is unbearable, but I can't look away until, once again, there's movement to the left. I stare in disbelief as the Goodson takes a running start across the east side of the bridge and jumps toward the west.

And he makes it.

The blood in my veins turns to ice. A memory bubbles to the surface, the image of him killing a telleg, bending and stretching and fighting in ways no normal man could.

My friend placed the seedpod in my hand, and it opened.

I just watched Goodson Anskar sail through the air like a Two-Swords.

Because he *is* a Two-Swords.

And now Tavik stands between him and DeRopa, the Sword of Wrath pointed at his captain, the Sword of Mercy—the Hand of the Father—trained on the Goodson. As they close in on him, he goes on the defensive, his blades moving in two different arcs, deflecting first one attack and then another. The Goodson swings his new sword at Tavik's belly, but Tavik sinks to one knee, and the blade rings through the air over his head as he lunges at DeRopa with the Sword of Wrath. The captain slides backward, but I think Tavik nicked him, because he's able to maneuver into the opening and get the tower's wall against his back.

For a breath, I think this gives him an advantage, until Brother Miklos, drenched in his own blood, climbs up Tavik's left side, brandishing a dagger just like the one he threw into Zofia's heart. Tavik jerks away, but not before the dying knight rams the blade into Tavik's back, just behind his shoulder.

I can feel his cry of agony in my bones as the Hand of the Father drops from his grasp and clatters to the ground in front of Goodson Anskar, who snatches it up. I cry out, a guttural sound without words, but it's drowned by Brother Miklos's last scream as

Tavik buries the Sword of Wrath into the man's chest. He pulls the blade free and turns to face the Goodson, standing crookedly, his left shoulder leaning toward the earth. He's going to kill himself trying to get that stupid sword.

"Tavik! Get out of there!" I scream up at him. The Goodson peers over the wall, but I don't return his gaze. I'm not here for him.

"Tavik!" I shout again, though I know he has nowhere to go and no way to get down to me.

Before either man can act, he sheaths his one remaining sword and staggers to the bridge. His assailants give chase, and DeRopa reaches him first, lashing out with one of his blades. Tavik rolls on the ground, heading straight for the gap. He clambers down the ragged slope cut into the bridge by the bomb, but he slips about ten feet above the water, barely catching himself on a brick with his right hand. I can't look away as he dangles over the Fev River below. Then his hand slips, and he drops like a rock.

I throw my head back and howl from my soul at the Father in heaven.

And I feel it, that same tug I felt when the Goodson placed the seedpod in my hand.

The air explodes with a sound that is both a cracking and a screech as the Fev's current turns to ice directly beneath Tavik, who lands on its surface with a dull thud. The ice slowly stretches out beneath him, forming an island around his body.

Elath pulses inside me, but Her fire could never turn water into ice. The song I feel now is coming from outside myself, not from within. I have no idea what's happening or why or how, and I could not possibly care less as long as Tavik moves.

"Get up, Tavik!"

He lifts his head and turns his bloodied face toward my voice. Then he heaves himself onto his hands and knees and begins to crawl toward me.

The ice grows, taking over more and more of the river—ten yards, fifteen yards, twenty yards.

Tavik gets to his feet and limps toward me as DeRopa lands on the ice behind him.

"Come on!"

He starts to trot, close enough now that I can see how his face twists with pain and determination, as the slippery solidity beneath his feet gets closer and closer to me.

DeRopa slides, unsteady on his feet, but he keeps moving, getting closer and closer to Tavik, as the Goodson climbs down onto the ice, too.

"Cover your ears!" I shout, but Tavik, knowing what I'm about to do, shakes his head and propels himself forward, gritting his teeth. I can't help him if he won't let me.

The ice has nearly reached the shore, and I back up to take a running lead so I can leap onto the ice with him.

"Stay there!" he cries, his voice pierced with a pain that's nearly as unendurable for me to hear as it is for him to feel.

DeRopa is only five yards behind him, but Tavik is still ten yards from shore as the ice finally meets the eastern bank. I slide onto the ice and reach out. "Come on!"

"Get back!"

"You can make it!"

He reaches out with his right hand, and I grab hold of him just as DeRopa thrusts one of his swords at Tavik. I yank back for all I'm worth. Tavik loses his footing and slides into the shoreline, leaving me face-to-face with a livid, panting DeRopa. He sneers at me with a hatred so profound I lose my breath.

The ice groans. Tavik wraps his arm around my waist and throws both of us to shore as the ice pops and splits beneath DeRopa's feet. The man doesn't even have time to register surprise or terror before the frigid waters of the Fev swallow him whole.

The frozen river continues to break into heaving shards like broken glass. From his position halfway between the bridge and the shore, the Goodson meets my gaze, his face stark with fear, before he goes scrabbling back across the ice the way he came. He skids into the rubble of the bridge's support and jumps as high as any Two-Swords to grab the same brick Tavik caught on the way down just before the ice breaks apart beneath him. He pulls himself up the jagged brickwork, collapsing when he makes it to the top. I watch the whole thing with a sick heart, worried for this man I should hate but don't.

Tavik sits on his heels, breathing hard, and I drop to my knees beside him. He touches my face with his right hand as he cradles his left arm to his stomach. "Are you all right?" he breathes, stroking my cheek with his thumb, examining me.

"Am *I* all right?" I repeat, my voice shrill. "I'm not the one who was stabbed!"

His fingers are freezing against my skin as he keeps studying my face, bewildered. "Your nose isn't bleeding."

"It wasn't me. Or Her. The ice didn't come from inside me."

We both turn our eyes to the river as it sends huge chunks of ice hurtling south.

"Father of death," Tavik utters.

"Literally," I whisper.

I prayed to the Father.

And, for once, I got an answer.

Forty-Two

Autumn shrouds the Dead Forest, lingering on the cusp of winter, never sleeping, never waking, always dying. But it's not the bare trees or the chilly bite of the air that makes me uneasy. It's the feeling that we've stepped out of reality into a world without time or care. There's a heartlessness here that freezes me to the bone more than any winter wind could.

Tavik shivers in front of the small, smoking fire I've managed to light, staring into the thin tendrils of flames as he pokes at it with a rotted tree branch. Dark smudges curve beneath his eyes, and his lips are chapped and ashy. He looks half dead, and that has me so worried I can barely hold myself together.

"We're screwed," he says.

"Don't talk like that." I don't know the meaning of the word *screwed*. I just know it's bad, very bad.

He unclasps his coat with his right hand as I kneel behind him and pull back the layers of clothing beneath to get a look at his wound.

"'Only the Vessel and the Sword may set Her free,'" he quotes. "Hey, you know what we don't have?"

"Let's just—"

"The telleg-licking Sword. Because I lost it. To the Goodson. I had it, and I lost it." He slams the heel of his boot into the branch, breaking it in half. The violence of the movement must make his shoulder wound hurt, because he grunts in pain before he draws his knees up and sets his forehead on top of them in defeat.

"One thing at a time," I tell him, the words that have become our mantra. "Right now, we need to focus on getting through the Dead Forest."

"Yeah. Need the Sword for that." His face is still hidden by his knees, his voice muffled.

"You have a sword."

"I have *a* sword, not *the* Sword."

By now, I'm staring at the raw puncture at the back of his left shoulder. There's blood everywhere, and the wound is still seeping. I put a hand over my mouth so I won't gasp out loud.

"How bad is it?" he asks, his voice throaty with pain.

Tears spring to my eyes, but I keep my voice steady as I dig through my pack for a bandage. "I'm sure it could be worse."

"Oh, good. I should live long enough to get myself ripped apart by a telleg."

I hold the bandage in my hand, but the world blurs as the angry red wound gapes at me. The forest around us goes translucent, transforming into a different time and place. I stand at the edge of a well.

I'm sorry! a child's voice calls to me from the dark water below. *Please!*

"Gelya?" Tavik sounds equally far away, as if I were suspended inside the well shaft with Tavik above and the child below.

Raran! Barri! His brothers' names echo up the shaft.

My spirit drifts into the well while my body stays beside Tavik. A will that is not mine takes my hand and covers the wound with my palm. Light flares inside me, a flash of lightning across a cloud, a firefly caught in a jar.

I fall, plunging toward the child at the bottom of the well, bringing the light with me, blinding, breaking apart the darkness. Then I slam back into a world of sight and sound and freezing air as if I fell from a great height.

"What just happened?" Tavik's voice is a thunderclap in my ears. He cranes his neck, tugging frantically at his clothes to stare at the smooth skin where his wound used to be.

"What did you do?" he demands, but I can't answer him, because my body goes boneless, and I slump onto the forest floor.

"Gelya!"

Tavik's distraught face hovers above me. His hands are warm once more, cupping my cheeks with a tenderness that makes me happier than I have any right to be at the moment. I can't move or speak, and blood is streaming out of my nose yet again, and Tavik is out of his mind with worry for me, and we are in the Dead Forest—the *Dead Forest*, for the love of the Father—and all I can think about is how much I love Tavik and how glad I am that he's still alive and how badly I want to kiss that infuriating, glorious, beautiful face of his, even though I have no idea how to kiss anyone.

"Blink twice if you can hear me," he says.

I can do that. I blink twice, and he's so relieved he keels over on top of me, pressing his forehead to mine. I must be truly unhinged to find this romantic, but at this point, I'll take my joy wherever I can get it.

I love Tavik.

I sing the Sanctus words in my mind—*I love Tavik*—and the Mother's life billows through me, not a lid to be ripped off but a buoy to cling to. I press against Her anyway, burying Her as deep as I can within me. She doesn't get any part of this. This belongs to me.

The first thing I do when my body returns to me is laugh.

Tavik is not amused. "You think this is funny?" he says as he helps me sit up.

How am I supposed to answer that? *A Daughter of the Convent of Saint Vinnica and a Vessel of the One True God fell in love with you on the floor of the Dead Forest, and it's hilarious, because who on earth does that?* It only makes me cackle harder.

He takes me by the shoulders and forces me to look into his eyes. Good Father, how I love those eyes.

"We had an agreement: You need to keep that lid pressed down."

"Or what? How could it get any worse?" My laughter transforms into something else, bordering on hysteria. I hold out both hands now, looking first to one and then the other, wondering what else they will do without my consent, terrified by the possibility that I'm losing control of them. Of me. "She's taking me body and soul, and I don't know where She ends and I begin anymore."

"Look at me."

But I can't tear my eyes from my hands. "Get Her out of me! I want Her out!"

The lid vibrates, clanking against the metaphorical pot.

"Look at me!" Tavik holds my face in his callused hands. "You are Gelya. You are *you*, and no one, not even Elath, can make you something other than you are. All right? So for the love of the Mother, don't let it happen again."

"For the love of the *Mother*? We wouldn't be here if it wasn't for your precious Mother." Resentment fills my mouth like blood pooling from a bitten tongue. Fury boils inside me, feeding Elath, who devours it like a baby at her mother's breast. "Look around you, Tavik. Is this the reward for your faith? Or for mine? Elath, the Father—they don't care about us. We are their instruments. That's all. We owe them nothing."

"You shouldn't say that." His words ooze not with love of the divine but with fear. Well, I may fear the telleg, but I am not afraid of gods anymore. My anger expands, feeds me, refills the marrow the Mother keeps sucking from my bones.

"Why not? Why should I worship something that cares so little for me, or for you? It's their loss, Tavik. They don't deserve you."

I skate right up to the edge of a feeling too big to speak aloud. Tavik doesn't answer right away. His hands are still on my face, and his thumbs brush my cheeks before he speaks again. "I'm not going to argue this with you. Just promise you'll try to keep that power contained, because it's not worth the price you're paying for it. If I get hurt again, you let my own body heal me."

Even now, Elath expands within me, as if She wants to crack my ribs and break through my skin. "I'll try," I tell him weakly.

"No. You promise me." His hands are warm and firm, and I remember the dream when I ran my fingers along the planes of the familiar face just inches from my own. The words I want to say to him are ready, heavy on my tongue.

Water of my thirst
Blood of my body

Instead, I tell him what he wants to hear: "I promise."

I wish we could stay like this, his hands pressed to my cheeks, his skin against my skin, as if simply touching each other could erase gods and monsters and leave us this one, tangible thing in the world. But we're still too close to the Great Wall of Saint Balzos, and I have no doubt the Goodson will follow us as soon as he's able.

"We should move," I say even as I lean my face into his left hand, wishing I could melt into him.

"I know." He purses his lips before he pulls away. The sensation of losing his warmth is so acute, it almost makes a tearing sound. He helps me up, and we walk north, blazing our own trail since there's no path to follow.

If I could, I would sing to him—*Come to me, my beloved*—so he would know, so he would understand what he is to me now. But since I promised I would keep Elath's power at arm's length, I hold the song inside myself.

The Fev's source is somewhere in the Rannig Mountains in the Dead Forest, but no one has mapped the river's path north of the Aurian border, for obvious reasons. Tavik and I stick to the western bank as we head north through the strange, muffled silence of the trees. Even the Fev's current seems oddly hushed as it murmurs from north to south.

"So this is where murderers and thieves go when they die?" Tavik says at last, his voice bizarrely loud in the quiet.

"And heathens," I add, trying to lighten the severity of our circumstances, but the word sticks uncomfortably in my throat. *Heathen.* How ignorant to think that one person is better than another. I'm ashamed of myself for believing it for as long as I did.

"Hopefully, we'll run into more heathens than murderers," Tavik jokes weakly. "Why do the . . . why do they only come out at night?"

He doesn't say the word, but it gallops between us anyway: *telleg.*

"I don't know."

"And they're drawn to light?"

"Yes." I decide not to tell Tavik how I know this. I'd rather not recall the moment when a knight lit his lantern and five telleg descended on him before he had a chance to scream.

"How do they track their prey? By sight? Smell? What?"

He turns toward me when I don't answer right away, and since

I'm using him as a human crutch, his face is only inches from mine. "I don't know that either," I admit. The urge to hug him for dear life pops when he gives me an exasperated huff and turns his attention back to the trees.

"I was young and really scared," I tell him defensively. "So, no, I didn't study their hunting patterns."

"Sorry. I'm just getting a little nervous. A lot nervous, actually. This place is eerie as death." I feel the shiver that runs up his spine.

"This place *is* death. It's the *Dead* Forest."

"Says Ovinists. From my perspective there are some things here that don't add up. Father of death, it's creepy."

Silence falls on us again, leaving ample mental space for Tavik and I to contemplate all the things we're not discussing, such as the fact that the telleg don't move the way living creatures do. They float and stretch. They attack with unnatural speed. They kill with their hands and their mouths.

They devour men.

I suspect that Tavik is carrying the same sick pit of dread in his stomach as I am.

"Think you'll be able to walk on your own two feet by nightfall?" he asks me as we hike in the shadow of a limestone escarpment shortly before twilight.

I'm still threadbare with exhaustion after healing Tavik—or after the Mother healed him—but I pull my arm away to demonstrate my ability to move of my own volition. In typical Gelya fashion, I immediately trip on something hard and fall onto my bottom beside it.

Tavik reaches down to help me up, but then he pauses, tilts

his head, and squints at a metallic wink beside my splayed hand. "What is that?"

I see glints of silver between freckles of rust.

And bones. Several bones.

And a human skull.

I shriek and scurry back like a crab as Tavik bends down and riffles through the skeletal remains of a human being.

"Oh, please, don't," I beg him, squeamish, but when he straightens, he's holding a sword that's so corroded, it's nearly the color of gelya berries.

"I need a second sword, and I doubt this man has a use for it anymore."

A memory stirs as I stare at the blade.

The Goodson slew a telleg here after the monster killed the last of his men. He stood over the creature for a good long while, frowning down at it. There's something about that memory that I'm missing, a piece of the puzzle I might be able to snap into place if I only stare at it long enough.

"Come on," says Tavik, giving me a hand up. "We need to keep moving."

First comes dusk.

Then night.

There's no rain or snow in the Dead Forest, and the moon bathes the trees in a ghostly light.

In the distance, a *crack* shatters the silence.

We watch and wait.

Fifteen yards ahead of us, a shadow oozes between the

night-blackened tree trunks, rattling their dying leaves like bells.

Ten yards.

Tavik's shoulders move up and down with each terrified breath.

Five yards, and I can sense Tavik's unuttered cursing: *Death, death, death, death . . .*

The telleg lunges.

Tavik grabs me by the shoulder of my jacket and hauls me after him as a small animal screeches in our wake. The wet, sucking sounds of the telleg's mouth feeding on its victim follow us for several yards, and we keep sprinting until the sounds are far behind us.

Our hearts beat in a syncopated rhythm when we stop at last to catch our breath. I wish to all the saints in heaven that we could find somewhere to hide, but it's night, and we must move at night because it's only safe to rest once the sun rises. So we walk, the sounds of our feet moving across the forest floor like whispered curses. We survive our first night in the Dead Forest, but I know it's only a matter of time before Tavik will have to fight the telleg with swords that are not destined to kill them.

At daybreak, we light a fire to warm ourselves. I lie in a huddle of blankets beside the flames. Tavik is too wound up to sleep. He cleans and sharpens the rusty weapon we found, and I doze off to the metallic pinging of the whetstone sliding across the blade.

"Stay alive, Gelya," Tavik whispers when he thinks I'm asleep. "Just stay alive, and I swear I'll get you there."

Forty-Three

We've almost made it through our second night in the Dead Forest when the skittering of an animal through the undergrowth brings us to a halt. An all-too-familiar fear thrums in our lungs, our hearts, our spines, our ears, while Elath remains nerve-rackingly still inside me.

Tavik's hand clutches the hilt of one of his swords behind his back.

We wait.

"It's all right," I breathe at last. "It was nothing."

Crack.

Right in front of us.

"That is not nothing." Tavik pulls both blades from their scabbards and keeps his eyes trained on the sharp fingertips emerging from the split in the bark, wiggling like maggots. The tree creaks and pops as the creature pushes the chasm apart with two abnormally long, hideous hands until the wound is large enough to birth the monster. The telleg seeps into the world, its black cape dribbling from concave shoulders until it envelops its wraithlike body. It hovers inches from the ground.

Elath retreats even deeper inside me, a life that does not belong in this world of death. I step back, watching the telleg over Tavik's shoulder.

"I can do this," he whispers, his grip tightening on the hilts, his focus grim and ready.

Another rustle. I look behind us, and terror fills me to the brim. "Tavik."

"Not now," he tells me through gritted teeth.

"Behind us," I warn him, my voice high and panicked.

He keeps the Sword of Mercy trained on the telleg in front of us as he swivels his head to see the other one even closer at our backs.

"Father of death!"

Before the curse is out of his mouth, an eerie hissing comes from our left—a third telleg, its pallid skin glowing in the night, its head faceless, as if someone had plastered over it with unearthly gray flesh. They close in, drawn to us like vultures to death.

I thought the intervening years had blunted my fear, that I could go on living, and the telleg would never find me again. But here I am—here we both are—face-to-face with our monsters once more, and we are powerless children.

The telleg closest to me attacks first, its body moving as if it has no bones. It lashes out with long knifelike fingers, and I barely dart out of the way in time before the first telleg we saw is on Tavik. He swings his swords in different directions, trying to jab one while decapitating the second, but he misses both. Their bodies contort around his blades, bizarrely elastic.

The third monster flies at Tavik so quickly, its whole body is a blur. Tavik ducks under the first two monsters and tries to skewer this newest opponent with both swords at once, but the telleg leaps and flies right over his head.

He can't figure out how to fight them or where to place me in relation to them. All he can do is swing and miss while trying to direct me with his hips and legs, and all I can do is try to stay out of the way and wish that I had taken that shiv when it was offered to me.

"Cover your ears!" I shout.

"No!" He makes a desperate unguarded strike against the telleg directly in front of him, and finally, his sword cuts through it as if the creature were made of gelatin rather than flesh and bone. The dull blade of the weaker sword slices it in half, and the creature goes down.

"Go!" Tavik thunders at me, and I run pell-mell through the forest with Tavik pelting after me, but the telleg give chase and trap us between them and the icy waters of the Fev River.

Tavik goes on the attack, stretching his body in ways that leave him alarmingly vulnerable. But it works. He's forcing the telleg to back up. His movements begin to imitate theirs, the strange elasticity, the favoring of quick violence over calculated risk. But just as he seems to be gaining confidence, one of them gets close enough to bite his outstretched arm. The telleg has no face, and yet a mouth appears on the monster's head, tearing through the pale skin with an audible *rip*, revealing dark gums and jagged, pointed teeth that nick Tavik's wrist before he can pull away. Blood beads on his skin and streams along the side of his arm. The telleg licks its horrid teeth with a thin, pointed tongue before the mouth disappears into its head.

They come at us again, and Tavik is completely on the defensive now. He dodges and blocks as they force him backward, closer and closer to me.

"Cover your ears right now!" I bellow, and he finally drops his weapons to cover the sides of his head with quaking hands.

My voice slices through the cold night as I sing the part of *The Ludoïd* where Ovin slays Ludo, the Hand of the Father cutting through muscle and tissue and bone. Even with his ears covered, Tavik cries out in pain.

It has no effect on the telleg.

I don't think they can hear the song.

I close my mouth as the stark realization washes over me.

Tavik grabs one of his swords off the ground and slashes at the nearest telleg, cleaving it in half horizontally, sending bits of bloodless gray flesh through the air like rain.

The last telleg reaches for me with long fingers, and with the river at my back, I have nowhere to go. Tavik tackles it to the ground. It oozes and slithers in his arms like a human-shaped slug, and he can't keep hold of it. Its strange, elastic body stretches, pushing apart Tavik's arms and rolling him beneath it.

I dart around them and fall to my hands in knees, patting the ground in search of Tavik's other sword. When I have it, I turn around in time to see Tavik get a hand under the creature's chest and push it back, but it uses the space between them to swipe its long fingers across Tavik's abdomen. He screams in agony as I swing the blade through the telleg's neck, and the monster's decapitated body flops on top of Tavik.

I shove the thing off him with my foot while clinging to the sword. He helps me, moaning as he maneuvers his wounded body out from underneath the telleg's dead weight. He manages to sit up with my help.

"How badly are you hurt?" I ask, crouching beside him, trying to remain calm.

"I'm all right," he slurs before vomiting down his front. I pull his hair out of his face and hold him up so he doesn't fall over into his own sick. When he's done, he makes a horrid whimpering noise.

"Can you sit up on your own? I'm going to get out the bandaging kit."

He nods. When I come back with the linen strips and a small flask of alcohol, he holds out a shaking hand as if I'm supposed to let him take care of this on his own.

"Let me see," I tell him, sounding rational when it's all I can do to hold myself together. He shakes his head. I think he might be sick again. "Tavik, let me see."

"Don't heal me." His voice his shot through with pain. He's suffering because of me, because he tried to save me.

"I won't," I tell him.

He gives me a long, hard look before pulling back his shoulder so that I can examine his stomach. The telleg cut through his heavy jacket and the layer of clothing beneath. There are three bleeding gashes in slanted lines from the edge of his rib cage to his navel. Between the shredded ribbons of his coat and tunic, I can see that two of the stripes are little more than scratches, but the one in the middle is deeper and bleeding.

For Tavik's sake, I keep myself composed. "I know it's cold, but I need to take off your jacket and shirt to bandage the wound."

He nods and tries not to give voice to his pain as I help him out of his clothes. Working quickly, I tear off a large strip of the bandaging and try to ignore the fact that the ripping sound brings the memory of the telleg's mouth back to life. I fold the cloth into a thick pad, douse it with the alcohol, and warn Tavik, "This is going to hurt."

"I know."

I press the pad to the wound, and he cries out, veins popping up along his neck as he clenches his teeth. I wind the remaining fabric tightly around his middle, pressing the pad against the bleeding, but a red stain is already seeping through to the outside.

"We have to keep moving," Tavik breathes when I doubt he can even get to his feet.

"One thing at a time. You need to get your jacket back on."

"You're the only girl on earth who tries to put my clothes *on*." The fact that he's joking fills me with a hope I dared not entertain seconds earlier, and I cling to that humor as tightly as I was clinging to the sword a minute ago.

"Oh, good, this is such a perfect time for lasciviousness," I tell him.

"You don't know the word 'barf,' but you know 'lasciviousness.' You really are adorable. Help me up."

I put his arm over my shoulders and heave him to his feet, a heroic effort on my part since my spent body feels like it will bend beneath the weight of him.

"All right?" I ask him.

"I'm not solid, but I'm not going to fall over. I'll take the swords, but I don't think I can manage the pack, too, so we need to consolidate. What can you carry?"

I make sure that what little remains of the bandaging kit is one of the things that make it into our single pack before we move on with me acting as Tavik's unreliable crutch and stealing concerned glances at him every thirty seconds.

"Tavik—"

"I'm fine. Just keep moving."

He is not fine. He is anything but fine.

By dawn, I'm beside myself with worry. His weight pushes down on my weary shoulders more and more with each passing minute. He doesn't even argue when I set out a blanket and order him to lie down on it. I cover him with my own blanket and raise the tent around him. Then I curl up against his back and wrap my thin arm around his shuddering body. Somewhere in the back of my mind as I fall into my own exhausted slumber, it occurs to me that he isn't just warm. He's burning up.

I wake in the afternoon to his moaning, "No!"

"Hmm?" I mumble, half asleep, my muscles leaden with fatigue.

He stirs, restless beneath my arm, his words slurring one into the next. "I'm sorry. Please. Raran. Barri."

He's so hot.

I bolt awake, throw the blanket off both of us, and put my

hand over his forehead. As the heat of the fever seeps into my palm, he opens two glassy green eyes.

"Gelya." He says my name with a tender relief that cuts me to the quick. When his eyes finally focus on my face, he says thickly, "I'm fine."

"You have a fever." I dig through our pack for the one remaining canteen as Tavik drags himself into a cross-legged position with a pained grunt and begins to take off his coat.

"Drink," I order, thrusting the canteen at him, but when I reach out to take over the examination of his wound, he drops it to block my hand, spilling water all over his blanket.

"Can you keep it under wraps?" he asks me, his voice worn to a thread.

"Just let me—"

"No. You promised me. Don't heal me."

Honestly, I'm not sure I can control what Elath decides to do with my body at this point, but I nod. Anything to get a look at that wound.

As I unwrap the bandage, Elath's power brims in my fingertips, and I have to concentrate to hold it at bay. Tavik says nothing as I work, which in and of itself is worrying. His skin is too hot, and his face is so drawn I think he might be sick again. He trembles and groans as I pull back the wad of fabric covering the wound. The skin around it is angry and red, and the opening, still weeping blood, is crusted in yellow pus. The sound he makes when I put the new bandage into place borders on sobbing. It's unbearable—for both of us—but he keeps saying the words over and over: "Don't heal me. Don't heal me. Don't heal me."

So I keep the lid over Elath for his peace of mind, not mine.

When I'm finished, he goes back to sleep, and all I can do is watch his lips move in some fraught, unconscious conversation I can't understand. The only word I recognize is *Gelya*. He rouses himself a few hours before dusk and gets stiffly to his feet.

"We have time. You should rest more," I tell him. He looks terrible, and I can't stand it.

"I've rested enough." He grimaces as he slides the scabbards into place over his shoulders.

"You can't fight tonight. You can barely move."

"If the telleg come for us, I'll have to fight whether I'm ready or not. If we start walking now, we can at least get a little closer to Hedenskia before the sun sets."

"Then let me carry the swords. Let me fight."

He regards me, his eyes bright with fever, before he takes the Sword of Mercy from its scabbard, gritting his teeth as he holds it out to me. I take the weapon from his hand, the same sword I used to cut the head off the telleg that wounded Tavik. It isn't as heavy as it looks, but even the extra two pounds in my grasp add an awkward heft to my arm I'm not used to.

"Show me what you've got," Tavik says.

I step back and swing the blade in the air, then jab, then swing again. One corner of his mouth ticks up as he shakes his head. "Your swordsmanship leaves a lot to be desired, but it's better than what I've got right now. Keep it. Consider it a wedding gift."

Just stringing together that many words winds him. He takes off the scabbard and hands it to me, and we walk side by side, each of us armed with one sword as we follow the Fev northward.

For the next few hours, Tavik moves like it's the only thing he can do, to put one foot in front of the other without falling over. I try to stop him only once. I get as far as "Are you all—" when he cuts me off.

"Don't."

He staggers. He stumbles. His breath goes in and out, a series of gasps and starts and grunts. But he doesn't fall.

Until he does.

I don't know what time it is—after midnight but long before dawn—when he trips. I try to catch him, but I'm too slow, and he crashes to the ground. I pull his arm over my shoulders and try to heave him to his feet again, but I'm too weak, and he slips out of my grasp.

"I'm sorry!" I cry, as if that could help him in the slightest. The wound is seeping dark blood through his coat, black in the night.

"Don't heal me." His breath rattles in his lungs. "You promised."

"Don't leave me!" I beg him. It's not the fear of being alone. It's the grief of losing him already snaking its way through my blood, feeding my heart with sorrow even before he's gone.

His lips barely move. "Don't."

"Tavik!"

He doesn't answer. His eyes lose focus.

"Please!" I press my hands over his fluttering heart.

His breath ceases.

His heart stops beating under my palms.

And I break my promise.

I break it with the ease of snapping a brittle twig in my hands.

I cast aside all that divides me from the life within, and I let Her fill my veins with Her light and fire. My breast thrusts toward heaven. I throw my head back as my mouth yawns wide, releasing a primal song from my throat.

There is movement in the trees, my light drawing the telleg to us like a fire calls to moths in the night. I could not tear my rigid arms away from Tavik's soul even if I wanted to.

Which I don't.

My muscles clench hard, forcing my life out of my body and into his in wave after painful, ecstatic wave, like the inevitable pulsing of a heart.

There is light.

So much light.

And then there is nothing.

Forty-Four

He falls into the water, drops into it like a stone.

Less than a stone.

A pebble.

A nothing.

He hangs in the water, suspended in the dark silence, until the thin gray light comes from below. And the telleg. The telleg come for him, mute and terrifying, there in the well with him, just as he knew they would be.

But he is not alone. She won't let him be alone in this.

His Mother swims between the monsters, and he reaches for Her, longing to be held when the object She carries is cold and hard and sharp.

He doesn't want this. He sinks further into the murk.

You must stand and fight. *She closes his hand around the hilt.* I chose you for a reason, and this is it.

The boy shakes his head in disbelief, sending tendrils of his hair floating in the water around him.

Every moment counts now, and you know it.

He looks at her with eyes the same green as his Mother's. She draws him into Her arms, where he is safe and warm. The monsters swim around them, but She keeps them away.

For now.

She rests her cheek against his curls and whispers the truth from which he can no longer hide.

I did not make you to kill men, my Sword. You were made to kill monsters.

When She pulls away and looks at him once more, he is no longer a child. She takes his chin in her fingertips and tilts his head, making him look into the light at the heart of Her being.

Be my Sword.

Forty-Five

"Father of death!"

The voice comes from the well shaft, faint and echoing as it reaches my ears. My body rolls, but I don't fall into the water. I land on soft earth.

I hear inhuman hissing and the startled, guttural cry of a man. Steel whistles through the air over my head. There is the slick sound of a blade cutting through flesh and rags.

"Gelya!"

I know this voice. I recognize the familiar touch of fingertips on my face.

"Open your eyes!"

I didn't know they were shut. When I open them, Tavik's face blurs before me.

Tavik.

I would say his name if I could.

A dry sob of relief comes hurtling out of his mouth. He takes my icy, limp hand and holds it to his warm cheek. "Why did you do it? You promised me! You promised!"

A slithering in the trees tugs at his attention. He snatches the Sword of Mercy from my scabbard and thrusts it into a telleg, slicing into its waist, cutting it all the way to its strange, rubbery spine. As he leaps to his feet, he yanks out the blade and thrusts it into another telleg bearing down on us.

The world comes into sharper focus, and all I can do is watch as a third monster attacks Tavik from behind. He releases his grip on the hilt of the sword to grab the third monster's head, slamming it down, forcing its neck onto the blade that's still jutting out of the other telleg's chest. He hurls the severed head at yet another telleg as it barrels in for the attack, and it flies backward, smashing into the tree behind it, and Tavik follows closely, drawing the blade from the scabbard at his back and plunging it deep into the creature's hideous body. He ducks in time to dodge the knifelike swipe of one more telleg's hand at his back before twisting at the waist and stabbing it clean through. Then he rips both weapons out of the monstrous corpses, and he stands there, panting, surveying the carnage.

I did not make you to kill men, my Sword. You were made to kill monsters.

The Sword is not a literal weapon.

It's Tavik, the Hand of the Father, reaching for me even as he holds back the things that would harm me.

I can see the exact moment he understands this as he stands above me, surrounded by the bodies of the five telleg he just slew.

"Um, all right," he says aloud, his voice strained and high-pitched, before looking down at me. "Blink twice if you can hear me."

I try, but my body and my mind are not yet in the same place.

"Death. Okay." He scans the perimeter as he takes the scabbard off my back, laying me down gently before he straps it onto himself. He's still scanning the trees for telleg as he thinks out loud. "So to review the bidding: You brought me back from the brink of death, and you probably put on a giant light show in the process, which means every telleg in a five-mile radius is heading this way to kill us right now. Our current position is open on all sides except for the river at our backs. I can't swim, and you are out of commission. Also, I'm going to be very blunt here and admit that I'm terrified, and I don't want to fight these things unless I absolutely have to, so . . . I'm going to get us to better ground. Yeah. That's what I'm going to do."

He picks me up like a baby and carries me through the forest, looking for a better position to defend while trying to make sure he doesn't whack my head into a tree trunk.

"Let's look on the bright side," he chirps. "We're both alive, and I'm the Sword, which—no offense—is so much more badass than being the Vessel. I'll be sure to rub that in when you wake up, so you can roll your eyes at me and give me that adorable Gelya scowl. Deal?"

I think I'd prefer to hug him than scowl at him, but since I can't do either, he gets no answer from me.

"Just please come back to me," he whispers, followed shortly by "Oh, death!"

A telleg darts out from between two trees, its hand stretching out unnaturally far to gut me, and my body has recovered enough to feel the sickening physical effects of terror.

Tavik kicks the creature's arm to the side, following with another kick to its chest. It buys him just enough time to slide me down to his side so that he can make my body duck with his to miss the telleg's next swipe. He draws the Sword of Wrath with his free hand, but all he can do is block.

"Sorry!" he says as he drops me and I slump to the ground. Tavik dodges and blocks, giving him an opportunity to draw his second sword. It doesn't put him on the offensive, but it makes the monster move to find a better position from which to attack us. Each of its reactions to Tavik's defenses buys a fraction of a second, and each fraction teaches Tavik how it moves, how it attacks, what it leaves undefended.

It reaches for me, but Tavik brings down his foot on its arm, pinning it to the ground so he can hack it off. A mouth rips its way across the telleg's face with a horrid screech that Tavik silences as he slashes his blades through the beast's torso.

"Sorry!" he calls to me again as he grabs me by the collar of my coat and tugs me along a slope, dragging my heels through the leaves. He follows a limestone ledge until it spreads into a broad vertical rock face with a lip just big enough to tuck me underneath.

He's got what he needs now: a wall at his back and a relatively safe place for me, the boneless Vessel who can't help him at all. As he ducks down to check on me, I try to make my hand reach out for him, but I still can't move. Maybe he senses what I want to do, because he takes my hand in his, forms a circle with my index finger and thumb, then locks his own ring with mine. He opens his mouth, but whatever he was going to say, he thinks better of it. Instead, he releases my hand and turns his back on me.

Tavik! I scream in my mind. My useless body has no choice but to watch him strip off his bulky coat and tunic, baring his skin to the frigid air from the waist up, sacrificing warmth to regain his full range of motion. He straps the scabbards back on just as a nearby tree cracks open and the first, ghostly telleg oozes out—the first, because I know there will be more, and Tavik is going to fight each and every one of them.

He draws both blades from his back as it attacks, zigzagging through the trees like lightning through a cloud, but Tavik also moves like a pulsing bolt of light, the Sword of Wrath cutting through the creature's body in jagged lines. The telleg is lightning, but Tavik is thunder.

The Sword of Mercy slices into the next telleg before he finishes dispatching the first.

They come. They all come for us, floating through the forest, cracking open the trees and sliding out to face Tavik, the Sword, the Hand of the Father.

His blades glow a faint blue-green as he fights them. His body moves between them like water, bending and stretching in ways I never imagined possible. His blades glow brighter as he cuts them down, slithering on the ground like a snake, flying into the air like an eagle. He is the Father's wrath, burning them, making their flesh hiss and sizzle with each blow.

He does not pray. He *is* the prayer.

The Greeting of the Morning Sun: Two swords pointing

directly skyward draws his body up, dodging a strike on either side as he plunges his swords into a telleg jumping onto him from the ridge above.

The Farewell to the Morning Star: His weapons slam into the telleg on either side of him.

Each prayer movement at full speed, one after another, allows him to dodge each blow while cutting the monsters to ribbons. His blades shine, lighting up the night.

The Supplicant Child: He bows low as a telleg flies overhead. At the same time, he jabs at two more coming at him from the front.

The Offering of Man to the Father's Service: The blades flow in two different directions, mowing down monsters at his sides while his right leg lifts, evading a telleg's low swipe.

The Sweeping Away of What Came Before kills three in a row, as easy as scything dry grass.

The Acceptance of Death: He does not falter. He arches his back so far that he's parallel to the earth as he crosses the swords over his head and kills the telleg behind him.

The Triumph Over the Dark Night: He doesn't fail, because he can't. It's as simple as that. The hilts flip over the backs of his hands, and the swords circle through the air to slam down into the outstretched necks of two telleg at once.

And I am still powerless to do anything but watch.

He recovers his stance and readies himself for the next attack, an entire horde just waiting for him. He bends like the willow around them. He flows like water between them. His swords blur and burn. His body dances, each lithe movement delivering the wrath of the

Father. He kills and kills and kills until nothing else comes at us.

The onslaught ceases. A gray carpet of slain telleg spreads out from Tavik's feet. In the eerie sword-lit silence that follows, he backs up to stand directly in front of my hiding place, keeping his eyes on the woods at all times, standing between me and a forest full of monsters with both swords faintly glowing, ready for the next attack. Even as dawn fills the world with gray light, he stands and waits, his skin steaming in the frigid air.

At last, my weak body returns to me. I stir, but Tavik doesn't turn away from the woods, not for one second. He promised he would defend me with the last breath of his body, and that is exactly what he intends to do.

I get to my knees. "Tavik?"

He doesn't answer. His eyes watch for any sign of the telleg's return.

My footsteps are muted by leaves and telleg flesh as I stagger in front of him, blocking his view. He tilts his head to continue watching the trees, ready.

"I think I got them," he tells me, his voice distant and mechanical.

I let out a fat sob and throw my arms around his neck, relishing the warmth and solidity of him. For a moment, he's stiff in my embrace, his arms at his sides, his weapons ready and waiting. Then he drops the swords onto the ground and hugs me back, holding me so tightly I think he might crush my rib cage, but I pull him closer anyway, and we cling to each other, two bodies knotted together, a pinprick of something good and right in a place that is horrible and wrong.

"That was terrifying, just so you know," Tavik says into the side of my head, setting my hat askew.

I let go so I can yell at him. "Put some clothes on, you lunatic! You're going to freeze to death."

"Oh, hey, I'm the Sword. It's so much more badass than being the Vessel," he informs me as I wade through the telleg corpses in search of his jacket. I look up long enough to roll my eyes, and he gives me a smug grin.

When I dislodge his coat from underneath a dead telleg, my eyes catch something familiar, and my mind goes back to that moment ten years ago when a telleg killed the last of the knights. Goodson Anskar had moved as swiftly as a Two-Swords to slice through the creature. Then he stared down at the body, just as I am staring at this slain telleg now.

"Tavik, come here."

He steps to my side, and we both study the body. It's missing an arm, but the torso is intact, and its filthy cloak is flung back, revealing the bony torso beneath. There's a familiar mark over its chest.

"What does that look like to you?" I ask him.

"Is that . . . ? It looks like the mark of the Order of Saint Ovin."

"Do you remember that part in the rubbing, the second half of *The Ludoïd*?" I translate it from memory into Kantari:

And the Father said,
The sons of Ovin have aligned themselves with death,
So they will live and live until the Sword cuts them down.

"Holy Mother, they're knights," Tavik utters. "This is what happens to them when they die."

"They don't get to die. They have to protect the Mother's body."

Tavik nods slowly, taking it in. "Until the Sword cuts them down."

"The Goodson saw this, and yet he still believed—and continues to believe—that the Father is the One True God."

Before either of us can say anything more, birdsong bursts from the trees all around us, impossibly lovely in the nightmarish landscape. One by one, the soulswifts descend upon the telleg scattered on the forest floor, and one by one, they fly away, singing a song that hurts to hear, carrying their invisible burdens with them.

Forty-Six

My whole life, I was taught to think of my body as a vessel, a human receptacle for the divine. In my mind, I pictured myself as a pitcher, something useful rather than lovely, pouring out the Father's Word for the faithful. But ever since I brought Tavik back from the brink of death, I feel more like an amphora—huge yet fragile, weighed down by its content, which is more valuable than the vessel that contains it, taking up more room than the vessel itself.

Herself.

Myself.

We follow the Fev River north, Tavik walking, me shuffling, bumbling, lurching, careening. He looks at me like I'm going to shatter into a million pieces before his eyes, and every five minutes he asks me if I'm all right. I'm not all right, but if I had it to do over, I wouldn't change a thing.

Very little breaks up the monotony of our trek except the

occasional telleg. For the most part, Tavik dispatches them with ease, although with a new sadness as well.

When we wake up on the afternoon of our sixth day in the Dead Forest, we linger beside the ashes of our fire, staring up at the treetops arching above our heads, their long bare twigs crisscrossing the cloudy sky. I can't speak for Tavik, but there's a part of me that doesn't want to leave despite the oppressive sense of infinity that stretches through the trees. What's so terrible about this? No knights on our tails. No loved ones lying to us. No war. Simply living. A world with only me and Tavik in it.

Except there *is* a knight on our tail. The Goodson is behind us somewhere, fighting telleg of his own. He'll do whatever it takes to keep Elath out of the world. If he's still alive.

That thought saps even more of my energy.

"I've been thinking—" I begin.

"When are you ever *not* thinking?"

I click my tongue at him before continuing. "The river turned to ice beneath you when you fell off the bridge, but it wasn't the Mother who did it."

"You think it was the Father?"

"We know from the text that he cursed the Knights of the Order to haunt the Dead Forest. What if he means for them to protect the Mother's body until She can return? What if the Father *wants* us to free the Mother?"

Tavik sits up and gives me a quizzical look. "I never thought He didn't. The Ovinists may have abandoned the Mother, but we Elathians have always remained faithful to the Father as well as to Elath."

I turn on my side to face him and curl my hands under my cheek. "Why have we never talked about this before?"

"I just assumed you knew. Of course the Father wants to bring Elath back. If someone took my wife from me, I'd move mountains to find her." He speaks with a conviction that reminds me of the night we met, when he knelt before me and promised to keep me safe.

With the last breath of my body.

He holds my gaze a moment longer, his eyes melting every organ inside me, before he rolls out of his sleep sack with his usual grace and heads toward the river with the canteen in hand.

I close my eyes and envision him kneeling before me again, only this time, I hold out my hand to him and feel his palm against my palm as I help him to his feet, and I lean in, and—

"Gelya, come here."

I moan in protest. Aside from my fluttering heart and Elath's blaring presence, my body feels like a deflated ball. And I was enjoying myself.

"Come on. You need to see this."

I groan again and drag my weak body after his. Tavik asks his burning question before I reach his side. "So is this the Fev River, or is that the Fev River?"

My sluggish brain catches up, and I see what we failed to notice when we set up camp at dawn. We have arrived at the juncture of two rivers, one on the opposite bank running from north to south, the other—a narrow tributary on our side—converging into the first from the west.

"I think that's the Fev," I guess, pointing at the river we can't reach without a bridge.

"Then what river is this?" Tavik asks, nodding toward the water at our feet.

My gaze drifts west, taking in the slow current snaking its way toward us. "No idea. There aren't many accurate maps of the Dead Forest or Hedenskia."

"Oh, death."

"I don't think it's a problem. We need to keep heading west anyway."

"No. Look."

I follow Tavik's dark gaze across the Fev. On the opposite bank, a man crouches beside the river and cups water to his mouth. Even from forty yards away, I recognize him.

The Goodson.

He looks up.

I can't see his eyes from this distance, and yet I feel them boring into me, those gray eyes that held such softness for a girl he thought of as his own daughter. I can still hear the heartbreak in his voice.

What the Father asks of me, I must do.

I don't know what to feel. Relief that he's alive? Fear that he's close? Both? Neither? It makes me want to drop to my knees and weep for days.

"How can he be here? How can he have made it this far?" Tavik asks, his words slathered with indignation.

"I don't think you're the only Sword. He was made to cross the

Dead Forest, just as you were. He's done it before, and now he's doing it again."

Goodson Anskar raises his hand. Is it a greeting? Is it his way of asking me to stop? Is he simply acknowledging the history between us?

Tavik's fingers twine with mine, warming my cold hand. "He can't lay a finger on you from over there, and I wouldn't let him near you if he were over here."

I nod. I know Goodson Anskar can't touch me now, but what happens if he catches up to us? What will Tavik do to him? Or he to Tavik? The longer we dally, the sooner that becomes a possibility.

"Come on," I say, pulling Tavik back to camp so we can pack up and be on our way, but not before taking one last look behind me at Goodson Anskar with a tight ache in my chest.

An hour after leaving behind the Goodson at the juncture of two rivers, things get a little troubling, which, considering everything we've been through, is saying something.

First of all, no matter how much I rest, I can't begin to recover my strength. I'm starting to wonder if I ever will. As we follow the river west, I have to lug myself after Tavik with the walking sticks he found for me. Thanks to me, our progress is glacial.

Second of all, the tributary quickly grows narrower. Soon the distance between shores will taper enough to cross without too much difficulty. If the Goodson finds a way to ford the Fev, he could follow this river on the north side and reach us at last, especially at our current pace. It's a threat as visceral as the Mother's spirit, ever present, weighing me down body and soul.

Lastly and most alarmingly, while the Dead Forest remains much as it has been for the past week—leafless trees, gray light, a world always on the verge of dying—the view across the river changes dramatically. An army of snow-clad spruce and pine stands sentry over a winter landscape, still and silent on a thick blanket of white as a light snow tumbles from the sky.

"What in the name of the Mother? Is this normal?" Tavik demands as he squints across the water.

I shake my head. "This is definitely abnormal. I think it must be a boundary of some sort. Maybe this is where the Dead Forest ends and Hedenskia begins."

That should be good news, but the unnatural fissure between here and there makes a dark unease take root in my belly, right alongside the Mother's quickening presence.

Tavik crosses his arms and bites the inside of his cheek. "I feel like I've been here before."

"Me too." My mind grasps at the memory of this place. I wasn't a child when I stood here before. I was me, as I am now, expecting to find Zofia on the opposite bank. The trees across from us were green then. There was no snow.

I saw this place in a dream, and Tavik was with me.

And I touched him.

A lot.

Oh.

But that wasn't real.

Was it?

I make the mistake of turning to Tavik at the exact moment

he turns to me. When our eyes lock, Tavik, of all people, turns as scarlet as I do. I didn't even know he was capable of blushing, and I'd be delighted if I weren't absolutely mortified.

We both turn our heads back to the river so quickly that our brains rattle in our skulls.

After a brutal five seconds of silence during which I repeat the words *It wasn't real* in my mind like a prayer, Tavik clears his throat. "I guess we should keep moving."

So we keep moving.

In more silence.

And in that silence, I remember the heat of his hands on my waist, pulling me close to him.

"Want to play a game of Ludo?" I joke, breaking the unbearable silence and holding up my sticks as I cling to humor, the language Tavik and I speak best.

He cocks a magnificent eyebrow at me. "Are you kidding? You'd have me beat in three moves, tops."

"I'm so weak I couldn't beat a mouse," I reply with a laugh as pathetic as my body.

"You're not weak."

I snort.

He stops me with a hand on my arm, and there's not a trace of humor in his voice when he says, "You're the strongest person I know."

He gives me an earnest look that makes it next to impossible for me to breathe. He's not lying. He really thinks I'm strong in a way that matters more than physical strength, and that admiration sends my pulse soaring through my veins.

Tell him, I think. *I love you.*

"And why would you want to beat a mouse? Heartless!" He shakes his head with a comical scrunching of his nose and removes my hat for the specific purpose of mussing up my hair.

"I'm not heartless! You're heartless!" I complain, dropping a stick to bat his hand away. He picks it up and beams at me with his perfect teeth on full display, and my insides melt all over again.

I don't think Tavik is heartless when it comes to me, and I know I'm not heartless when it comes to him. I just don't know how to broach the subject. It's like crossing a river without a bridge. I might make it to safety, but there's an equally good chance I'll fall in. Is that a risk worth taking?

Eventually, we find ourselves at a place where the unknown river takes a sharp turn north, but the uncanny boundary between the Dead Forest and the winter landscape to the north continues west as if the river still divided them. Two groves of snow-clad gelya trees create a wide lane in front of us, their red berries vibrant against the gray sky and white snow. If we cross the boundary, we'll have to walk through it to get to the other side.

"Holy Mother, just when I think things can't get weirder, they get weirder," says Tavik. "What do you think?"

The Mother hums like a bee greeting an open bud, although I'm not sure if it's the presence of the Father or the call of Her body nearby that inspires Her. "I think someone rolled out the welcome mat for us." When I catch Tavik studying me with a lopsided grin, I add, "What?"

"It's funny. I think you're more dedicated to the Father now than you were when you were His Vessel."

"I don't know about that. I'm only saying that, if He's real, He's a greater god than I was led to believe."

"Considering the fact that you were taught to believe He was a jerk, your opinion didn't have anywhere to go but up."

As we get closer to the odd boundary, I say, "I'm starting to get nervous about this."

"Starting? I've been nervous since I got my marching orders back in Kantar."

"I mean that we're close now, but we still have no idea what's going to happen if we—"

"When," Tavik corrects me with a wag of his finger.

"When we find the tree."

"There's only one way to find out."

"And it couldn't be worse than what would happen if we *didn't* find the tree," I add. A stark look flutters across Tavik's face, disappearing as soon as I catch sight of it.

By now, we've made it right up to the line. Our toes mere inches away from the snow that falls on one side but not the other. Close up, the gelya berries blaze against the white winter. I've never seen so many all in one place, and their beauty here, where death ends and the living world begins, clogs my throat with emotion.

"What are they?" Tavik asks me.

A tearful smile spreads across my face. "Gelyas. They're gelya trees. That's where my name comes from. Goodson Anskar said my gift is like their berries in winter, bright and alive and lovely when all else seems to have died. Not a very fitting name for me, is it?"

The sight before us is stunning, but Tavik turns to look at me instead. "I cannot imagine a more appropriate name for you."

He is better than all the gelya berries of the world combined.

"Come along, dearest wife." He offers me his arm, and I drop a stick to put my hand in the crook of his elbow.

"Let us be off, darling husband."

And we step out of the Dead Forest and into Hedenskia.

V.

The Soulswift

Forty-Seven

The crisp air nips my nose as a breeze whispers through the pines. Everything feels loud and overwhelming, a land filled with sights and sounds and smells, even in winter. I had no idea how much the Dead Forest muffled the living world until Tavik and I crossed over into Hedenskia.

I lean more and more on him as the chill pierces my flesh, freezing my limbs, making it hard to move. The Mother's fire blazes inside me, but since She's using my body as kindling, I don't enjoy the benefit of Her warmth.

I can feel Tavik watching me. He tries to turn away when I catch him in the act, but I always get a glimpse of his concern before he resets his face and tries to cheer me up with a joke.

"I've heard the Hedenski don't bathe. Think we'll smell them before we see them?"

"May I remind you that you were not exactly a fragrant rose when I met you?" I point out.

"The Tovnians transported me to the summit in a circus wagon. It's not my fault I smelled like tiger piss."

"Oh, so that's what that smell was."

He laughs, but I don't, which seems to worry him even more. And he already has so much to worry about, such as the fact that the Hedenski have a reputation for executing foreigners. Even if they don't want to murder us, will they help us, or will they stand in our way? And what will the Hedenski make of me? Will they see me as one of them, or do I simply not belong anywhere in this world?

We've come so far that our last hurdle seems like our hardest, and even if we manage to get past it, neither of us truly knows what we're supposed to do once we find Elath's body. An undercurrent of doubt pulls up a chair right next to the Mother's enormous presence inside me.

Tavik releases me to adjust his boot, and I take the opportunity to totter ahead a few paces to see how far I can go on my own two feet without him.

"Whoa," he breathes.

I turn back, but he's not looking at me. His eyes are on the ground between us. I follow his gaze to the footprints I left behind, every one of them melting the snow within, leaving behind a trail of foot-shaped patches of bare earth from which tiny green shoots begin to spring up: the fiddleheads of fern fronds, the jagged lines of miniature oak leaves on straight red stems, the first delicate needles of an infant pine tree.

For a moment, we gawk at the miracle between us. Then I take a step toward Tavik and turn to watch as the snow melts in the footprint I leave behind, sending up small sprouts of life. All at once, the Mother's power surges inside me, buoys me. With unbridled laughter, I leap and bound through the trees like a deer, stopping only to watch in delight as the earth turns green behind me. I am full of life, giddy with it.

"Gelya!" Tavik calls to me, but how can I stop? I race past him in pure joy as the world comes to life all around us.

"Stop!"

But I don't stop. I'm a child again, dancing by the cliffs over the salt sea, too caught up in my own game to listen. I stretch my hand to a tree branch above my head and watch in utter delight as the snow melts at my touch and the first buds of spring leaves burst along the tip, then down the branch, all the way to the trunk, breathing life into the slumbering oak until the whole tree awakens beneath my fingertips.

The skin of my hand gleams gold. My sleeve falls back as I reach higher, and veins of power snake down my arm, glowing bright, like a candle's light shining through a crack. And I am laughing with the joy of it.

Life.

"Stop!"

A boy grabs me by the shoulders and pulls me away from the tree, and the world that was full of life and joy and music goes suddenly silent. I look back at him in dismay, this boy whose name I think I know, as all that power drains out of my body, and my legs give out beneath me. My dead weight makes him stumble, but he keeps us both upright with a crushing grip around my upper arms. He eases me slowly to the ground and leans my back up against the oak tree I just woke from its winter slumber.

"Gelya?" He still holds me up, but gently now. Thick blood drips from my nose, dribbling down my lips and chin.

"Mother and Father, speak to me."

But I don't, because I can't. My body is not mine to control. A long time passes before I can move or think or remember. And then I recall his name: "Tavik."

His body is strung taut as a bow, and he's yelling at me, so upset that tiny red veins stretch across the whites of his eyes. "You have got to stop doing that! Can't you see what it's doing to you?"

But I still feel only half here while the rest of me floats in the air we breathe, trembles in the earth beneath us, skims the green surface of the oak leaves above. My gaze drifts, taking in the scene beyond Tavik's face, a mismatched forest of green and white.

Tavik gives my shoulders a shake. "Gelya? Gelya!"

My gaze falls away from his face, down and down to the long, freckled hands in my lap. The Mother's light lingers in them, making them shimmer. My veins are gold beneath the surface, like fissures, like a candle's flame burning between the splints of a basket.

His hands are on mine, grasping them with his fingers. "Let her go," he says.

"I can't," I tell him, disoriented, pushing the words past my lips with heroic effort.

"I'm not talking to *you*!"

My soul recoils inside the shell of my body. I'm only the Vessel. He's speaking to the far more valuable thing I carry inside me. He may as well slap me across the face.

"Why are you doing this to her?" he demands of his goddess, his face contorted, his eyes wet and raw. "Whatever you need me to do I'll do it! I'll do anything!"

You'll do anything for Her, I think bitterly. If he were still looking into my face, surely he'd see the hurt and anger in my eyes—*my* eyes. But instead, he unclasps his coat and yanks down on the neck of his shirt, exposing the handprint over his heart—*my* hand. Then he snatches up the same hand that branded him and presses it over the mark, a perfect fit.

"Just tell me what to do!"

I blink, and when I open my eyes, we are back in the courtyard of the Convent of Saint Vinnica.

Her prison has been opened, but She is not yet free.

She looks on the world with Her burning fire, bright with heat, glowing in the night. The Sword before Her has eyes the color of life, but he scrabbles away from Her, terrified of his own Mother.

She moves within Her Vessel, sitting up, leaning into the Sword to place Her new hand over his heart. Her light flows into him, pierces his being, fills him to overflowing, makes every muscle go rigid, an ecstasy so sharp it sears him.

He believes that he is only a little boy in a well, but She sings inside him. He tries to close himself against it, but the song pushes its way into his nose, his mouth, his ears, his eyes, insistent, needling its way into the pores of his skin.

She will be heard.

She will be known.

You must keep the Vessel safe and whole.

He shakes his head.

A mortal Vessel cannot contain something as infinite as the Mother's soul for long.

Already, the Vessel begins to crack, and the Mother's light seeps out of a fissure no bigger than a hair. The Sword thrashes in the water. Time is running out. She pushes him toward the surface, but She leaves him with one word, so clear and pressing he can see it blazing on the insides of his eyelids.

Hurry.

The Vessel is cracked.

The Vessel is breaking.

The Vessel is my body.

Me.

I heave the lid over the cauldron that is Elath and press down on Her boiling poison until it stops steaming out from underneath. Then I grab hold of my own body with a talon-like will and tear my hand from Tavik's heart, glaring at him with a fire that is all my own. The blade of truth is sharp and heavy on my tongue.

"I'm dying. She's killing me."

Tavik blinks hard. His silence is louder than cannon fire.

"And you've known from the beginning." I am breathing flames and speaking fire.

He buries his face in his hands. "I'm sorry," he says into his palms.

I pull his hands from his face. He doesn't get to hide from me. "I don't want your apologies."

His nostrils flare and redden. A tear streaks down his cheek.

"Don't you waste your water on me," I spit before clawing my way up the side of the tree, its bark rough beneath my fingernails. Tavik springs to his feet, his hands out to steady me, but I push him away.

"You lied to me, every day and all the time. You lied to me over and over and over." With each *over* I pound his chest with fists made weak by the thing that is slowly devouring me. "All you've ever done is lie to me!"

I shove myself off the tree and stagger past him.

"Where are you going?"

"I don't know," I answer, my voice cold and dead.

Dying.

He scurries in front of me. "I'm sorry. Mother and Father, I'm so sorry. You'll never know how sorry I am. I should have told you."

"Yes, you should have told me," I agree as I shoulder past him.

"Where are you going?"

"I need to be alone right now."

"I can't protect you when you're alone," he pleads.

"You can't protect me at all, not from this." My words hit their mark. Two more tears fall from his eyes.

Good.

He lets me go.

I stumble to the river, where I drop to my knees beside the water's edge, letting the snow soak my woolen clothes all the way through to my skin. I splash the brutally cold water on my face to clean off the blood before sinking the canteen's mouth into the river and drinking down a few icy gulps. The frigid water does nothing to revive me, and now my hand is painfully cold. I tuck my aching fingers into my armpit and sit there like a lump, converting my ignorance and my stupidity and my naivete into a fiery anger. Anger at Tavik. Anger at the Goodson. Anger at the Father. Anger at the Mother who took up residence in my body as if it belonged to Her and not to me. But most of all, anger at myself. My stupid, childish self.

I knew. On some level, I knew all along. I simply chose not to see it, and now it can't be unseen.

It isn't much farther now, a familiar voice comes from the opposite bank.

I raise my head. Zofia-who-is-not-Zofia watches me from across the river.

Who's to say I'm not Zofia? Or that Zofia is not Me?

"Get out of my head."

I think you know by now that I'm in every part of you.

"Get out!" The words scrape my throat, and my cry sends birds panicking from their branches into the safety of the sky.

Soulswifts.

Dozens of them.

Will I still become one of these birds when I die? Or is that another future Elath has stolen from me? I control nothing, not my fate, not even my own self. My shoulders slump, pressed down by the crushing weight of who and what I am.

"I'm dying," I tell Her. It's so much easier to think of Her as Zofia, even if She isn't.

Yes, She agrees.

"When?" I ask, the word bitter on my tongue. "How long do I have?"

She shrugs in her elegant Zofia way. *I can't answer that.*

"You can't, or you won't?"

She raises an eyebrow in response, a gesture so completely and utterly Zofia that my resentment boils over. This thing who is not Zofia—who is responsible for her death—doesn't have the right to use my memory of her like this. I swipe at the air as if I could banish the vision, like waving smoke away from my eyes. "I'm your Vessel! You *chose* me!"

She crosses her arms, as unflappable as ever. *There are many Vessels. There are many Swords. I only needed one of each. Are you any more precious than the rest? Is your life worth more than anyone else's?*

Her words crush me, like Tavik's arm wrapped tightly around me in that alley in Varos da Vinnica before I even knew his name, squeezing the air out of my lungs.

"So I'm nothing to you? And Tavik? Is he nothing?"

I think you ask the wrong questions sometimes.

"I just want to know how much time I have left. Is that such a ridiculous thing to ask?"

Would the answer change anything?

I hate that I don't have a ready response, and I hate how easily She's turned my anger into defeat.

You may have hours or days or weeks, just like anyone else. She crouches down so that She's eye level with me, just as Zofia did when I was very small and she, herself, was still quite young. *So let me ask you, Daughter: How will you spend the life you have left?*

The river narrows. She's so close that if I reach out far enough, I might be able to touch Her and feel the warmth of Zofia's familiar hand against my fingertips once more. She gives me a sad smile and says, *I can't go where you are, so you must come to me where I am.*

And then She's gone, and winter stares back at me from across the river.

I get to my feet, feeling a little stronger. My footsteps are only footsteps as I return to the place where I left Tavik. When I walk into the strange, half-waking world of my creation, I find him sitting with his back against the oak's thick trunk, hugging his knees to his chest, his misery writ large across his face as the snow I melted drips down on him. I go to stand at his feet, and he looks up at me with reddened eyes.

"I'm sorry," he says, the words coming out in a tearless sob as I kneel beside him.

"I know."

"I promise you, on my life, I will get you to the Mother's body in time."

I put a hand on his knee. He's so warm when I am chilled to the bone. "Don't make promises you may not be able to keep," I tell him gently.

"I'll get you there," he insists.

When Tavik makes a promise, he has every intention of keeping it. If he says "on my life" or "to my dying breath," it's not hyperbole. He means it. I love him for that, but I also envy it. I'll never have that kind of conviction, that level of hope. I'll always question and doubt. His faith in me is the only thing I can really believe in.

I reach out for him just as I did in my dream, tracing the long, crooked line of his nose with my fingertips. I slide my fingers across his thick eyebrows, downward to his cheekbones, the sharp line of his jaw. I touch my fingers to his mouth, and he watches me, perfectly still, his eyes soft and scared and waiting.

I lean over the tops of his knees and kiss him.

His lips are warm and dry and a little chapped. He startles beneath me, and then his mouth responds, the softest hint of movement against mine. I pull away, putting a few inches between the tips of our noses. I'm shy of him and unsure of myself as he looks back at me with wide, lovely eyes.

"Did I do that right?" I ask him, my lips humming with the memory of his mouth against mine.

He nods. Then he reaches for me, tentatively, cupping my cheek in his palm. I put my hand over his as he brushes my cheekbone with his thumb. We stay like that for a minute, watching each other until we both see that there's nothing—not one thing—standing between us now.

He gets to his knees, torso to torso with me. When he leans in, he stops right before he presses his lips to mine, and I wonder if he's savoring this moment as I am, tucking it safely into the vault of memory, the excruciating want just before the having.

And then he kisses me, opening my mouth to his the way the sun unfurls the petals of a rose, not all at once, but slowly, inevitably.

He kisses me, and I kiss him back, and I never knew just how many ways two mouths could join together in so many iterations of one gesture. Why did it take so long for us to do this? How much time and life have we wasted focusing on all the wrong things when we could have been doing this one right thing?

His lips skim across my cheek, all the way to my tender earlobe. They follow the line of my jaw, dipping lower, brushing along the skin of my long neck.

And I am no longer cold.

His fingers hold me at the nape of my neck, spreading into the rough thicket of my hair. His thumb brushes the indentation of my chin, and he kisses that, too. His hands travel down my shoulders and arms, all the way to my waist.

"I'm covered in freckles," I breathe in apology.

"Entire constellations of them," he agrees, utterly unapologetic. When he kisses my mouth this time, he communicates very, very clearly that being covered in freckles is an excellent thing to be. But just in case I missed the message, he pulls away and says, "I'll kiss each and every one of those freckles, if you let me." His lips touch mine again, lightly. "Water of my thirst." He kisses me again, not so lightly. "Blood of my body."

And then the kissing is not at all light. There's just us, me and Tavik, and I don't think about the Mother, and I don't worry about the cost. There is only the sensation of his lips pressed to mine, the salty taste of his skin, my hands warming themselves against his body.

He finally pulls away, still kneeling on the ground, the snow long since melted beneath him, and he grins stupidly at me.

"It would take a lifetime to kiss them all," I tell him, flushed and deliriously contented.

His grin goes from stupid to rapacious. "Good."

An arrow hits the ground near Tavik's knee, sending up a cloud of snow on impact. Tavik leaps to his feet and places himself between me and eight men, standing shoulder to shoulder about five yards ahead of us, closing off our northern route along the river.

Hedenski.

Forty-Eight

The Hedenski men are bundled in colorful quilted jackets with fur collars, and some of them wear bright knitted caps embellished with twigs or antlers. While some are shorter than others, they are all tall. Most of them carry a battle-axe, but a couple are armed with longbows.

"That was a warning shot," Tavik tells me, keeping his eyes on the men. He doesn't unsheathe his blades, but he doesn't hold his hands up in surrender either.

"Hedenski! I'm Hedenski!" I call from behind him. The words are old and rusty, but I manage to pull them out of some long-closed drawer in my mind, the sounds strangely familiar.

The tallest of the men, hatless and redheaded, pushes his neighbor's arrow downward with one hand as he steps forward, closing the distance by a third. His companions glance at each other, unnerved. Tavik, equally on edge, draws his weapons, ready to defend us both. The Hedenski respond in kind, grasping their axes. The archers, their arrows already nocked, pull back their bowstrings.

The man stops halfway between the two sides.

"Tavik, stop! Put down your swords!" I hurl myself in front of him and call out to the redheaded man, "Please! I'm one of you!"

He stares at me for one long, nerve-racking moment, before he says, "Oh, my soul. Kristorna?"

Kristorna, the Hedenski word for *gelya*.

Bright and alive and lovely.

My heart hurts, and my breath hitches. This has always been my name.

I take a step toward him.

"Gelya," Tavik hisses behind me.

"It's all right," I tell him, and he doesn't try to stop me as I take another cautious step, then another, bringing the Hedenski man into sharper focus: red hair, freckled skin, deep-set brown eyes, just like mine.

"Kristorna!"

He runs the last few feet to me, taking me in his arms and weeping into my cap. He's so tall I can fit snugly under his chin. I have no idea who he is, but my heart bounds in my chest.

I think I've come home.

"You're sure they're not going to kill me?" Tavik asks for the third time, speaking so low he's not even moving his lips.

"They're not going to kill you," I assure him.

"Because the guy with the green-and-blue hat and the guy with the extra-big axe definitely want to kill me. Probably that lady to your left, too, and, frankly, I think she could take me."

The enormous blond woman in question makes me feel small by comparison. Personally, I find it comforting to blend in rather than stand out for a change, but Tavik sticks out like a sore thumb here. I've decided not to tell him that there was some debate over his fate, although it was hard to follow. I have only a child's understanding of the language at best.

I think the entire village has crowded into the longhouse to get a look at the lost girl, Kristorna. Me.

The redheaded man makes sure we're seated closest to the fire, which I think is a place of honor. Well, actually, he makes sure *I* am seated close to the fire. I had to beg them to let Tavik stay beside me, which probably didn't help his ratcheted nerves. The man leans over and lays a giant hand on mine. "Do you remember me, Kristorna?"

Despite his size, he looks at me with the eagerness of a child, and I feel ashamed of myself for having to admit, "No. I'm sorry. Are you my . . . ?" I can't remember the word for *father*. I'm not entirely sure there is a word for *father* in Hedenski.

"I'm Sevlos. Your mother's brother."

"Sevlos," I repeat, and he smiles at the sound of his name from my mouth. He's missing a couple of teeth, but the ones that remain are strong and white.

"Is my mother . . . ?" Again, I'm at a loss for words. How do I finish that question? *Here? Nearby?*

Alive?

But I don't need to finish it, as it turns out. Sevlos's face falls, and he shakes his head.

"She died when Ovin's men came. They killed so many."

I expected as much, but grief twists my heart anyway. I mourn the loss of what she might have been to me if the Goodson hadn't taken me away. I put my other hand over Sevlos's and tell him, "I don't remember. Can you tell me what happened?"

He speaks slowly so that I can understand him. "Ovin's men sailed into South Harbor, thousands of them, and they brought us their thunder. It was as if lightning had struck the town again and again."

"Yilish gunpowder?" Tavik guesses when I translate for him. "Those Ovinist dogs."

"They went from town to town, slaughtering their way north along the coast, searching for the Great Goddess. But there is no life without Her, so the people refused to tell Ovin's men where to find Her. By the time the murderers reached our village at the mouth of the Western Path, our warriors had assembled, and we taught Ovin's men what we do to those who threaten what we hold most dear. The few who survived our wrath fled south into the Land of the Dead." He presses his hand more firmly against mine. "We thought you must have died, but here you are. Where did you go, and how did you get here?"

"One of Ovin's men took me far away. I have traveled a long time to come home."

Sevlos lifts my hand and presses a fatherly kiss to my wrist, making my eyes water with affection for this man who is both a complete stranger and my uncle.

"Does the Western Path lead to the goddess? Can you take us there?" I ask him.

"Yes, but . . ." He glances suspiciously at Tavik, while my mind latches onto the word *yes*. Yes, he will take us to the Mother's body. Yes, after everything we've been through, we made it to our goal. I'm not sure if I should dance for joy or cower in fear of whatever awaits us when we unite body and soul at last.

"That man is looking at me like he could bore a hole through my torso with his eyeballs," Tavik murmurs, recalling me to the conversation where Sevlos's *but* still hovers in the air.

"But what?" I ask my uncle, praying that he's not about to throw up another obstacle for us to circumvent.

"The Hedenski may only be in the goddess's presence at the solstice festivals, when we wake Her in the spring or bid Her farewell in autumn. Ever since Ovin's men came, She has awoken later and later each year and has returned to her slumber sooner and sooner. This spring, She did not wake at all when we offered Her the yearly stag. You must not offend Her."

I remember my nightmare, when Tavik wore a crown of antlers and my mother drew her blade across his throat at the foot of Elath's body. The memory of that dream makes me sick to my stomach and adds to my sense of foreboding. I've wanted to get Elath out of me for weeks, but now that we're so close, now that everything seems to be happening so quickly, so inevitably, I'm getting cold feet. It's like that moment I stood at the exit of the parlertorium's escape tunnel, when it seemed easier to hide than to face the unknown.

"What's wrong?" Tavik asks me. "What's he saying?"

I take my hand from Sevlos's and touch Tavik's arm before telling my uncle, "We have come to wake Her. That is why he's with me. He's not one of Ovin's men. He's one of us."

Sevlos narrows his eyes at Tavik, studying him in this new light.

"Gelya?" Tavik asks uncertainly.

"It's all right."

If Sevlos finds Tavik wanting, he doesn't say so. He nods and pats my hand. "Would you like to see your mother's tree first?"

"The goddess, you mean?"

"No, your mother, Lanya."

I turn to Tavik, confused.

"Don't look at me. You stopped translating five minutes ago. I'm completely lost."

"I don't understand," I tell Sevlos.

He shakes his head again and clicks his tongue. "Those men stole so much from you. When a Hedenski dies, she or he is buried in the Great Goddess's forest. From each human heart grows a new tree. Would you like to see Lanya's tree?"

"My mother's name was Lanya?"

Sevlos nods. A single giggle bubbles up my throat, and my eyes fill with tears. I turn back to Tavik and tell him, in Kantari, "My mother's name was Lanya."

Nobody but Sevlos offers to accompany us on the half-hour trek west to the village where I spent the first years of my life. When we arrive, I understand why he's the only one willing to come. It feels like we've entered a graveyard, one in which the dead are listening and waiting. Few houses remain here, and a new forest has overtaken the ones that do. Saplings and vines have infiltrated the cottages, and the walls left standing are singed at the edges.

"Mother and Father," Tavik utters, keeping his distance. I don't blame him. It must remind him of his own lost family, his own obliterated home.

We can't see the ocean from here, yet it fills every inch of this town, from the salty scent of the air to the sound of the waves crashing against the cliffs, a familiar presence I took for granted as a child and cherish now that I've been separated from it for over half my life.

I walk ahead, past the crumbled remnants of the well and the burned-out husk of a longhouse, my destination inevitable, as if the tide were carrying me there.

You must remember where you came from.

Zofia's voice skates past my ears, so near I'd swear she was standing beside me. I wish she was, the woman who willingly became my mother when I lost mine. And I never even thanked her for it.

Home, I tell her in my mind. *I've come home.*

The door is gone, as is most of the roof. Inside, ten years of rain and snow have rotted the table, the chairs, and the child's bed by the blackened hearthstones. I walk over to the bed's frame, where the straw of the tick has given way to nests of mice. It seems impossible that I could ever have fit on it.

The more I stand here, the more I remember my home, the life that came before: sitting by the hearth, the flames of a newly lit fire licking the peat; holding a rag doll in my arms; the sound of my mother singing, so visceral I could pluck the melody out of the air.

Tavik follows me inside and puts a hand on my shoulder. I turn in to him, clinging to his solidity in a house full of death and loss. He holds me and waits, which is exactly what I need from him. When I finally let go, he asks, "Are you all right?"

"I don't know," I admit. "Are you?"

"I think being not all right is our baseline normal at this point."

I put my hands on his chest to feel his life beating inside him, careful to keep my touch away from the handprint seared into his flesh. "Remind me: How do you think this is going to work? When we get to the tree, do you think the Mother will just . . ." I make a vague exiting gesture with my hand.

Tavik laughs softly, mimicking the gesture and repeating my own words from ages ago. "What does *this* mean?"

"Do you think She'll just leave my body and enter Her own?"

"I don't *think* that's what's going to happen. I *know* that's what's going to happen."

"Kristorna?" Sevlos's voice calls from outside, cutting off our conversation. Reluctant to leave, I poke my head through the doorless doorway. He stands several feet from the house. I suppose he has more reason than Tavik or I to feel sad here. He nods his head to his right and says, "This way."

We follow him in silence, the three of us making a somber trio as he takes us into the trees and stops at last at a pale, slender birch.

Sevlos places his hand on the bark for a moment, then steps away. Tavik also stays back, both men giving me space to be here.

With her.

I don't know what to do or say, so I follow Sevlos's example and place my hand on the tree. I feel a pulling at my stomach, a tugging ache in my heart. I remember the weight and softness of the doll in my arms before I dropped her in the mud the night the men came. I remember screaming for my mother, the Hedenski word lingering on my lips: *Ati! Ati!*

For the first time, I feel the full force of my loss. Grief racks my body. I grasp the slender trunk, and I sob my pain into the tree.

"*Ati,*" I call to her.

I close my eyes so I can see her—my mother—the face I couldn't remember until now. Her eyes are dark like mine, her skin freckled, her hair red. And she sees me, too.

She sees me.

I reach for her, and she stretches her hand out to me, even as she says, *I can't come to you, my soul, not where you are.*

But I don't accept that. I've come all this way. How can I let her go now? I touch my fingertips to hers and feel the warmth of her. My mouth opens in a song I pull from the depths of my being, a song to bring her back to me. Elath's power pours out of me, pulsing with the beating of my heart as She takes and takes and takes what little of my own life remains.

Tavik wraps his strong arms around my body and pulls, but my soul clings to my mother's spirit. "Gelya!" he shouts, pulling so hard on my body I feel I might break in two.

My mother's eyes soften, searing my heart, but she lets go of my hand. My soul crashes back into my earthly body, to the place beside my mother's tree where Tavik holds tight to me and calls my name again and again.

Then there is darkness.

I drop like a stone.

Less than a stone.

A pebble.

A nothing.

Are you any more precious than the rest? Is your life worth more than anyone else's?

"Gelya." Tavik's voice is very faint.

"Kristorna," Sevlos calls to me.

My soul.

I open my eyes and feel my blood seeping from my nose, my ears, my eyes, my mouth, even rimming my fingernails. Tavik looks on me in grief, as if I were already dead. His breath stutters as he holds my wasted body in his arms. It breaks my heart to see him hurt, but I can't speak or give him comfort. Even drawing breath requires staggering effort.

"Which way?" he begs my uncle in Kantari, but Sevlos is staring at me, wide-eyed and terrified. "The tree!" Tavik bellows. "The path! Where is it?"

There is a language that goes beyond words, because Sevlos, who does not speak a single word of Kantari, shows Tavik the way to the path's beginning. And all I can do is sway in his arms like a baby.

Forty-Nine

I long to sing life back into the dead branches of winter and wake the seeds nestled and waiting in the earth. Or is that what *She* wants? Does it matter? Do *I* matter?

I don't know where She ends and I begin.

"Tavik." I say his name, my anchor, the hand in the darkness.

He shushes me. "Save your strength." As if anything in this world could be wasted on Tavik.

I am a little girl, dancing along the forest path to the rhythm of drums, spinning until my hair comes loose of its plaits and tickles my cheek, leading a line of all the Gelyas who came after: the one who told stories to a new rag doll in her hiding places, the one who tried to erase all that came before, the one who learned everyone else's words and everyone else's truth, the one who quailed before a captured soldier and thought, *He is every bit the dangerous Kantari heathen I always imagined.*

"Look," Tavik tells me as he approaches the enormous tree at the center of a wide clearing, its roots sprawling across a spring that gives life to a brook, a stream that becomes a river running all the way to the Fev.

The tree.

The body.

Her.

For weeks, the idea that we would reach this place felt as unlikely as the sun rising in the west, but now that we've arrived, our presence before the tree brims with finality, like the period at the end of a sentence. I feel the tremor that runs through Tavik's body, a certainty, a knowing. The Mother's spirit has walked beside him all this time, and here is Her physical self, alive and waiting.

"I told you," he speaks into the top of my head with raw emotion. "I promised you I would get you here."

"You did," I breathe, giving him a weak smile he can't see.

He picks his way closer to the body's great girth until he finds a spot where the roots make a cradle. He hugs me very gently against him before he sets me in this hollow, carefully sliding me out of his arms. He kneels in awe and reverence and waits for the Mother to receive Her soul. His eyes are lit up like a beacon.

I work up the strength to ask him with the remaining shreds of my voice, "What will you do once the Mother is free?"

He takes my hand in his and plays with my fingers. "I've always wanted to see the ocean."

"We were so close in my village. You should have told me."

"Seemed like bad timing. I mean, there you were, facing the ghosts of your past. I'm not going to say, 'Hey, can we take a quick detour to the ocean?' I do want to see it, though, once we're finally finished with all this. It's hard to imagine so much water in one place."

"Then I will take you to the sea," I tell him softly.

A smile tugs up on one corner of his mouth. I've kissed those lips. "And we'll sail to the Empire of Yil and drink the tea of Ulu Province until our bladders are nearly bursting," he tells me.

We. I like the idea of we.

"Will you take me to Kantar?" I ask.

"Of course. That goes without saying. We'll dance in the Prima's palace in Nogarra."

"Yes. And I want to see where Zofia came from in Auria." My voice thins as I sink between dream and reality.

"Then I will take you to Auria, beloved wife."

"Dearest husband," I murmur, my eyes drifting shut.

"Do you want to hear something funny?"

I try to nod, but my head and neck won't cooperate. "Yes," I whisper instead.

"You accidentally married me."

"Hmm?" I ask him, opening my eyes to slits.

The smile tugs up on both corners of his mouth, but he manages to look sadder rather than happier. He runs his fingertips along the slender bones of my hand as he speaks. "In Kantar, when people want to get married, they pray each other's prayer. And you prayed mine." He looks at me shyly from under his thick lashes. "But it's not like you knew what you were doing. I promise you're not stuck with me."

"Unless I want to be?"

He nods, and I feel like I'm standing before the statue of the nameless saint. Here is Tavik, holding out his own heart and wondering what I'm going to do with it. He lets go of my hand and musses up my hair, far more lightly this time than on previous occasions, but I moan my annoyance anyway.

"You know you love me," he says, his grin going lopsided.

"It's true. I do," I tell him, because there's no reason not to.

My words erase the grin from his face, but I don't regret saying them. I may not get another chance. Tavik releases a shaking breath, then scoots a couple of feet away on his knees.

"You stop me if this isn't what you want, all right?" he says.

I wish I could ask him what he's doing and what I'm supposed to stop, but I'm not sure I have enough strength left to string together that many words. I simply say, "All right."

He presses his forehead to the frosty earth, the position I used to assume when I still prayed to the One True God. Tavik speaks in Kantari, but I recognize it as "The Vessel's Prayer" from *The Song of Saint Lanya*, the words as he understood them whenever I sang my song.

> *Father, most high and most exalted,*
> *I am your humble Vessel.*
> *You have made my mouth clean to sing Your praise.*

His voice is dampened by leaves and snow, and yet I can hear the notes of longing threaded through it, the same music I put into my own prayer on my hands and knees in Ambrus's attic. The execution isn't perfect, but the sanctity of it is.

You have made my tongue straight to spread Your word.
You have made my body pure to receive Your spirit.

He pauses. I think he's waiting for me to stop him.
I don't.

You have given me life to reflect the light of Heaven for all to see.
You have given me death that I may live eternally
In the light of the Father.

He sits back on his heels and gazes at me with beatific reverence. He switches to Rosvanian to speak the words I thought he barely understood when he repeated them so long ago on our fake wedding day. "My body shall be your body, and my soul shall be your soul."

He doesn't say *your body shall be mine* or *your soul shall be mine.* He's not telling me that I belong to him. He's telling me that he belongs to me. My throat swells with an emotion so enormous, I feel like I might burst. I don't know how to respond. What could anyone say at this moment that would be anything other than inadequate?

Many girls don't get a say on their wedding day. I'm glad I

had a choice to make after all.

He comes back to me and takes my freezing hands in his deliciously warm grasp. "I love you, Brother Elgar, Kicker of Ass."

We burst out laughing—or Tavik does at least. The best I can do is smile feebly. At least I can feel the joy of it, of loving and being loved. Happiness tethers me to the earth at the point where our hands meet, a firm knot that keeps me from floating away like the tufts that burst from the seedpod of the Grace Tree when it opened in my hand.

Tavik's laughter peters out, and we fall into silence. After a few moments of waiting for the Mother to take Her soul into Her body, Tavik speaks again with an ominous doubt creeping into the low notes of his voice.

"I was chosen to free the Mother. It was supposed to be my life's purpose. But I've got to tell you, I don't care about that anymore. I just want you to be all right. I want you to get your life back. That's the only thing I want now."

He wears his burden. My life weighs as heavily on him as his life tugs on me. I watch his face as despair seeps into the taut lines of him with each passing second. He didn't mean to make me the Vessel of the Mother. He didn't mean to love me. And now he watches and waits, powerless, as my body cracks and breaks while nothing—*nothing*—is happening.

Time stretches on. A minute. Five minutes. Ten. My shallow breath grows slower and slower, but the tree is only a tree, and Elath's life still thrums inside me.

The Mother is also waiting, but for what?

There was another girl hundreds of years ago who was the first Vessel, the prison and the prisoner. And there was another boy, a Two-Swords, who was both the breaker and the broken.

Some vessels are made to be shattered.

The Mother is waiting for Tavik to destroy me. She's waiting for me to break apart and free Her.

I look into Tavik's tortured eyes, feeling as though my heart beats in his chest rather than my own. I don't want to leave him. I don't want to leave *me*. I don't want to leave the world I've barely come to know. But I use my expiring strength to whisper the truth anyway. "She's waiting for me."

He presses my palm to his cheek. "But you're already here. I brought you here in time. We made it."

My skin to his skin. Tense muscle. Hard bone. Ticklish beard. I can finally understand why he didn't tell me what he knew all along. It's a hard thing to face.

"No," I tell him gently. I have no choice but to be gentle. My body won't let me be anything else now. "She's waiting for me to die."

He freezes beneath my hand, an unmoving statue, turned to stone by an unwavering denial.

I draw on the strength I have left to speak again. "You opened Her first prison, and now you must open Her last."

"No," he breathes.

Somewhere along the way, that lid I kept so tightly over the life inside me slid off. I've lost track of it and see no point in searching for it now. The Mother fills every part of my body, taking hold of my voice to sing to him, to help him understand.

Call down the Mother's voice, the song of the soulswift, to sing the tale of Tavik, Breaker and Broken.

"No!" His pain is a blade that stabs me where it hurts most. He releases me and climbs over the roots of the Mother's body, right to the great trunk of Her tree. He pulls the Sword of Wrath free of its scabbard and slams the blade against Elath's body with both hands on the hilt as if he could open the tree and let the Mother's soul slip inside.

Nothing.

"Tavik," I call to him, but he hacks at the tree, over and over, dulling the blade, crying out with each impact.

Nothing.

"Stop."

He throws the damaged sword away, and his hands tear at the bark until his fingers bleed, and when that doesn't work, he pounds the trunk with his fists.

"Please," I beg him, but he refuses to stop.

"I brought her to You!" he shouts, slamming his open palms against the rough bark. "We came all this way! And I promised her! I promised!"

Nothing.

"Tavik." I'm crying when I thought I had no tears left.

"You chose us!" He grips the tree with both hands like a child clutching his mother's hem.

Nothing.

He sinks in on himself, his spine curving, bent by his own

helplessness, his hands and face pressed to the tree's rough surface. The accusation grinds its way through his clenched teeth one last time, a prayer of resentment and fury and defeat.

"You chose us."

Fifty

He refuses to break me, and I don't blame him. I wouldn't break him either, not for anything.

I'm honestly not sure if that's a good thing or a bad thing. If he doesn't break my body now, what happens to the spirit inside me? Does She finally return to the world? Or will She be trapped forever inside Her mortal Vessel? Do I even care at this point?

Tavik won't break me, but he'll hold me until I'm gone.

He'll probably hold me for a long time after that, too.

We sit at the foot of the Mother in Her tangle of roots, Tavik upright and cross-legged, me draped across his lap, my head leaning against his shoulder.

"Are you cold?" he asks me.

"No." It's true. My body feels very little now. Even my voice is disappearing in slow, painful increments.

"I'm sorry," he whispers. "I shouldn't ask you to speak. Save your strength."

"For what?"

His chin trembles. He clutches me more tightly, nestling my forehead into the crook of his neck.

I make my hand move to his chest and press my fingertips over the place where his heart beats beneath the mark of my handprint, and I sing inside him.

What the Mother joins in life cannot be separated in death.

He gasps and kisses the top of my head.

I press my face into his neck. "I should tell you not to waste your water, but I won't."

"Shh."

I'm the one who's breaking, yet Tavik is the one who is falling apart.

"It doesn't matter now." And then I sigh his name just for the simple pleasure of saying it. "Tavik."

He bursts like a broken dam, weeping, clinging to me as if I were a doll. He rocks us back and forth as he sobs, and still I live. When he has cried himself out, he shifts, cradling my head in the crook of his arm to watch me die, breath by breath, while he can do nothing to stop it. He strokes the cooling skin of my hollowed cheeks with his fingertips. He looks to the sky for a moment, but his eyes return to my face, and he speaks one word—prays it—"Please"—and I don't know what it is he's asking or from whom.

There's a rustling in the woods to the south, movement, and

I can sense Tavik's hope surging inside him, his trampled faith assuring him that his Mother and his Father have not abandoned him. But it is not hope that approaches us. Goodson Anskar emerges into the clearing, walking along the stream. He must have found a way to cross the Fev River so he could follow us on the north side of the tributary. As he comes into view, Tavik and I both understand, finally and completely, that our lives are nothing to the gods. We are only a Vessel and a Sword to them, objects to be used, then cast aside when we are no longer useful.

The Goodson startles when he spots us cradled in the roots of the Mother's body. He steps across the brook and comes to a halt several yards away, keeping a cautious distance from the tree. He speaks to Tavik rather than to me. "Is she . . . ?"

"No," Tavik answers shortly. He can't bear to hear the word spoken aloud in any language, not by the Goodson, not by anyone.

"Goodson Anskar," I call to him, weak and mewling, but his eyes are on the tree, gazing up and up, taking in the expanse of Elath's earthly body before turning his troubled face back to Tavik.

"Have you done it then? Have you released the Great Demon?"

Now that my own belief has been demolished, it seems impossible that the Goodson's faith should continue to burn so brightly. Tavik gapes at him, then barks an incredulous, bitter laugh. "You have eyes," he answers in Rosvanian.

The Goodson wears his relief as clear as the Hand of the Father emblazoned on his chest.

"Goodson," I call again with a voice that refuses to go far. I want to reach out to him, but my hands will no longer obey me. "It's over."

He steps closer and finally addresses me. "No, Daughter, it's not over. It will never end until the body is cut down once and for all, and the Vessel is secured."

"Me," I murmur.

He nods, his eyes curving down with sorrow. "You."

I know what he is, and yet it stings more than words can say that his faith is stronger than his love.

"I'll make you hurt for this," Tavik spits at him in Kantari.

"Calm down, heathen. You know that I am not going to kill her. That would only set the Great Demon free. The Vessel must be put somewhere safe before it's too late."

Tavik pulls together the Rosvanian words he needs. "What you do to her is worse than death."

"It's a mercy. I will carry the Vessel to Saint Balzos—"

"The 'Vessel' has a name."

"—and the world will thank me for it. Don't you see? If only you had taken Rusik's hand."

"If only I had killed you at the convent when I had the chance," Tavik answers in Kantari.

"I can see you care for her. I understand. I have loved her as a father loves his daughter. But what we want, whom we love—none of that matters. There are things that are bigger than you or I. As hard as this is, there are things that matter more than just one girl."

Tavik slides himself out from underneath me, taking his

warmth and comfort away when I need them most.

"Don't," I plead, but he lays me down in the cradle of leaves between the roots. He kisses my hands. "Water of my thirst, blood of my body."

"No," I beg him as he rises and pulls the Sword of Mercy from its scabbard.

He turns his back on me to face the Goodson. "Nothing matters more than her."

Goodson Anskar nods again, but there's nothing sad about it this time. He draws his sword and takes the crouching, offensive stance of a man long used to fighting. "Let's get this over with."

Tavik can't not fight the Goodson now, and I know it. Even as his blade meets Goodson Anskar's, I remember when I asked him about *The Ludoïd*, what it means.

So by that logic, it is better to die for the love of one person than to sacrifice what you most love for the benefit of the many? You think entire nations should fall for the sake of the love between one man and one woman?

And what did he say in response?

Love trumps hate. Every time. Even in the face of world destruction, love is the better choice.

And that's why Tavik is winning.

When the Goodson strikes, he blocks, and when Tavik attacks, he gets closer to victory. He pushes Goodson Anskar on the defensive. He makes him step back, moving him farther and farther away from me. When the Goodson lunges, he feints and shoves the seasoned knight down with his foot, sending him sprawling to the ground, as ungainly as the Mother's roots, knocking the Hand of the Father out of his grip. The ancient sword slides away through the carpet of rotting leaves and snow as Tavik holds his one blade to the Goodson's neck, ready to strike down his enemy at last.

"No!" I whimper.

I'm sure Tavik can't hear me, and yet he stops, his blade unmoving. When he speaks at last, it's in Kantari.

"I'm not going to kill a man as pathetically deluded as I have been, not when Gelya still loves you."

He casts aside the sword in disgust.

"There. I offer you the Sword of Mercy," he says in Rosvanian before giving up and switching once more to Kantari. "It doesn't matter now. Nothing matters now but her."

He turns back to me, and I'm glad to see his face again, to watch his chest rise and fall with life.

Then, with a sudden, violent jolt, Tavik's body arches backward, bending into the searing point, the place where his own blade has pierced his back. The Goodson rams the Sword of Mercy so hard through Tavik's body, it emerges from his stomach. His eyes widen. His mouth contorts. His whole face becomes a mask of agony, sending a shaft of anguish into my own chest. He cries out as the Goodson withdraws the blade, and he drops to the ground. He manages to roll onto his back, but already the hungry earth soaks in his blood, feeding the roots of the great tree that cradles me.

The Goodson stands above him, holds the sword high, and

drives it down into Tavik's heart, pinning him to the ground like a moth to a board. Tavik takes his last breath, then looks on the world with eyes that no longer see, and there is nothing left but pain and the Goodson and the Mother's arms stretching to the gray sky above.

Fifty-One

The sword that tore Tavik's life away from me drips red as the Goodson pulls it free of his body.

Silence looms over me, so incongruous in the aftermath of fighting and death that I want to scream into the void. There is only the creaking of frozen tree limbs, the call of a crow in the distance, Goodson Anskar's ragged breathing. The color of the world is a desolate gray-white from the sky above to the frost-coated ground below.

My heart shatters. My entire body breaks. And still I live when Tavik doesn't.

His left hand, swordless and empty, splays without intention in my direction, the back resting on the earth while his fingers curl toward the sky, the skin under the nails purpling already. I smell his blood, like rust and woodsmoke, cutting through the crisp air.

He is so close, but I am so weak.

I force myself to roll onto my stomach and crawl toward him, clawing my way inch by inch, grunting with effort even as the effort of grunting pushes me closer to my own death.

"Gelya." The Goodson's voice cracks with heartbreak.

I will not turn toward that voice.

I press forward and reach for Tavik's hand. I have done it before. I can do it one last time. This is how I choose to die.

The Goodson's footsteps crush the frost beneath his feet as he crunches his way to me and lifts me in his strong soldier's arms. "Poor little Gelya. Come. I shall carry you now."

"No." I stretch my hand toward Tavik, but his touch has been stolen from me almost as quickly as it was ever given.

"It's done," Goodson Anskar whispers, holding me high, cradling me as he did so long ago.

I look down at Tavik. His skin has turned the same dull color as the sky, as if he was a blazing fire, and now all that's left are the ashes. The only color left in the world is the green of his blank, open eyes.

Where has he gone, the blood of my body, the water of my thirst? To his underworld? To a heaven he doesn't believe in?

I try to push myself free of the Goodson's arms, but he holds more tightly to me, and I am too cold and feeble to resist.

We failed, Tavik and I. We came all this way for nothing. What does it matter now? Why did any of it matter in the first place? Gods and demons and wars and monsters . . . it all seems so small and ridiculous now that I've reached the end.

I sway in the Goodson's arms as he carries me away, my head

lolling. I watch Tavik's body, determined to keep him in my sight for as long as I can. From the earth at his Mother's feet, where his blood has soaked into the soil, a small green shoot curls upward and fans out two tiny green leaves.

The son gives his death so that the Mother may live, Elath sings inside me.

I feel no joy, but I understand now: we didn't fail after all. This is not the end. This is the beginning.

In my mind, I stand at a stream so narrow, I could jump across it without even dampening my boots. *Is it time?* I ask the woman who stands across from me, a goddess who somehow manages to be both Zofia and my own mother. She nods and smiles and reaches out a strong hand to steady me. I put my small, grubby child's hand in hers and take the last step.

I feel a pulling at my stomach, a tugging ache in my heart. I am a song trapped in a cave, the newly lit wick of a lamp, brightly burning in the darkness. The seedpod cracks and bursts open, and from within the husk of my body comes light, so much light.

And wings.

And feathers.

The lithe body of a small blue bird.

The weight of the Mother's soul soars out of me as I surge into the air, free of the burden. My entire being turns inward until there is nothing left but the burning pinpoint that is the heart of the bird I have become. The Goodson cries out as I take flight, a dazzling thing, alive and vivid in a colorless world.

I did not know how heavy my body was until I became light. I am freed by feathers. I am buoyed by song and air. I hear the soft breath of animals waking in their winter burrows, taste the promise of spring on my tongue, smell the loamy soil that waits beneath its frozen blanket of earth.

I know what I am now.

My new eyes see what my human eyes could not: Tavik's soul buried within the flesh and bone of his own heavy body, a pulse made of laughter and pain and love, all the things he is.

I fly to him, landing on his still and cooling chest, and call to him in my birdsong. He comes to me, rising from the shell of his body to the place where I perch on the handprint over his heart. I take the light of his soul in my tiny bird's grip, holding the luminescent threads of his colorful life in toes as thin and delicate as strands of melted glass, and I lift him up.

All around us, the world wakes in the Mother's footsteps, in the air that the goddess breathes, warm and green and brimming. The Father wipes away the bleak clouds with His great hand, and I soar into the blue sky as if it were an open window, holding Tavik close to me as I circle higher and higher. I sing as I raise him up, a song so excruciatingly beautiful it could pierce any living soul.

The Goodson listens to my heart-wrenching call, watching me climb into the heavens until he can see me no more. Then he falls to his knees, so broken he cannot even weep for me.

And still I fly, up and up, carrying Tavik's precious soul with me.

Epilogue

A HYMN FROM *THE SONG OF SAINT ANSKAR*

There is no poetry in the Spear of the Father.
There is only death.
I wear my name to remember what I have been.

When I drove my sword into Saint Tavik's body
And felt the flesh yield,
And heard the slick sound of blade against blood,
I gave the Mother his death for Her life.
Death for life, all things in balance.

Saint Gelya became blue feathers and birdsong,
Excruciating in her beauty,
Circling into the sky until I could see her no more.
Such a tiny bird to carry something so vast, so heavy as a soul.

THE SOULSWIFT

We set the goddess free, the three of us,
And when I saw the world turn green and good around me,
I understood that my life as the Spear of the Father had been a lie.
I thought I could not bear to have been wrong.
But the Mother called my name,
And who am I to defy Her again?

I sing The Song of Saint Gelya to anyone who will listen,
And The Song of Saint Tavik,
The Song of Saint Zofia,
The Songs of the Mother and the Father,
Life and Death,
All things in balance.

They are the only songs worth singing.

Acknowledgments

Many thanks to A'ishah Amatullah, Rebecca Coffindaffer, Christie O. Hall, Natasha Hanova, and Alejandra Olivia for their insightful feedback and suggestions at various stages of this project. Thanks also to the KS/KCMO writing crew for the support, comradery, and excellent food (and, more recently, for the comforting Zoom sessions). To my critique partners Kathee Goldsich and Jenny Mendez, and to my fellow Nebulous Dread Cloud band members Miranda Asebedo and Amanda Sellet: thank you for lighting my way time and again.

I hereby dedicate my most impressive dance moves to my agent, Holly Root, who is the literal best. Air fives to the whole Root Literary gang and to Heather Baror-Shapiro as well.

Heaps of gratitude go to Renée Cafiero, Alison Donalty, Jacqueline Hornberger, Catherine Lee, Maxime Plasse, Sasha Vinogradova, the Balzer + Bray team, and everyone at Harper-Collins who played a part in this book's journey to publication.

Caitlin Johnson has been stellar throughout the editorial process, and my editor, Kristin Daly Rens, deserves canonization for her patience and guidance. Thank you for seeing what this book was meant to be when I couldn't, Kristin, and for sticking with me until I could. I shall sing your song for many years to come.